ANN M. MARTIN

# BABY-SITTERS LITTLE SISTER

follow
chimney
ENGLISH
sailor
believe
sugar
banana

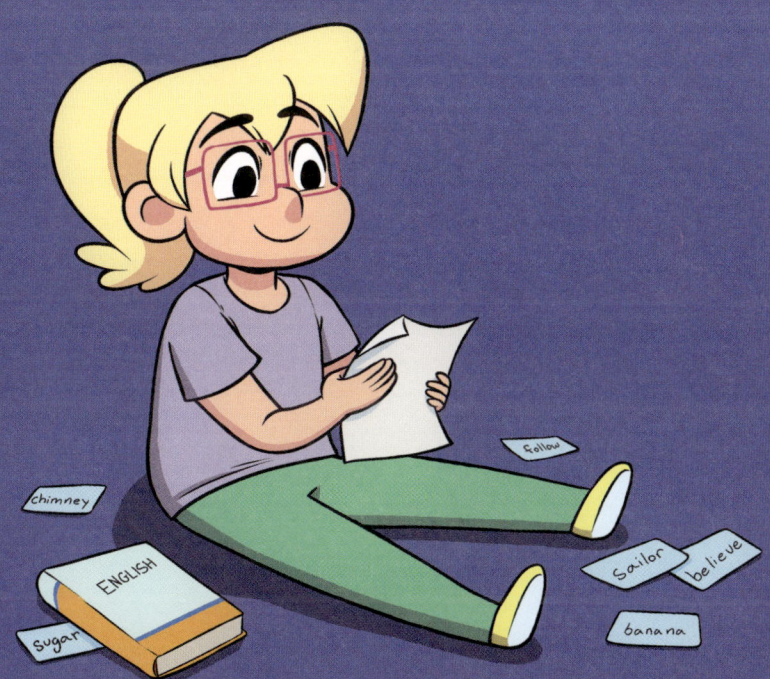

## KAREN'S PRIZE

A GRAPHIC NOVEL BY

SHAUNA J. GRANT

WITH COLOR BY BRADEN LAMB

graphix

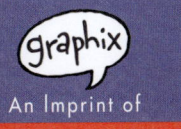

An Imprint of

SCHOLASTIC

The author gratefully acknowledges
Stephanie Calmenson for her help with this book.
**A. M. M.**

This book is for my friends, my sisters.
Thank you for your endless love and support.
**S. J. G.**

Text copyright © 2025 by Ann M. Martin
Art copyright © 2025 by Shauna J. Grant

All rights reserved. Published by Graphix, an imprint of Scholastic Inc., *Publishers since 1920.* SCHOLASTIC, GRAPHIX, BABY-SITTERS LITTLE SISTER, and associated logos are trademarks and/or registered trademarks of Scholastic Inc.

The publisher does not have any control over and does not assume any responsibility for author or third-party websites or their content.

No part of this publication may be reproduced, stored in a retrieval system, or transmitted in any form or by any means, electronic, mechanical, photocopying, recording, or otherwise, or used to train any artificial intelligence technologies, without written permission of the publisher. For information regarding permission, write to Scholastic Inc., Attention: Permissions Department, 557 Broadway, New York, NY 10012.

This book is a work of fiction. Names, characters, places, and incidents are either the product of the author's imagination or are used fictitiously, and any resemblance to actual persons, living or dead, business establishments, events, or locales is entirely coincidental.

Library of Congress Control Number: 2024935921

ISBN 978-1-5461-1007-1 (hardcover)
ISBN 978-1-339-00507-2 (paperback)

10 9 8 7 6 5 4 3 2 1    25 26 27 28 29

Printed in China    62
First edition, April 2025

Edited by Cassandra Pelham Fulton and Megan Peace
Book design by Natalie Padberg Bartoo
Creative Director: Phil Falco
Publisher: David Saylor

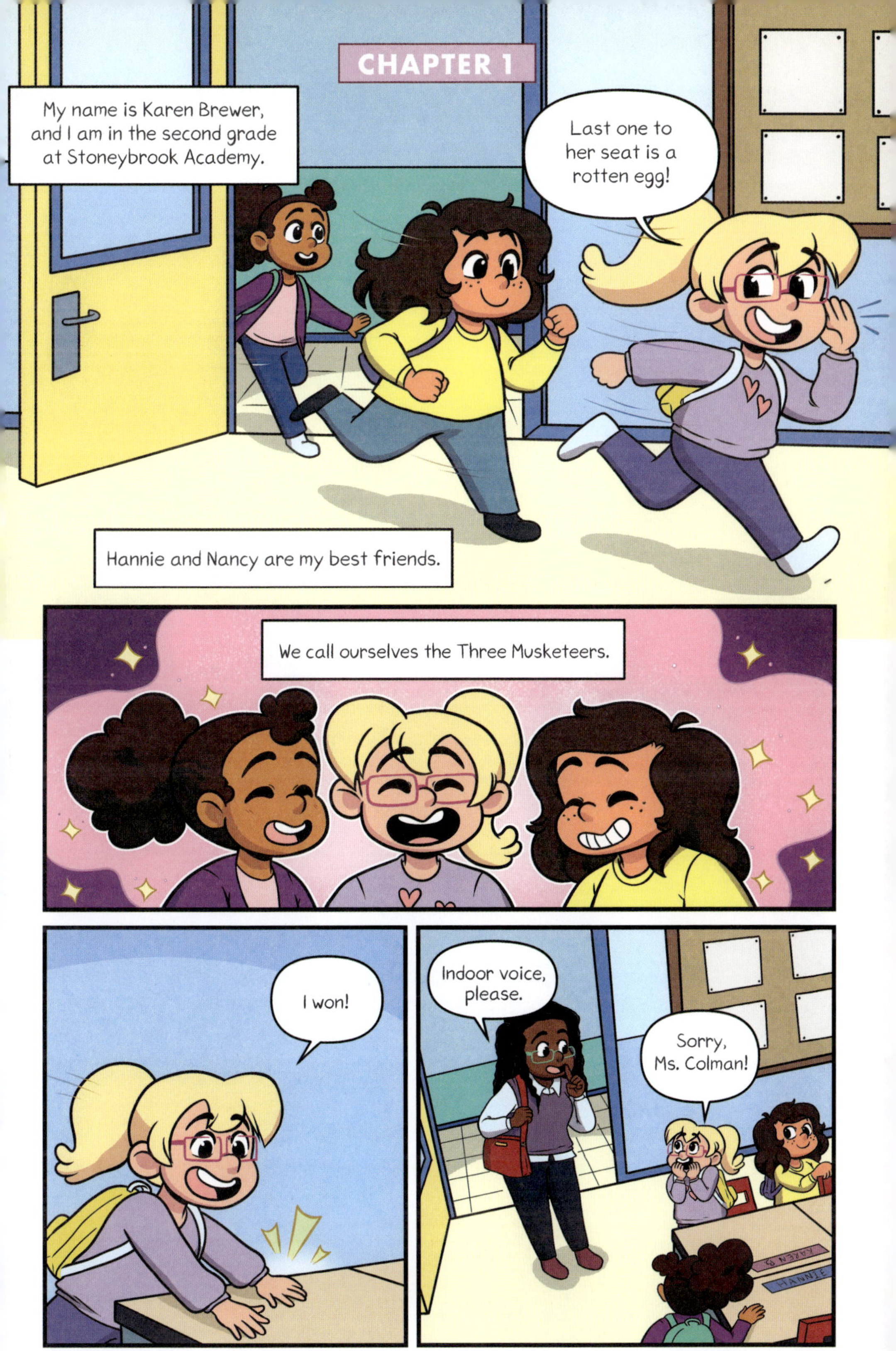
CHAPTER 1
My name is Karen Brewer, and I am in the second grade at Stoneybrook Academy.
Last one to her seat is a rotten egg!
Hannie and Nancy are my best friends.
We call ourselves the Three Musketeers.
I won!
Indoor voice, please.
Sorry, Ms. Colman!

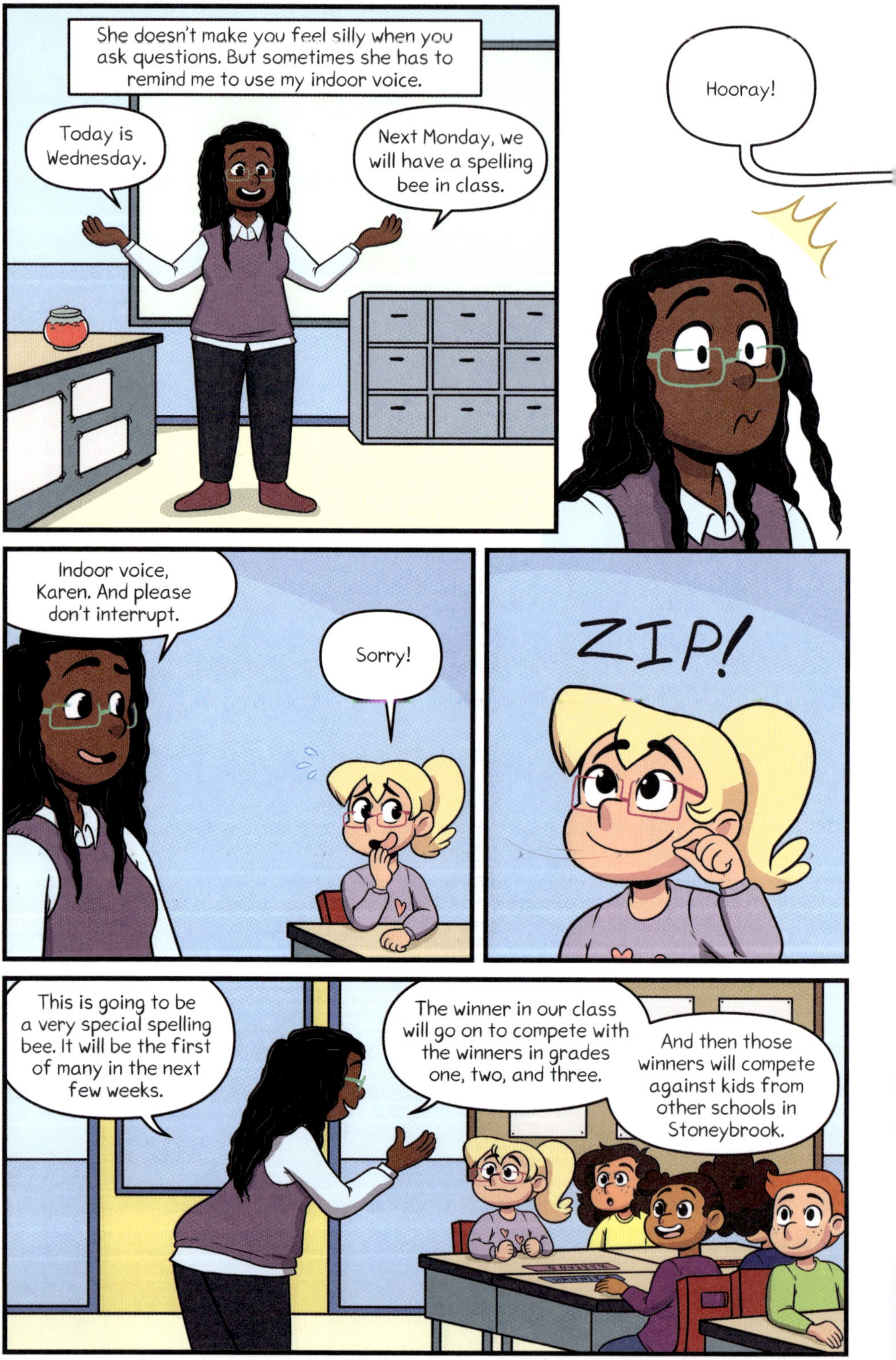
She doesn't make you feel silly when you ask questions. But sometimes she has to remind me to use my indoor voice.
Today is Wednesday.
Next Monday, we will have a spelling bee in class.
Hooray!
Indoor voice, Karen. And please don't interrupt.
Sorry!
ZIP!
This is going to be a very special spelling bee. It will be the first of many in the next few weeks.
The winner in our class will go on to compete with the winners in grades one, two, and three.
And then those winners will compete against kids from other schools in Stoneybrook.

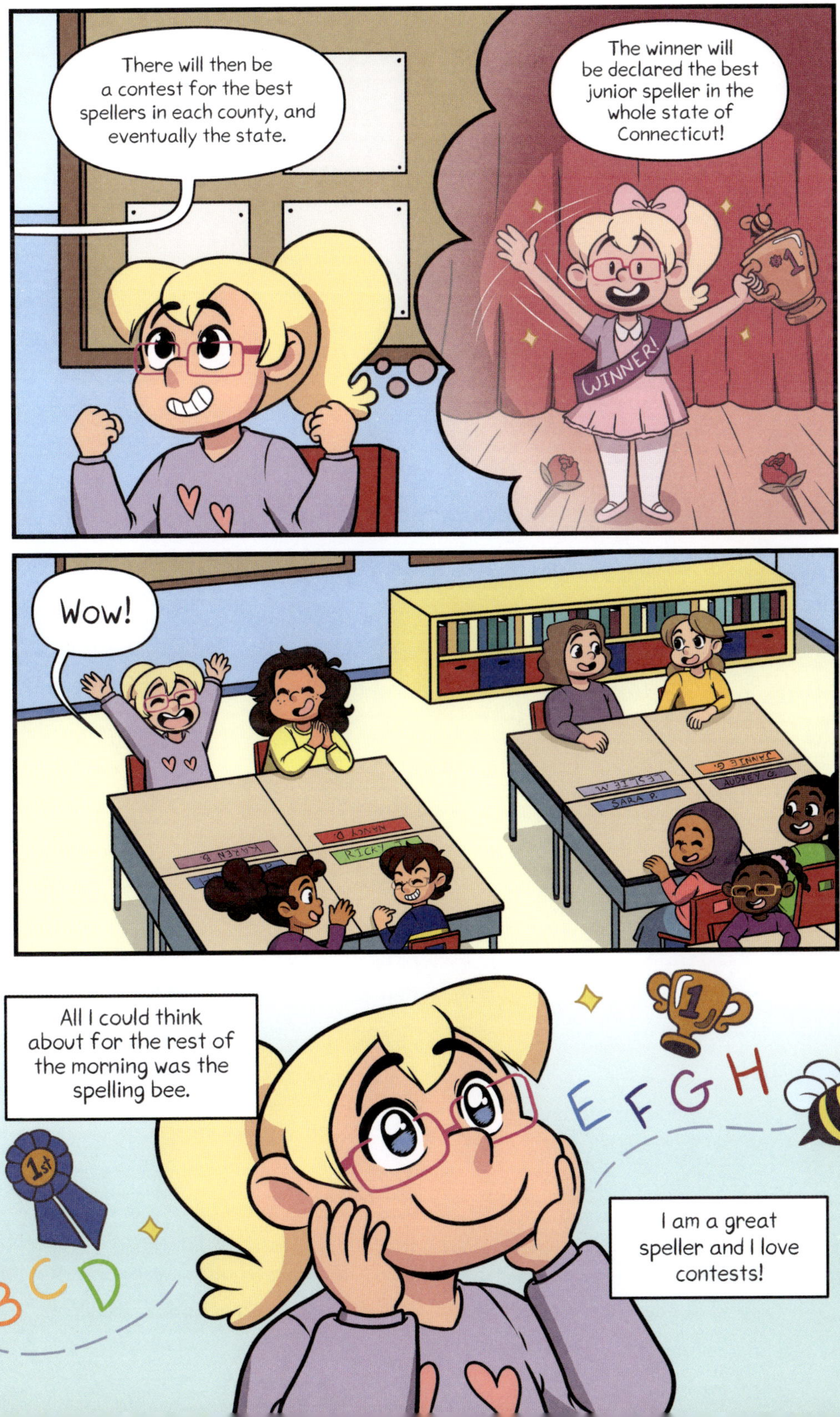
There will then be a contest for the best spellers in each county, and eventually the state.
The winner will be declared the best junior speller in the whole state of Connecticut!
WINNER!
WOW!
All I could think about for the rest of the morning was the spelling bee.
E F G H
1st
A B C D
I am a great speller and I love contests!

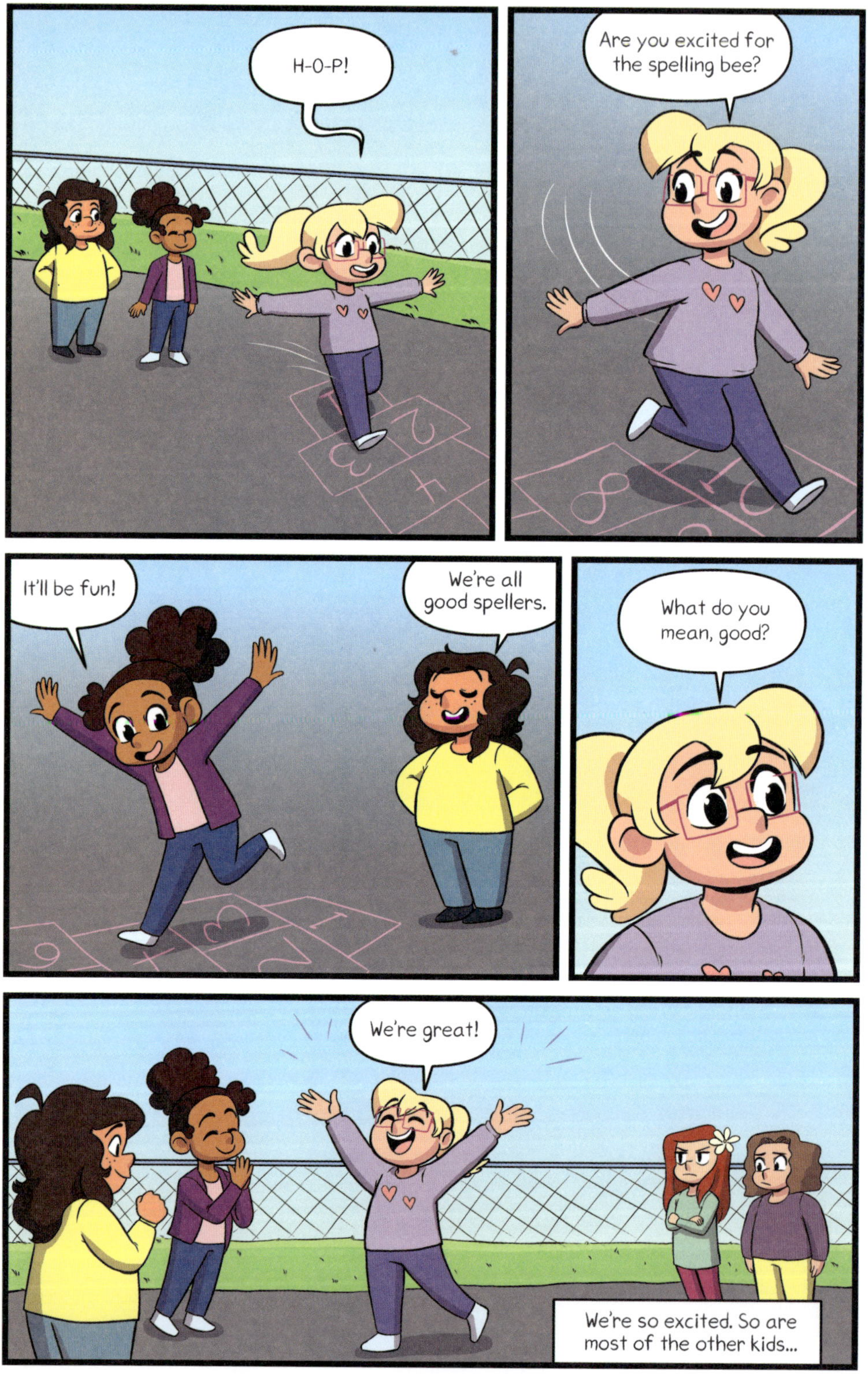
H-O-P!
Are you excited for the spelling bee?
It'll be fun!
We're all good spellers.
What do you mean, good?
We're great!
We're so excited. So are most of the other kids...

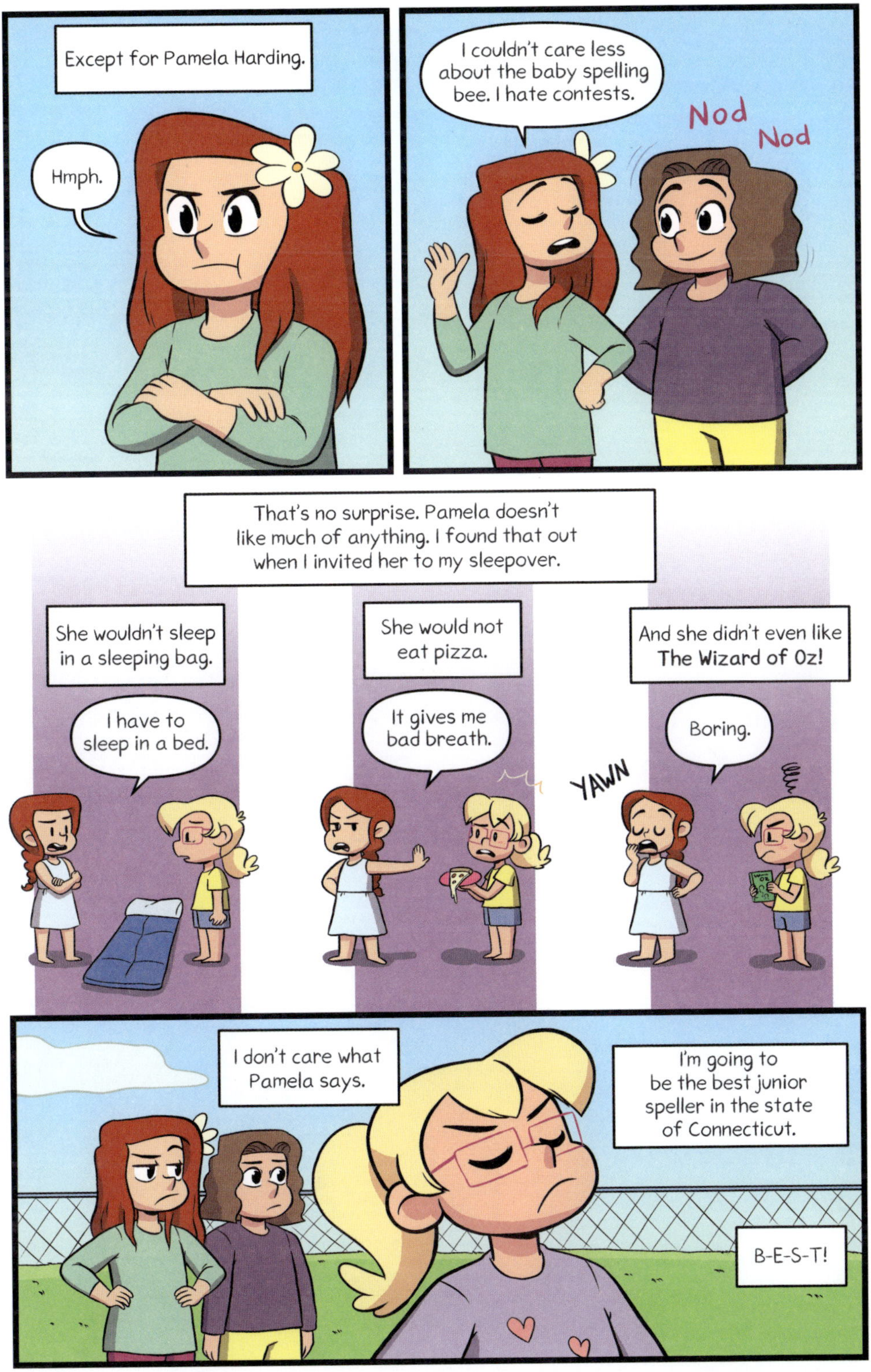
Except for Pamela Harding.
Hmph.
I couldn't care less about the baby spelling bee. I hate contests.
Nod
Nod
That's no surprise. Pamela doesn't like much of anything. I found that out when I invited her to my sleepover.
She wouldn't sleep in a sleeping bag.
I have to sleep in a bed.
She would not eat pizza.
It gives me bad breath.
And she didn't even like **The Wizard of Oz!**
YAWN
Boring.
I don't care what Pamela says.
I'm going to be the best junior speller in the state of Connecticut.
B-E-S-T!

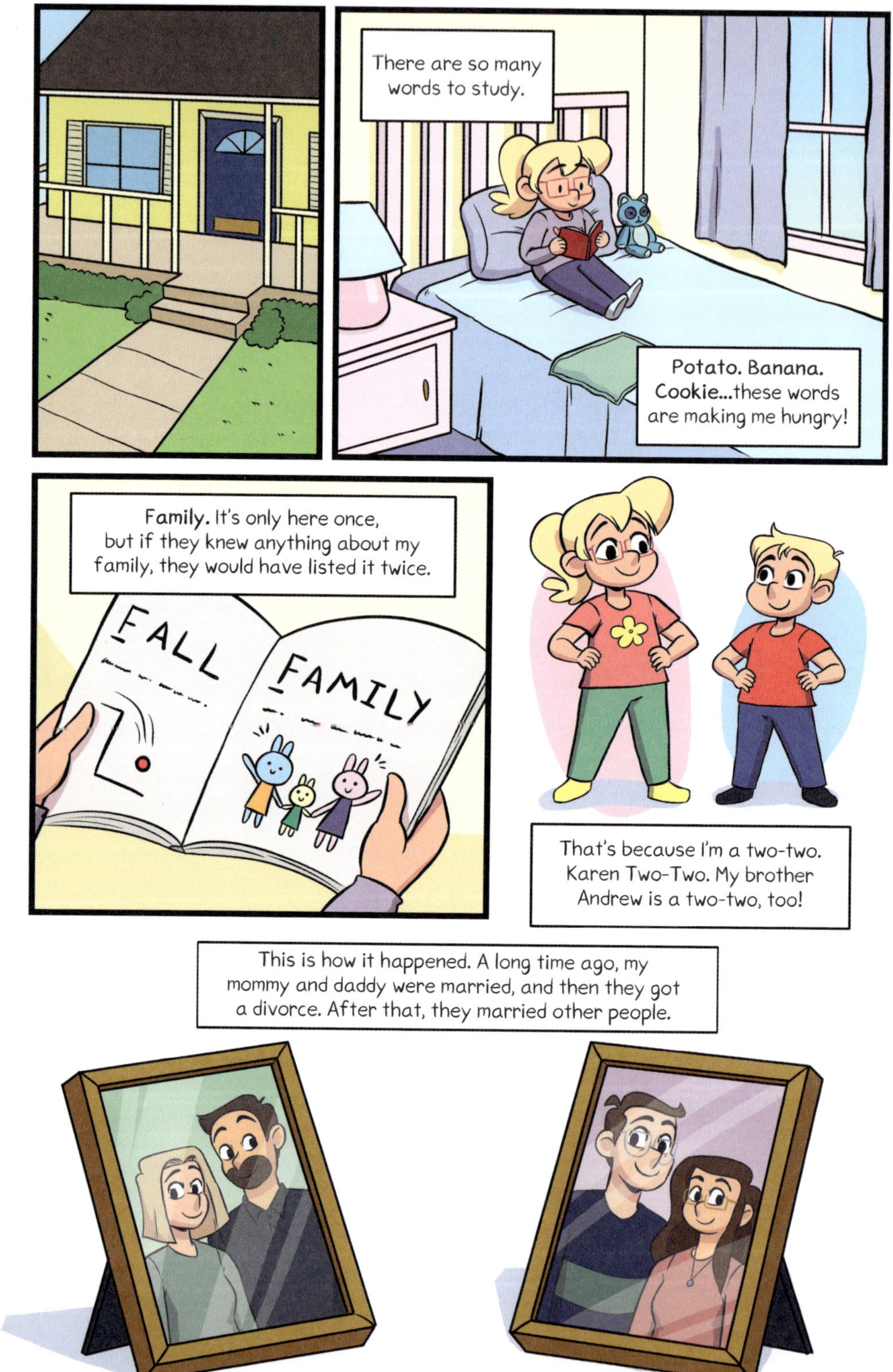
There are so many words to study.
Potato. Banana. Cookie...these words are making me hungry!
Family. It's only here once, but if they knew anything about my family, they would have listed it twice.
FALL
FAMILY
That's because I'm a two-two. Karen Two-Two. My brother Andrew is a two-two, too!
This is how it happened. A long time ago, my mommy and daddy were married, and then they got a divorce. After that, they married other people.

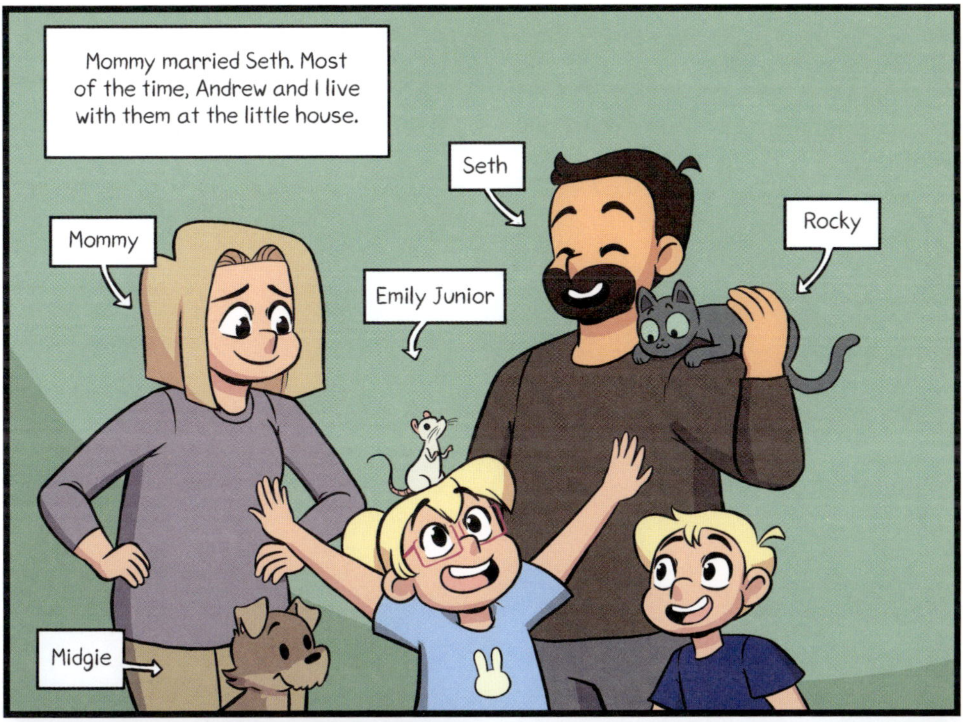
Mommy married Seth. Most of the time, Andrew and I live with them at the little house.
Seth
Mommy
Emily Junior
Rocky
Midgie

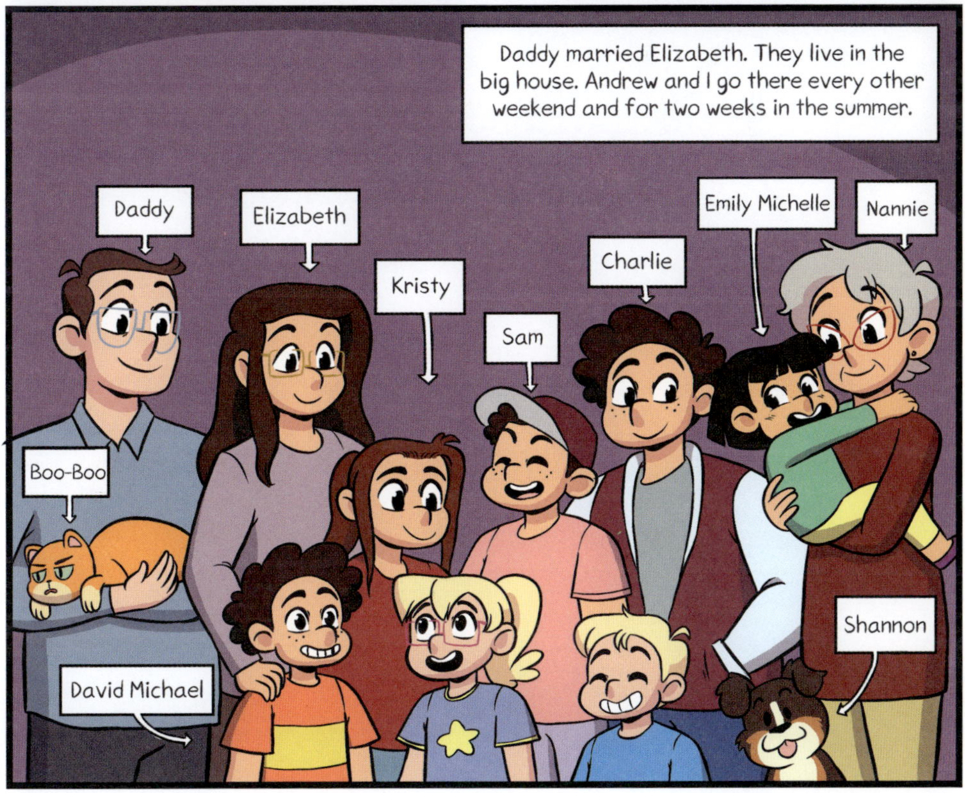
Daddy married Elizabeth. They live in the big house. Andrew and I go there every other weekend and for two weeks in the summer.
Daddy
Elizabeth
Kristy
Sam
Charlie
Emily Michelle
Nannie
Boo-Boo
David Michael
Shannon

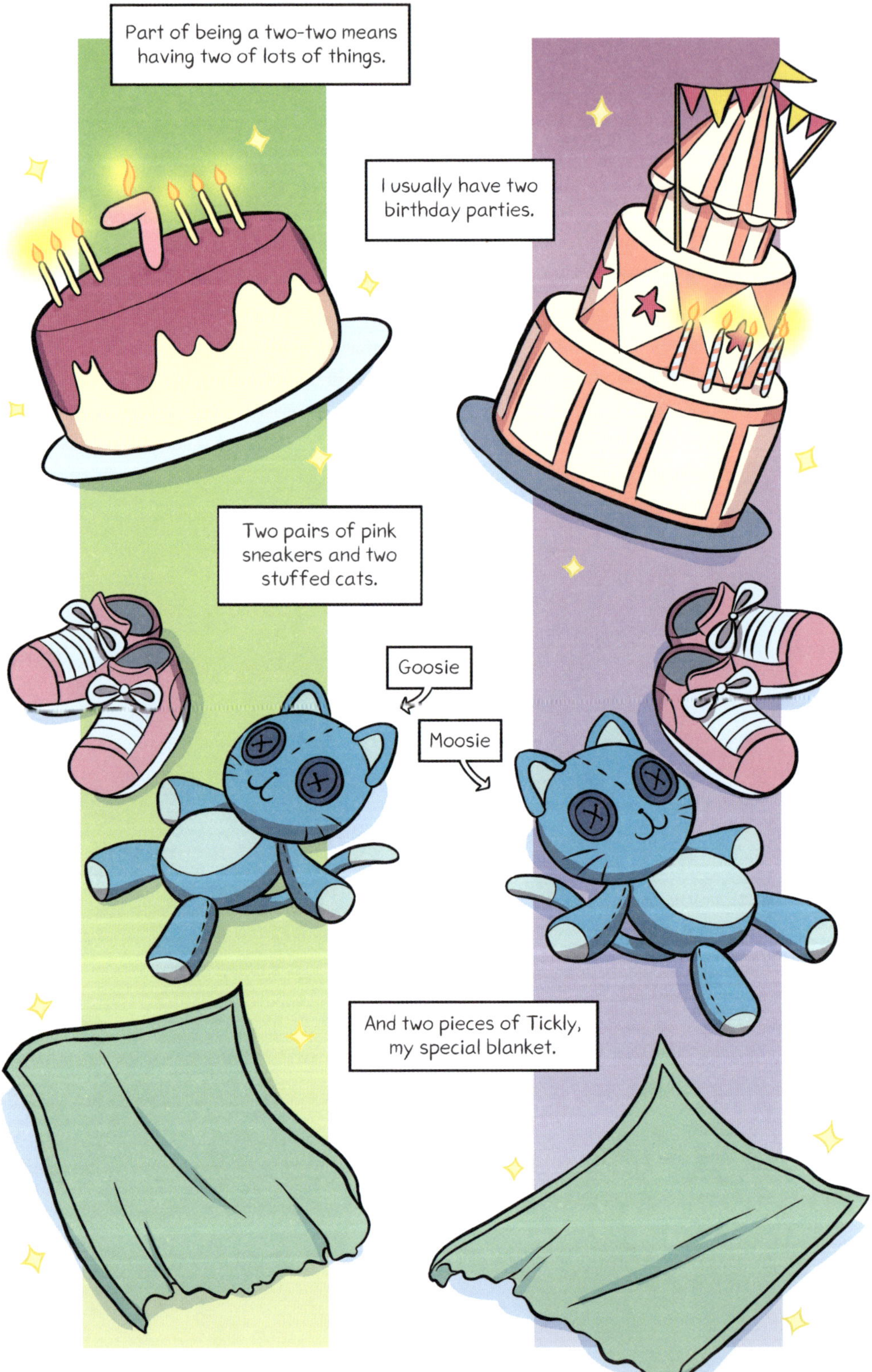

Part of being a two-two means having two of lots of things.
I usually have two birthday parties.
Two pairs of pink sneakers and two stuffed cats.
Goosie
Moosie
And two pieces of Tickly, my special blanket.

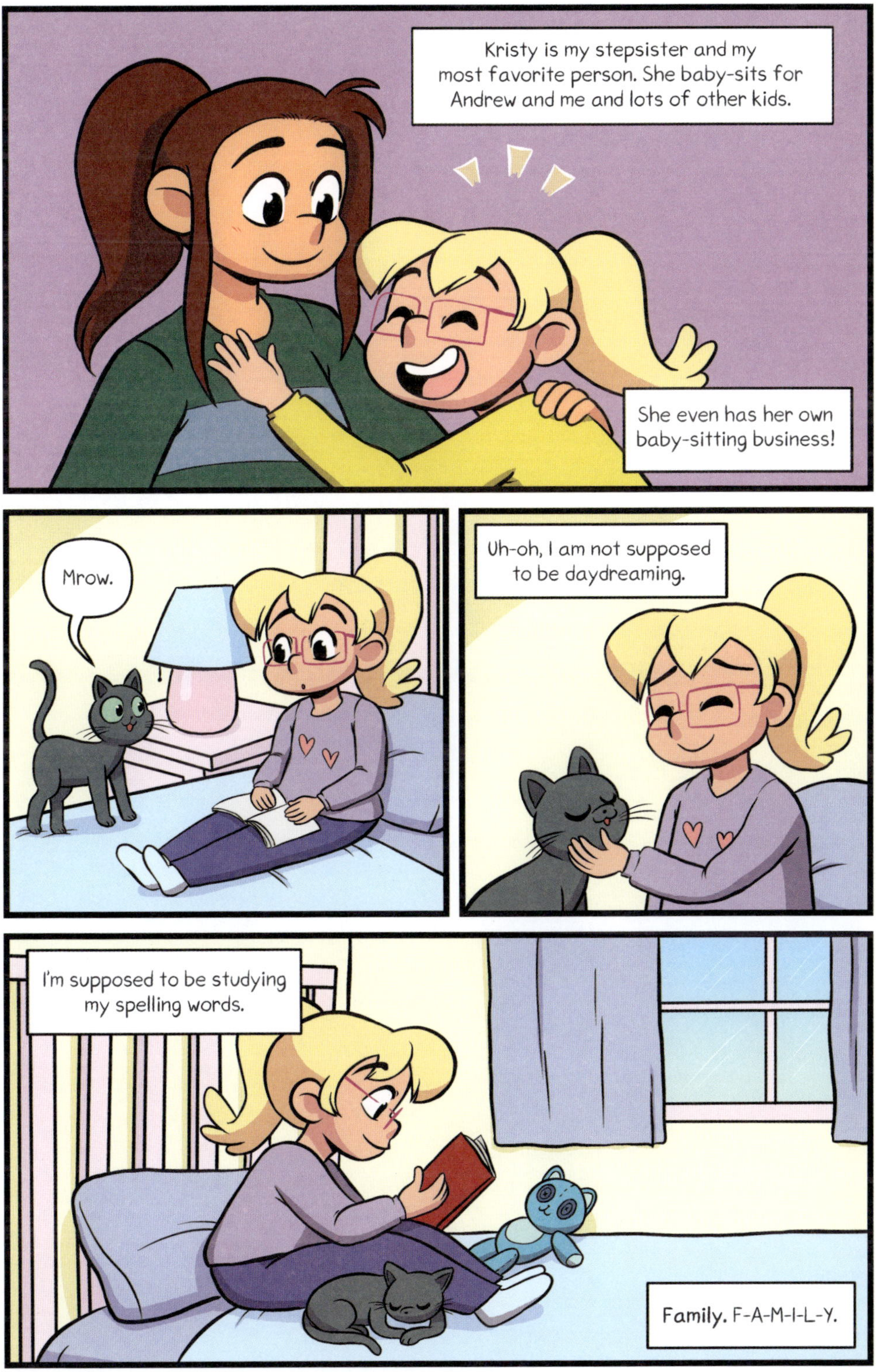
Kristy is my stepsister and my most favorite person. She baby-sits for Andrew and me and lots of other kids.
She even has her own baby-sitting business!
Mrow.
Uh-oh, I am not supposed to be daydreaming.
I'm supposed to be studying my spelling words.
**Family.** F-A-M-I-L-Y.

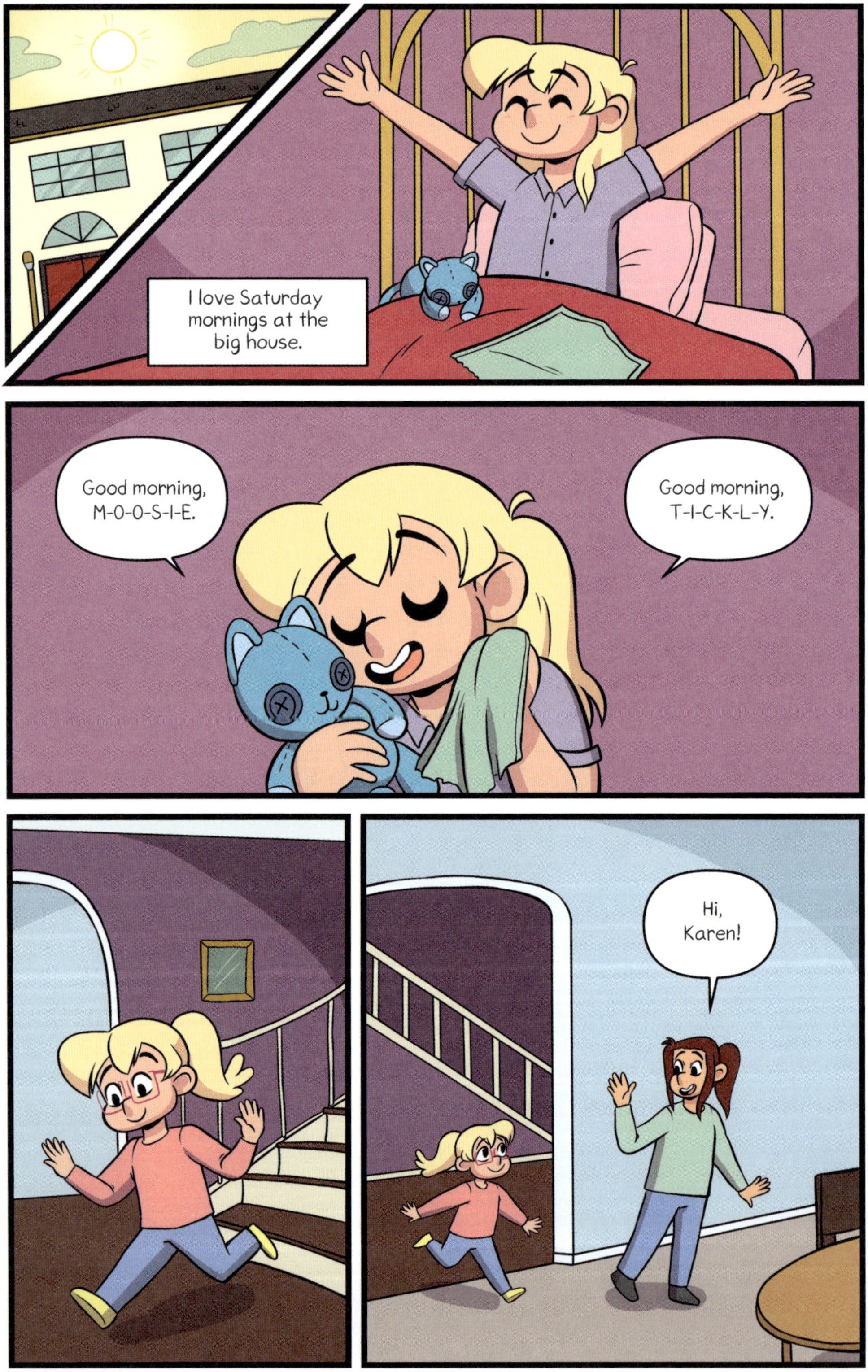
I love Saturday mornings at the big house.
Good morning, M-O-O-S-I-E.
Good morning, T-I-C-K-L-Y.
Hi, Karen!

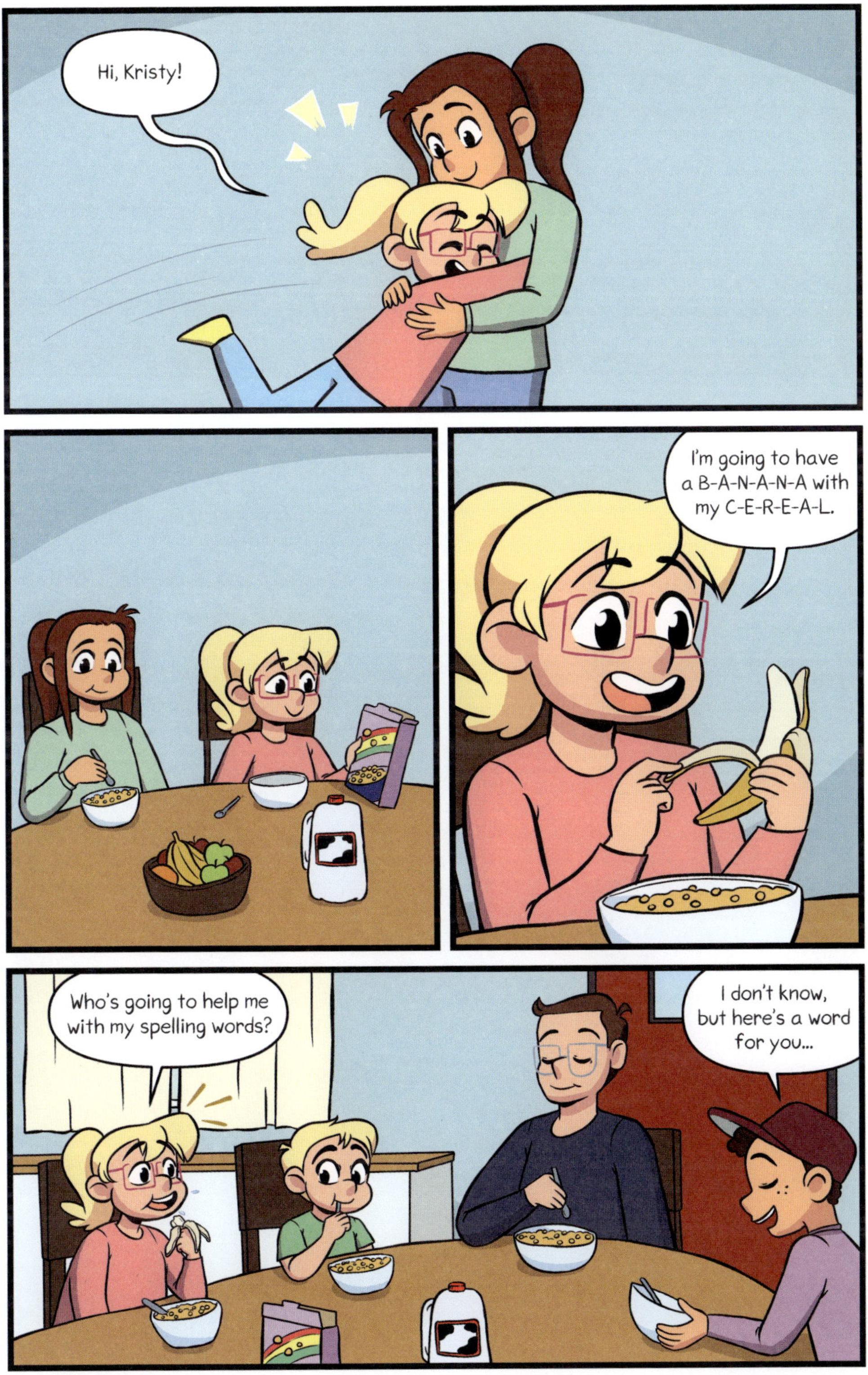
Hi, Kristy!
I'm going to have a B-A-N-A-N-A with my C-E-R-E-A-L.
Who's going to help me with my spelling words?
I don't know, but here's a word for you...

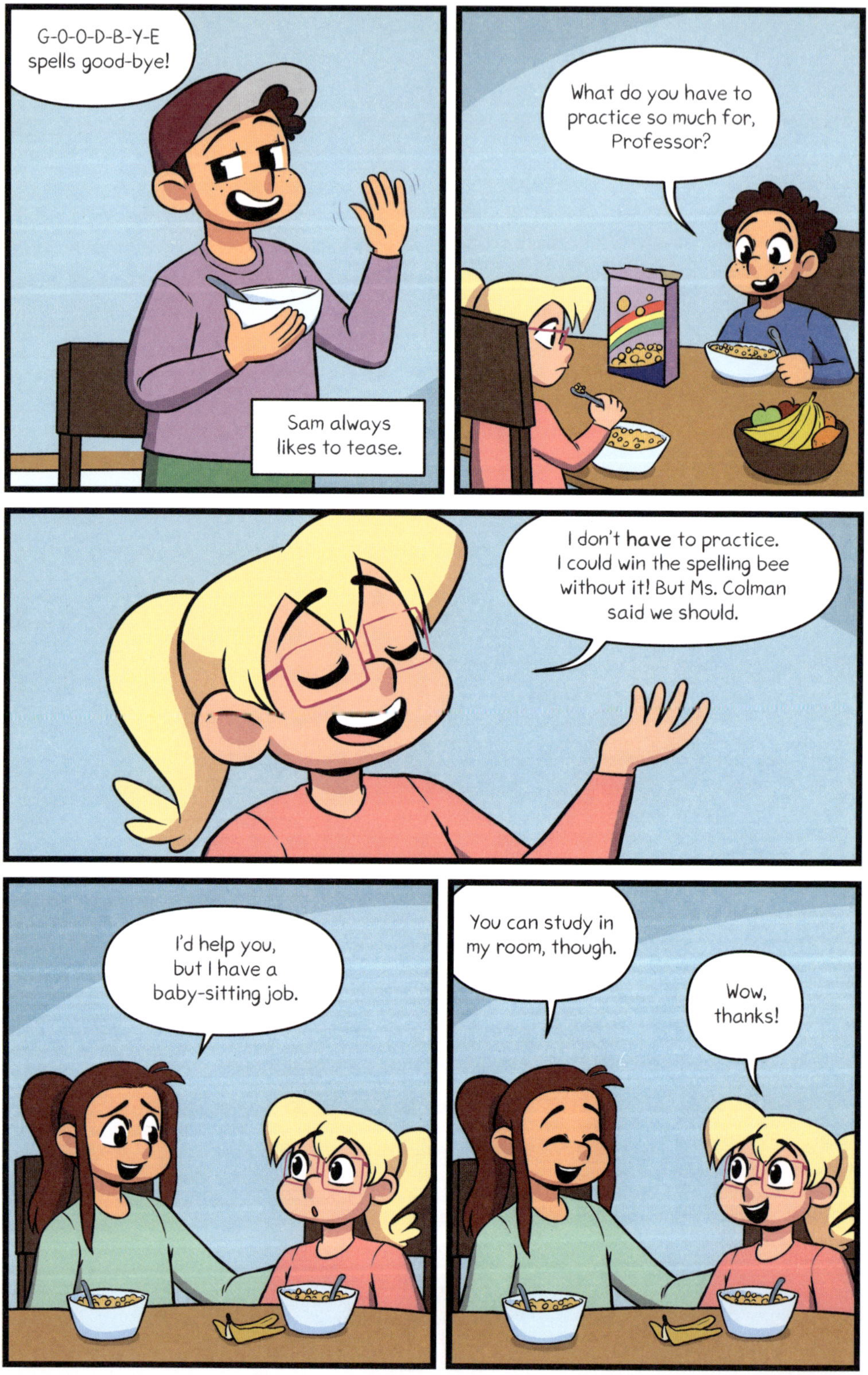
G-O-O-D-B-Y-E spells good-bye!
Sam always likes to tease.
What do you have to practice so much for, Professor?
I don't **have** to practice. I could win the spelling bee without it! But Ms. Colman said we should.
I'd help you, but I have a baby-sitting job.
You can study in my room, though.
Wow, thanks!

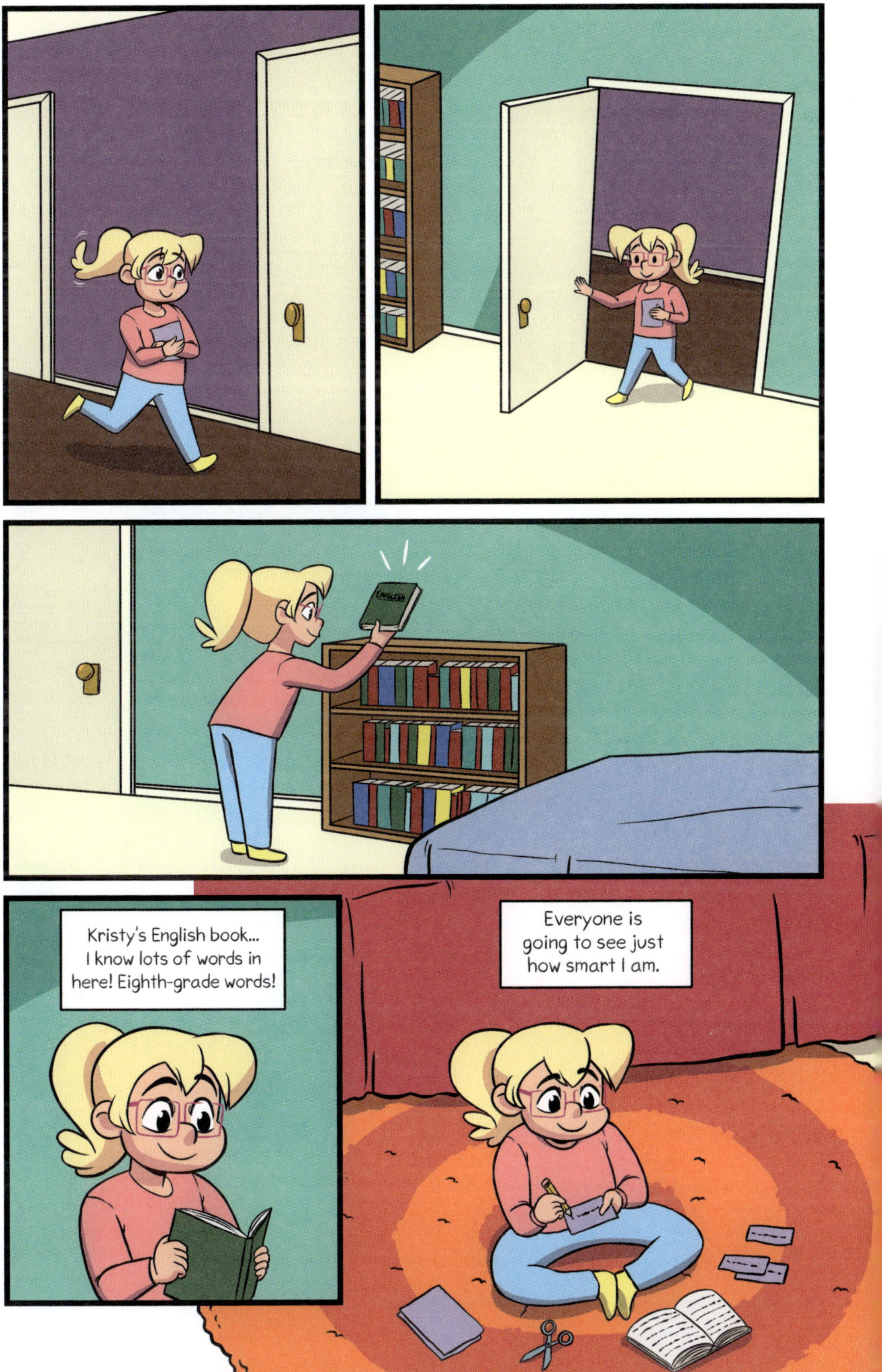
ENGLISH
Kristy's English book... I know lots of words in here! Eighth-grade words!
Everyone is going to see just how smart I am.

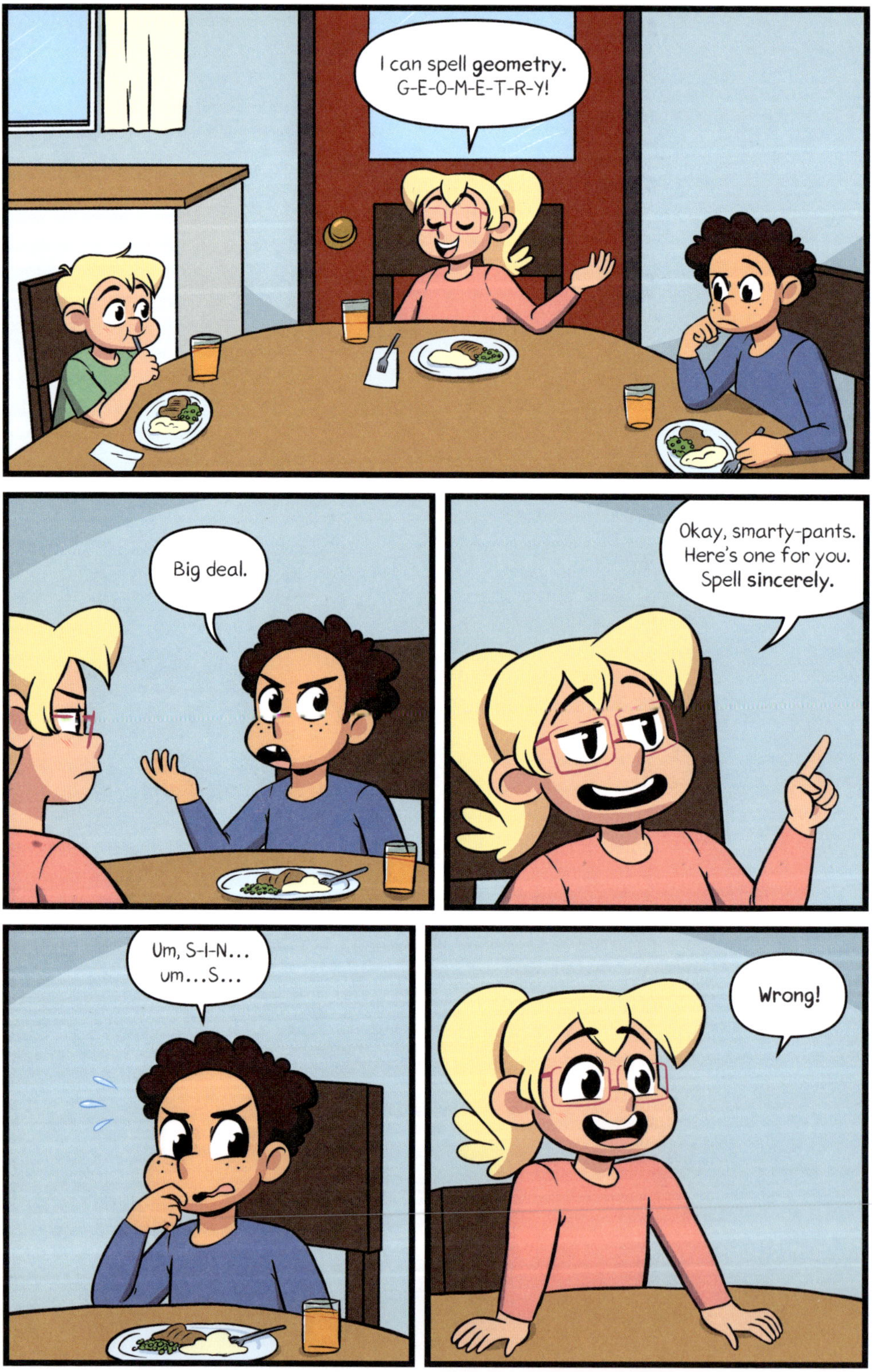
I can spell **geometry.** G-E-O-M-E-T-R-Y!
Big deal.
Okay, smarty-pants. Here's one for you. Spell **sincerely.**
Um, S-I-N... um...S...
Wrong!

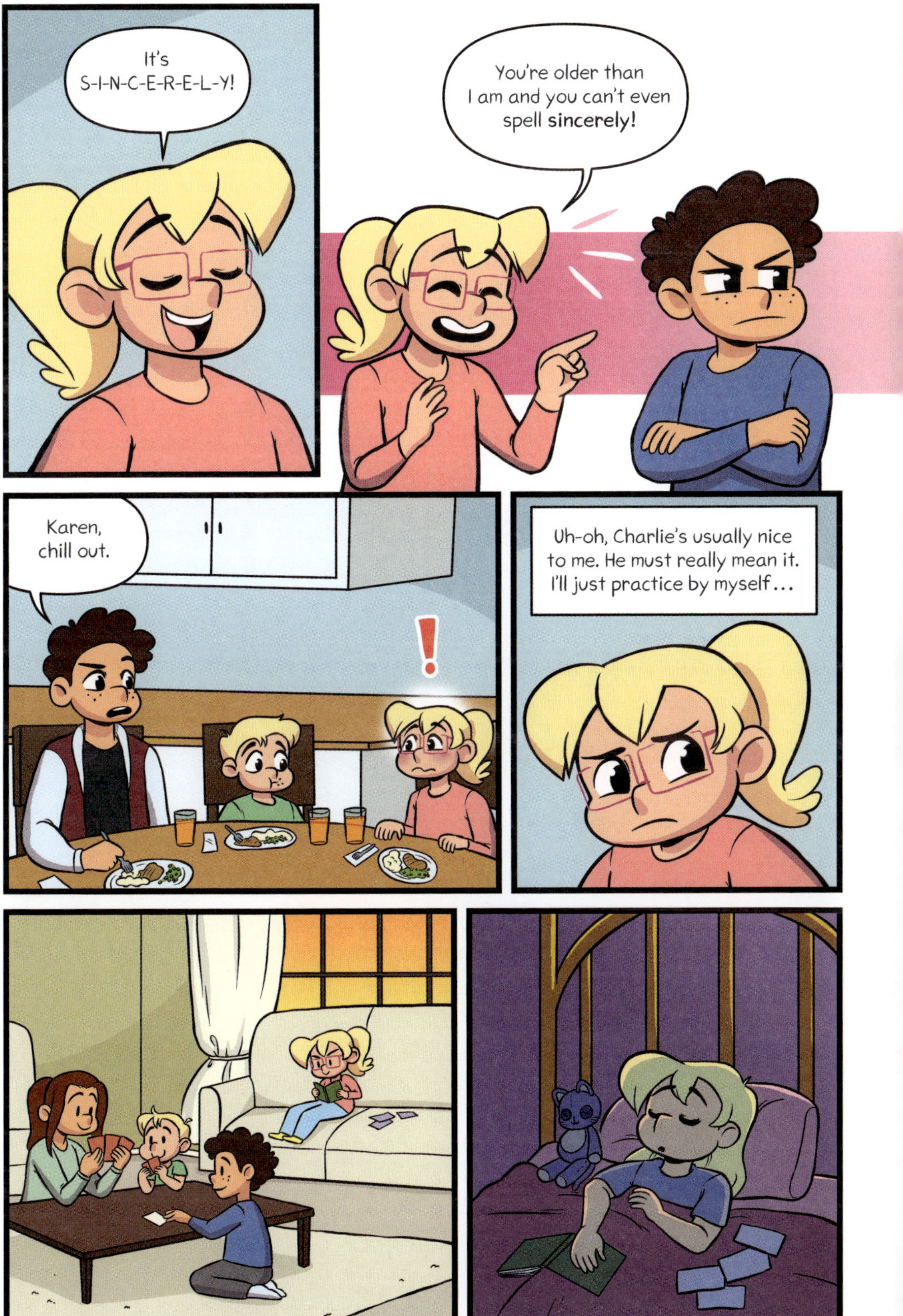
It's S-I-N-C-E-R-E-L-Y!
You're older than I am and you can't even spell **sincerely**!
Karen, chill out.
!
Uh-oh, Charlie's usually nice to me. He must really mean it. I'll just practice by myself...

# CHAPTER 2

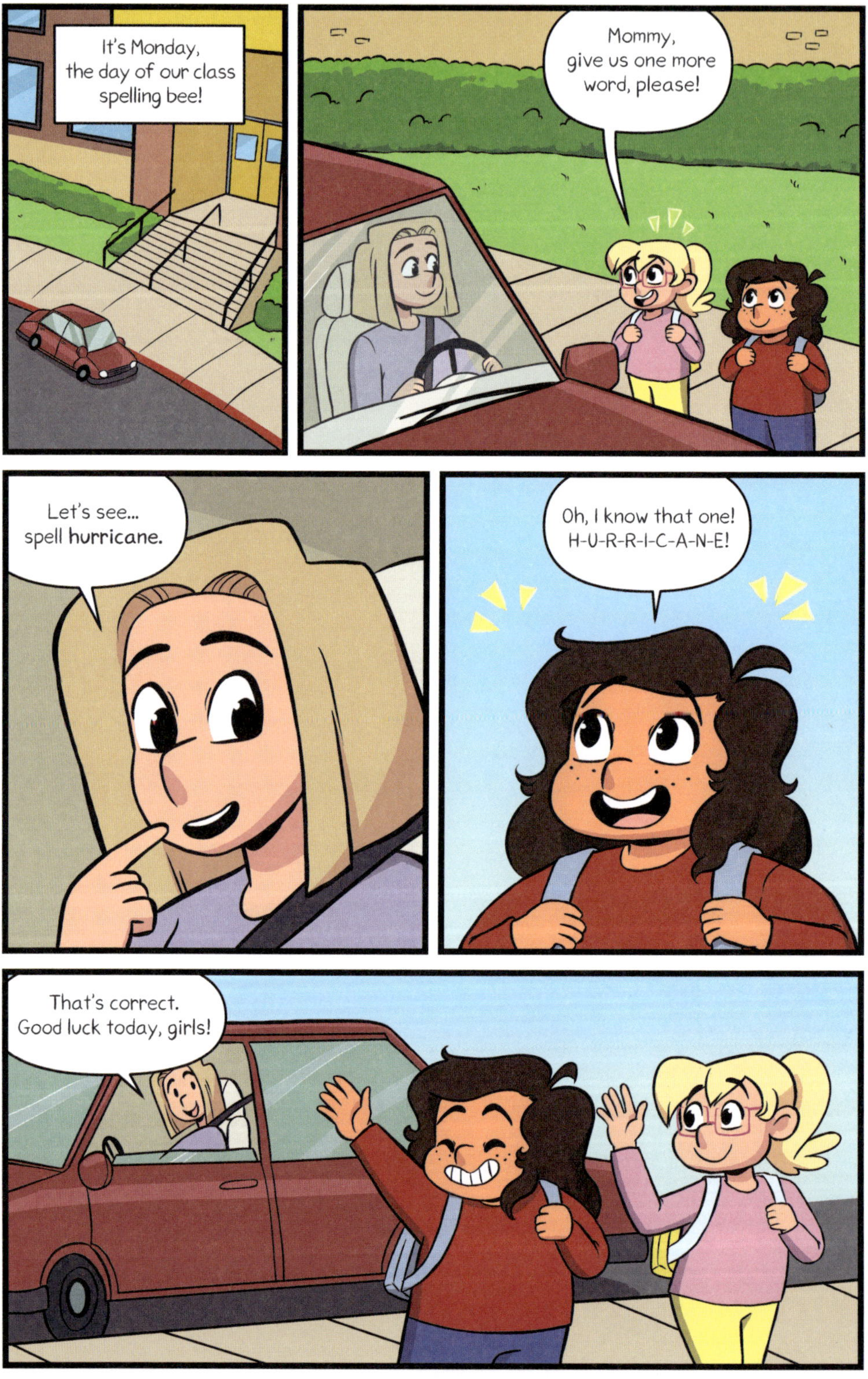
It's Monday, the day of our class spelling bee!
Mommy, give us one more word, please!
Let's see... spell **hurricane.**
Oh, I know that one! H-U-R-R-I-C-A-N-E!
That's correct. Good luck today, girls!

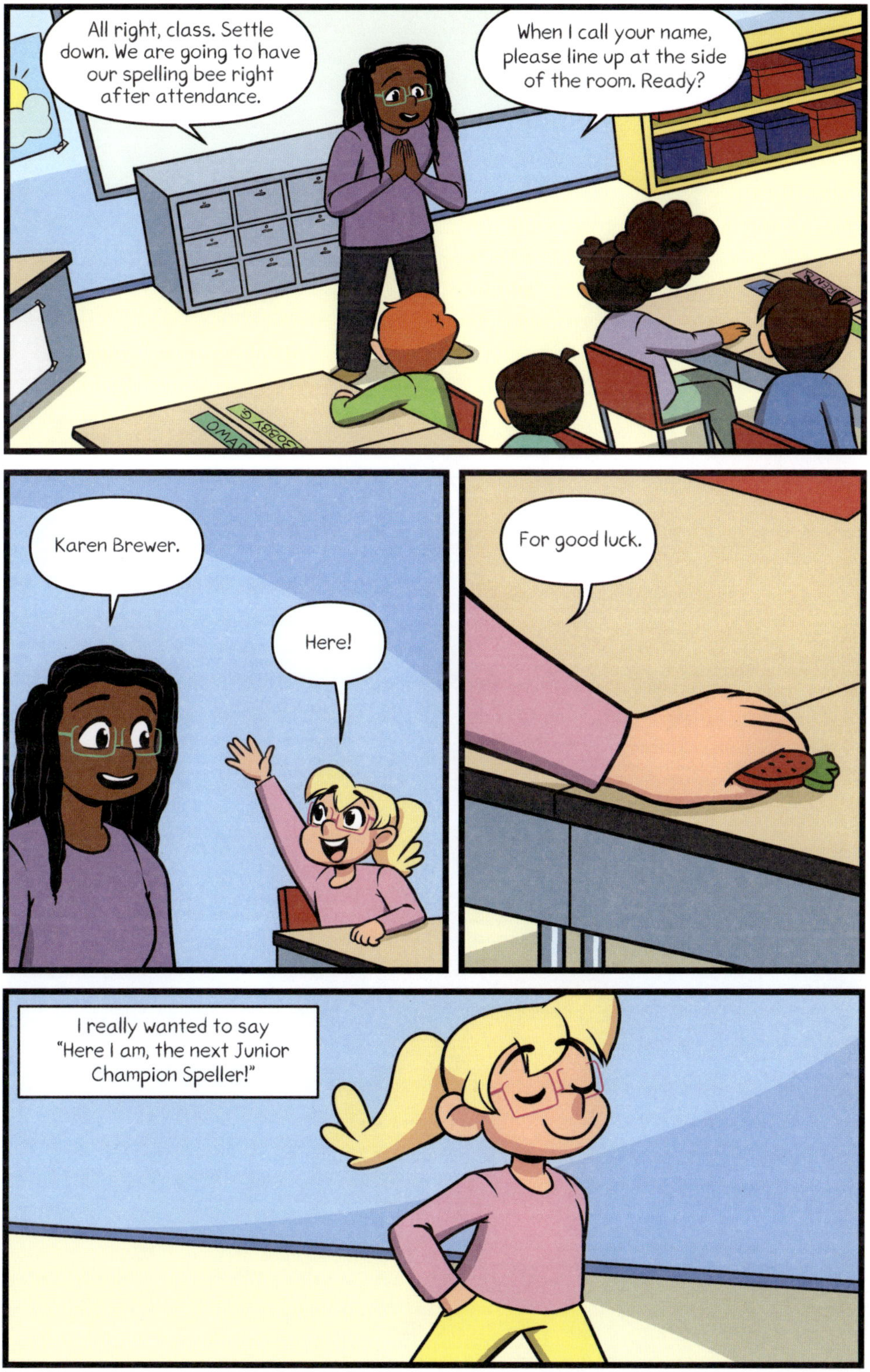
All right, class. Settle down. We are going to have our spelling bee right after attendance.
When I call your name, please line up at the side of the room. Ready?
Karen Brewer.
Here!
For good luck.
I really wanted to say "Here I am, the next Junior Champion Speller!"

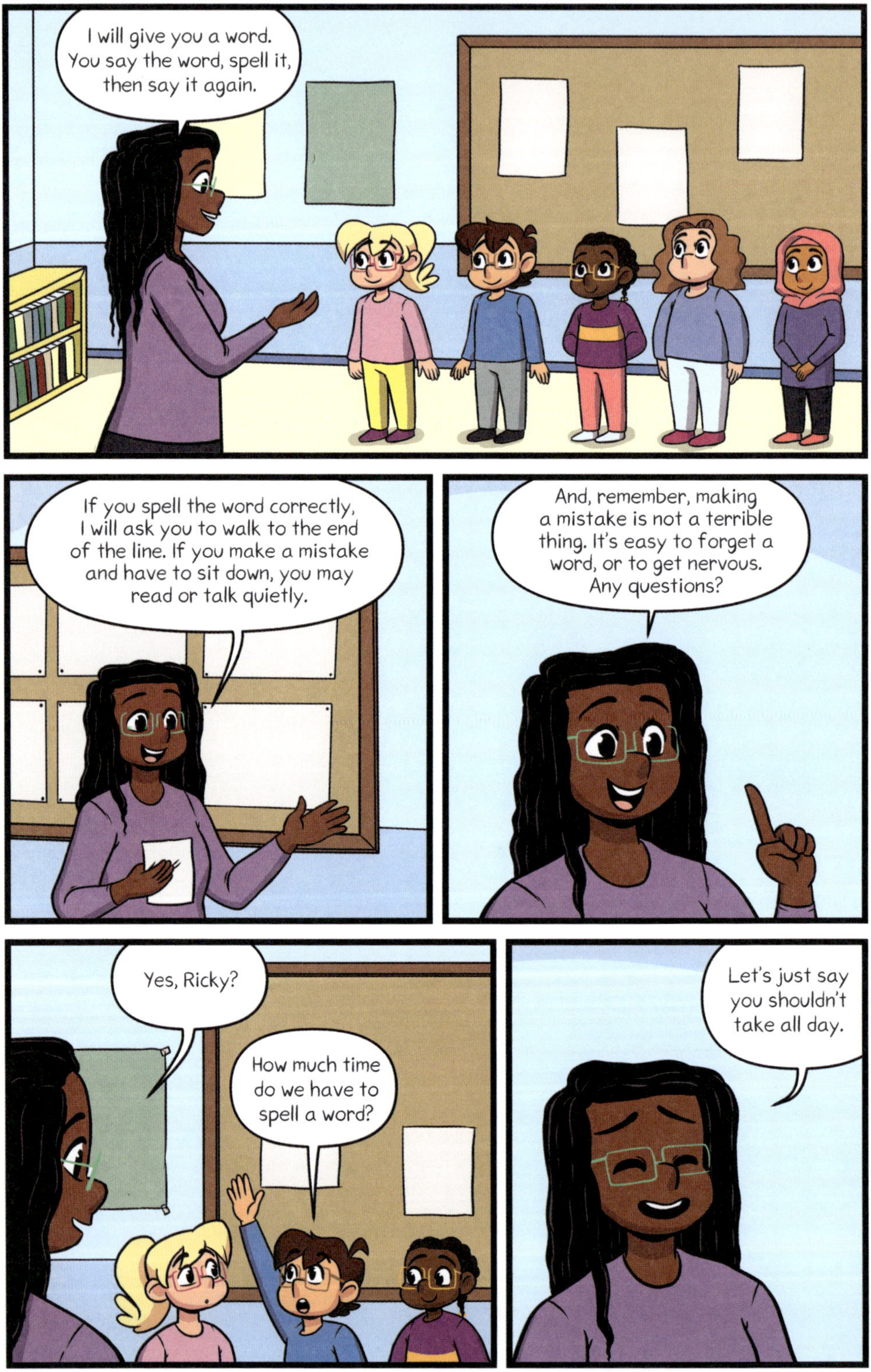
I will give you a word. You say the word, spell it, then say it again.
If you spell the word correctly, I will ask you to walk to the end of the line. If you make a mistake and have to sit down, you may read or talk quietly.
And, remember, making a mistake is not a terrible thing. It's easy to forget a word, or to get nervous. Any questions?
Yes, Ricky?
How much time do we have to spell a word?
Let's just say you shouldn't take all day.

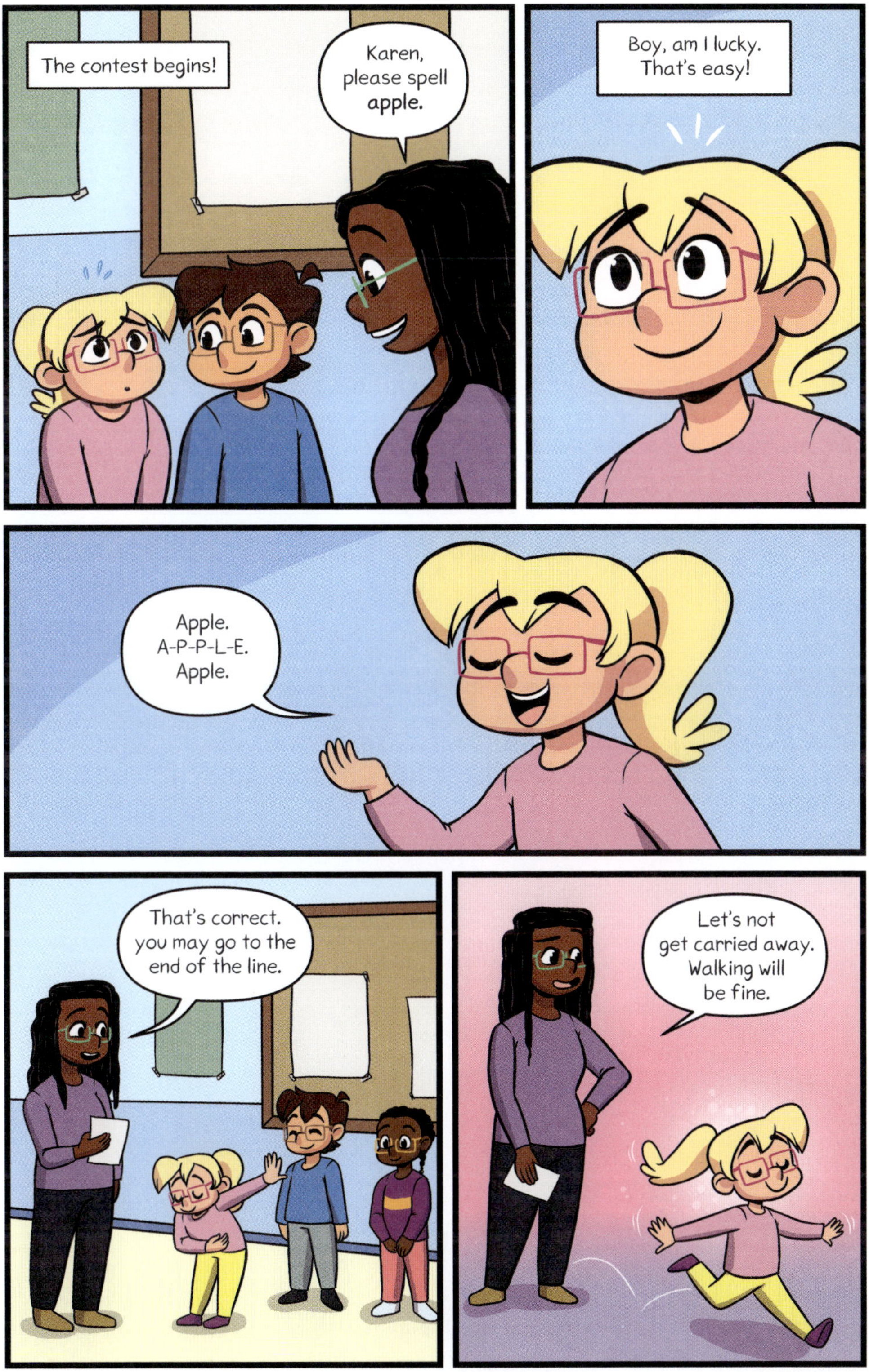
The contest begins!
Karen, please spell **apple.**
Boy, am I lucky. That's easy!
Apple. A-P-P-L-E. Apple.
That's correct. you may go to the end of the line.
Let's not get carried away. Walking will be fine.

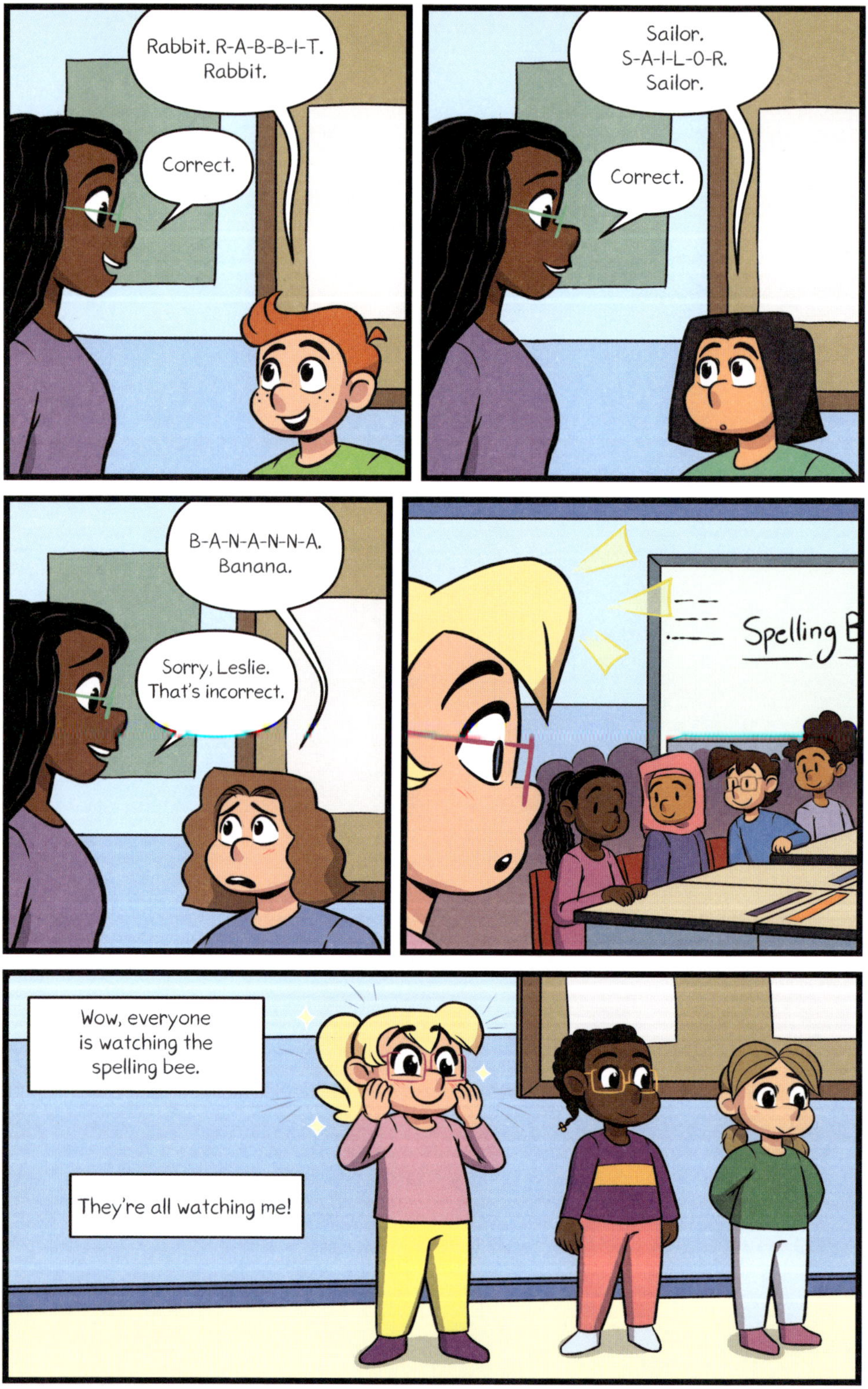
Rabbit. R-A-B-B-I-T. Rabbit.
Correct.
Sailor. S-A-I-L-O-R. Sailor.
Correct.
B-A-N-A-N-N-A. Banana.
Sorry, Leslie. That's incorrect.
Spelling B
Wow, everyone is watching the spelling bee.
They're all watching me!

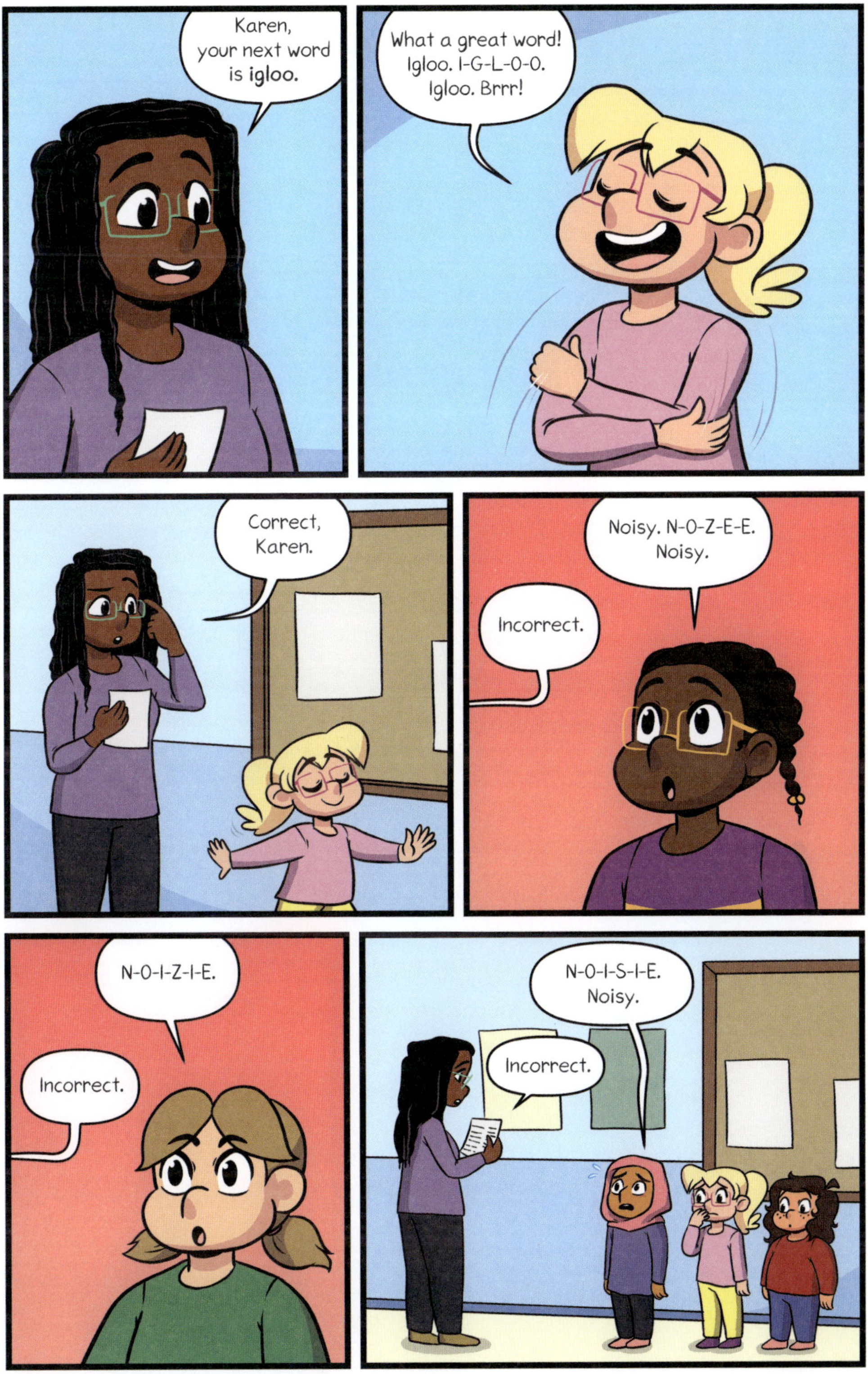
Karen, your next word is **igloo.**
What a great word! Igloo. I-G-L-O-O. Igloo. Brrr!
Correct, Karen.
Noisy. N-O-Z-E-E. Noisy.
Incorrect.
N-O-I-Z-I-E.
Incorrect.
N-O-I-S-I-E. Noisy.
Incorrect.

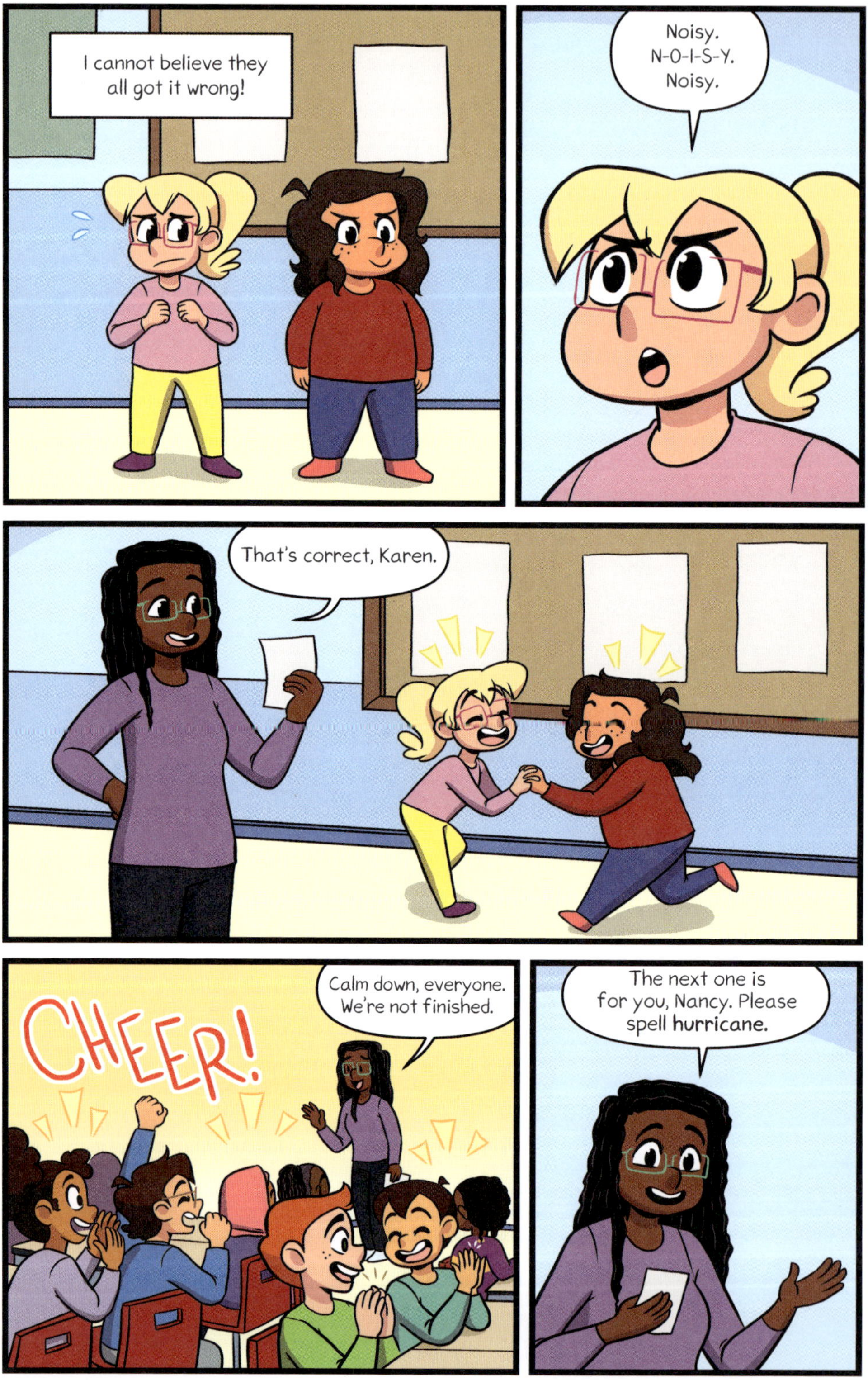
I cannot believe they all got it wrong!
Noisy. N-O-I-S-Y. Noisy.
That's correct, Karen.
CHEER!
Calm down, everyone. We're not finished.
The next one is for you, Nancy. Please spell **hurricane.**

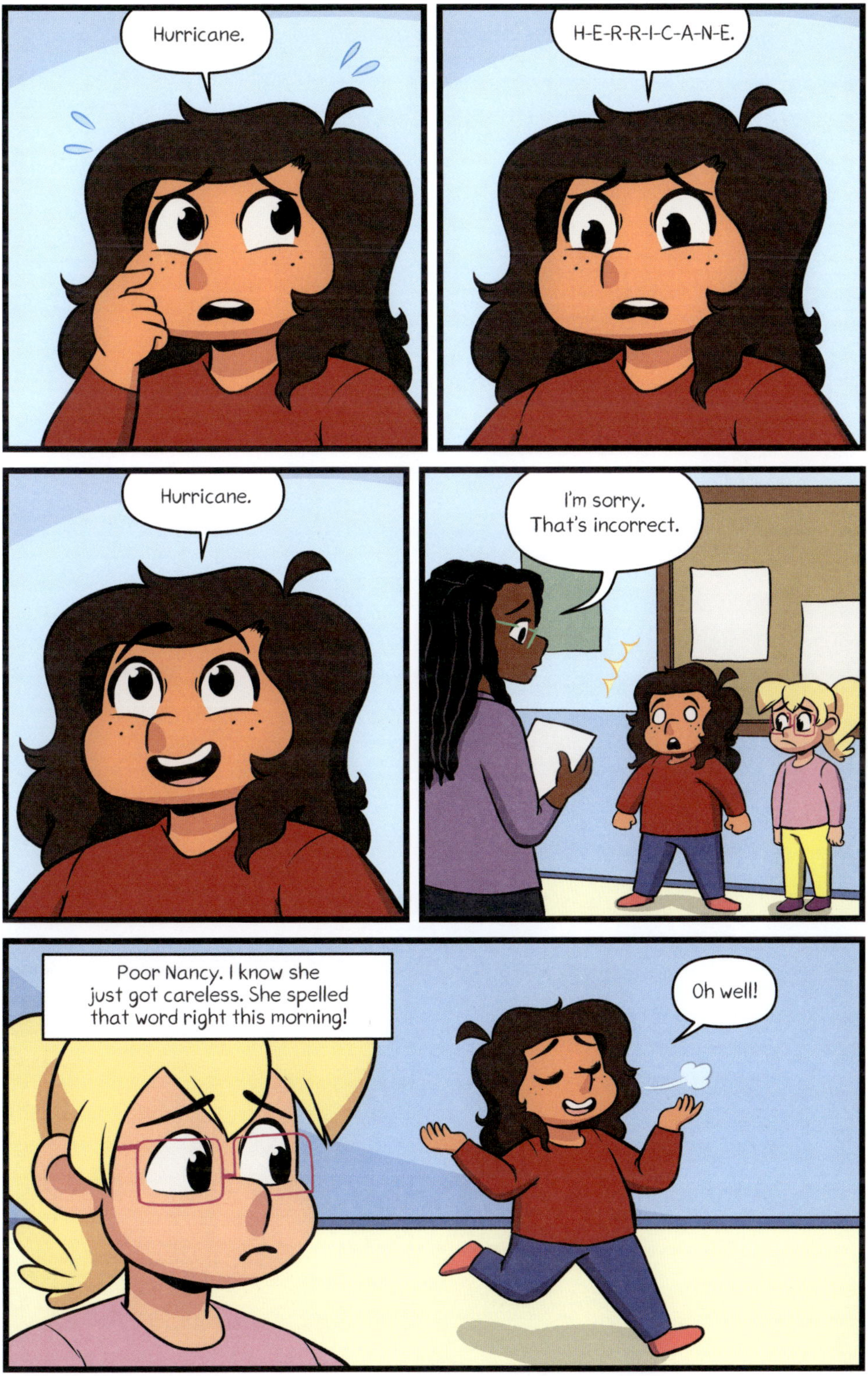
Hurricane.
H-E-R-R-I-C-A-N-E.
Hurricane.
I'm sorry.
That's incorrect.
Poor Nancy. I know she just got careless. She spelled that word right this morning!
Oh well!

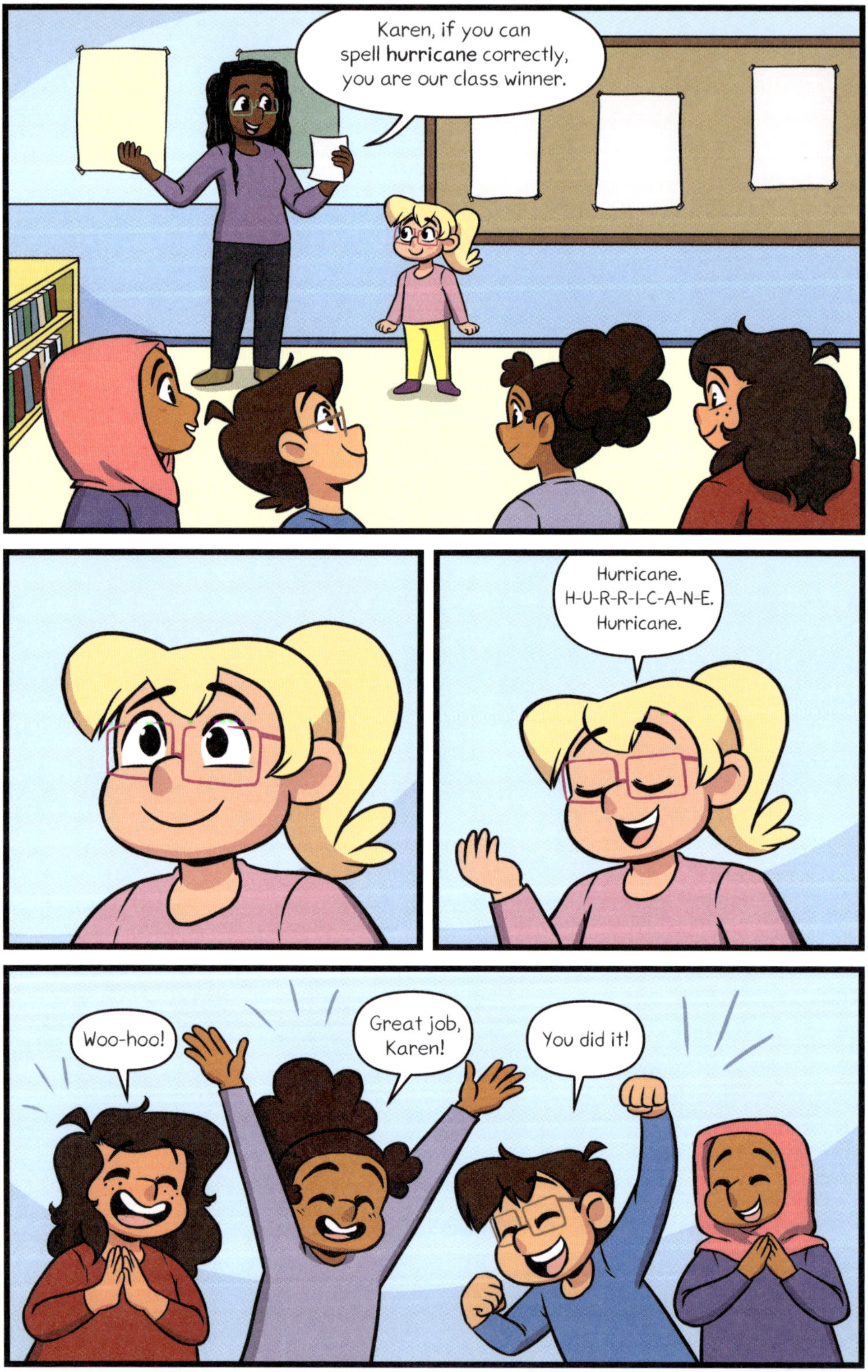
Karen, if you can spell **hurricane** correctly, you are our class winner.
Hurricane. H-U-R-R-I-C-A-N-E. Hurricane.
Woo-hoo!
Great job, Karen!
You did it!

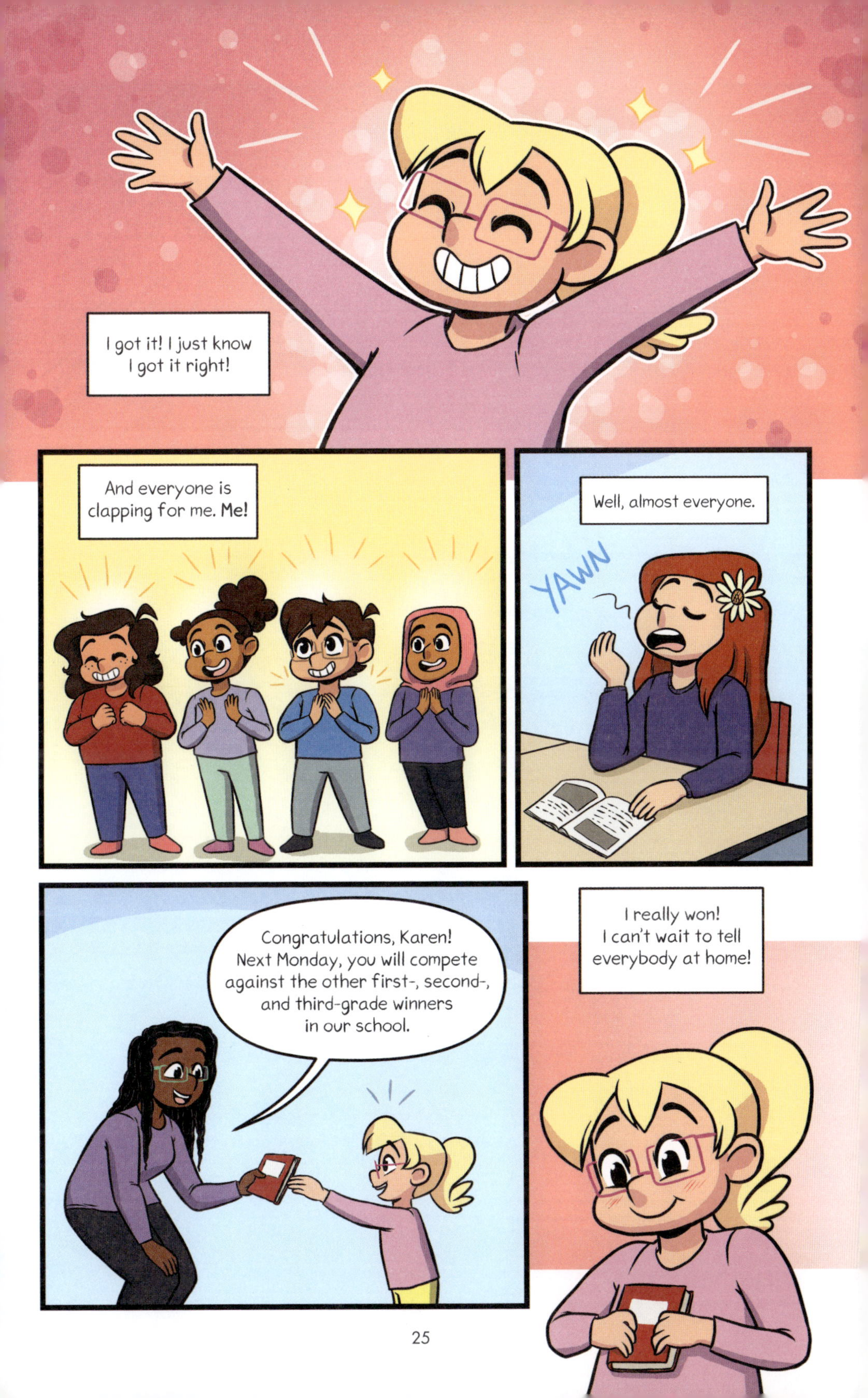
I got it! I just know I got it right!
And everyone is clapping for me. **Me!**
Well, almost everyone.
YAWN
Congratulations, Karen! Next Monday, you will compete against the other first-, second-, and third-grade winners in our school.
I really won! I can't wait to tell everybody at home!

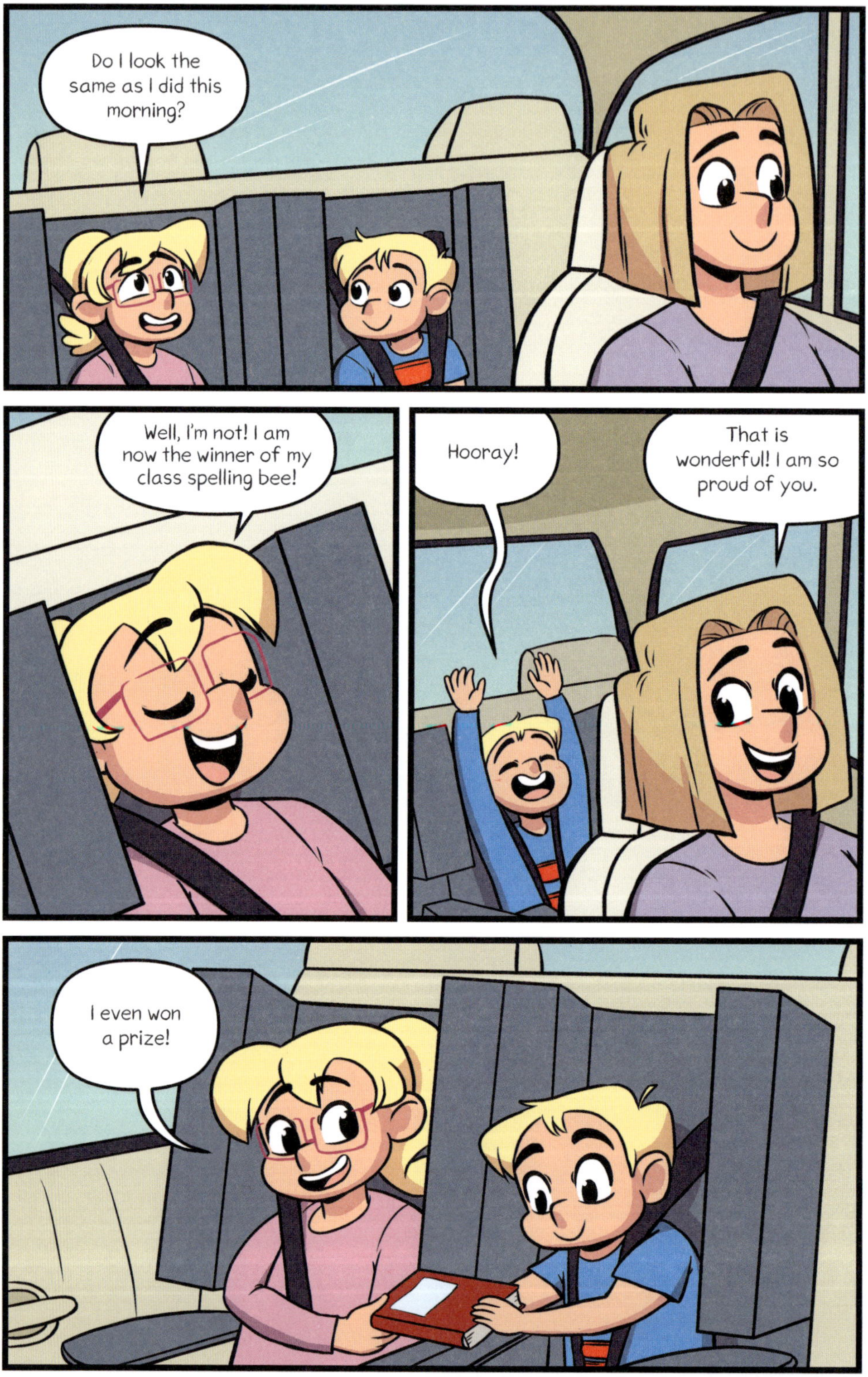
Do I look the same as I did this morning?
Well, I'm not! I am now the winner of my class spelling bee!
Hooray!
That is wonderful! I am so proud of you.
I even won a prize!

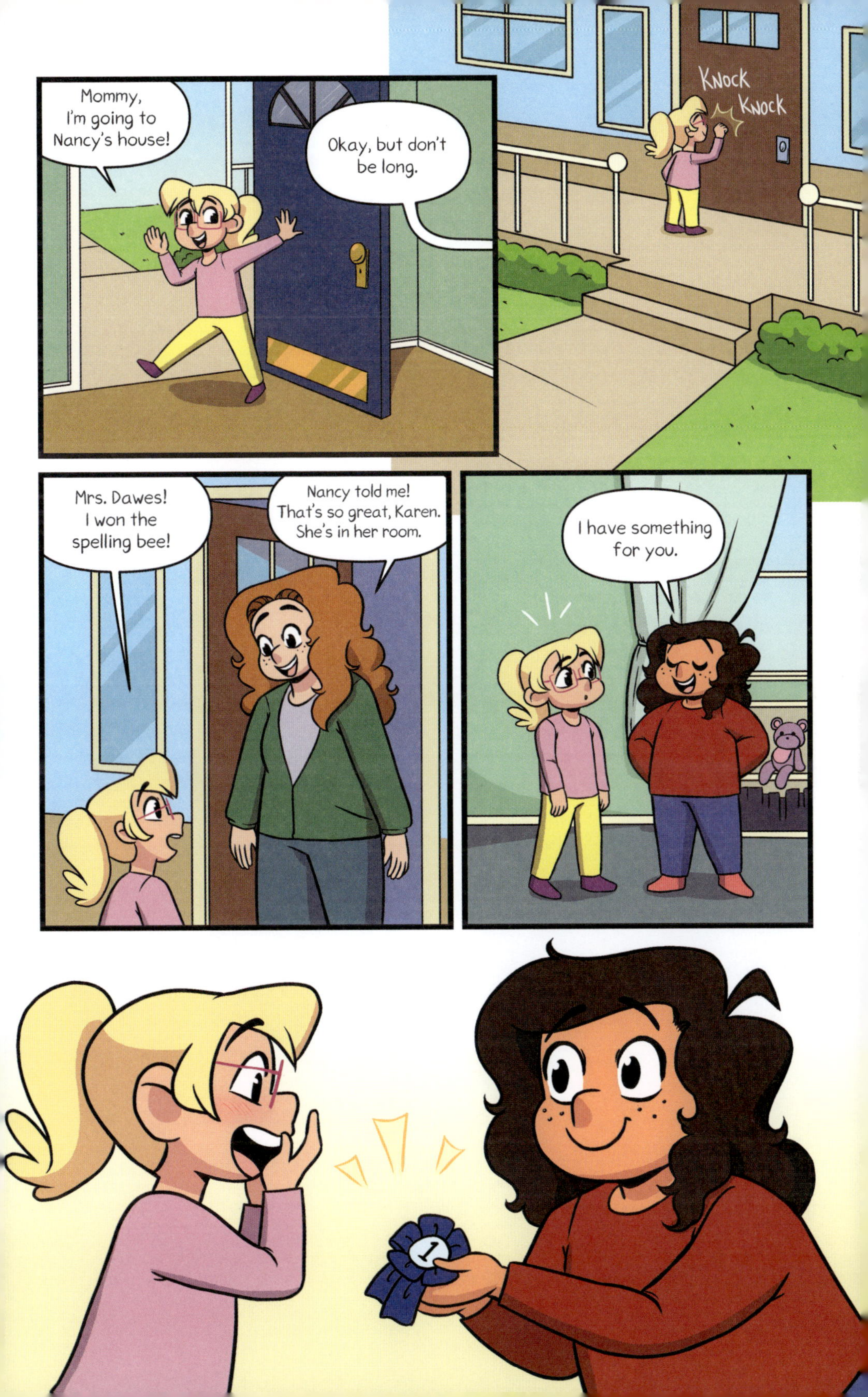
Mommy, I'm going to Nancy's house!
Okay, but don't be long.
KNOCK KNOCK
Mrs. Dawes! I won the spelling bee!
Nancy told me! That's so great, Karen. She's in her room.
I have something for you.
1

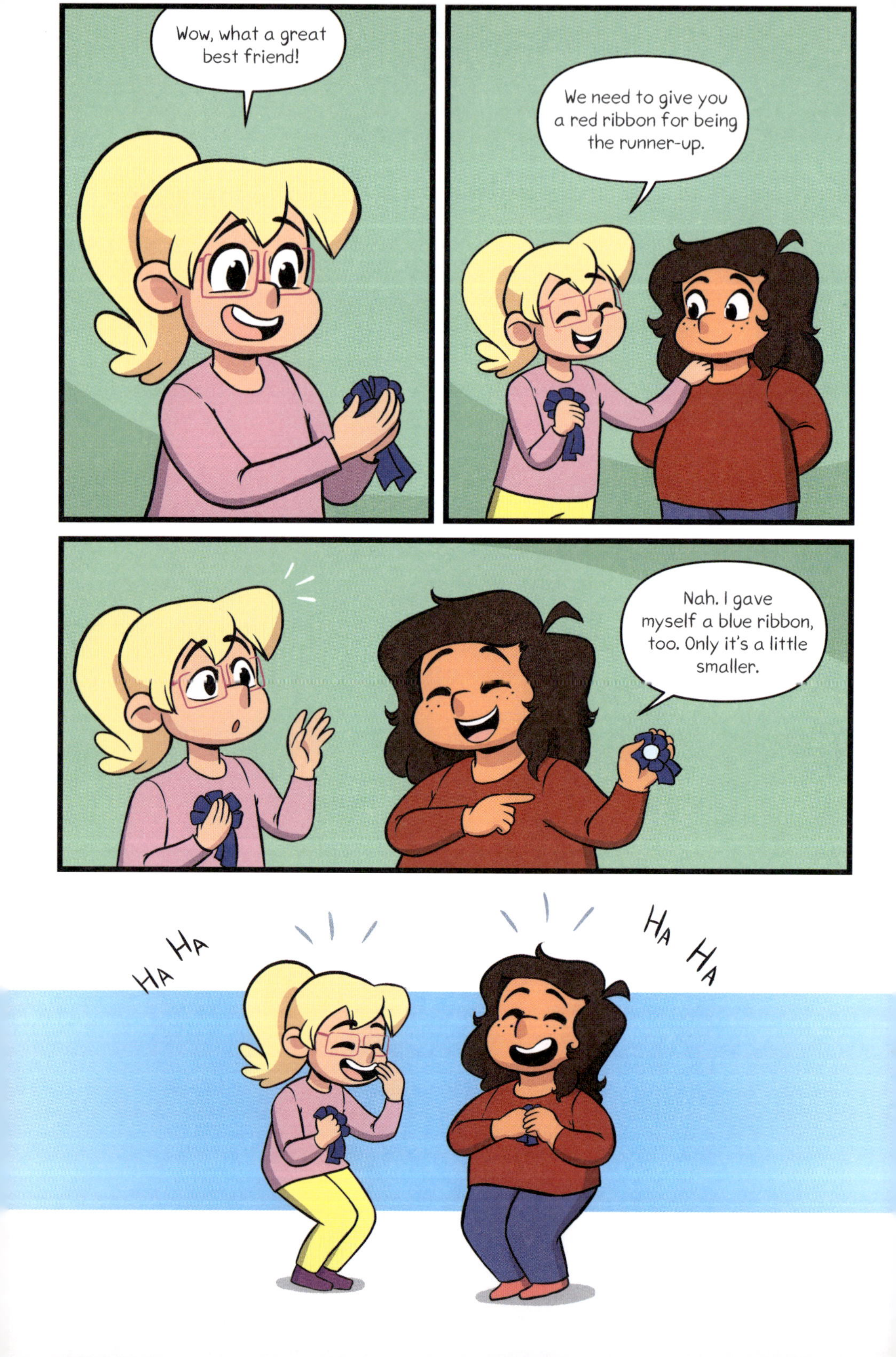
Wow, what a great best friend!
We need to give you a red ribbon for being the runner-up.
Nah. I gave myself a blue ribbon, too. Only it's a little smaller.
HA HA
HA HA

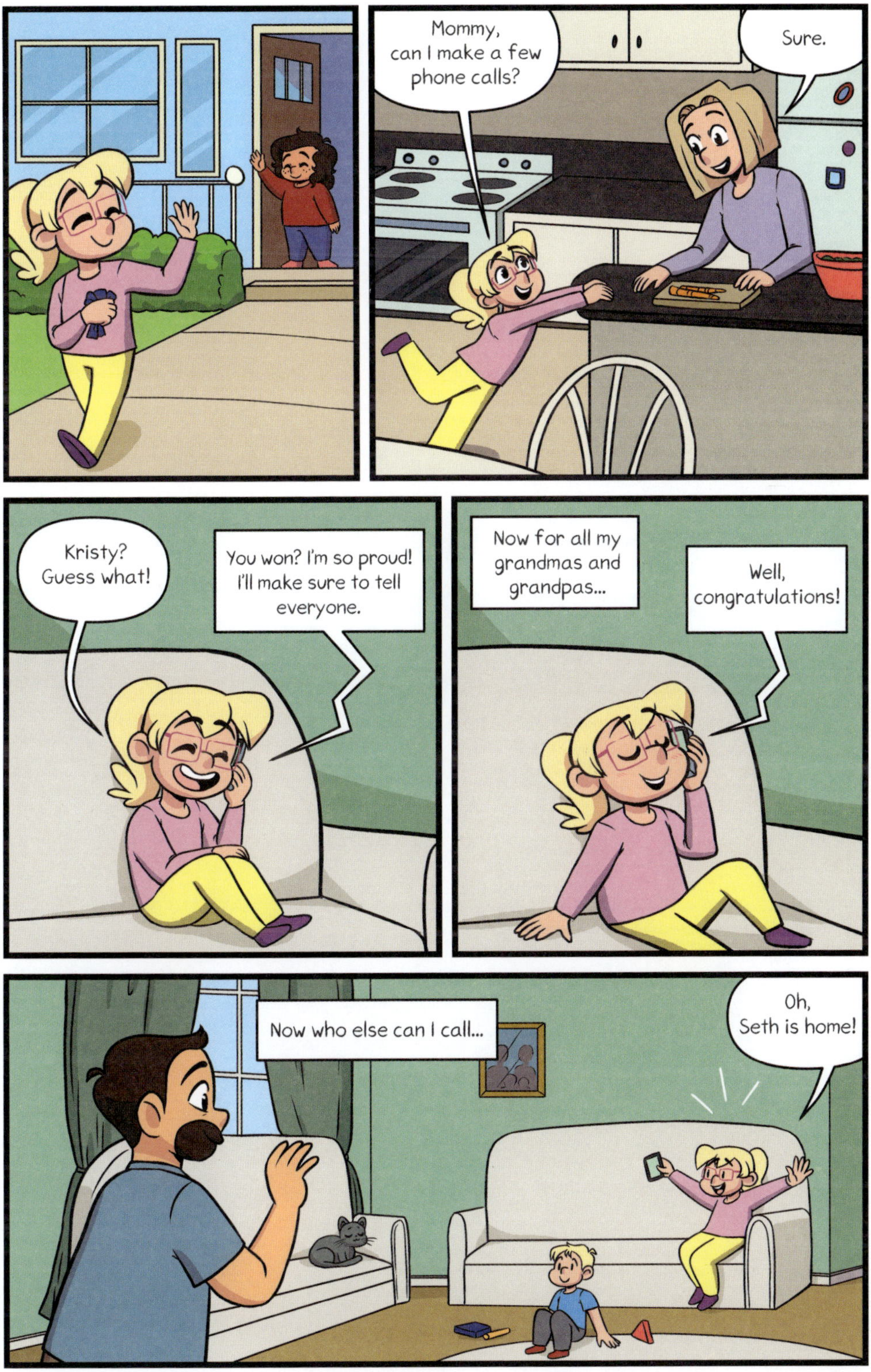
Mommy, can I make a few phone calls?
Sure.
Kristy? Guess what!
You won? I'm so proud! I'll make sure to tell everyone.
Now for all my grandmas and grandpas...
Well, congratulations!
Now who else can I call...
Oh, Seth is home!

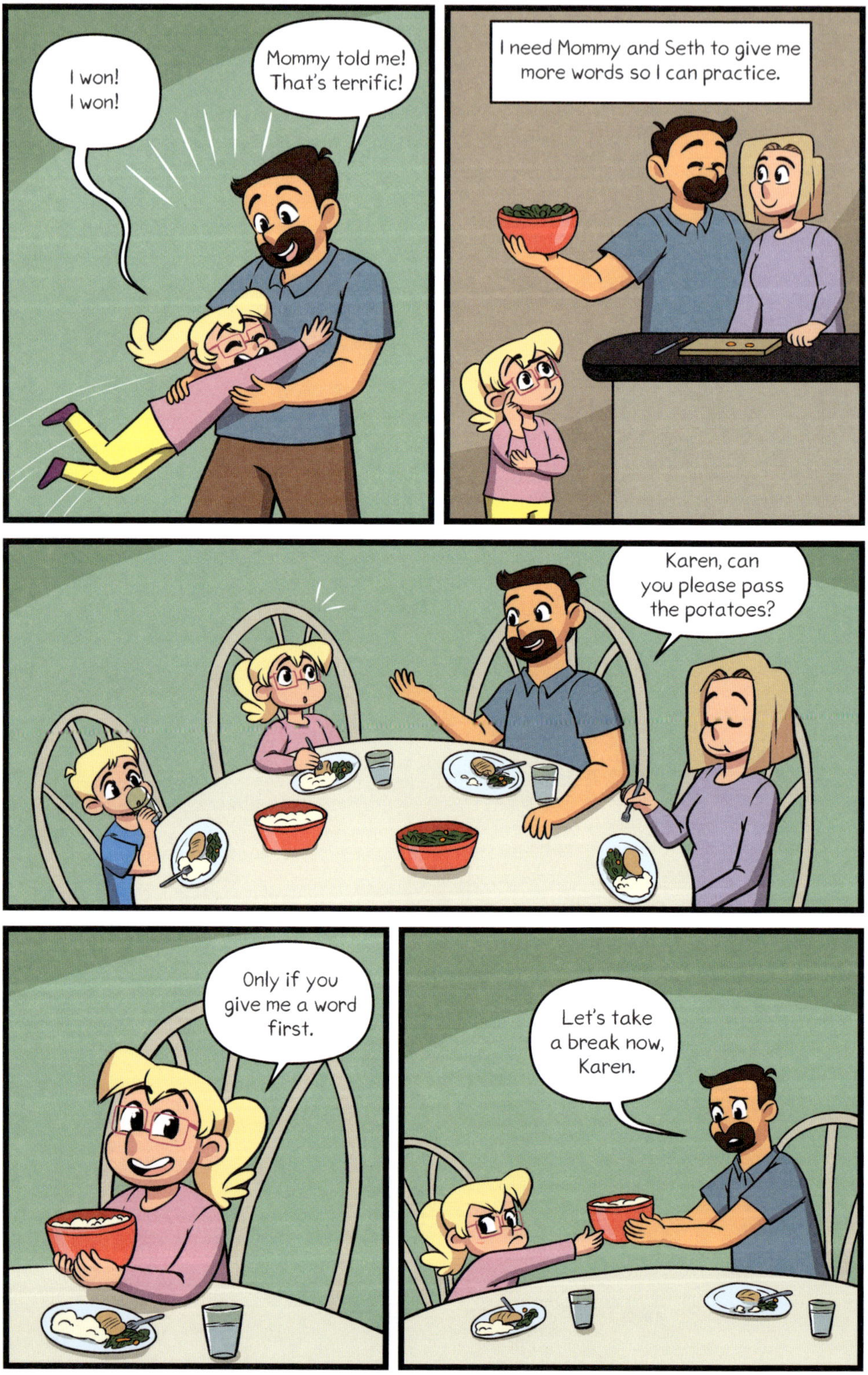
I won!
I won!
Mommy told me! That's terrific!
I need Mommy and Seth to give me more words so I can practice.
Karen, can you please pass the potatoes?
Only if you give me a word first.
Let's take a break now, Karen.

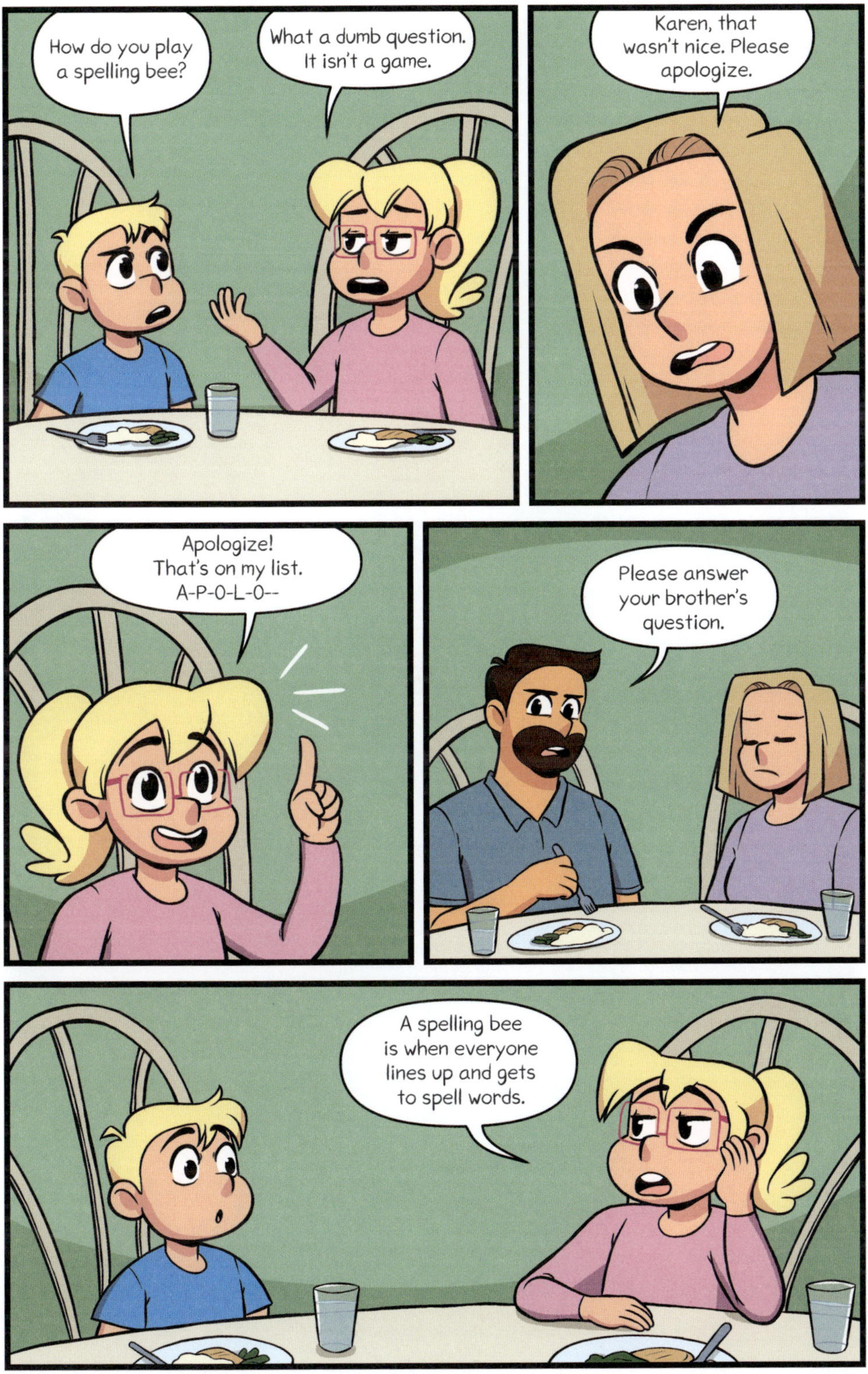
How do you play a spelling bee?
What a dumb question. It isn't a game.
Karen, that wasn't nice. Please apologize.
Apologize! That's on my list. A-P-O-L-O--
Please answer your brother's question.
A spelling bee is when everyone lines up and gets to spell words.

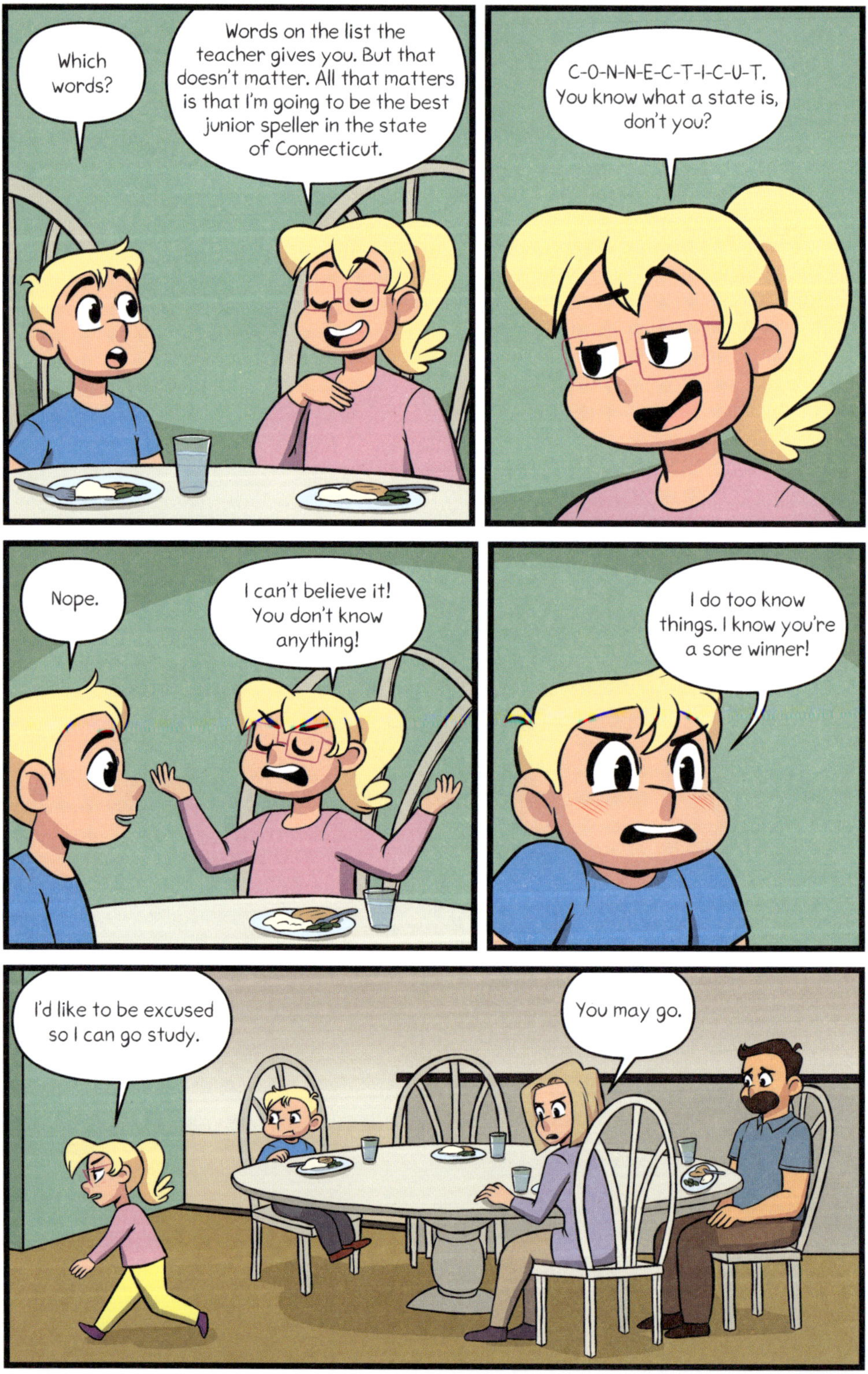
Which words?
Words on the list the teacher gives you. But that doesn't matter. All that matters is that I'm going to be the best junior speller in the state of Connecticut.
C-O-N-N-E-C-T-I-C-U-T. You know what a state is, don't you?
Nope.
I can't believe it! You don't know anything!
I do too know things. I know you're a sore winner!
I'd like to be excused so I can go study.
You may go.

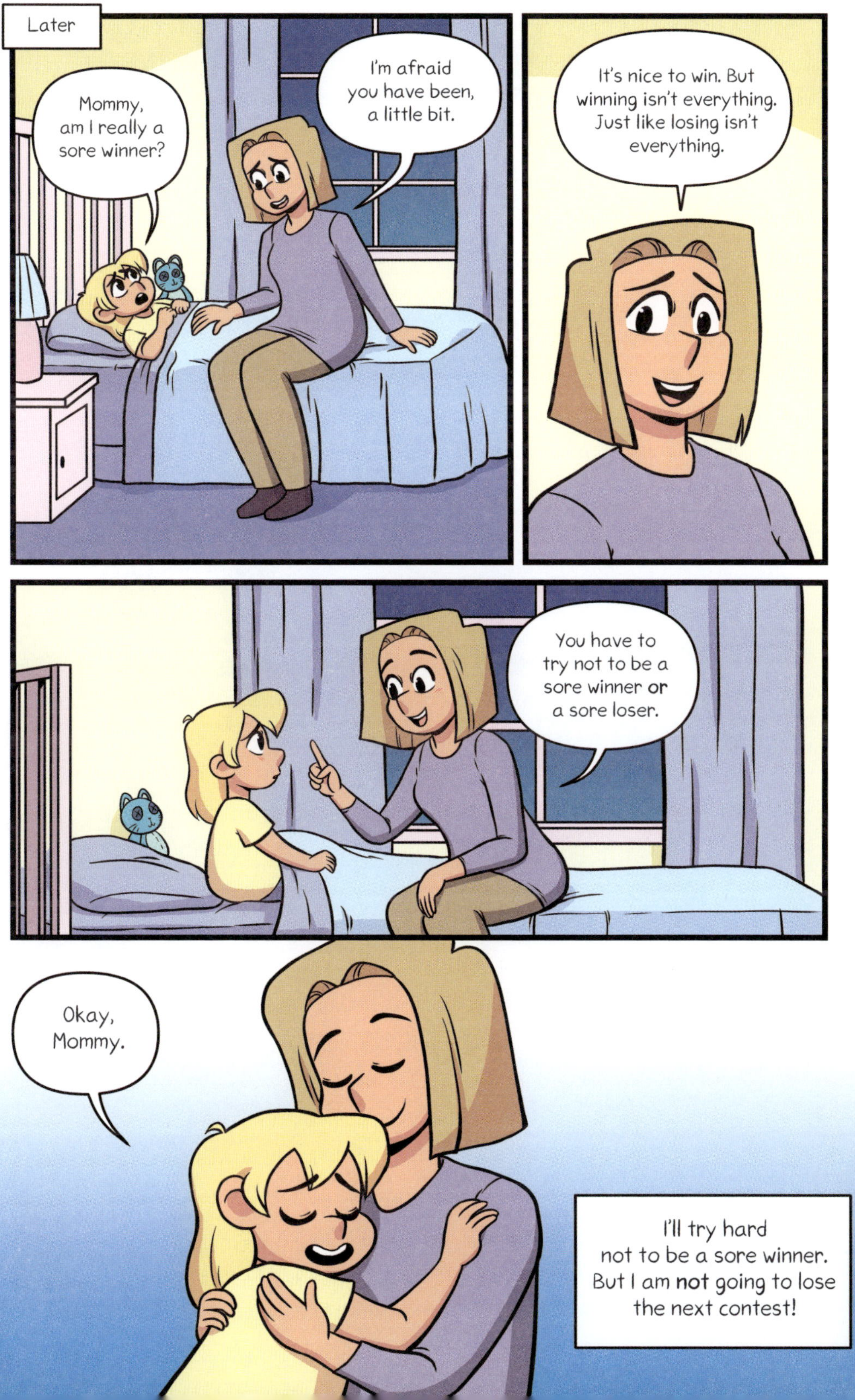
Later
Mommy, am I really a sore winner?
I'm afraid you have been, a little bit.
It's nice to win. But winning isn't everything. Just like losing isn't everything.
You have to try not to be a sore winner **or** a sore loser.
Okay, Mommy.
I'll try hard not to be a sore winner. But I am **not** going to lose the next contest!

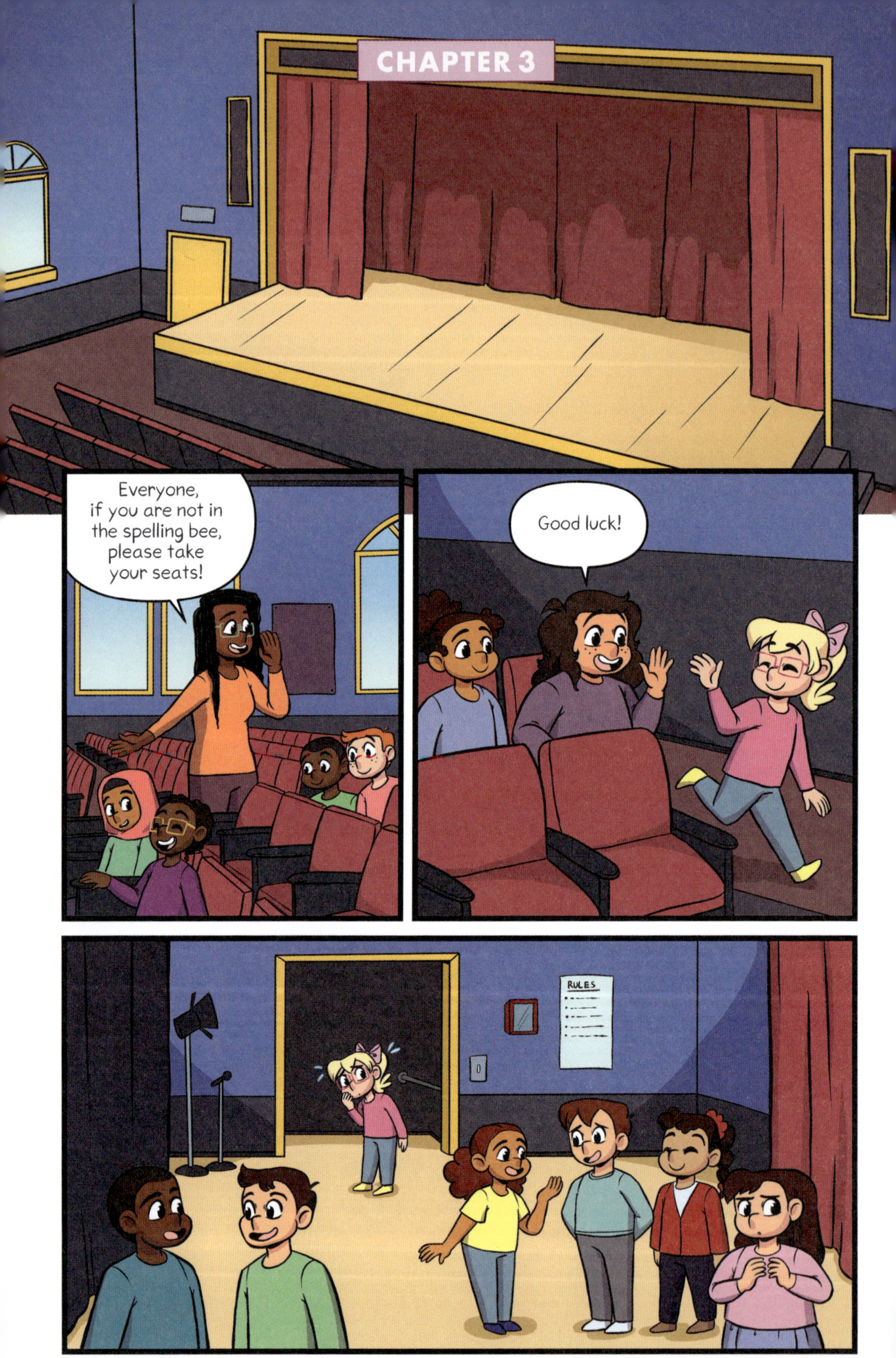
CHAPTER 3
Everyone, if you are not in the spelling bee, please take your seats!
Good luck!
RULES

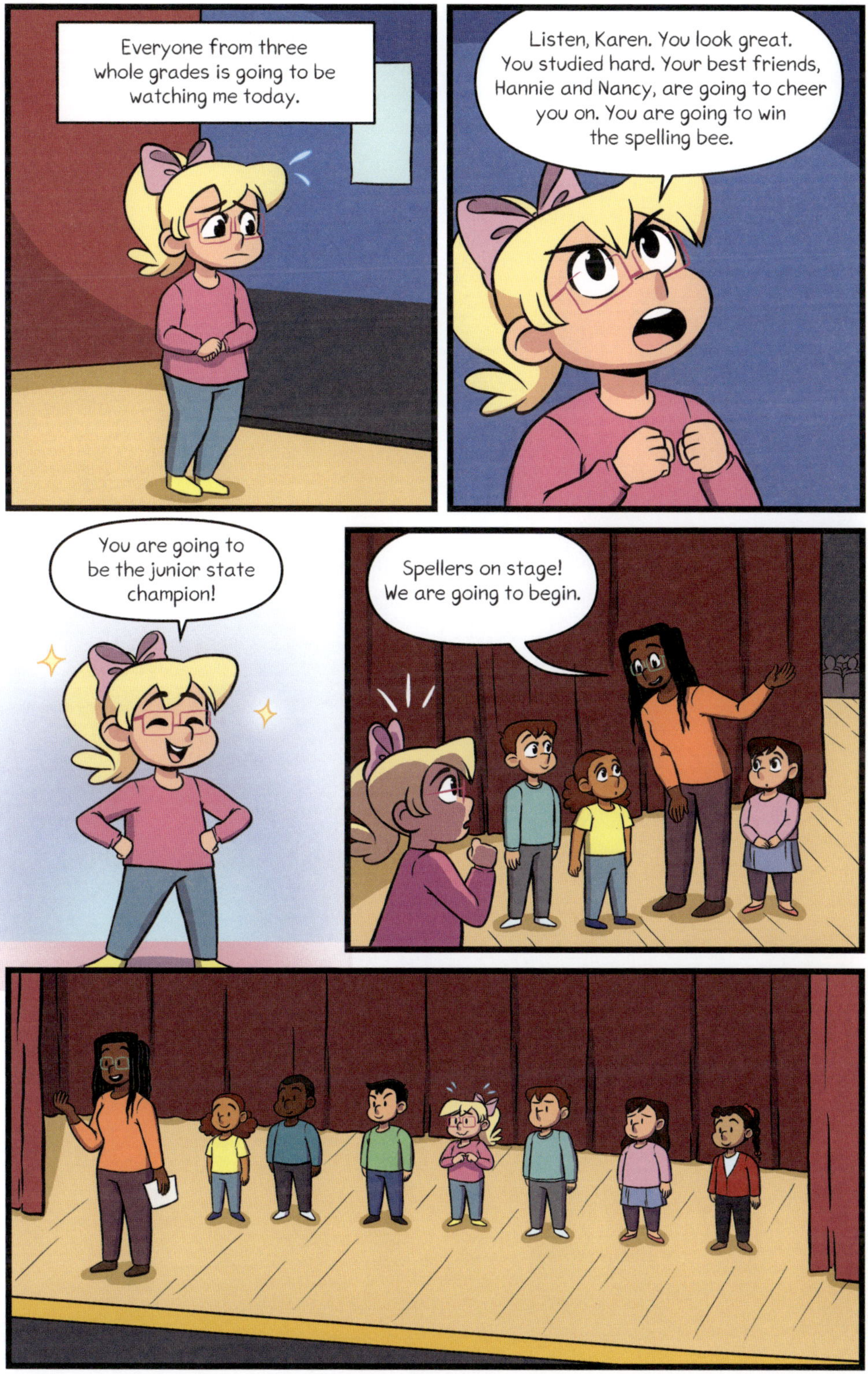
Everyone from three whole grades is going to be watching me today.
Listen, Karen. You look great. You studied hard. Your best friends, Hannie and Nancy, are going to cheer you on. You are going to win the spelling bee.
You are going to be the junior state champion!
Spellers on stage! We are going to begin.

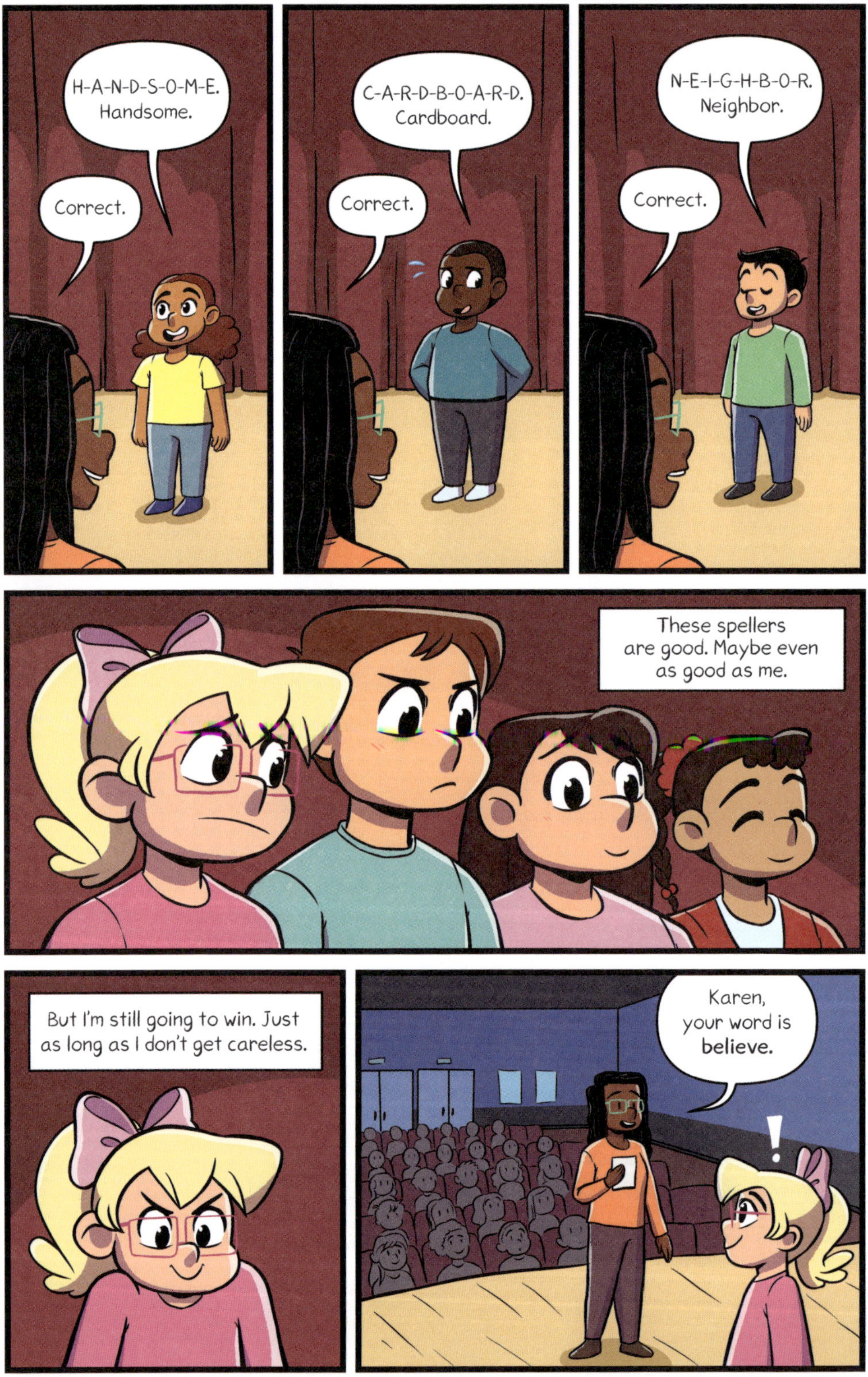

H-A-N-D-S-O-M-E. Handsome.
Correct.
C-A-R-D-B-O-A-R-D. Cardboard.
Correct.
N-E-I-G-H-B-O-R. Neighbor.
Correct.
These spellers are good. Maybe even as good as me.
But I'm still going to win. Just as long as I don't get careless.
Karen, your word is **believe.**
!

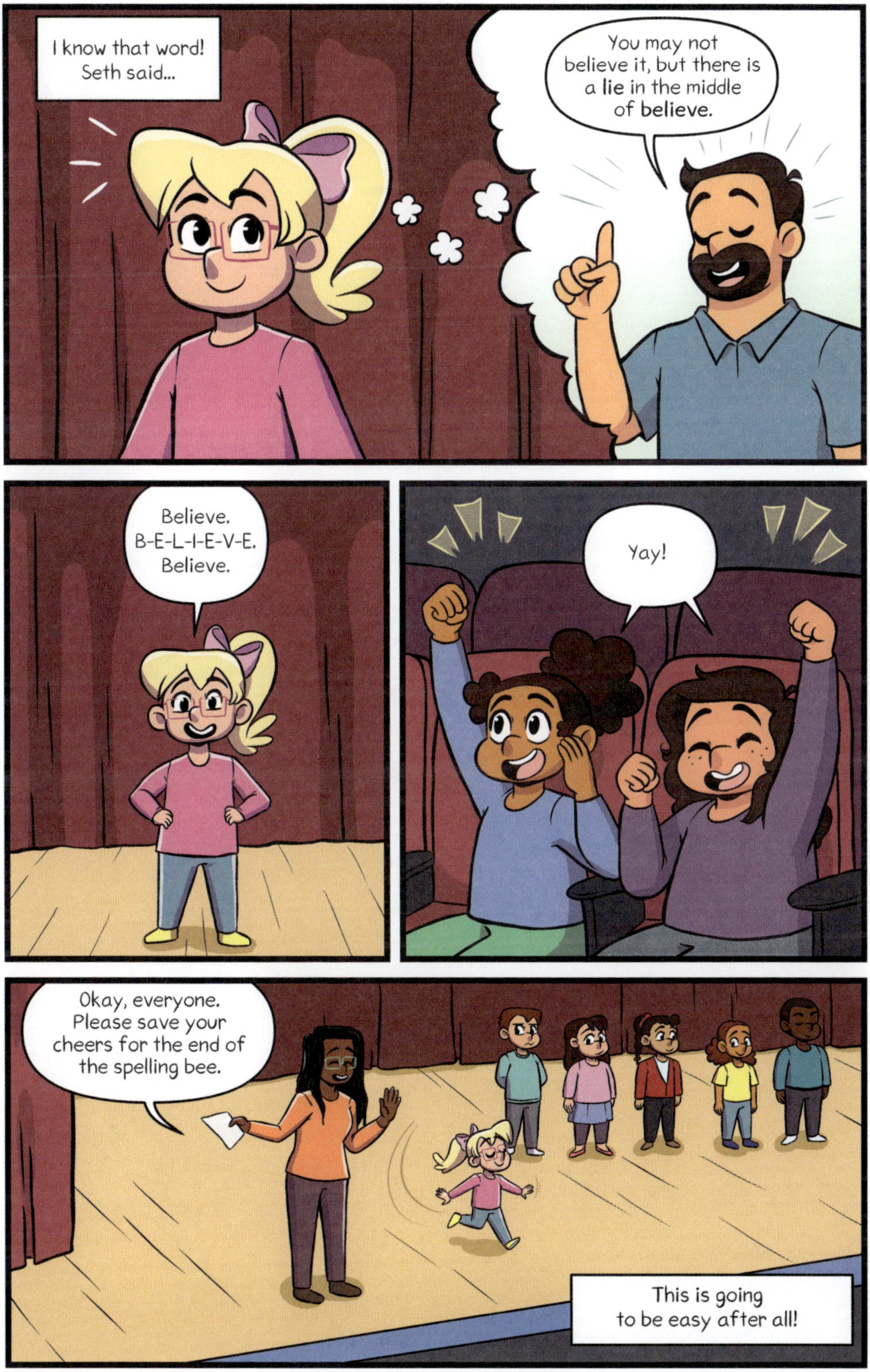
I know that word! Seth said...
You may not believe it, but there is a **lie** in the middle of **believe**.
Believe. B-E-L-I-E-V-E. Believe.
Yay!
Okay, everyone. Please save your cheers for the end of the spelling bee.
This is going to be easy after all!

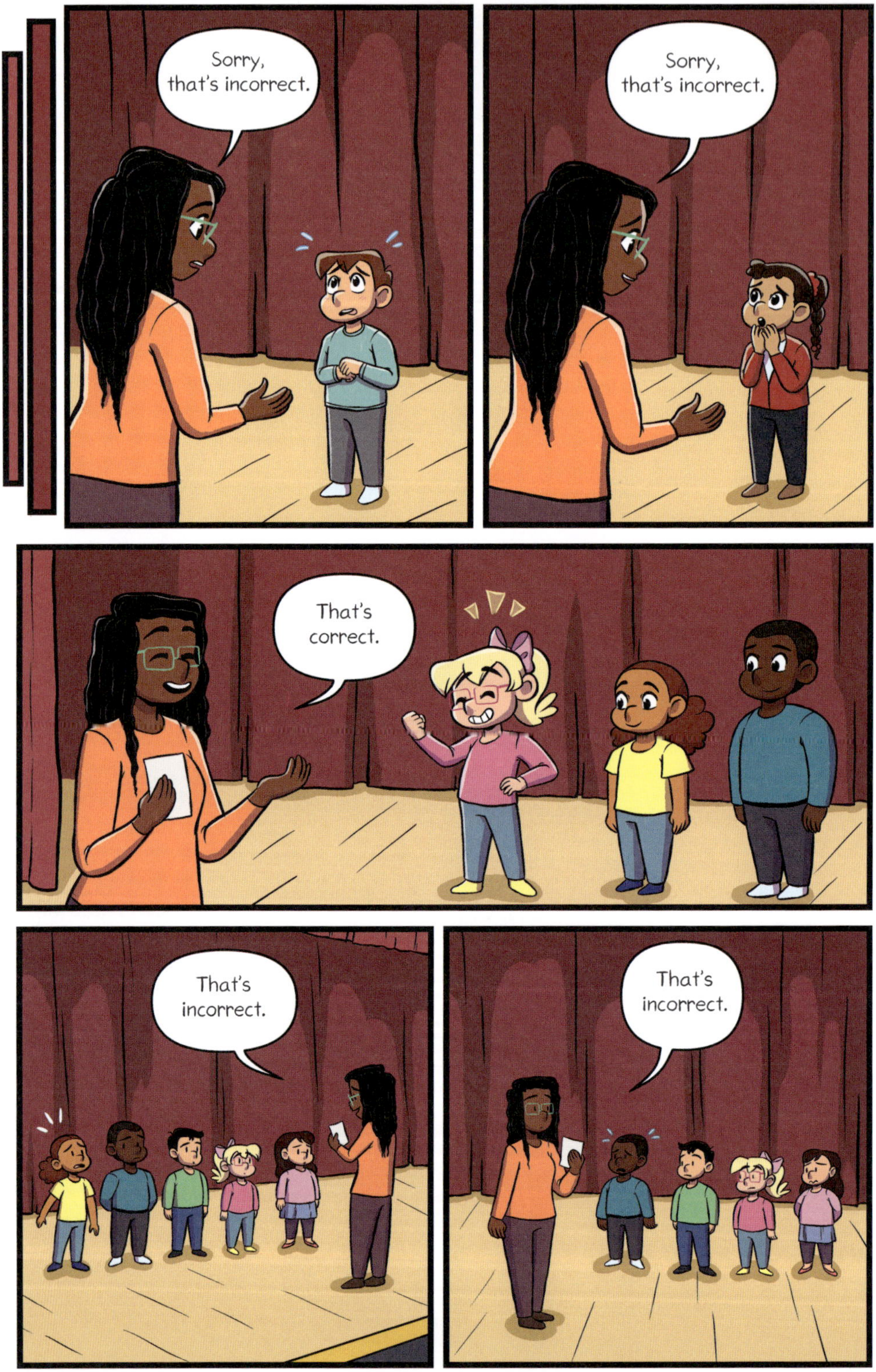
Sorry, that's incorrect.
Sorry, that's incorrect.
That's correct.
That's incorrect.
That's incorrect.

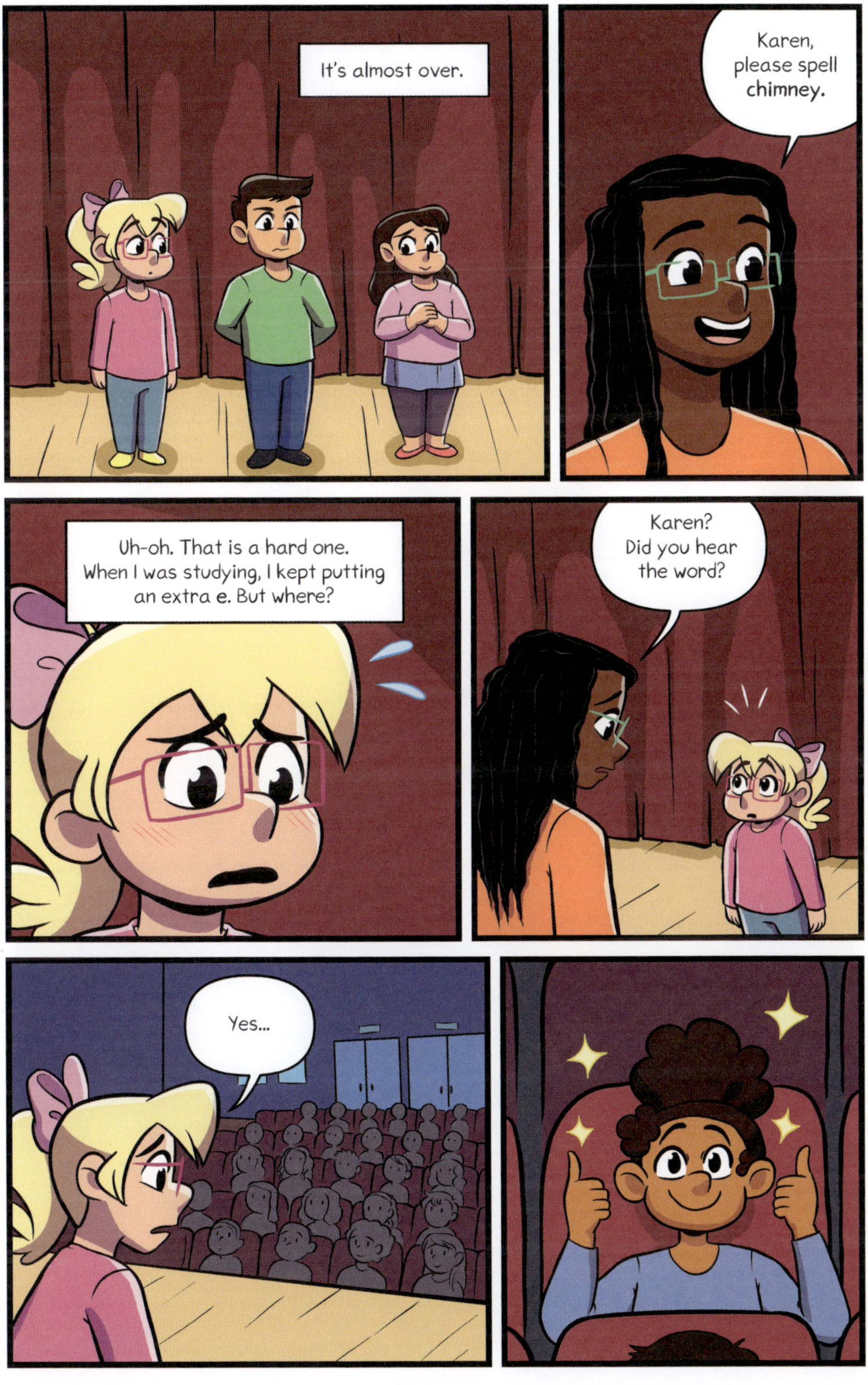
It's almost over.
Karen, please spell chimney.
Uh-oh. That is a hard one. When I was studying, I kept putting an extra e. But where?
Karen? Did you hear the word?
Yes...

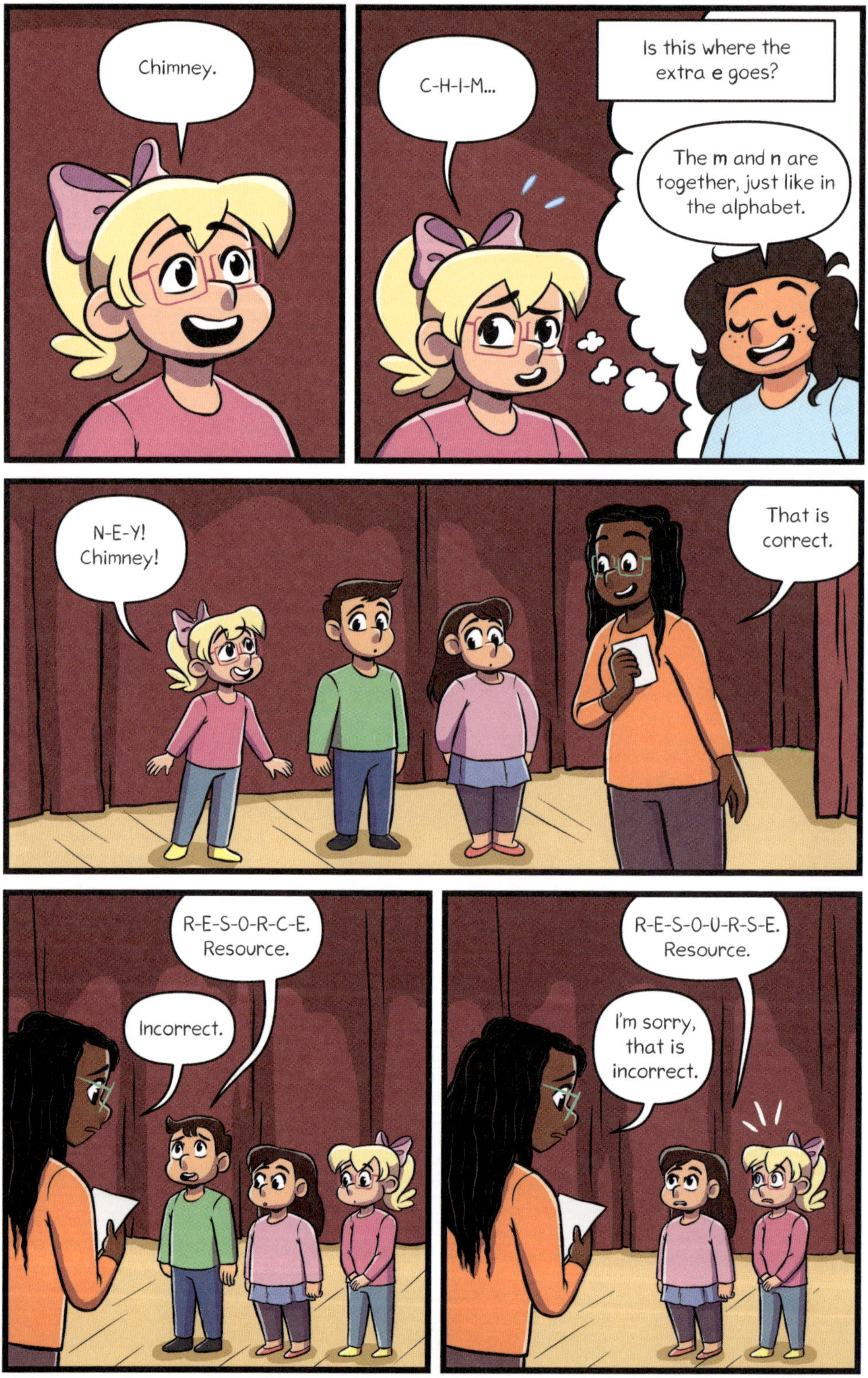
Chimney.
C-H-I-M...
Is this where the extra e goes?
The m and n are together, just like in the alphabet.
N-E-Y! Chimney!
That is correct.
R-E-S-O-R-C-E. Resource.
Incorrect.
R-E-S-O-U-R-S-E. Resource.
I'm sorry, that is incorrect.

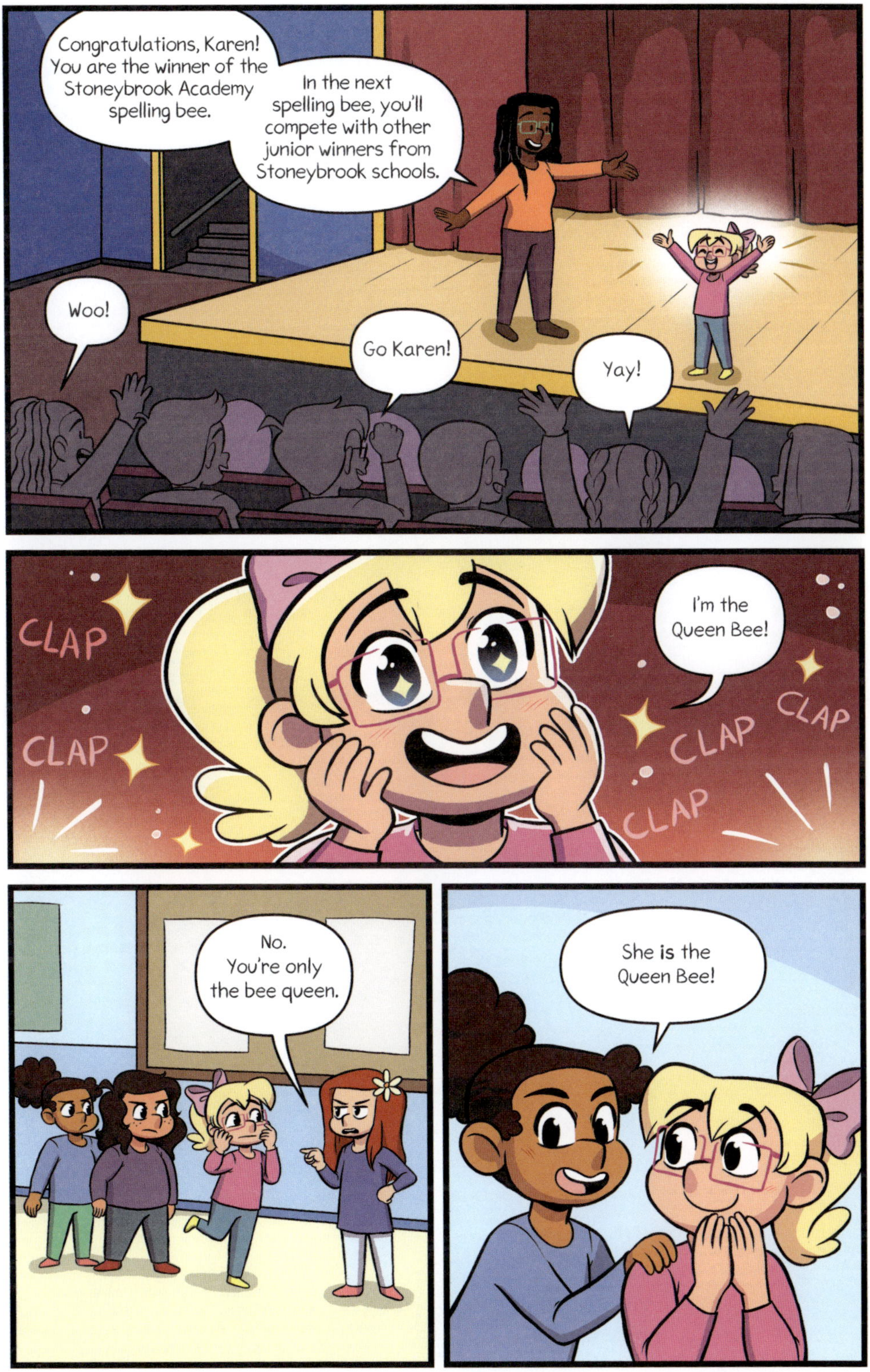
Congratulations, Karen! You are the winner of the Stoneybrook Academy spelling bee.
In the next spelling bee, you'll compete with other junior winners from Stoneybrook schools.
Woo!
Go Karen!
Yay!
CLAP
CLAP
I'm the Queen Bee!
CLAP
CLAP
CLAP
No. You're only the bee queen.
She **is** the Queen Bee!

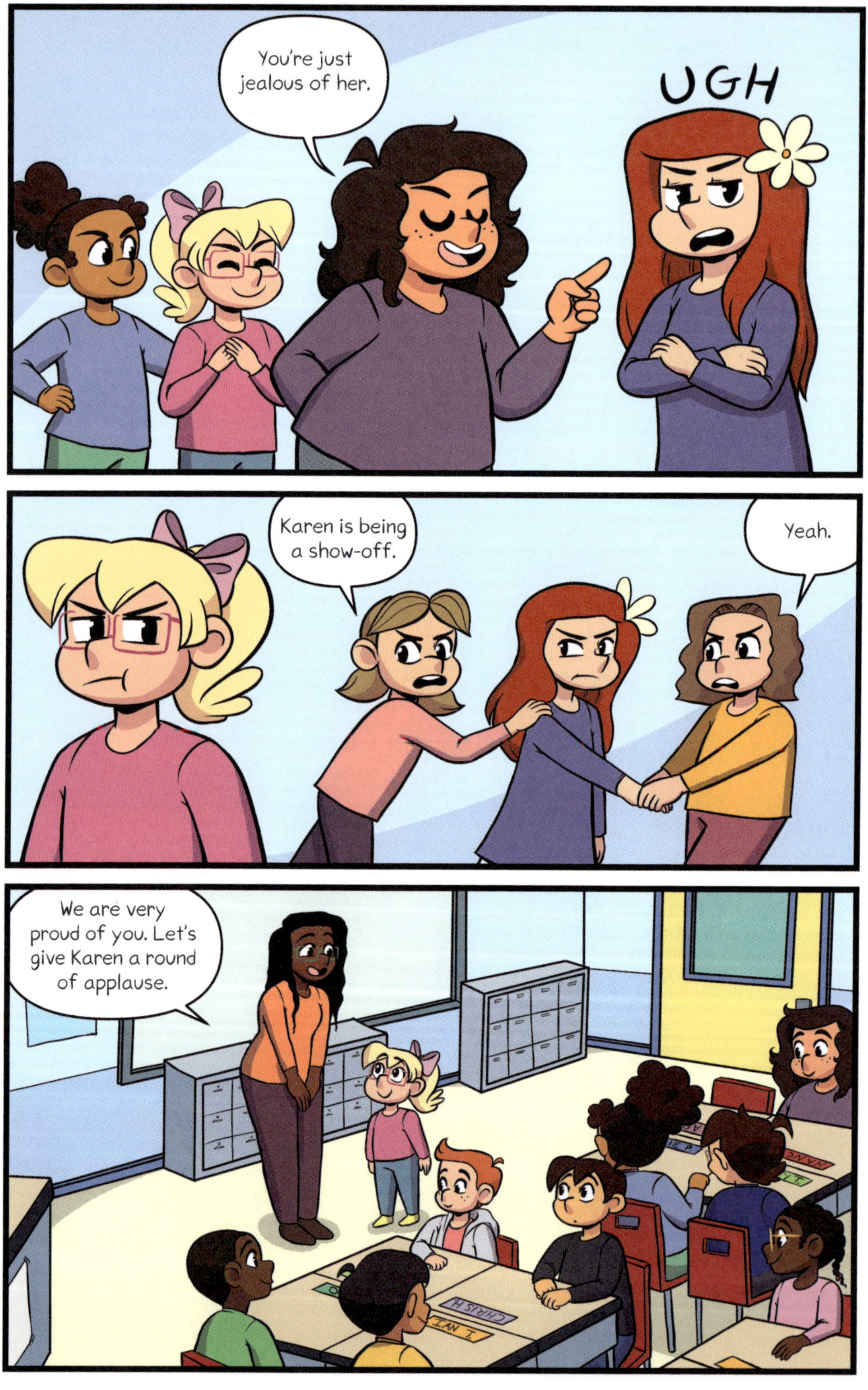
You're just jealous of her.
UGH
Karen is being a show-off.
Yeah.
We are very proud of you. Let's give Karen a round of applause.

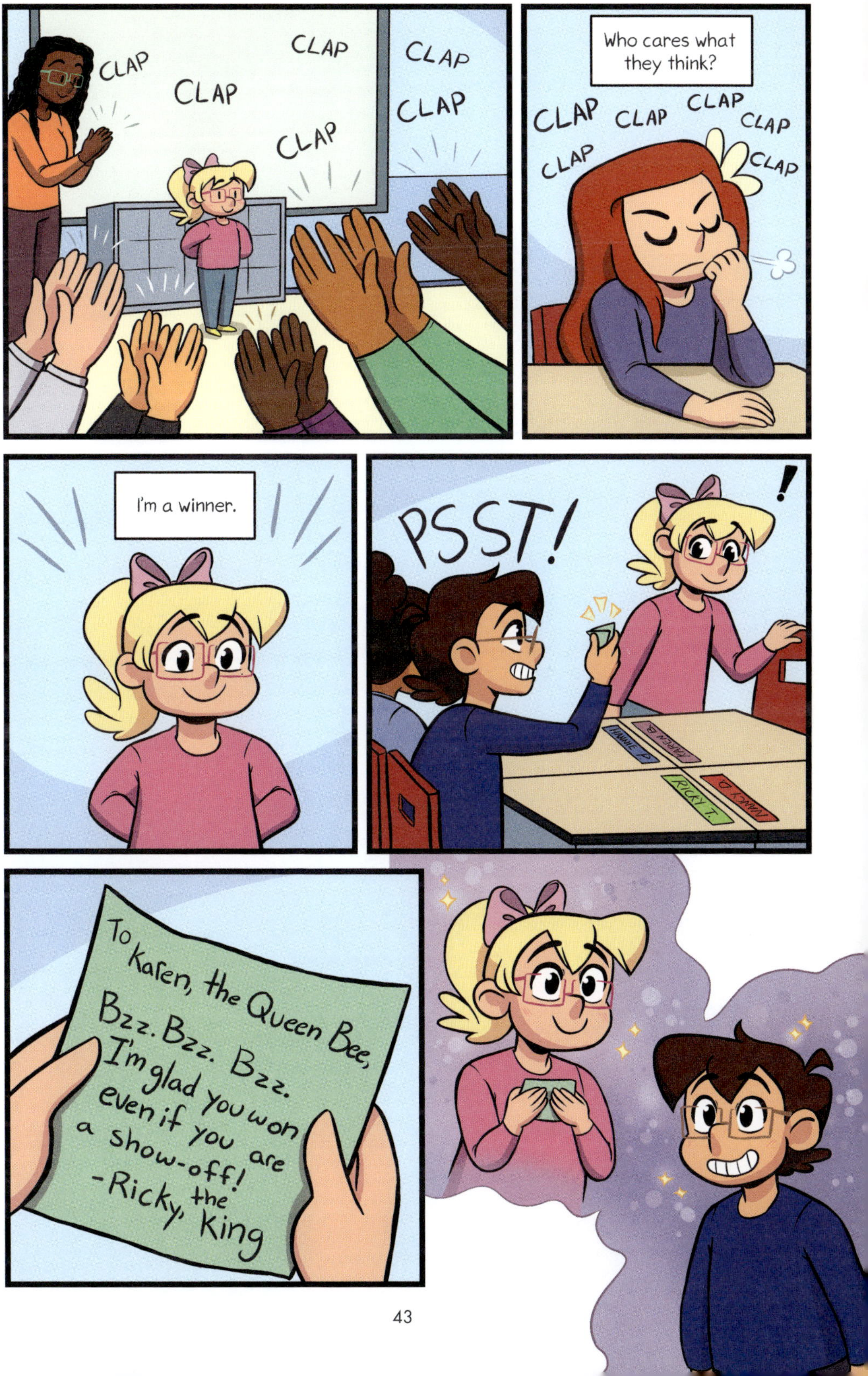
CLAP
CLAP
CLAP
CLAP
CLAP
CLAP
Who cares what they think?
CLAP
CLAP
CLAP
CLAP
CLAP
CLAP
I'm a winner.
PSST!
!
RICKY T.
To Karen, the Queen Bee,
Bzz. Bzz. Bzz.
I'm glad you won even if you are a show-off!
-Ricky, the King

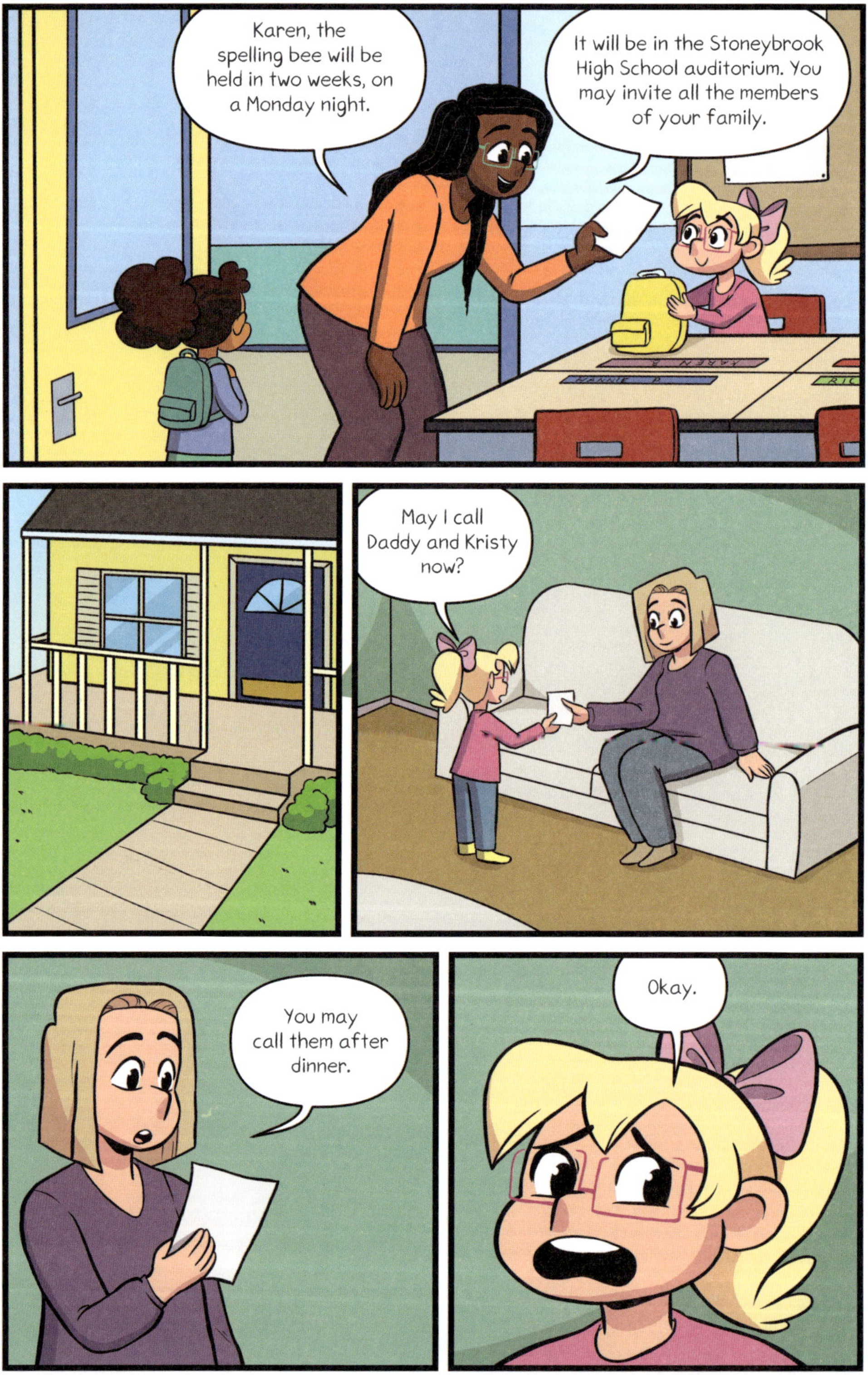
Karen, the spelling bee will be held in two weeks, on a Monday night.
It will be in the Stoneybrook High School auditorium. You may invite all the members of your family.
May I call Daddy and Kristy now?
You may call them after dinner.
Okay.

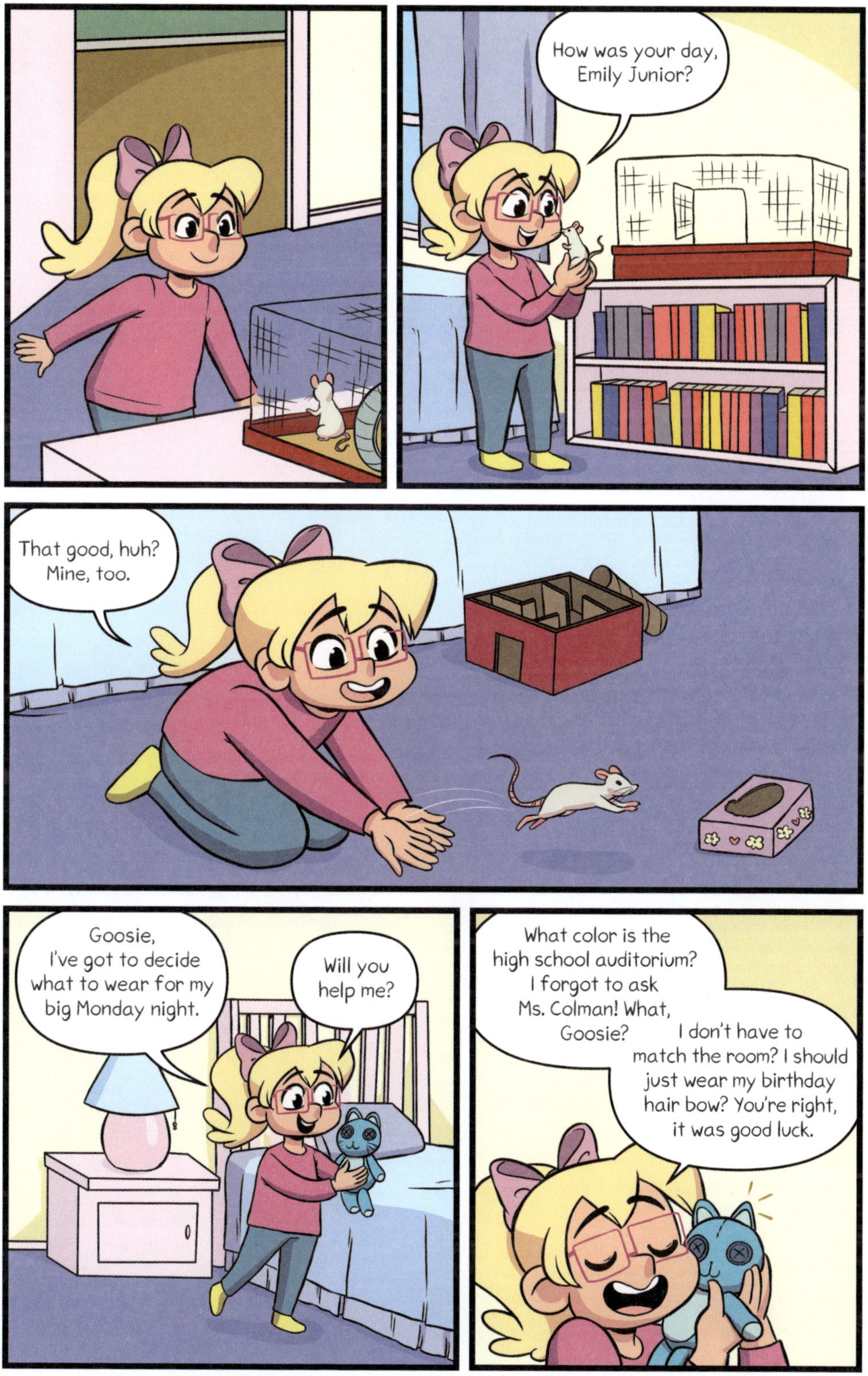
How was your day, Emily Junior?
That good, huh? Mine, too.
Goosie, I've got to decide what to wear for my big Monday night.
Will you help me?
What color is the high school auditorium? I forgot to ask Ms. Colman! What, Goosie?
I don't have to match the room? I should just wear my birthday hair bow? You're right, it was good luck.

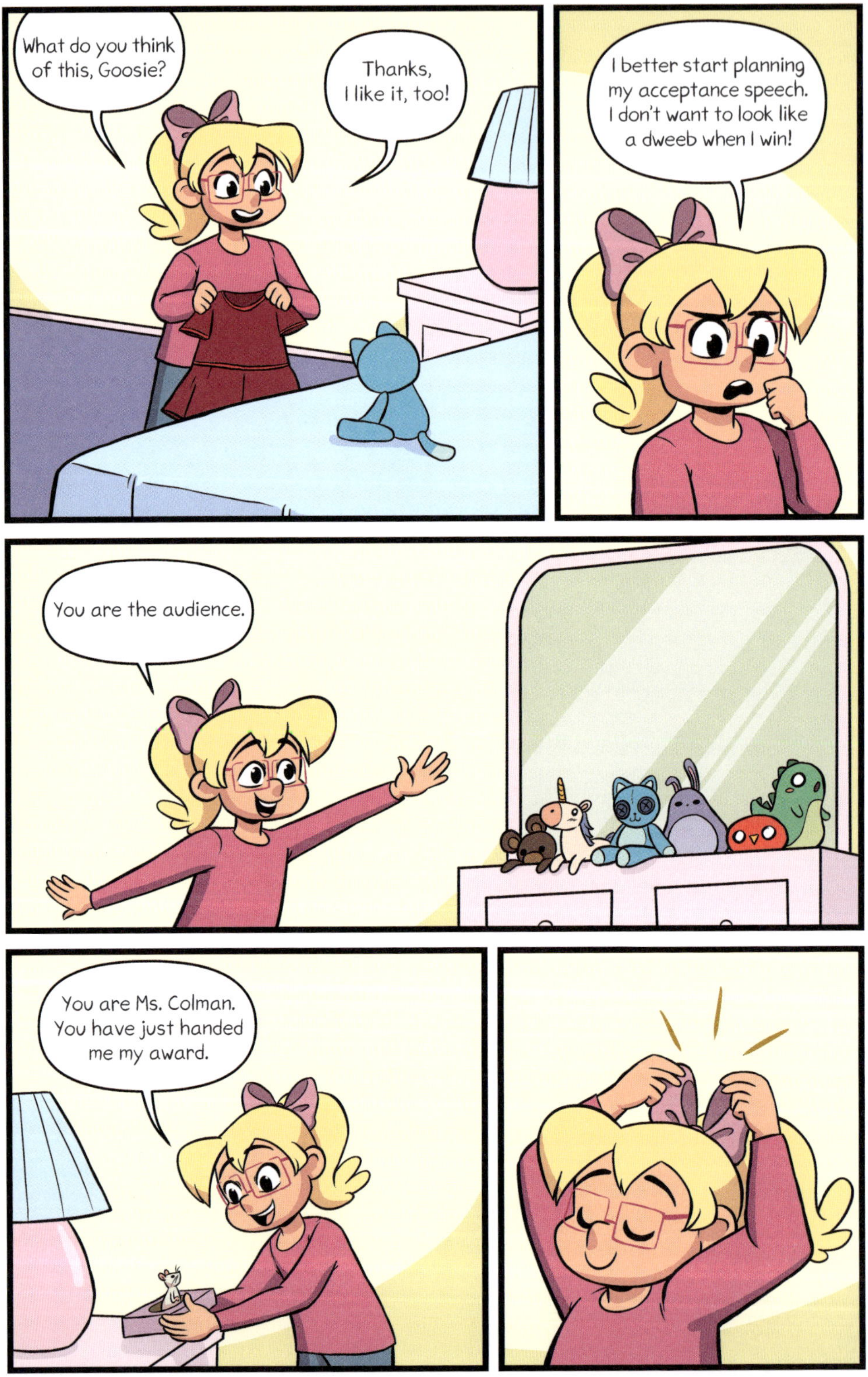
What do you think of this, Goosie?
Thanks, I like it, too!
I better start planning my acceptance speech. I don't want to look like a dweeb when I win!
You are the audience.
You are Ms. Colman. You have just handed me my award.

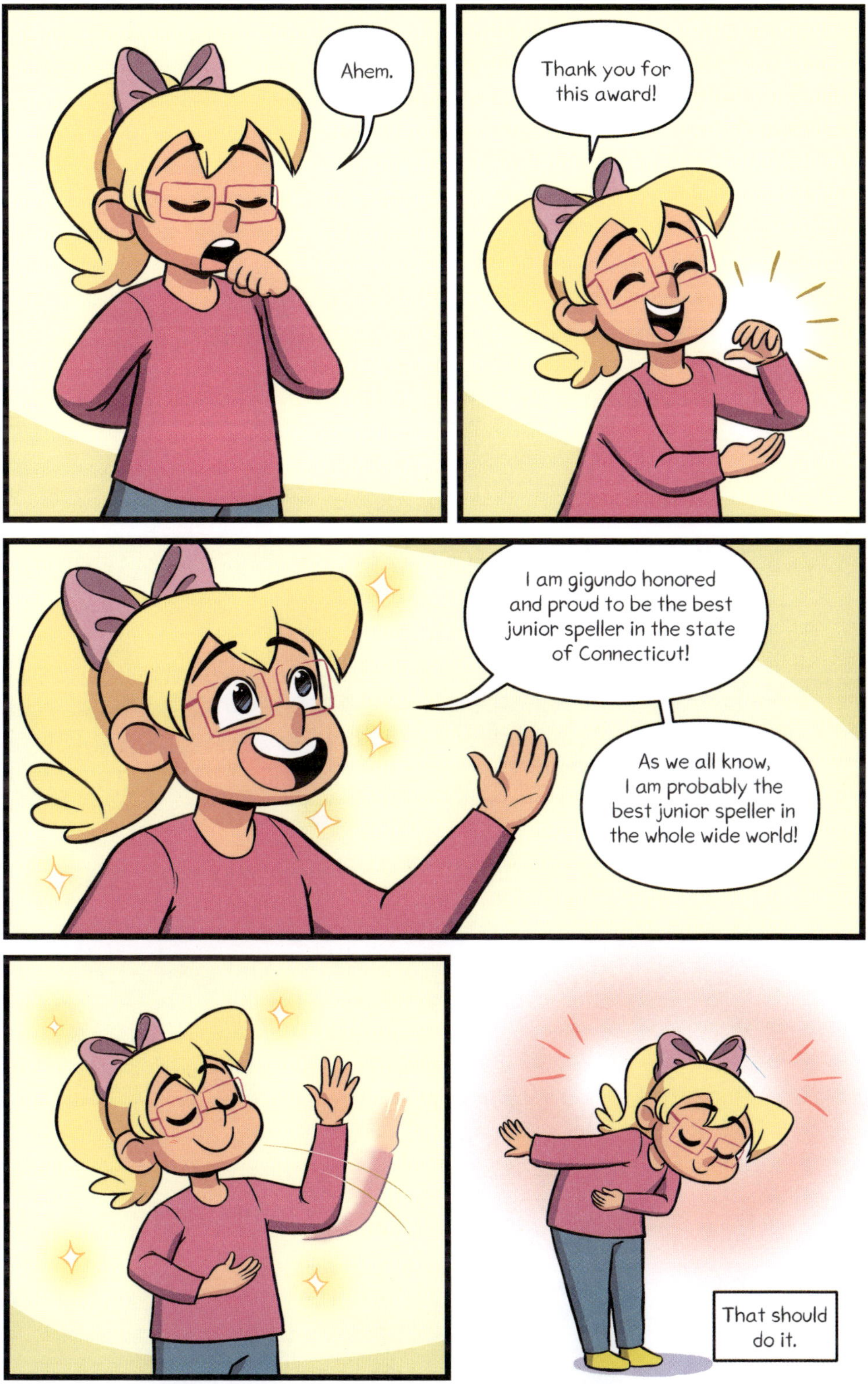
Ahem.
Thank you for this award!
I am gigundo honored and proud to be the best junior speller in the state of Connecticut!
As we all know, I am probably the best junior speller in the whole wide world!
That should do it.

# CHAPTER 4

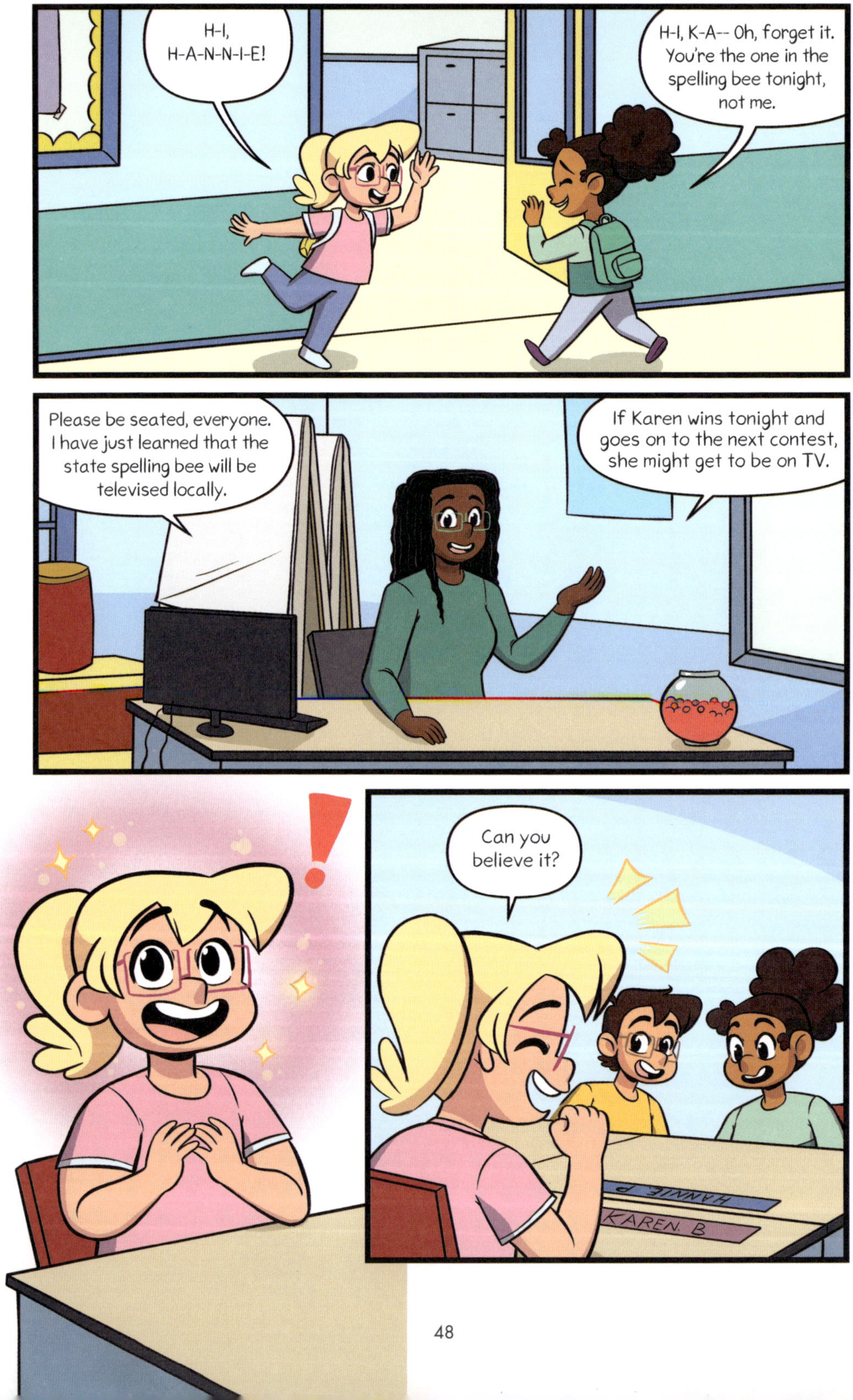
H-I, H-A-N-N-I-E!
H-I, K-A-- Oh, forget it. You're the one in the spelling bee tonight, not me.
Please be seated, everyone. I have just learned that the state spelling bee will be televised locally.
If Karen wins tonight and goes on to the next contest, she might get to be on TV.
Can you believe it?
HANNIE P
KAREN B

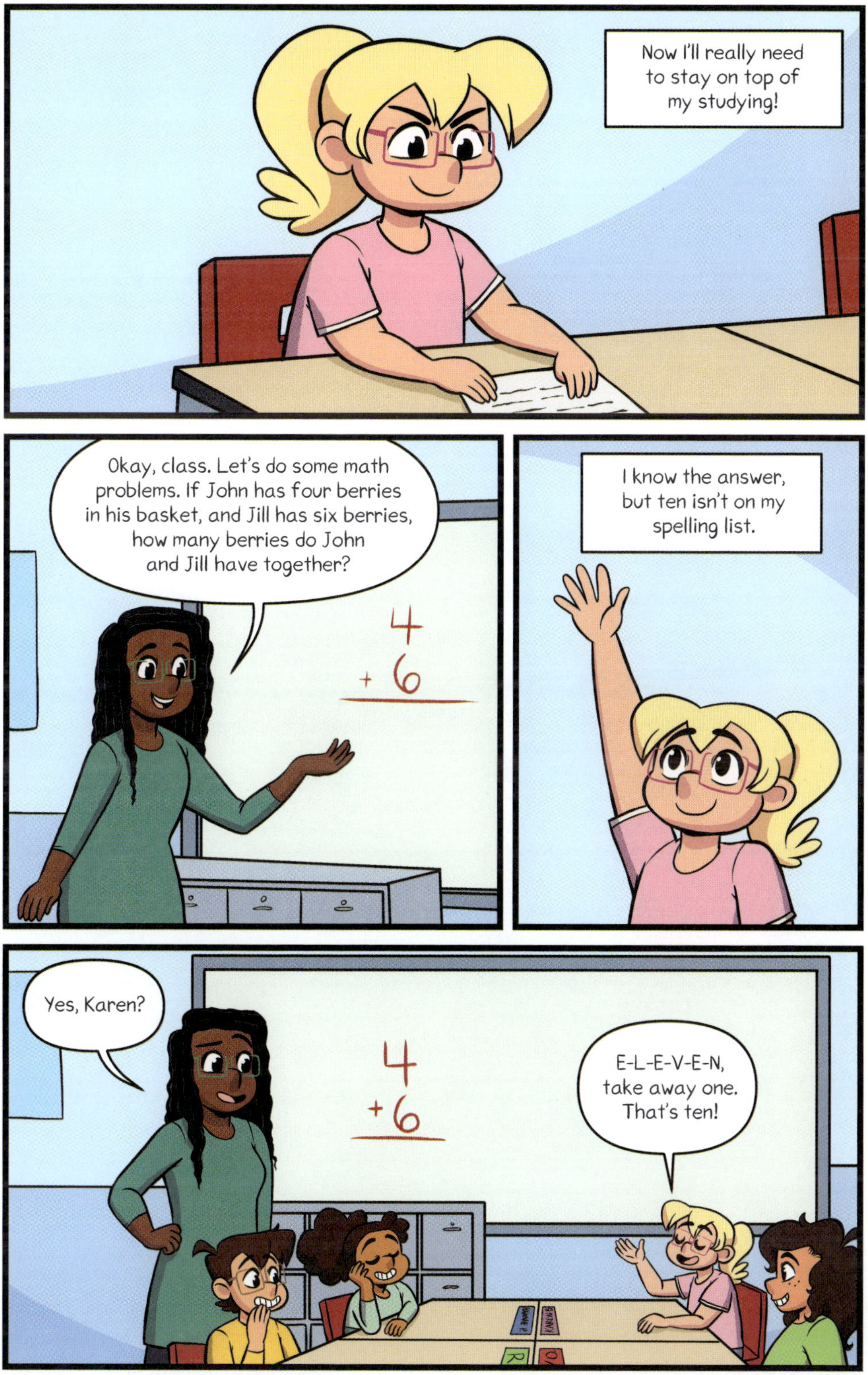
Now I'll really need to stay on top of my studying!
Okay, class. Let's do some math problems. If John has four berries in his basket, and Jill has six berries, how many berries do John and Jill have together?
4
+ 6
I know the answer, but ten isn't on my spelling list.
Yes, Karen?
4
+ 6
E-L-E-V-E-N, take away one. That's ten!

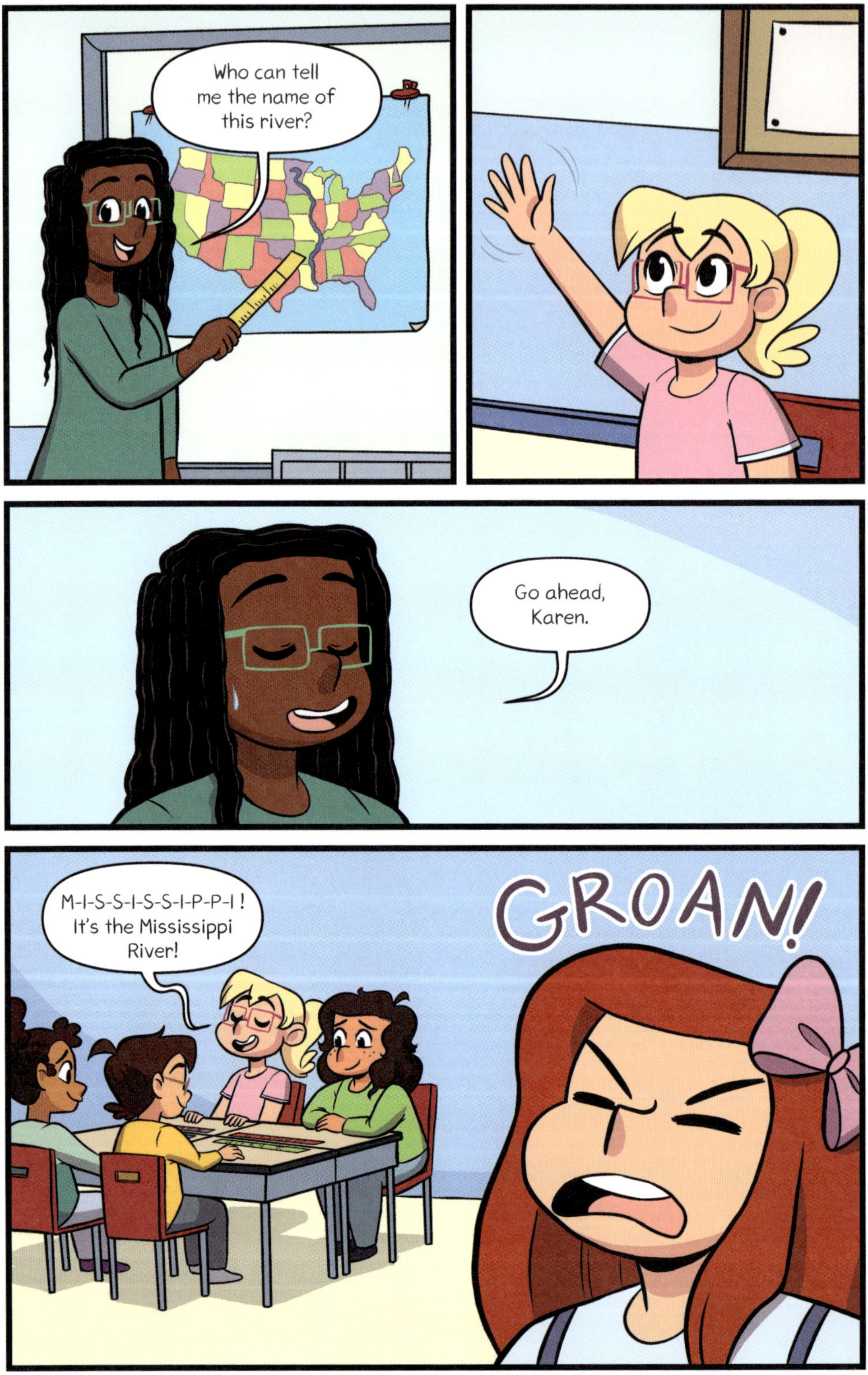
Who can tell me the name of this river?
Go ahead, Karen.
M-I-S-S-I-S-S-I-P-P-I! It's the Mississippi River!
GROAN!

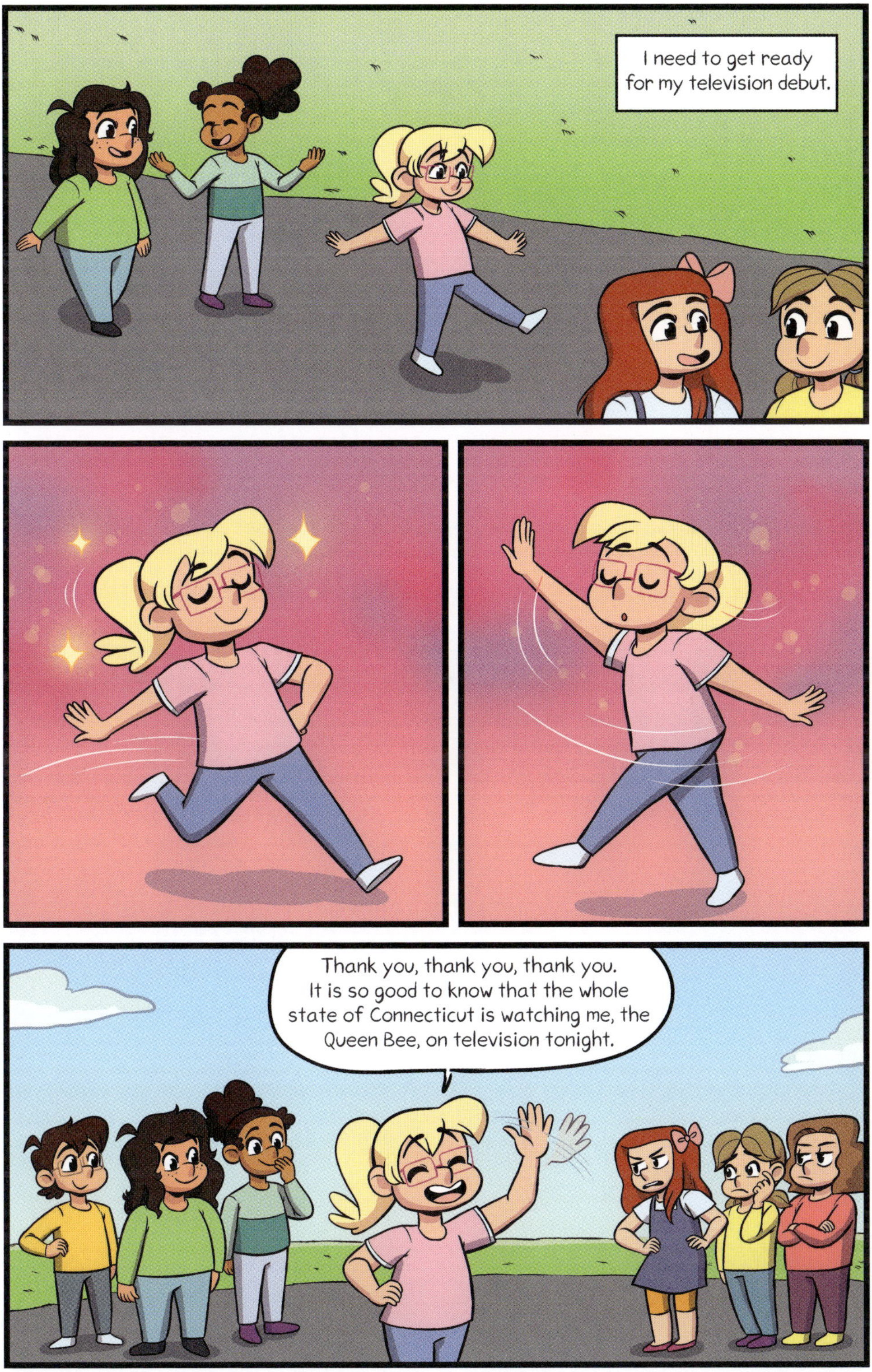

I need to get ready for my television debut.
Thank you, thank you, thank you. It is so good to know that the whole state of Connecticut is watching me, the Queen Bee, on television tonight.

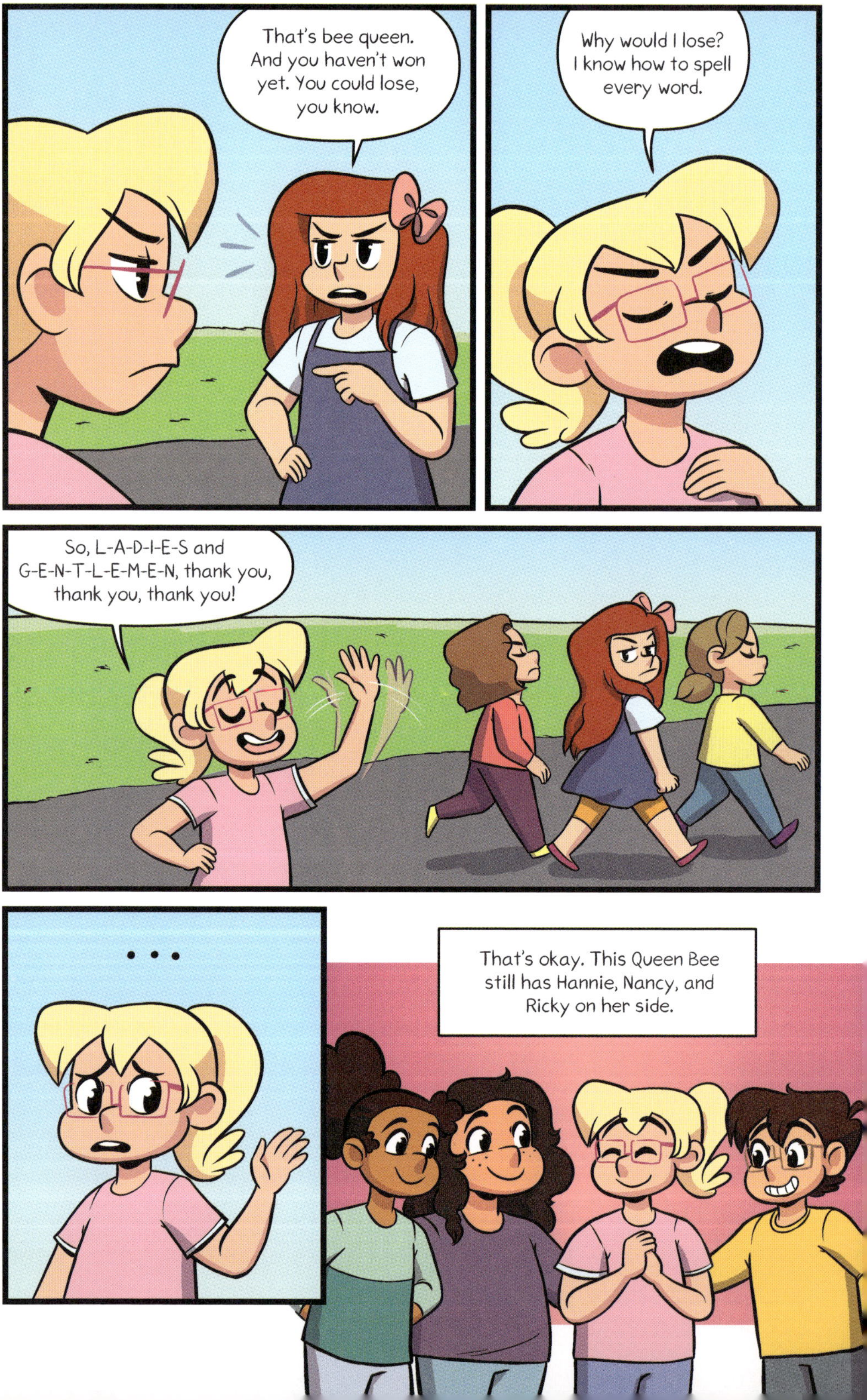
That's bee queen. And you haven't won yet. You could lose, you know.
Why would I lose? I know how to spell every word.
So, L-A-D-I-E-S and G-E-N-T-L-E-M-E-N, thank you, thank you, thank you!
. . .
That's okay. This Queen Bee still has Hannie, Nancy, and Ricky on her side.

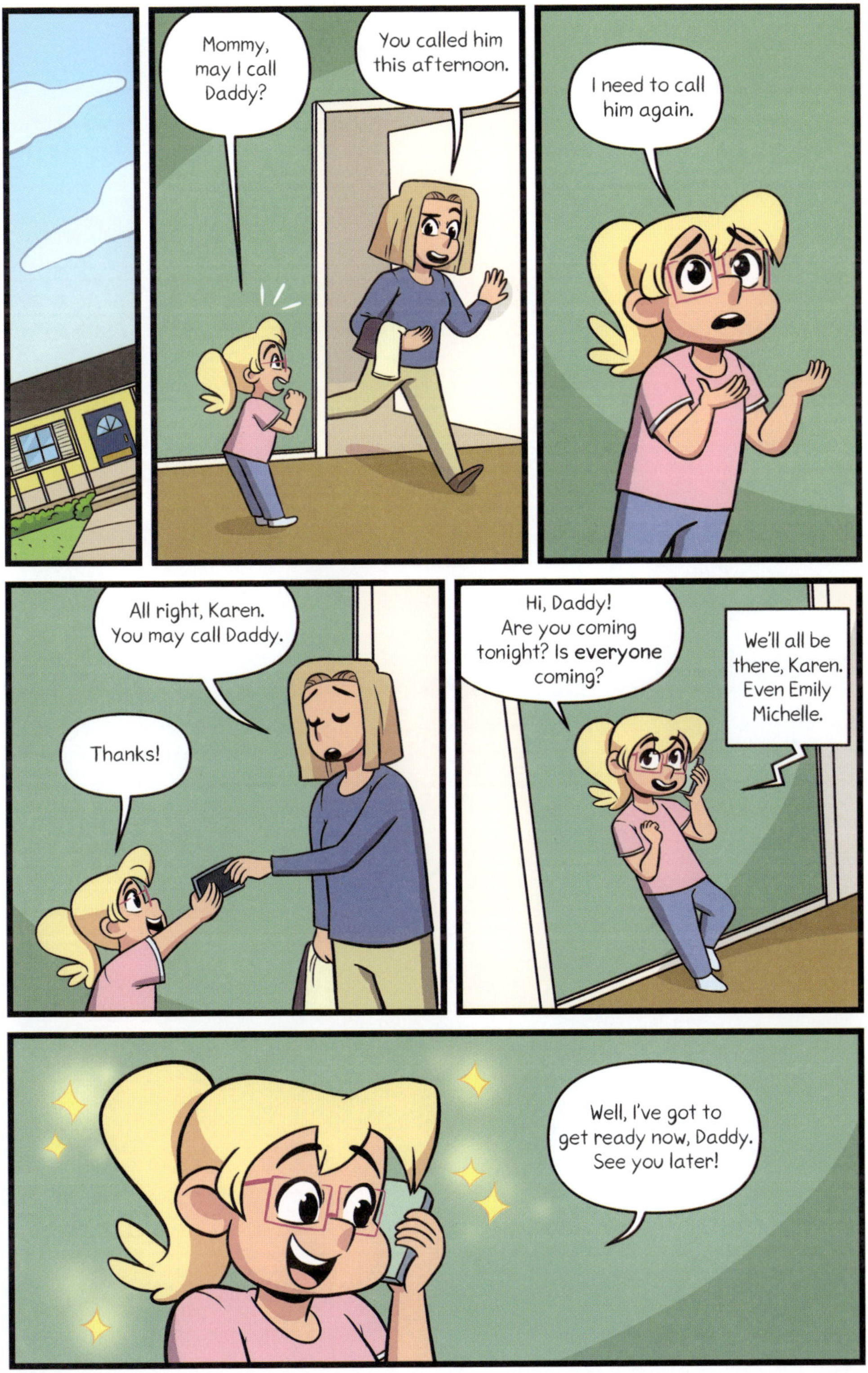

Mommy, may I call Daddy?
You called him this afternoon.
I need to call him again.
All right, Karen. You may call Daddy.
Thanks!
Hi, Daddy! Are you coming tonight? Is **everyone** coming?
We'll all be there, Karen. Even Emily Michelle.
Well, I've got to get ready now, Daddy. See you later!

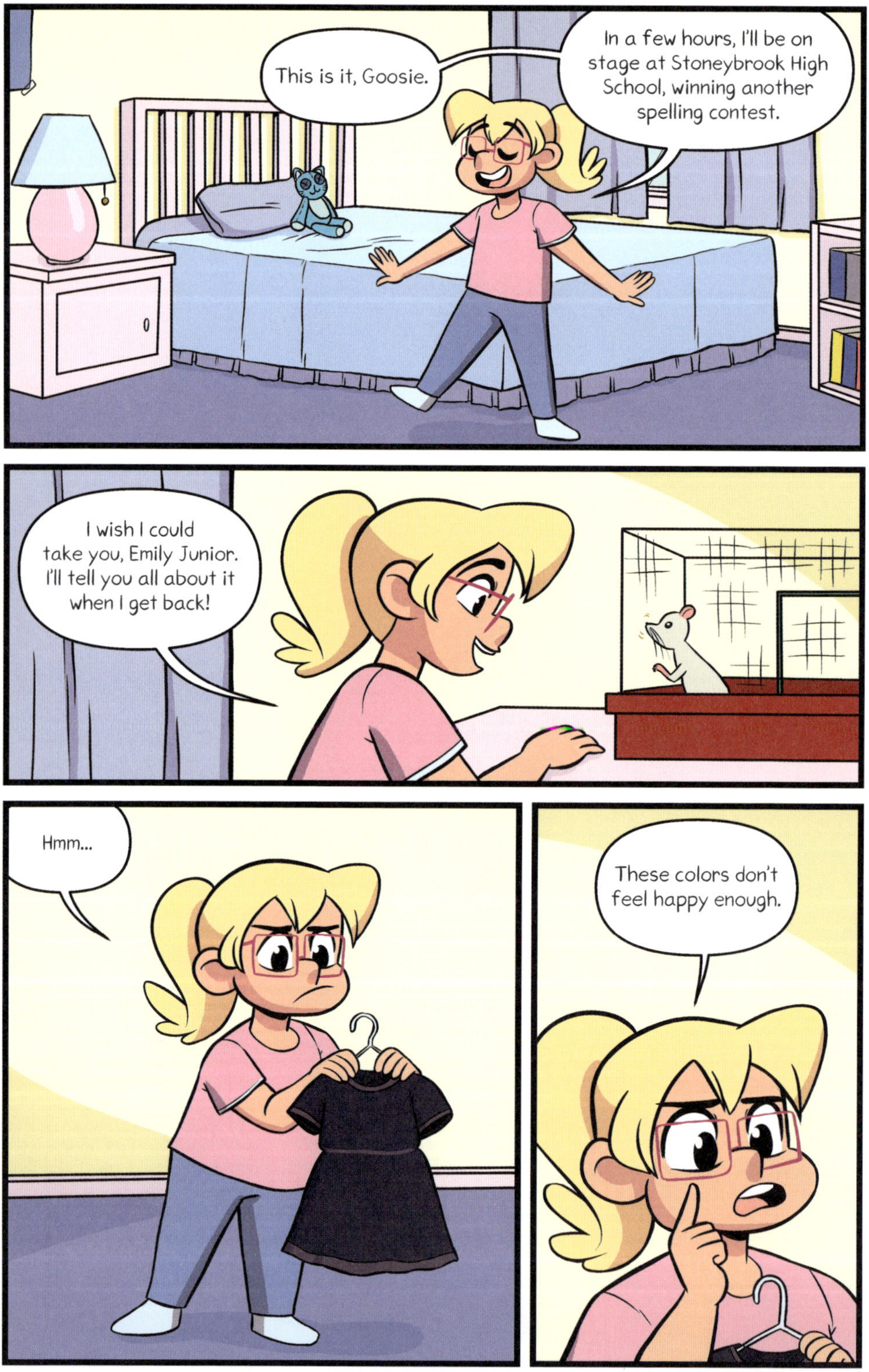
This is it, Goosie.
In a few hours, I'll be on stage at Stoneybrook High School, winning another spelling contest.
I wish I could take you, Emily Junior. I'll tell you all about it when I get back!
Hmm...
These colors don't feel happy enough.

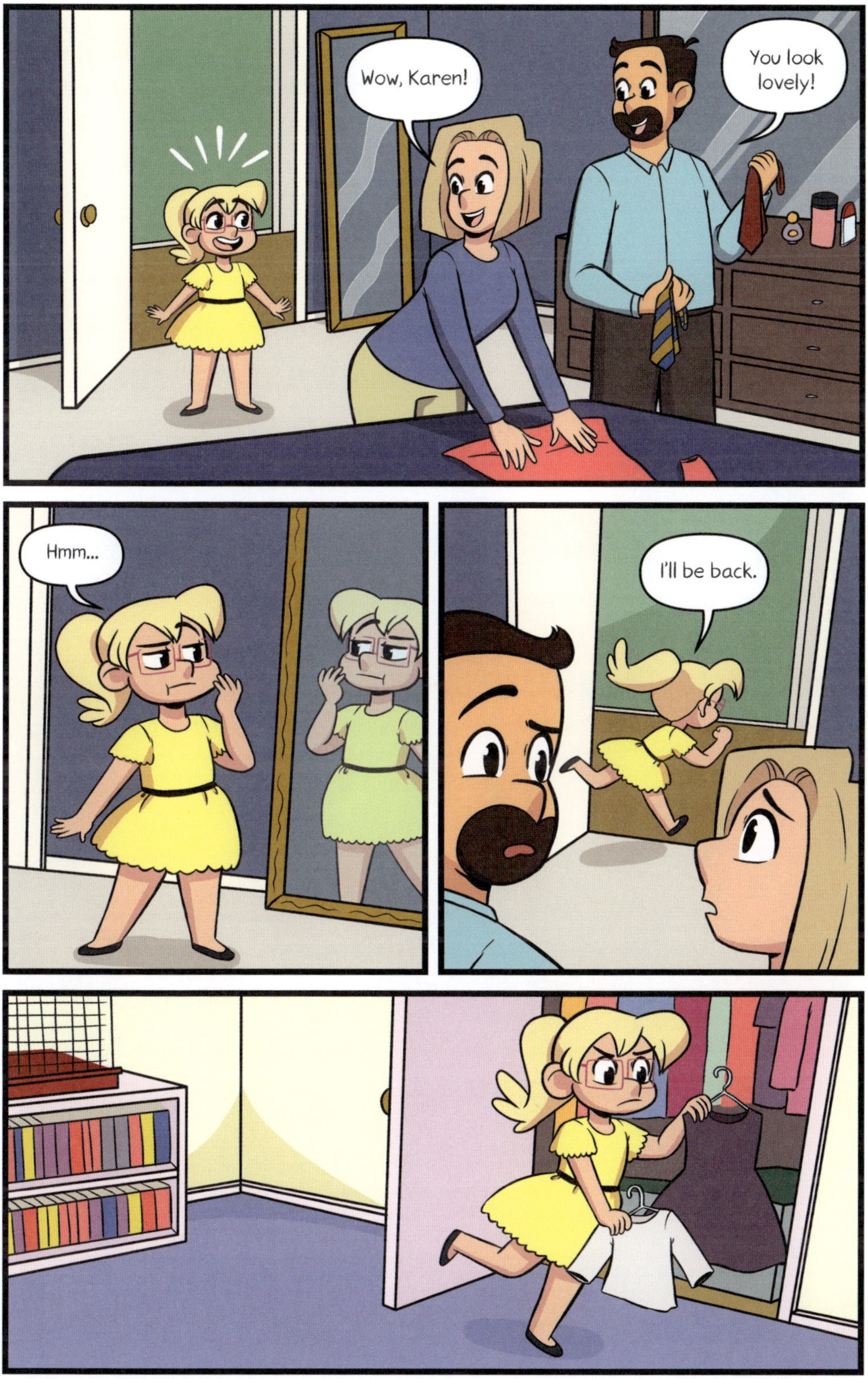
Wow, Karen!
You look lovely!
Hmm...
I'll be back.

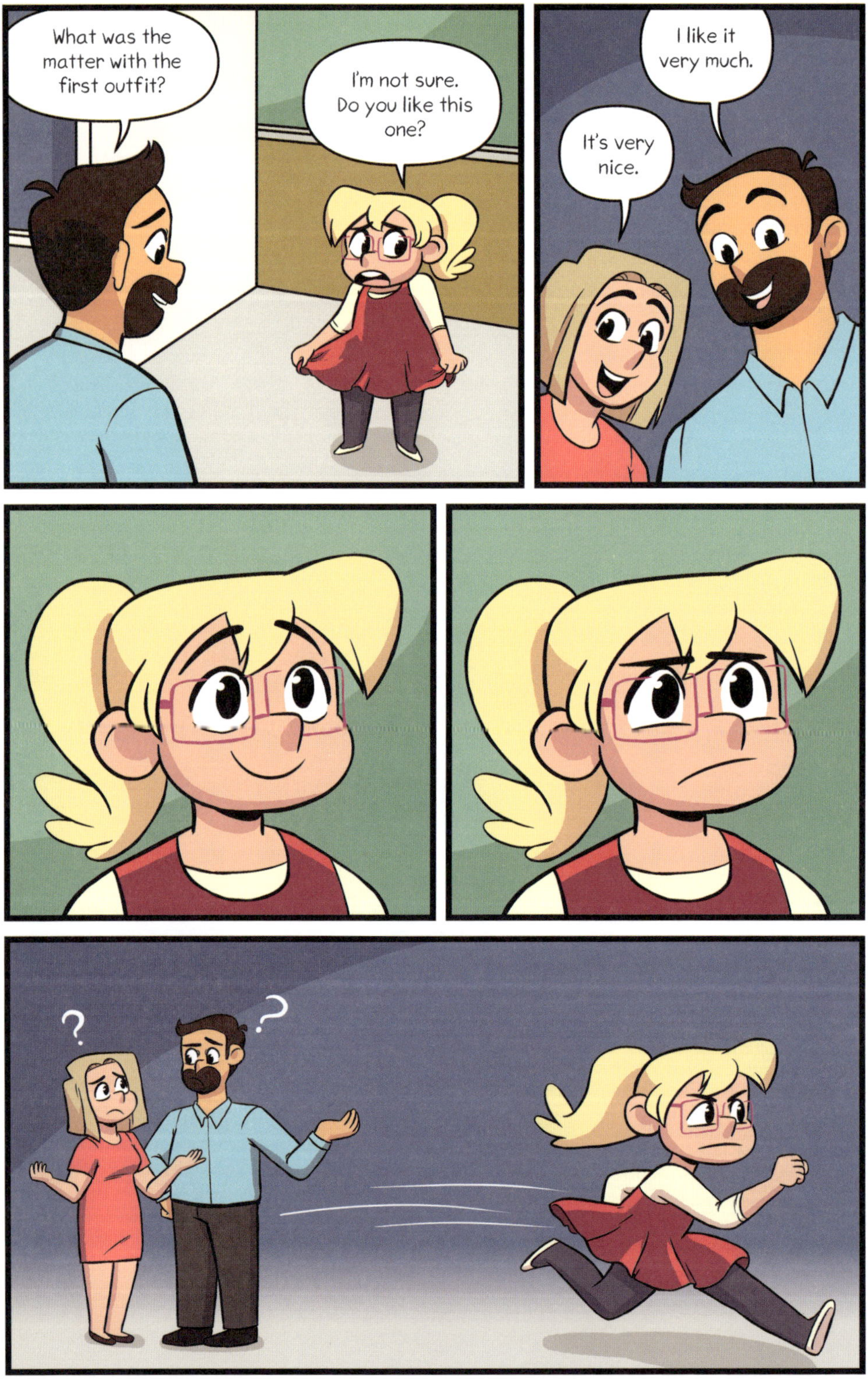
What was the matter with the first outfit?
I'm not sure. Do you like this one?
It's very nice.
I like it very much.
?
?

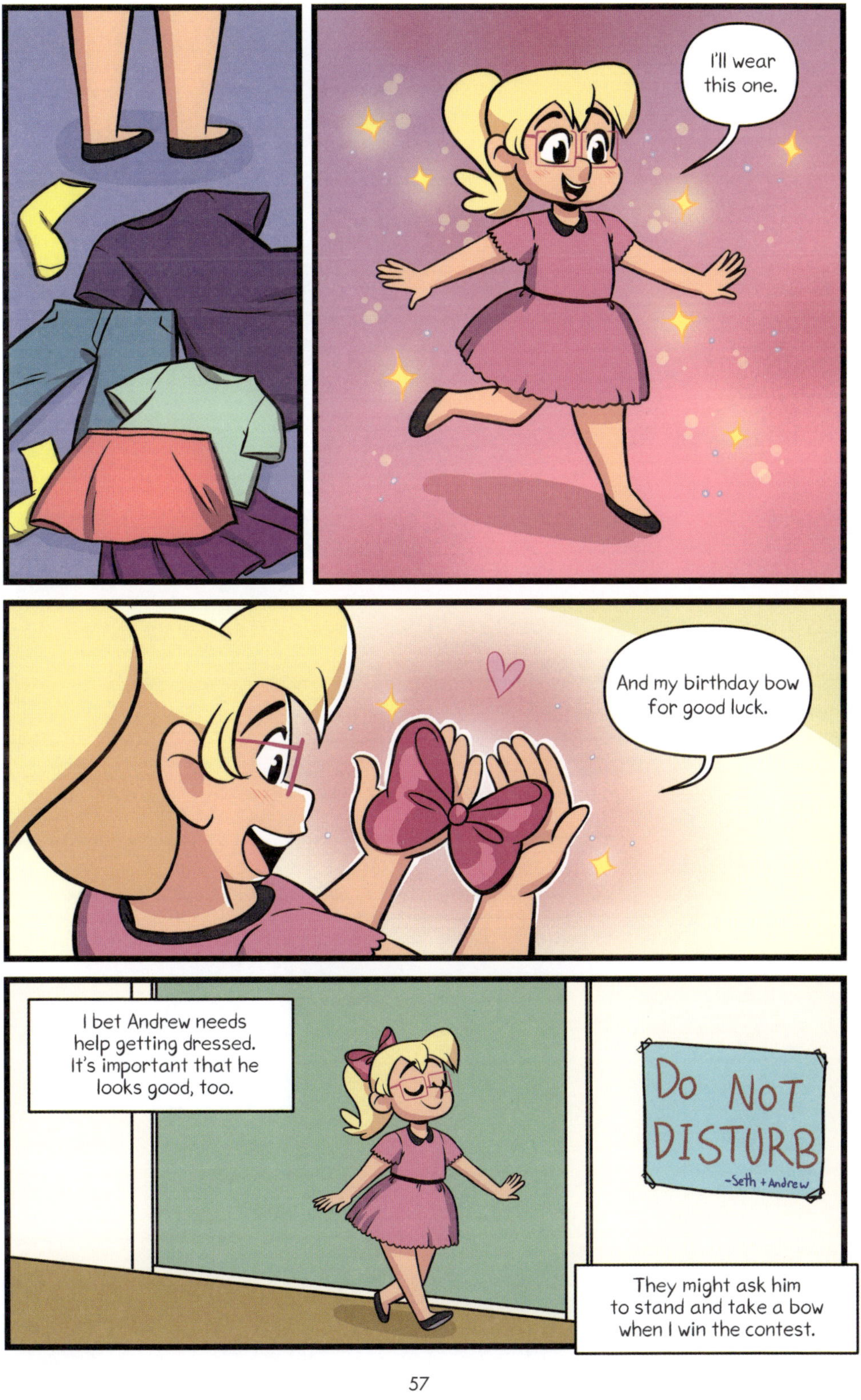
I'll wear this one.
And my birthday bow for good luck.
I bet Andrew needs help getting dressed. It's important that he looks good, too.
Do NOT DISTURB -Seth + Andrew
They might ask him to stand and take a bow when I win the contest.

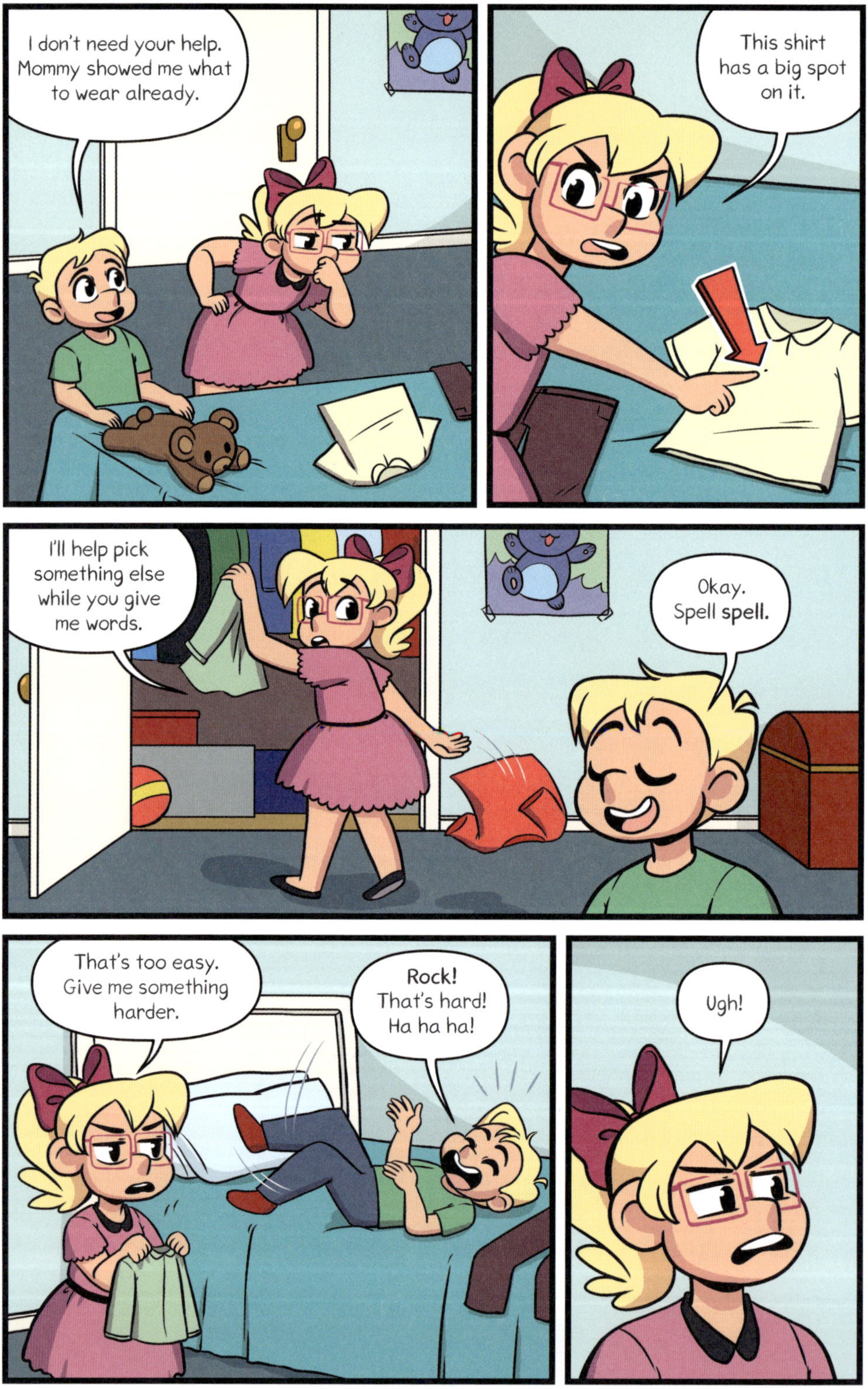
I don't need your help. Mommy showed me what to wear already.
This shirt has a big spot on it.
I'll help pick something else while you give me words.
Okay. Spell **spell.**
That's too easy. Give me something harder.
**Rock!** That's hard! Ha ha ha!
Ugh!

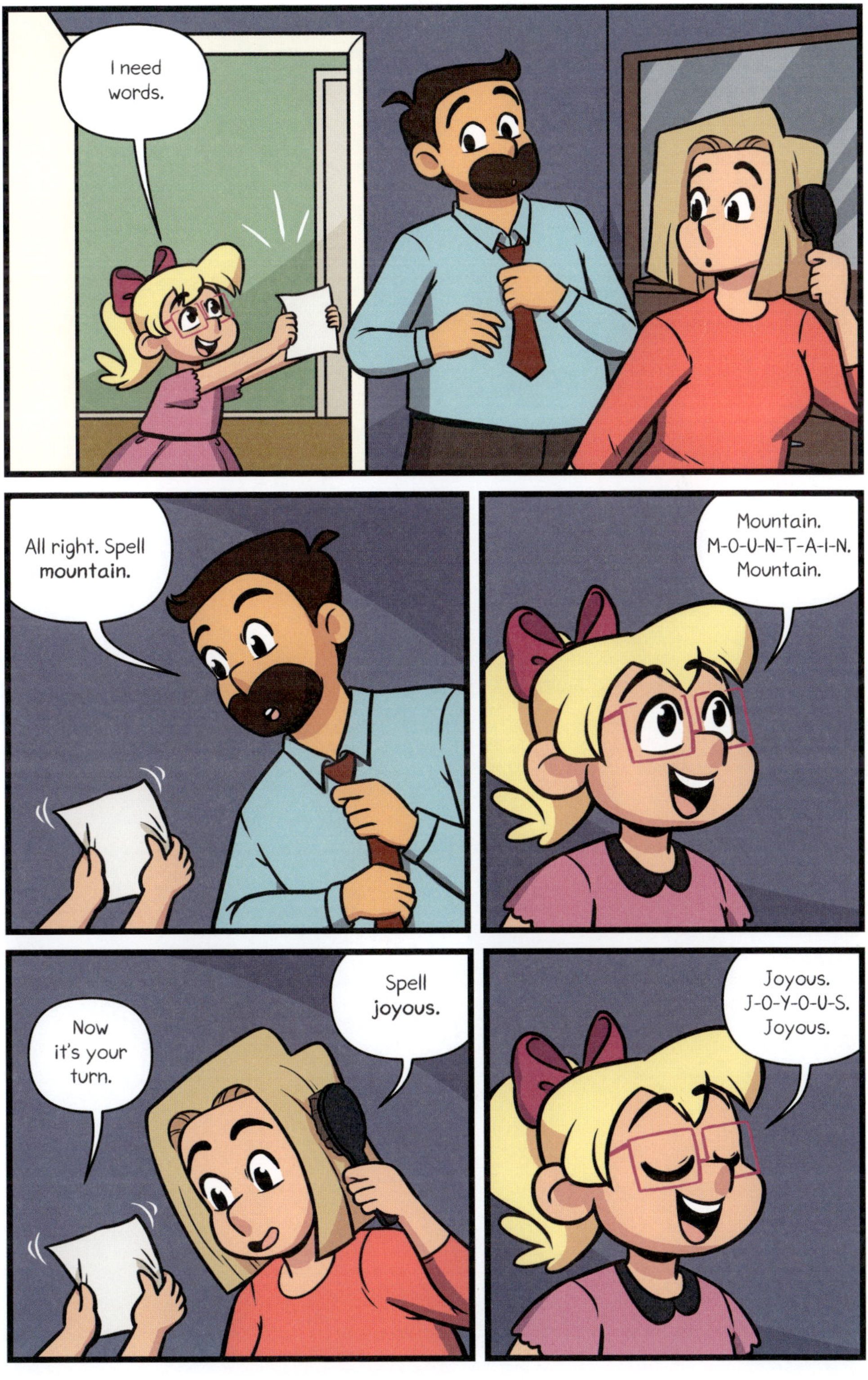
I need words.
All right. Spell **mountain.**
Mountain. M-O-U-N-T-A-I-N. Mountain.
Now it's your turn.
Spell **joyous.**
Joyous. J-O-Y-O-U-S. Joyous.

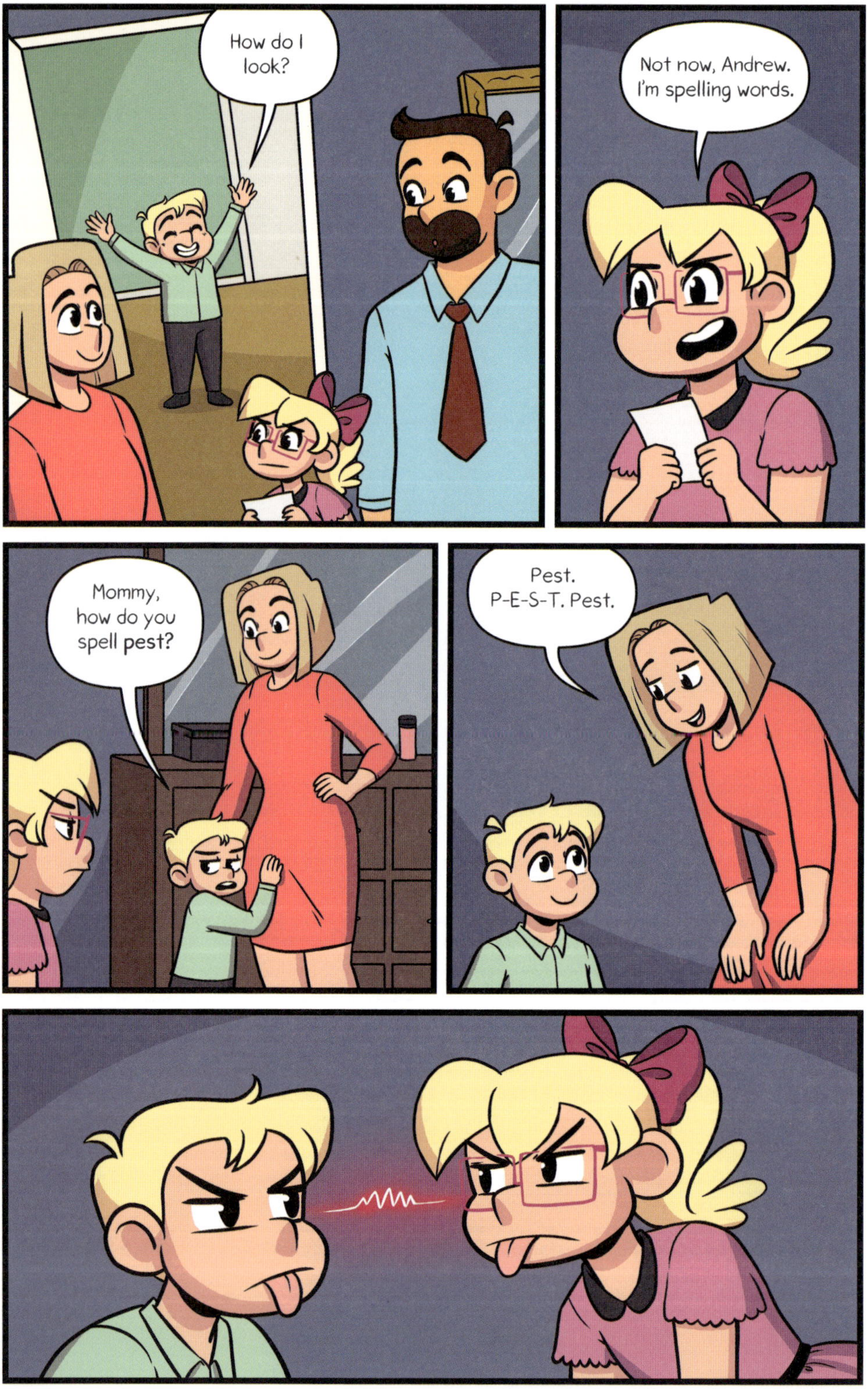
How do I look?
Not now, Andrew. I'm spelling words.
Mommy, how do you spell **pest**?
Pest. P-E-S-T. Pest.

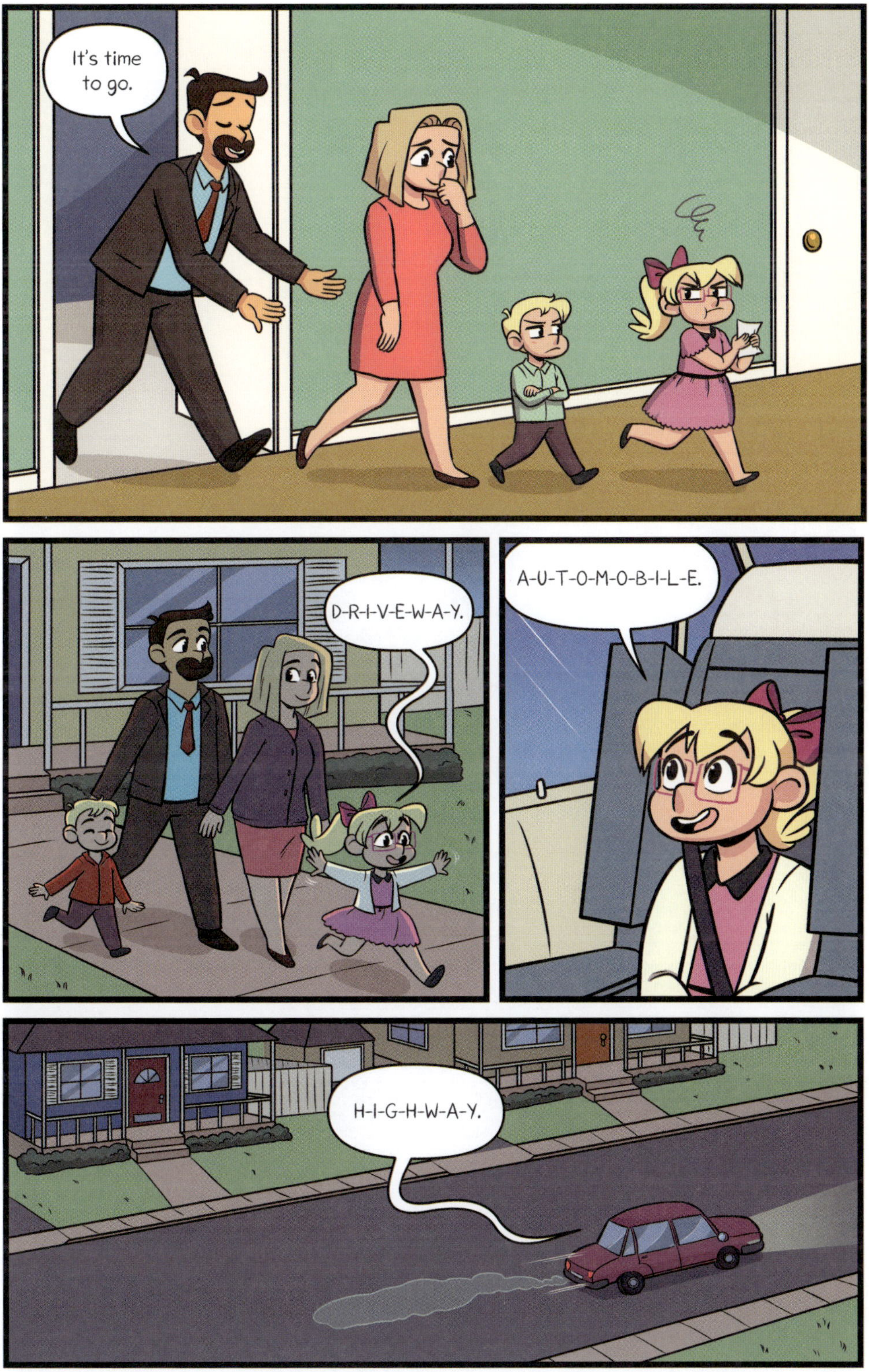
It's time to go.
D-R-I-V-E-W-A-Y.
A-U-T-O-M-O-B-I-L-E.
H-I-G-H-W-A-Y.

# CHAPTER 5

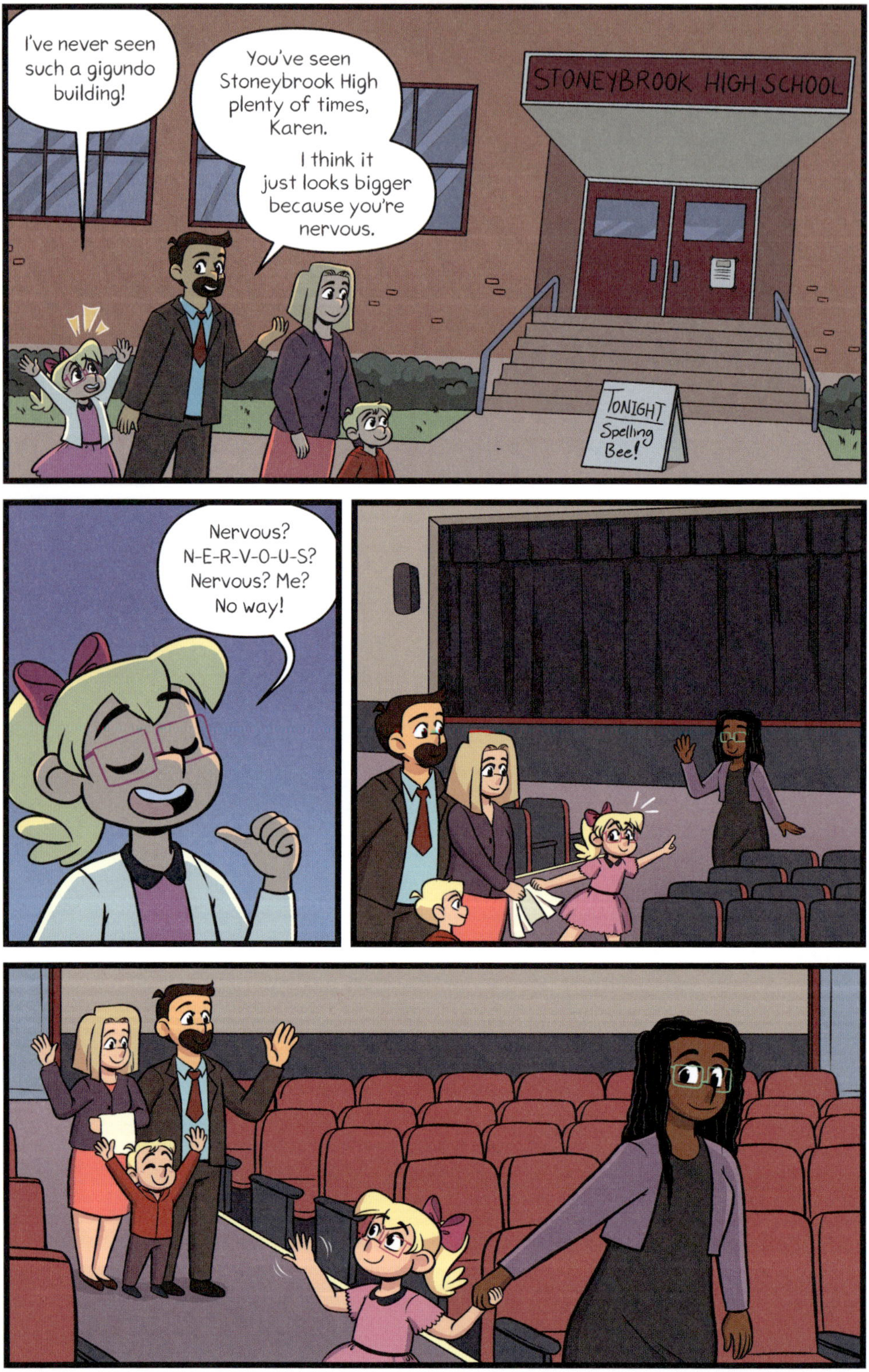
I've never seen such a gigundo building!
You've seen Stoneybrook High plenty of times, Karen.
I think it just looks bigger because you're nervous.
STONEYBROOK HIGH SCHOOL
TONIGHT Spelling Bee!
Nervous? N-E-R-V-O-U-S? Nervous? Me? No way!

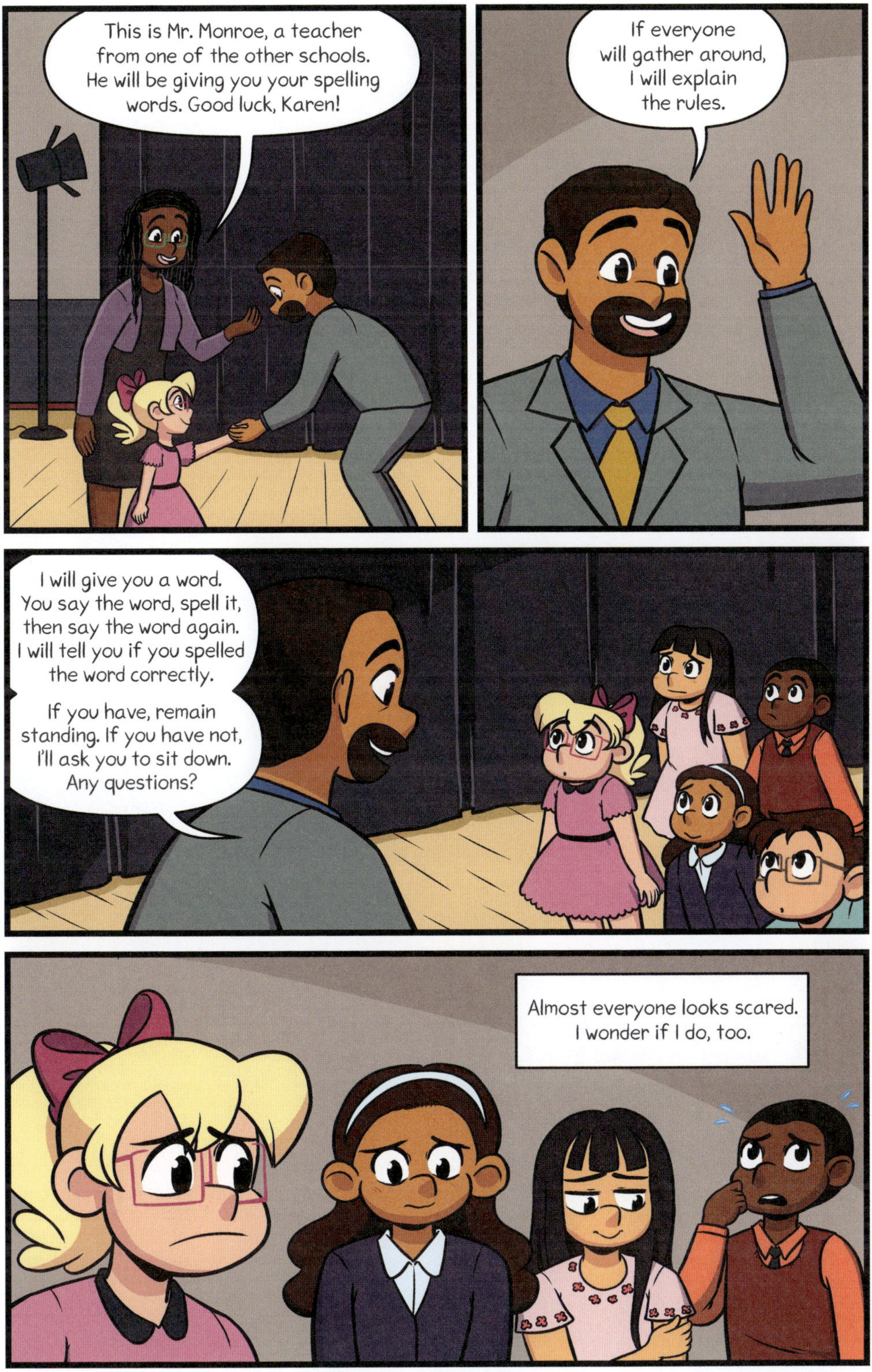
This is Mr. Monroe, a teacher from one of the other schools. He will be giving you your spelling words. Good luck, Karen!
If everyone will gather around, I will explain the rules.
I will give you a word. You say the word, spell it, then say the word again. I will tell you if you spelled the word correctly.
If you have, remain standing. If you have not, I'll ask you to sit down. Any questions?
Almost everyone looks scared. I wonder if I do, too.

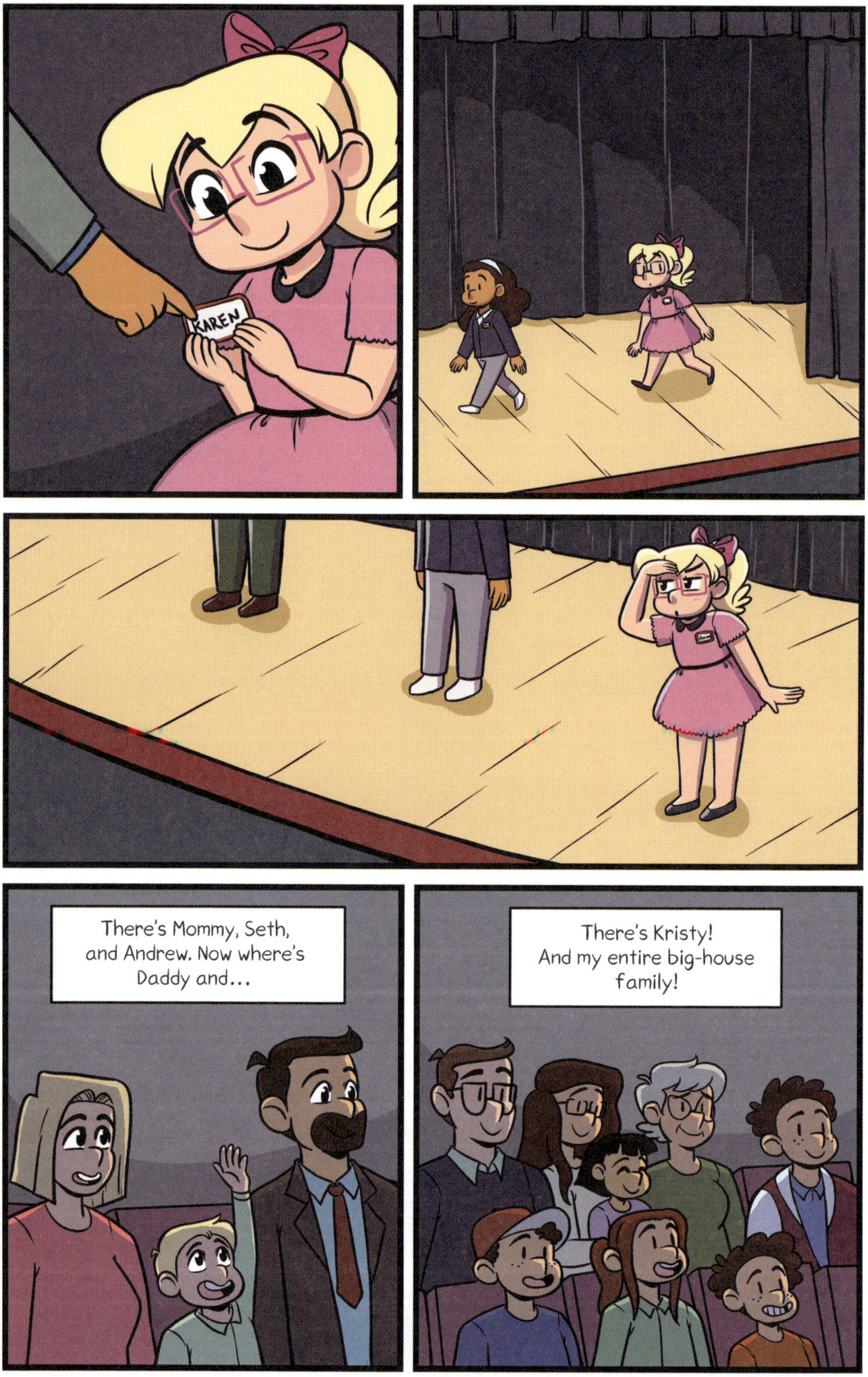
KAREN
There's Mommy, Seth, and Andrew. Now where's Daddy and...
There's Kristy! And my entire big-house family!

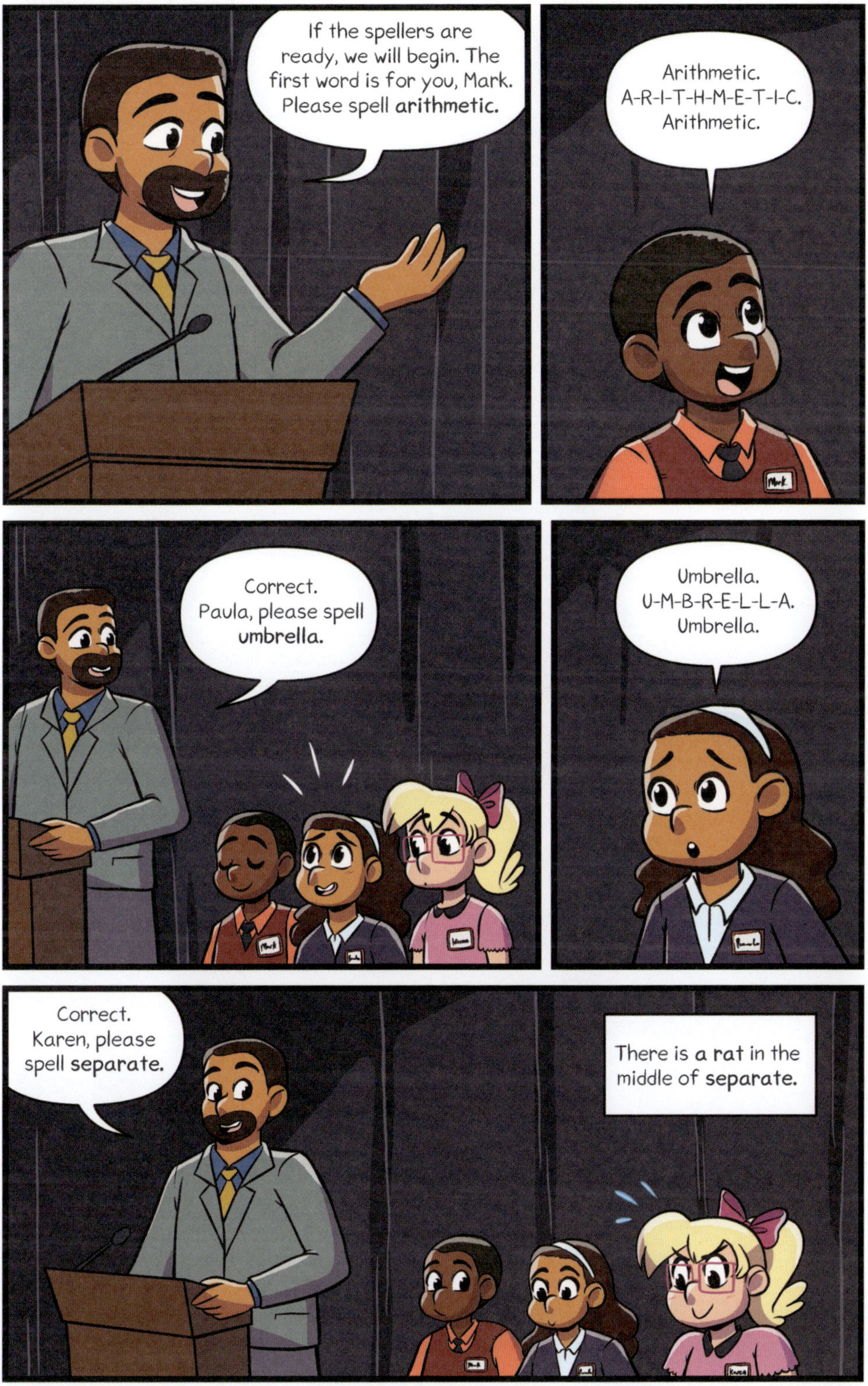

If the spellers are ready, we will begin. The first word is for you, Mark. Please spell **arithmetic.**
Arithmetic. A-R-I-T-H-M-E-T-I-C. Arithmetic.
Correct. Paula, please spell **umbrella.**
Umbrella. U-M-B-R-E-L-L-A. Umbrella.
Correct. Karen, please spell **separate.**
There is **a rat** in the middle of **separate.**

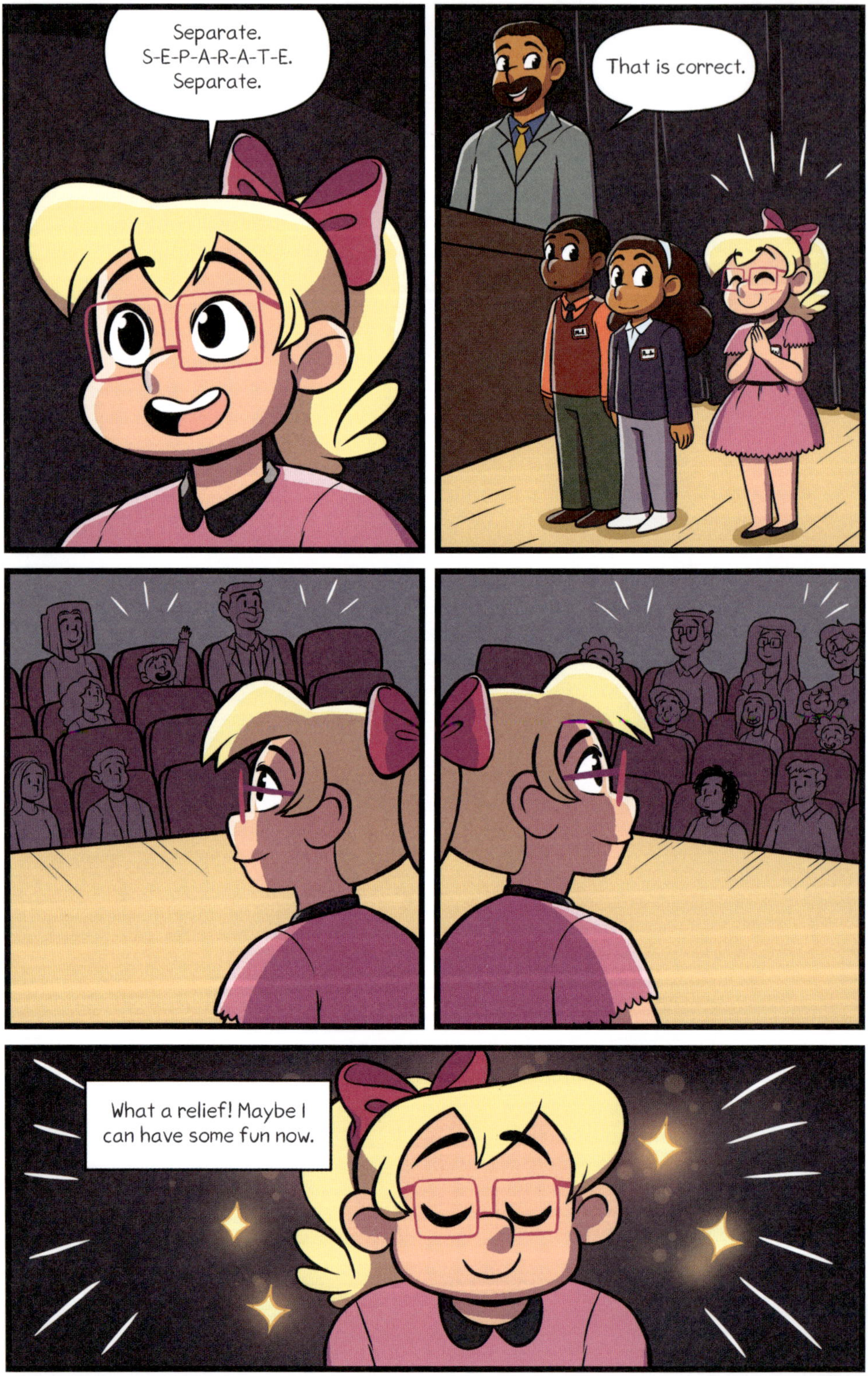
Separate.
S-E-P-A-R-A-T-E.
Separate.
That is correct.
What a relief! Maybe I can have some fun now.

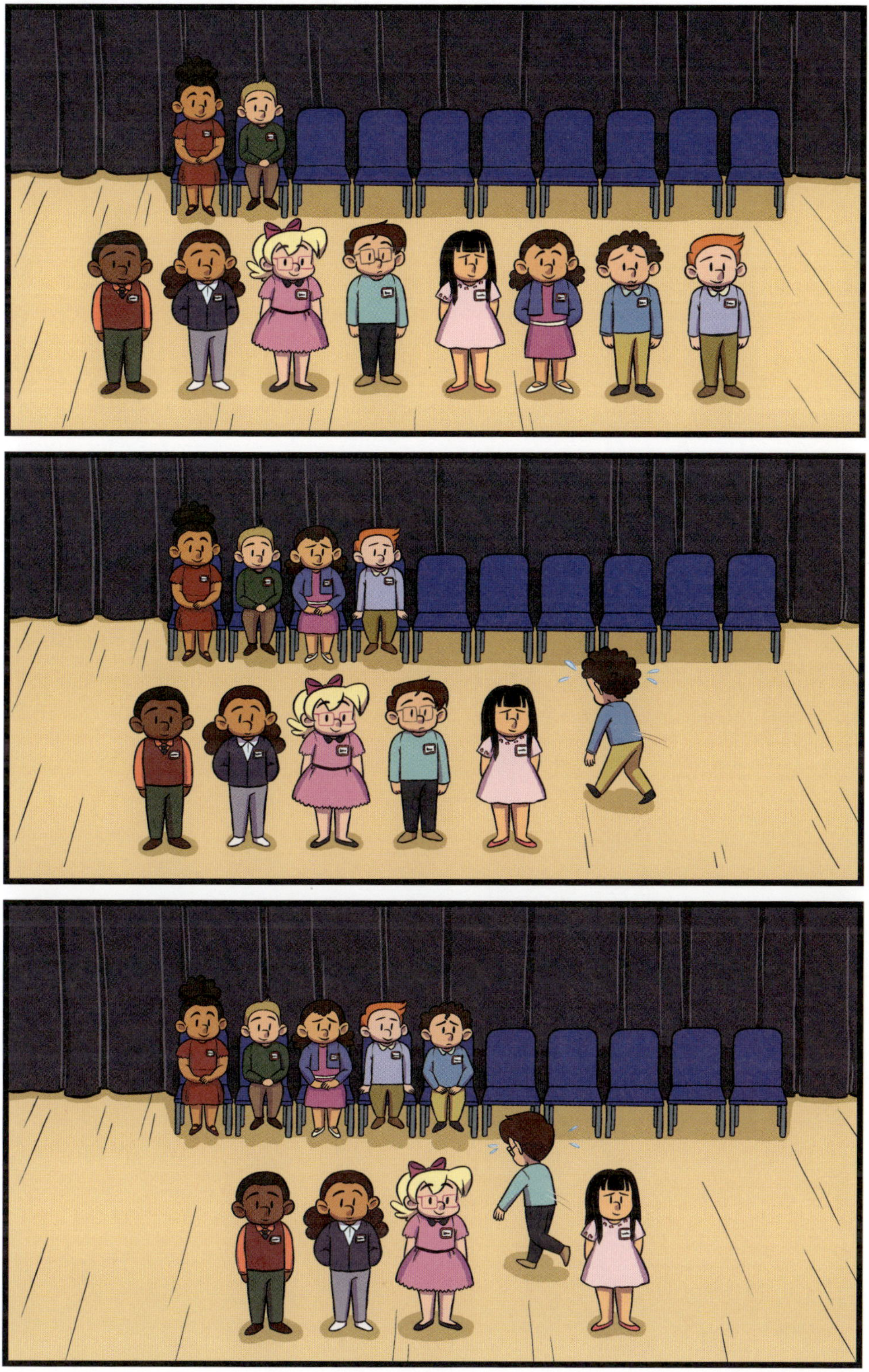

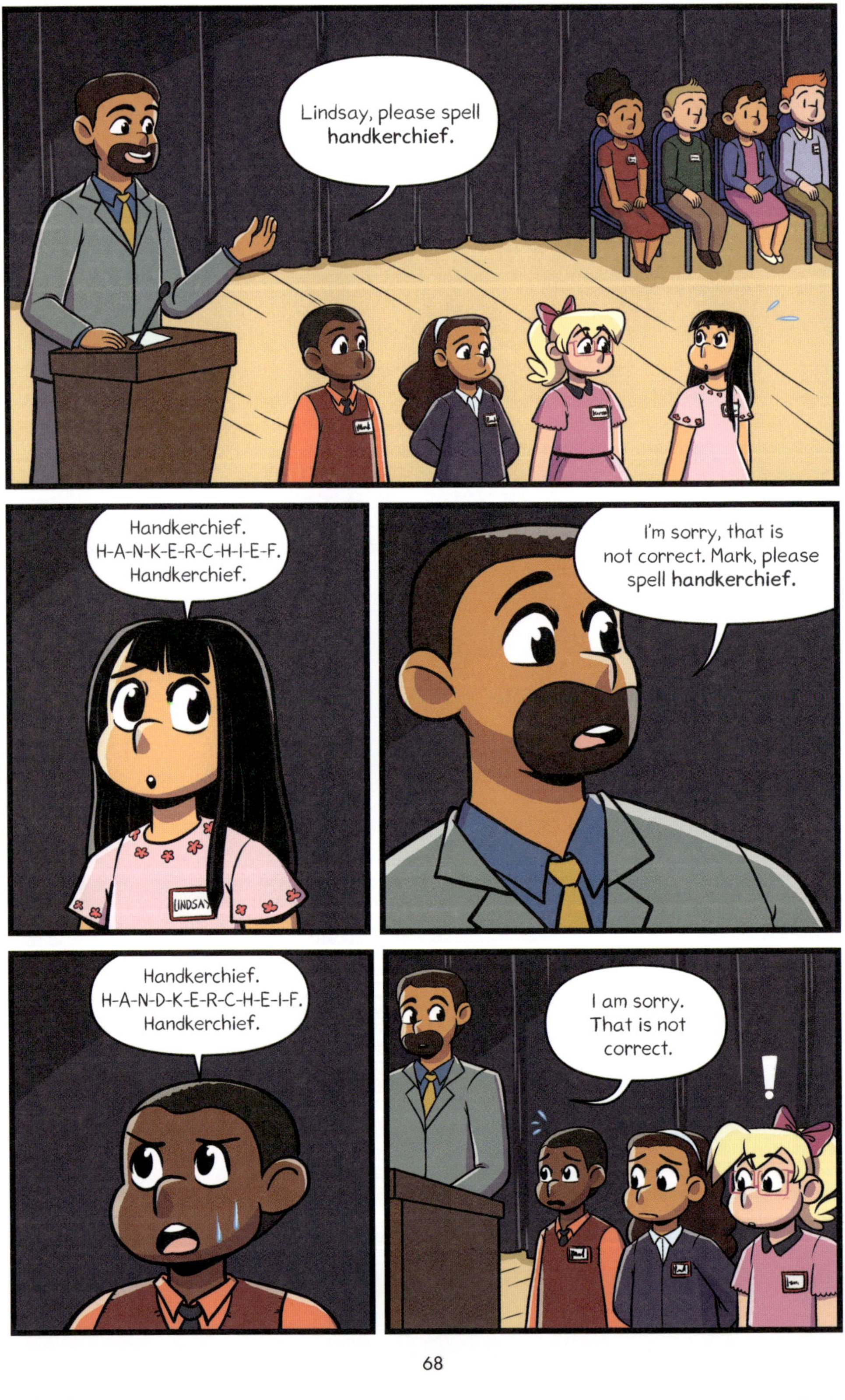
Lindsay, please spell handkerchief.
Handkerchief. H-A-N-K-E-R-C-H-I-E-F. Handkerchief.
I'm sorry, that is not correct. Mark, please spell handkerchief.
Handkerchief. H-A-N-D-K-E-R-C-H-E-I-F. Handkerchief.
I am sorry. That is not correct.
!

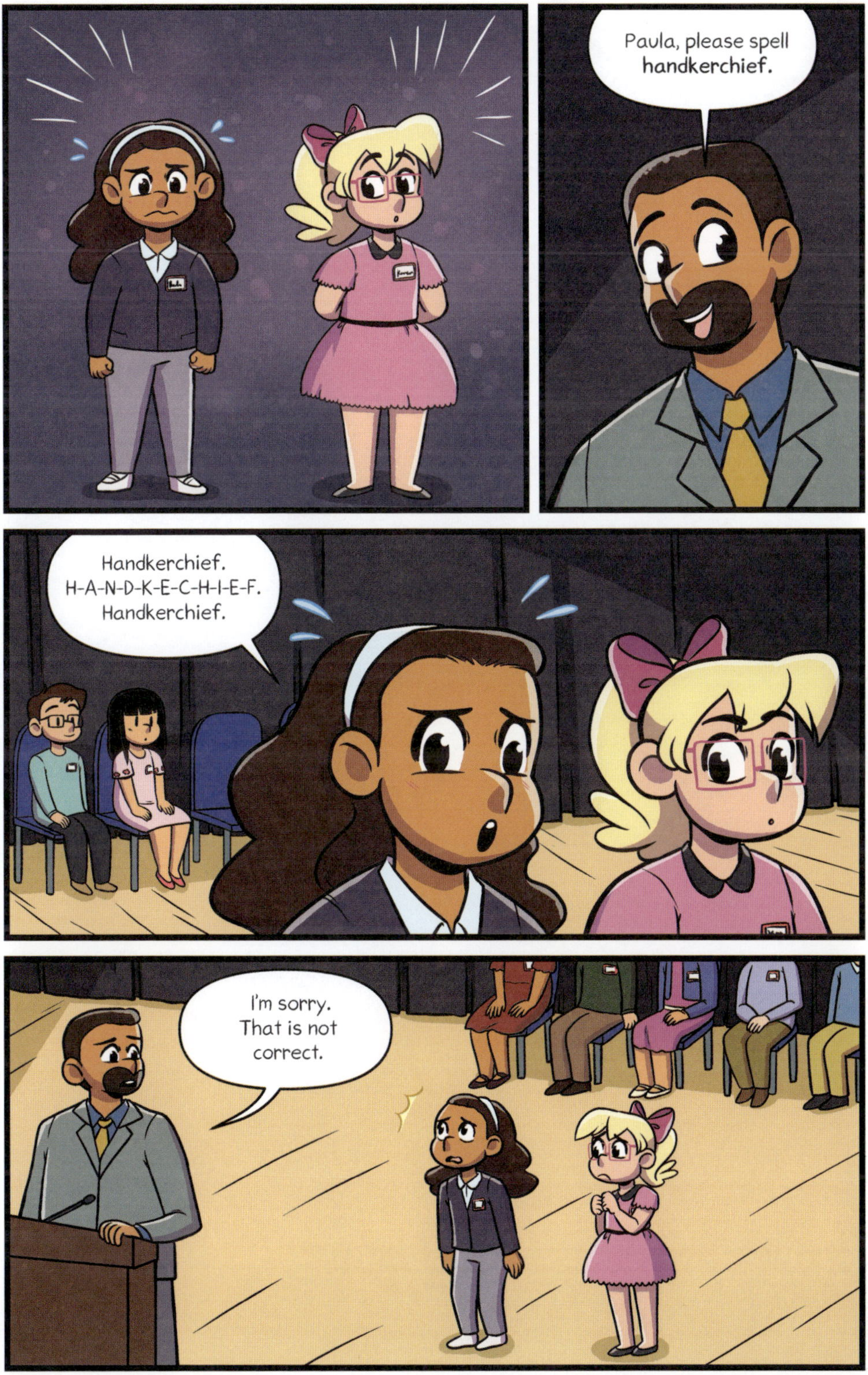
Paula, please spell handkerchief.
Handkerchief. H-A-N-D-K-E-C-H-I-E-F. Handkerchief.
I'm sorry. That is not correct.

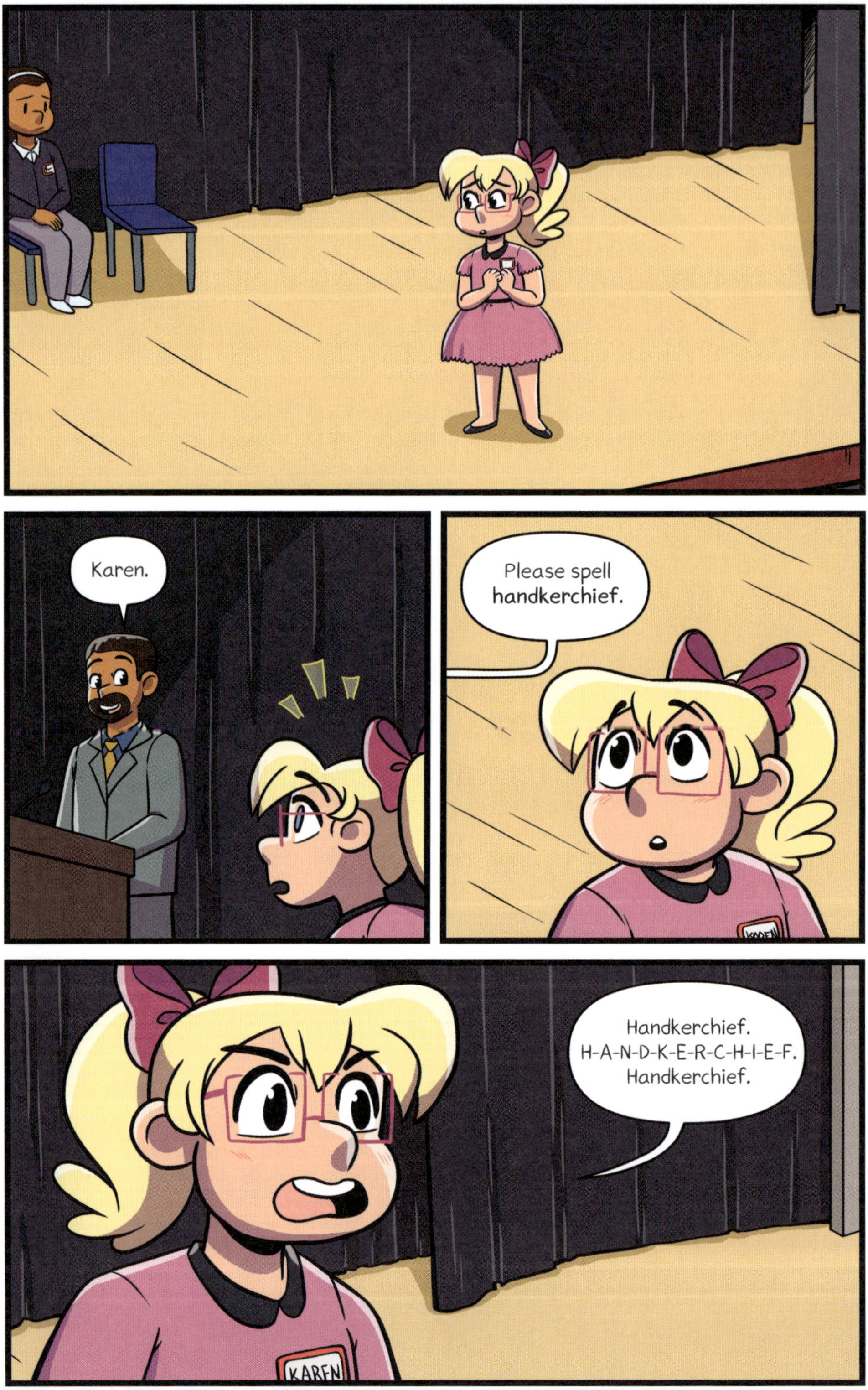
Karen.
Please spell handkerchief.
KAREN
Handkerchief. H-A-N-D-K-E-R-C-H-I-E-F. Handkerchief.
KAREN

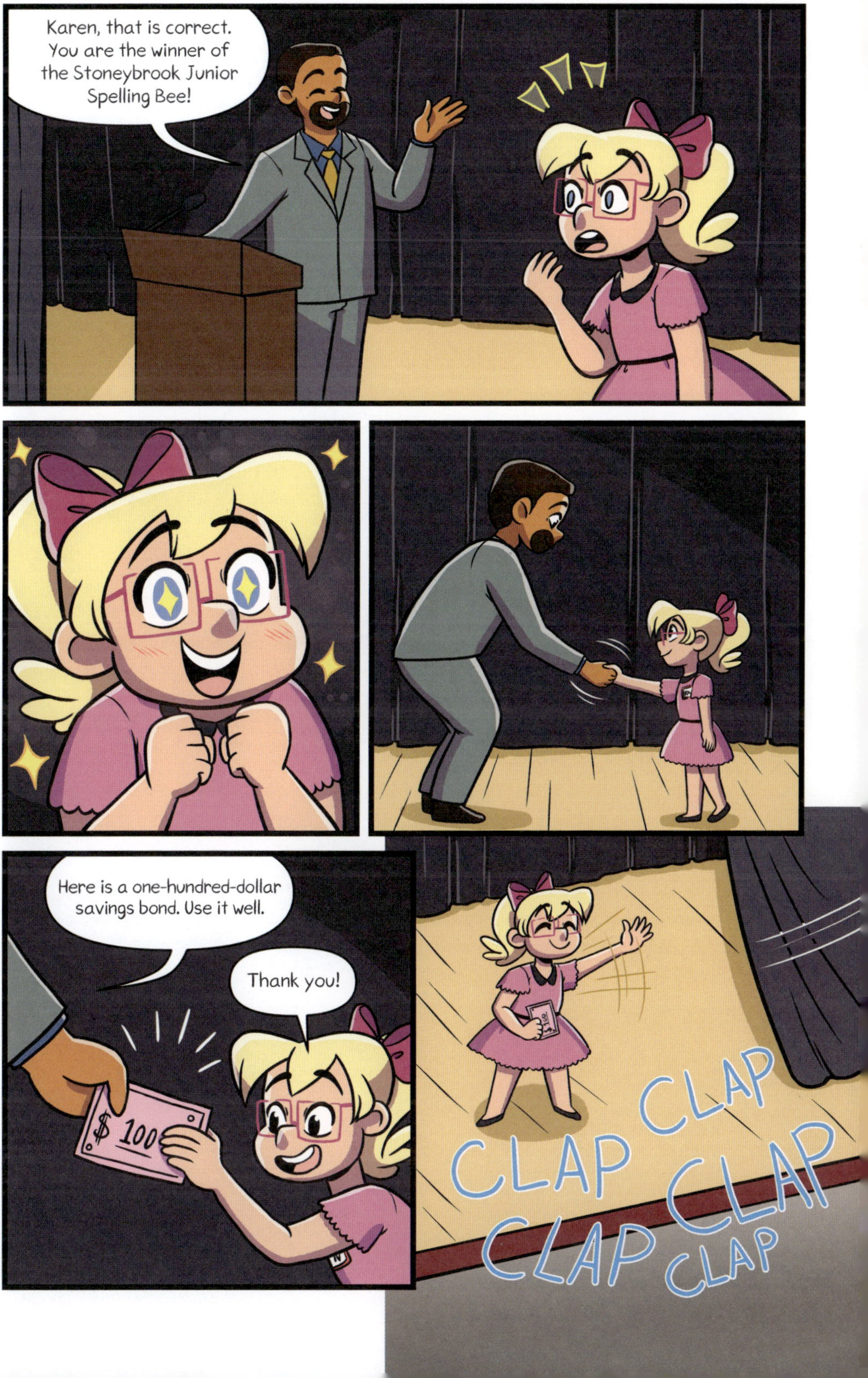
Karen, that is correct. You are the winner of the Stoneybrook Junior Spelling Bee!
Here is a one-hundred-dollar savings bond. Use it well.
Thank you!
$ 100
CLAP CLAP
CLAP CLAP
CLAP
CLAP

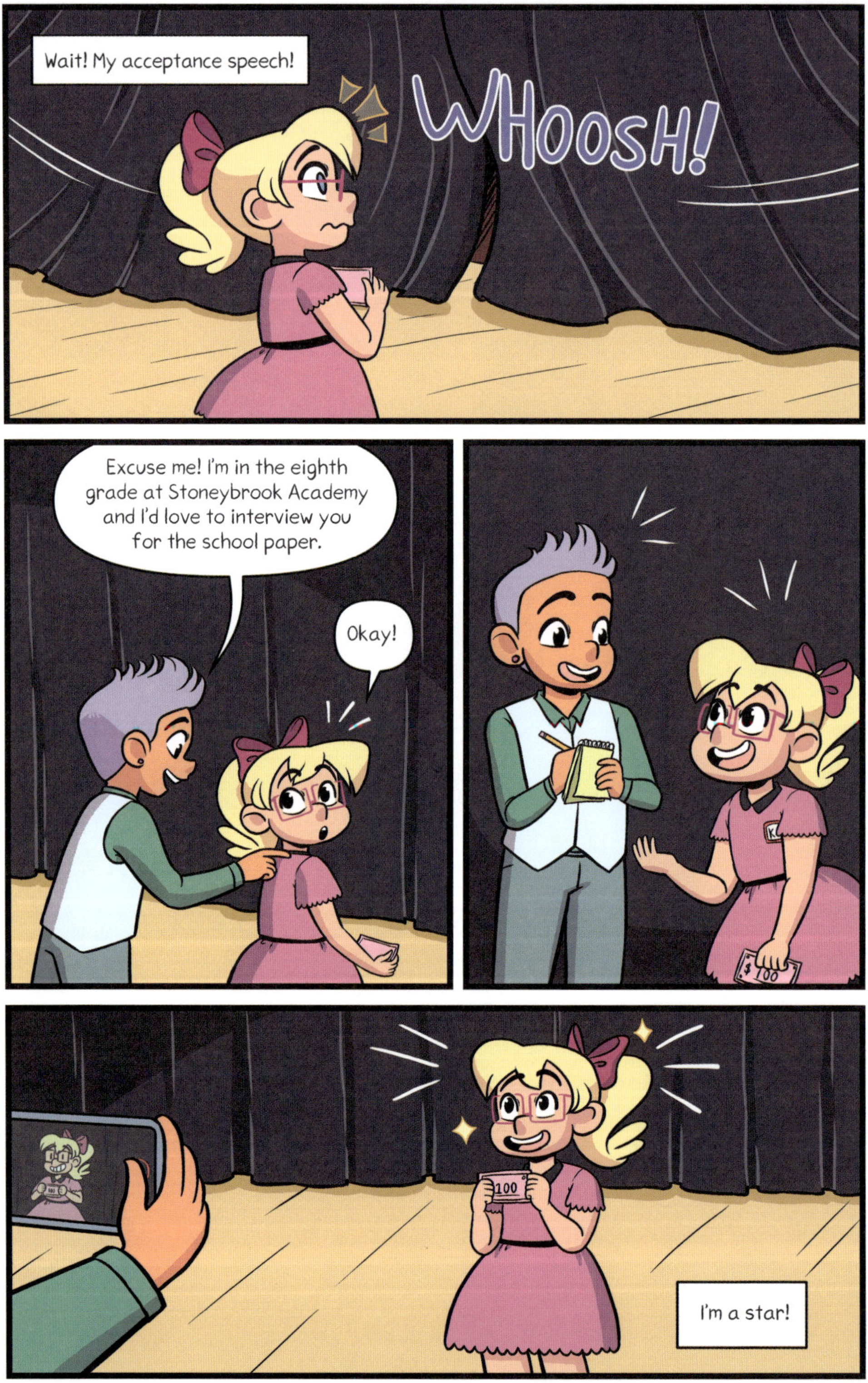
Wait! My acceptance speech!
WHOOSH!
Excuse me! I'm in the eighth grade at Stoneybrook Academy and I'd love to interview you for the school paper.
Okay!
I'm a star!

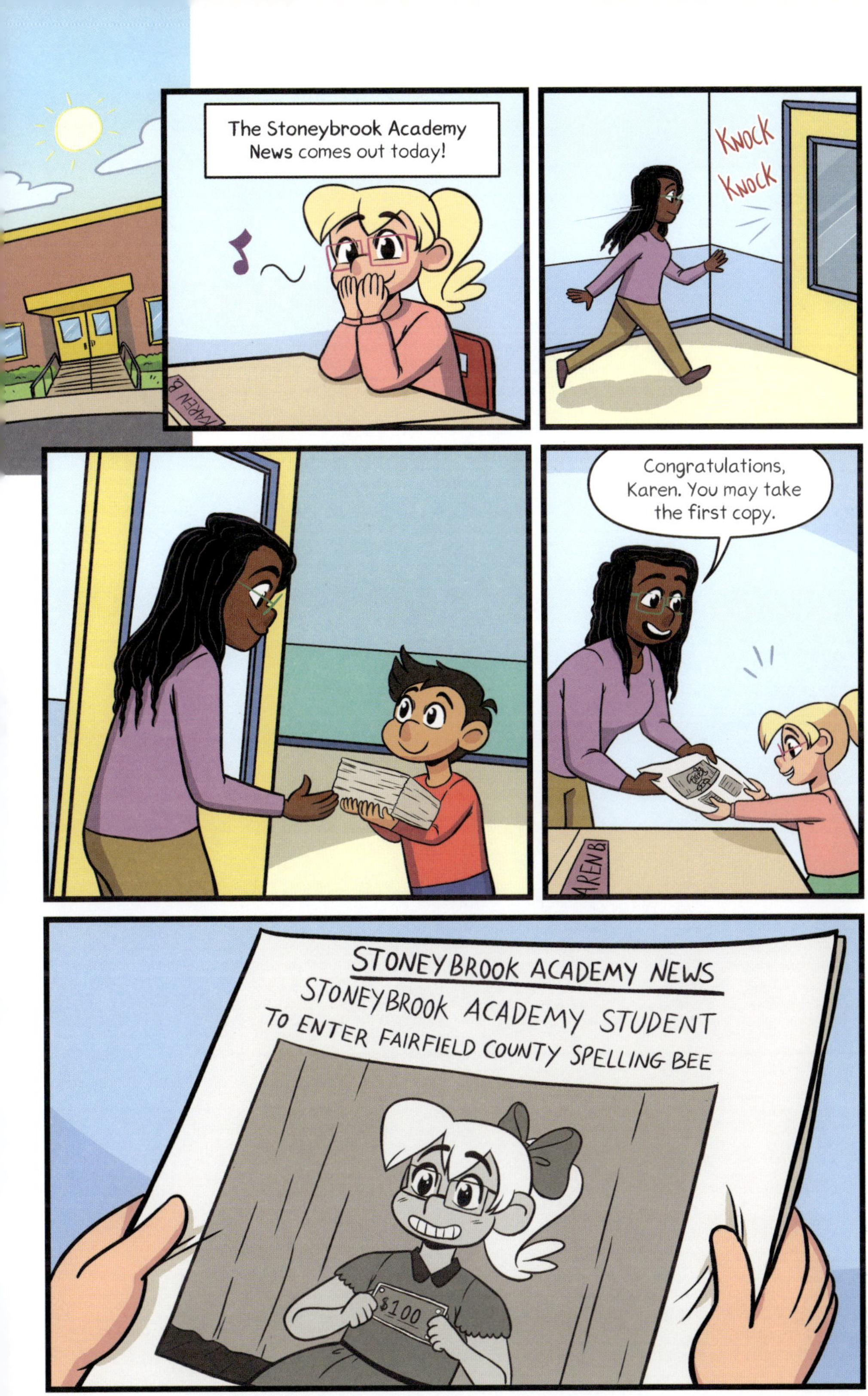
The Stoneybrook Academy News comes out today!
KAREN B.
KNOCK KNOCK
Congratulations, Karen. You may take the first copy.
KAREN B
STONEYBROOK ACADEMY NEWS
STONEYBROOK ACADEMY STUDENT TO ENTER FAIRFIELD COUNTY SPELLING BEE
$100

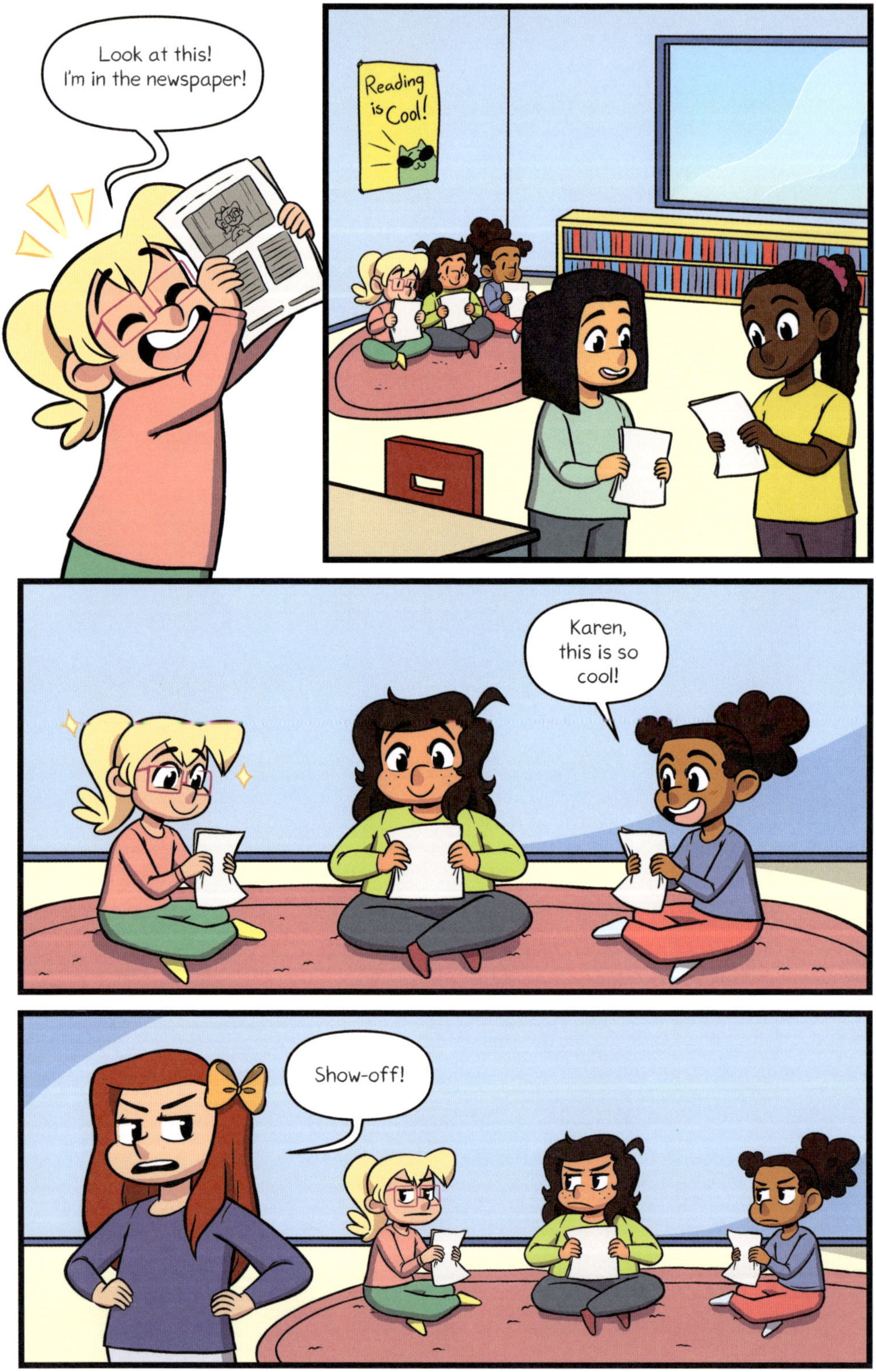
Look at this! I'm in the newspaper!
Reading is Cool!
Karen, this is so cool!
Show-off!

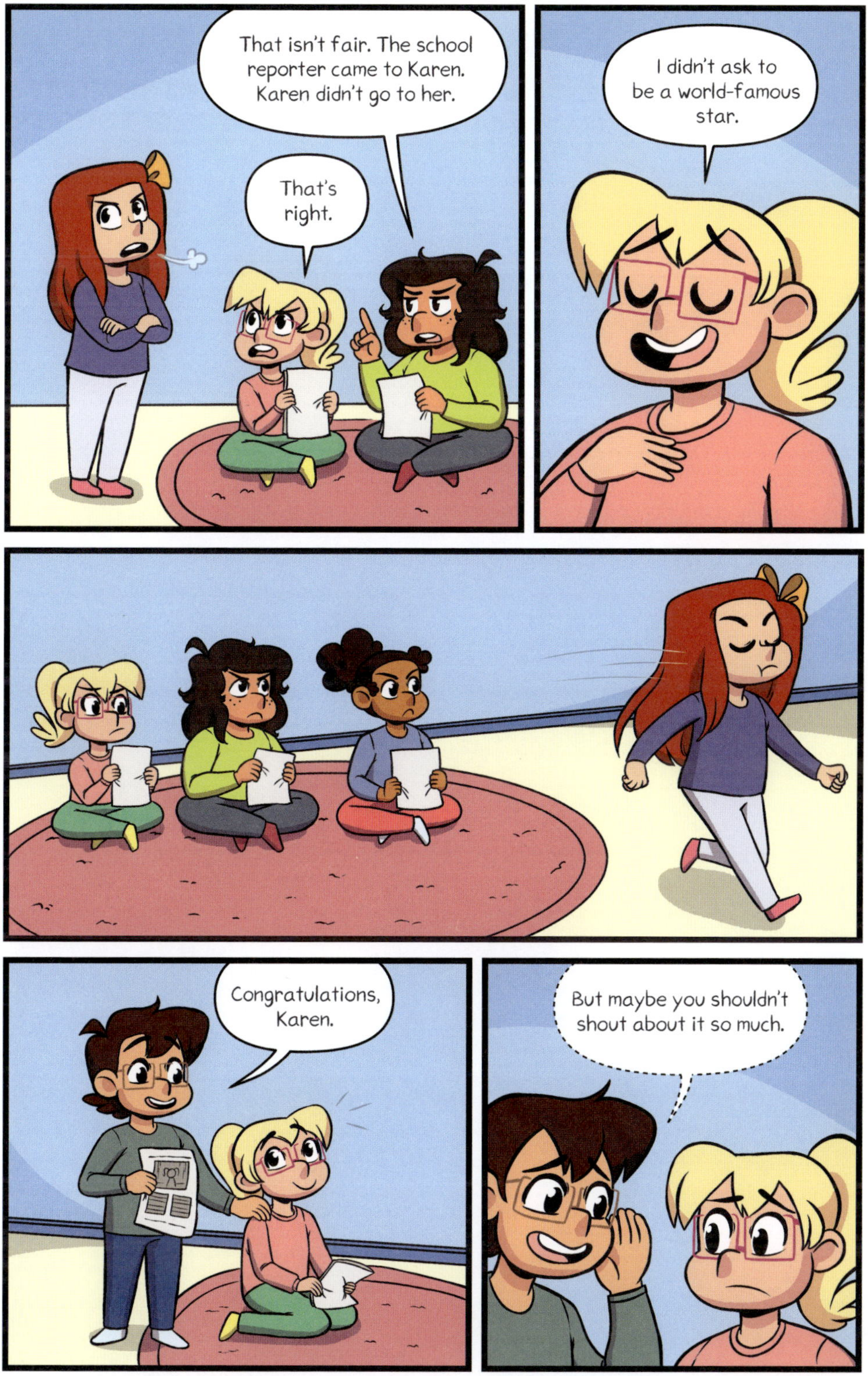
That isn't fair. The school reporter came to Karen. Karen didn't go to her.
That's right.
I didn't ask to be a world-famous star.
Congratulations, Karen.
But maybe you shouldn't shout about it so much.

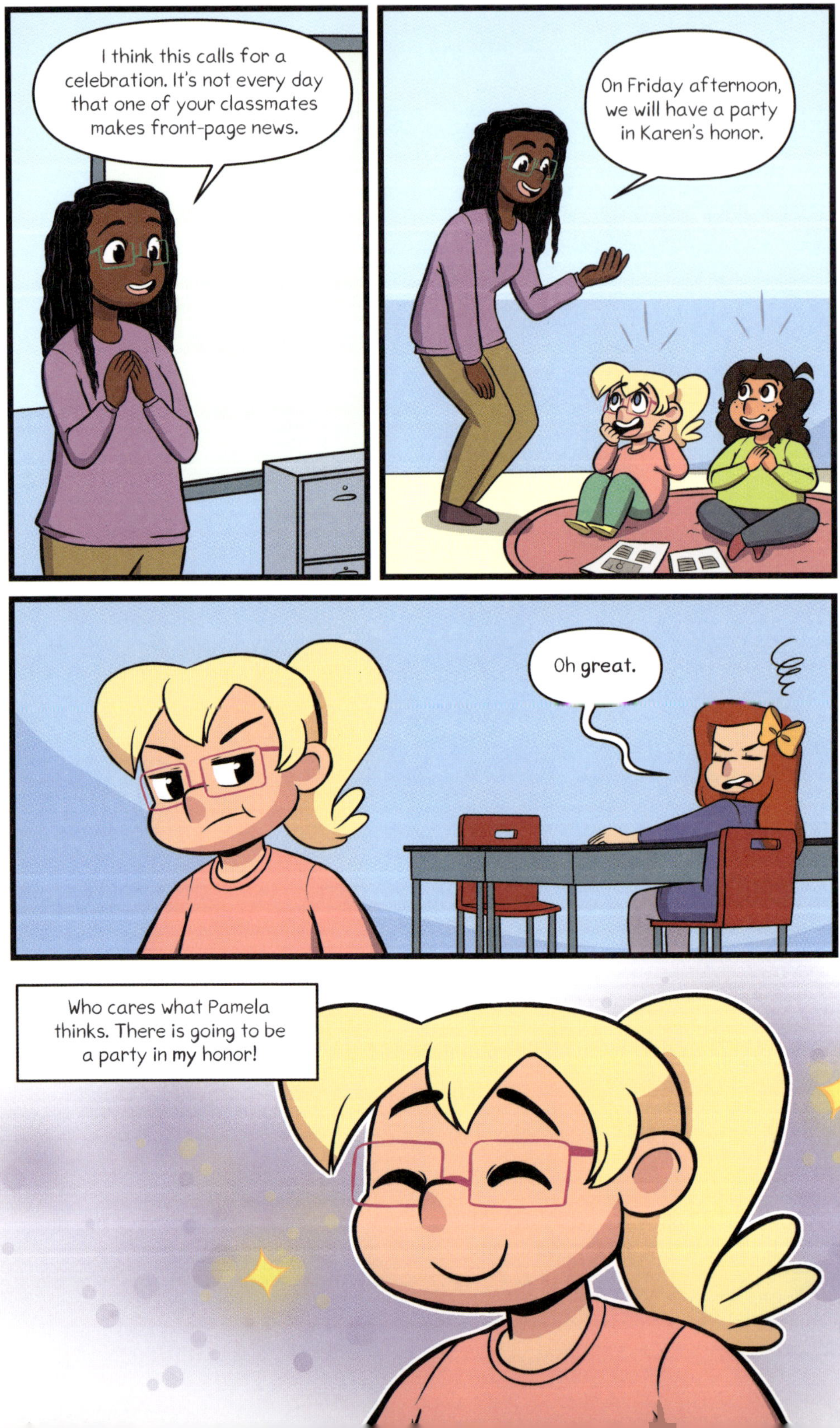
I think this calls for a celebration. It's not every day that one of your classmates makes front-page news.
On Friday afternoon, we will have a party in Karen's honor.
Oh great.
Who cares what Pamela thinks. There is going to be a party in my honor!

# CHAPTER 6

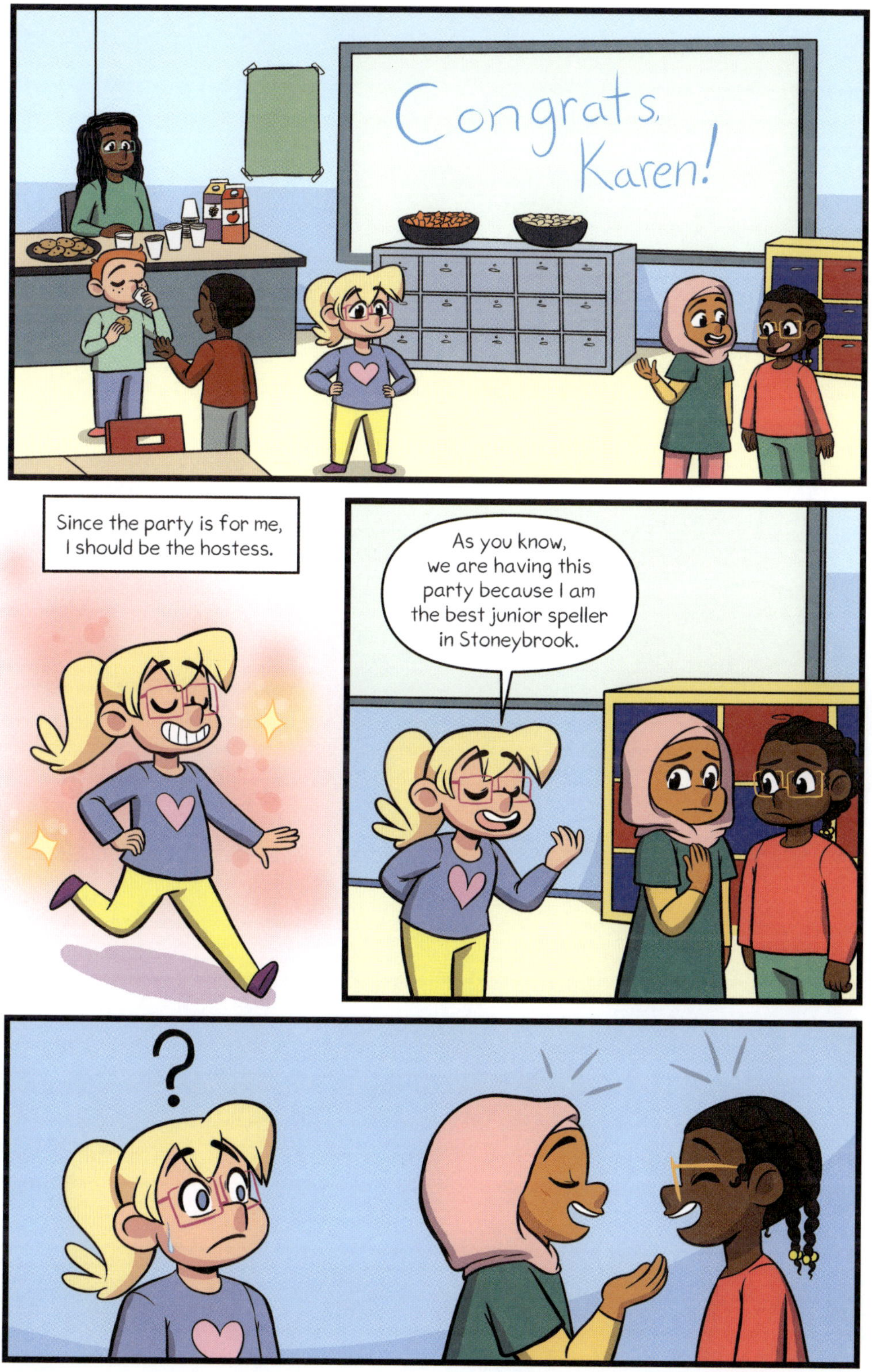
Congrats, Karen!
Since the party is for me, I should be the hostess.
As you know, we are having this party because I am the best junior speller in Stoneybrook.
?

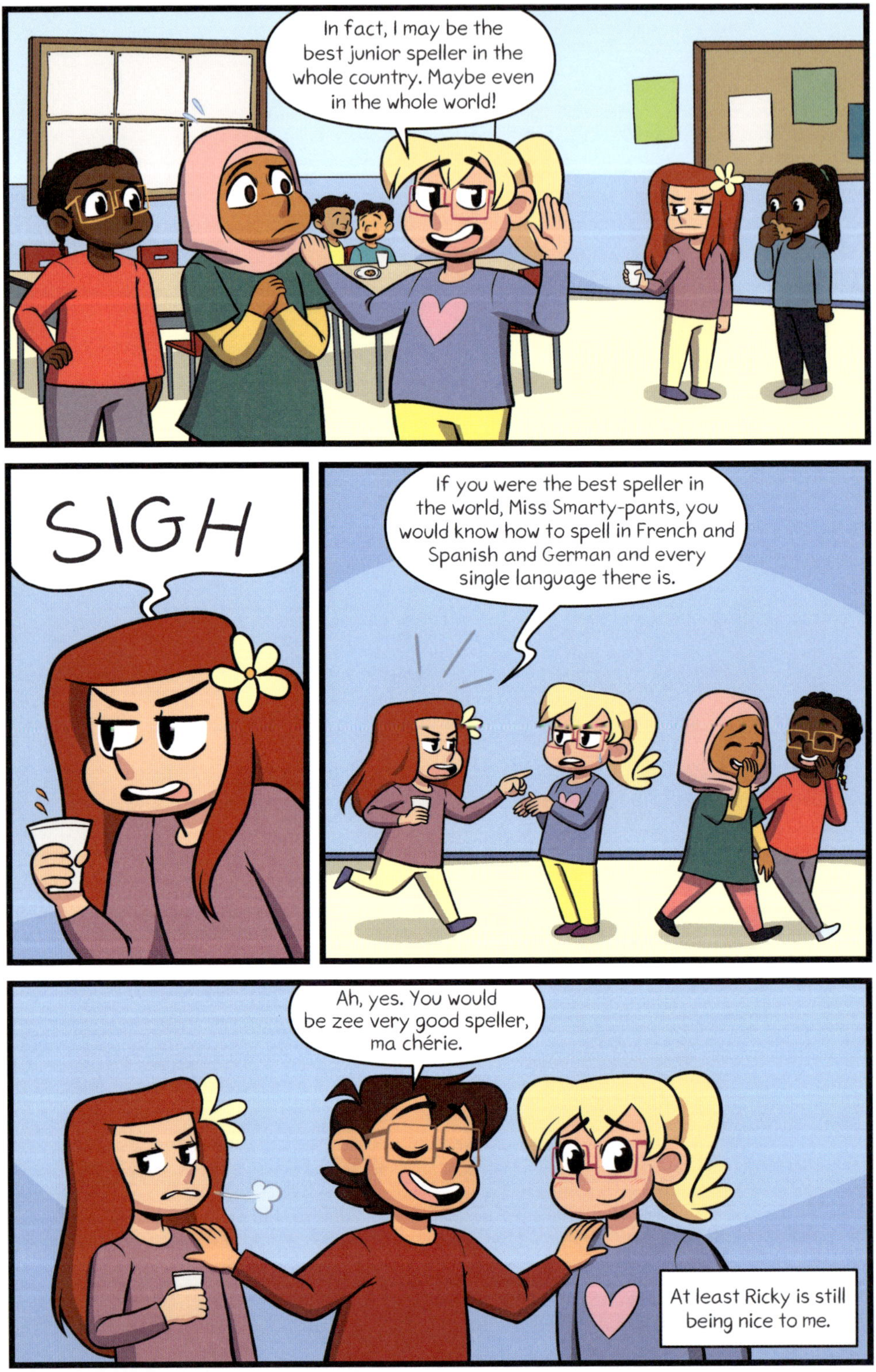
In fact, I may be the best junior speller in the whole country. Maybe even in the whole world!
SIGH
If you were the best speller in the world, Miss Smarty-pants, you would know how to spell in French and Spanish and German and every single language there is.
Ah, yes. You would be zee very good speller, ma chérie.
At least Ricky is still being nice to me.

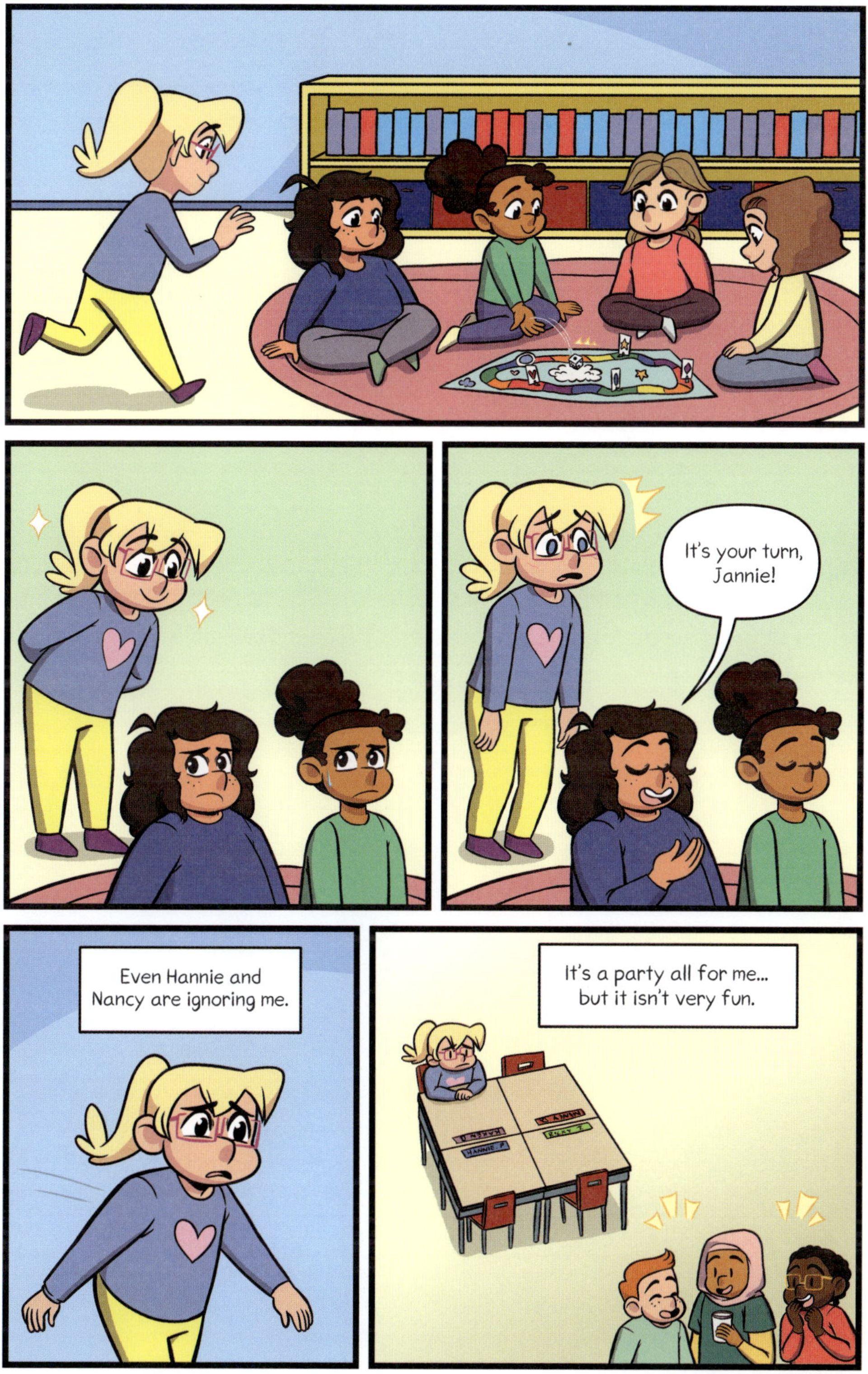
It's your turn, Jannie!
Even Hannie and Nancy are ignoring me.
It's a party all for me... but it isn't very fun.

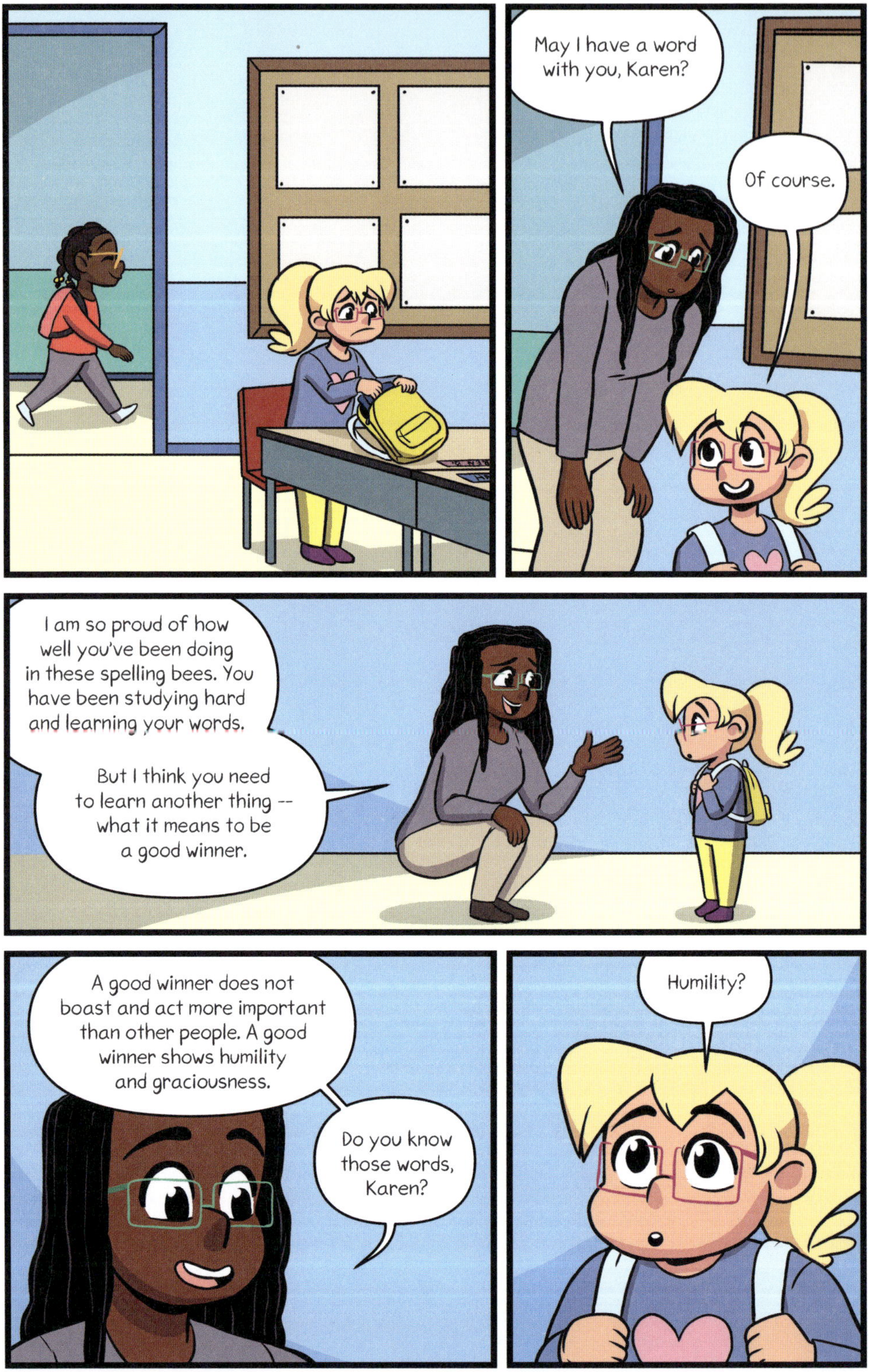
May I have a word with you, Karen?
Of course.
I am so proud of how well you've been doing in these spelling bees. You have been studying hard and learning your words.
But I think you need to learn another thing -- what it means to be a good winner.
A good winner does not boast and act more important than other people. A good winner shows humility and graciousness.
Do you know those words, Karen?
Humility?

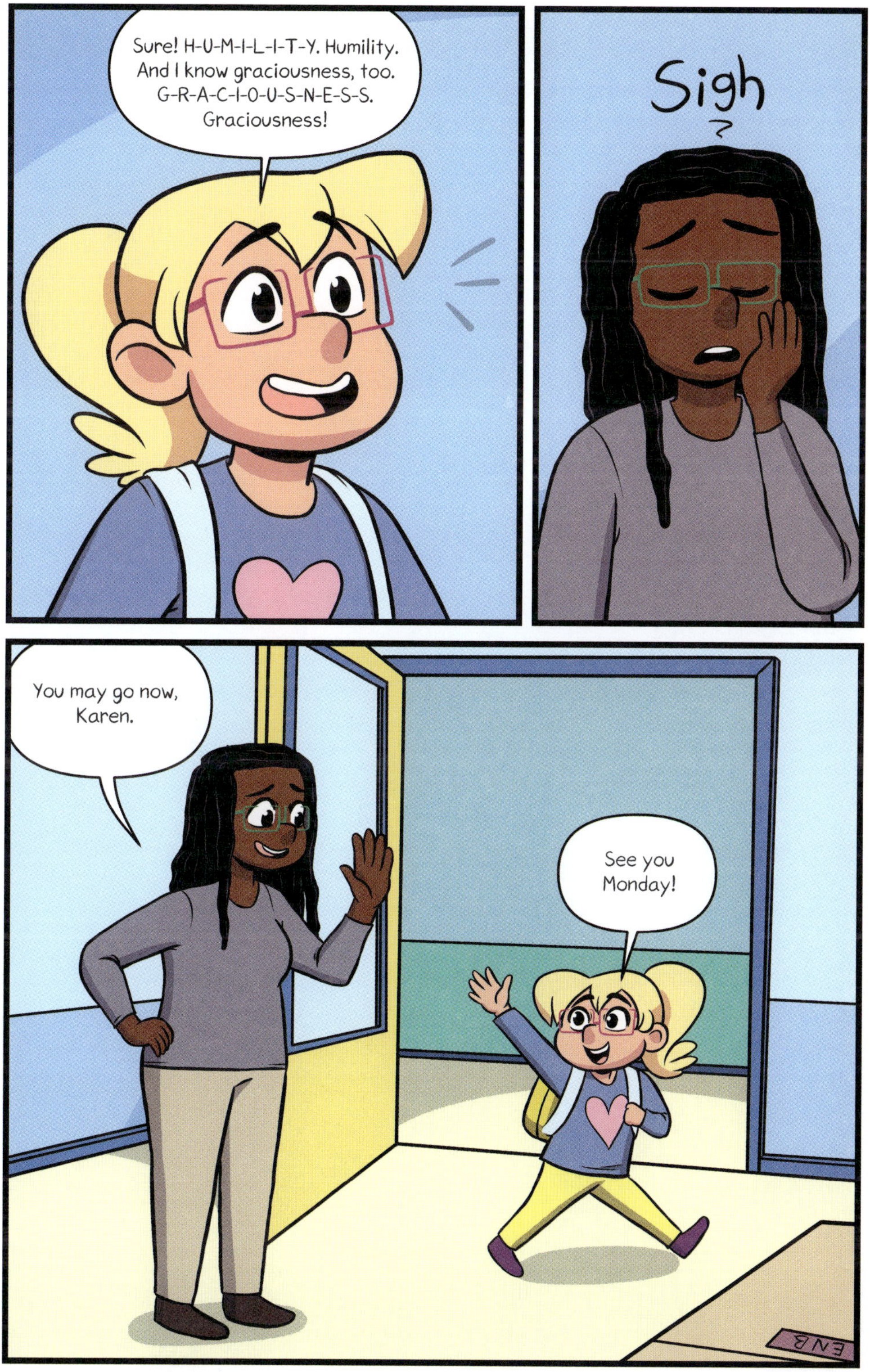
Sure! H-U-M-I-L-I-T-Y. Humility. And I know graciousness, too. G-R-A-C-I-O-U-S-N-E-S-S. Graciousness!
Sigh
You may go now, Karen.
See you Monday!

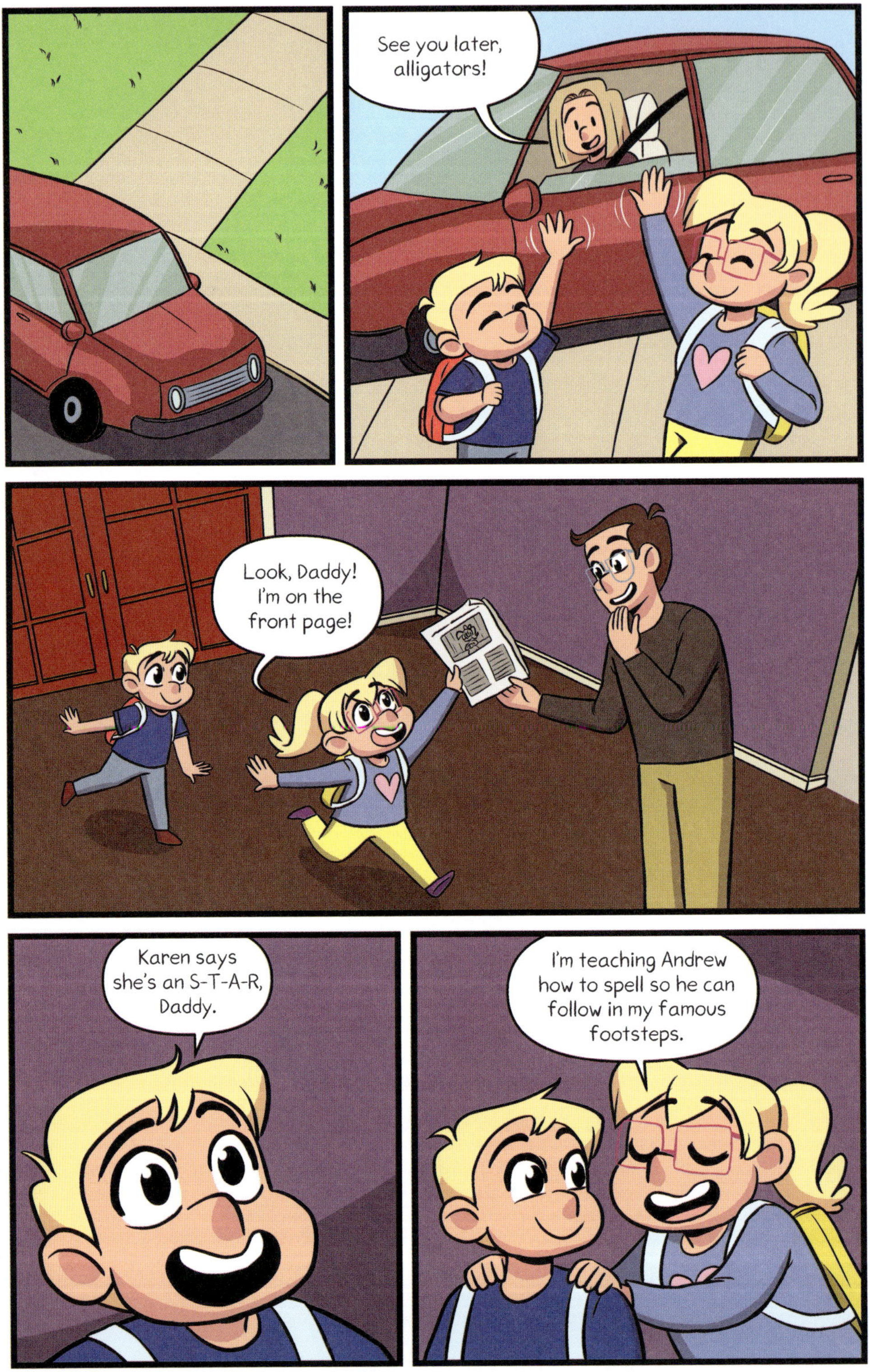
See you later, alligators!
Look, Daddy! I'm on the front page!
Karen says she's an S-T-A-R, Daddy.
I'm teaching Andrew how to spell so he can follow in my famous footsteps.

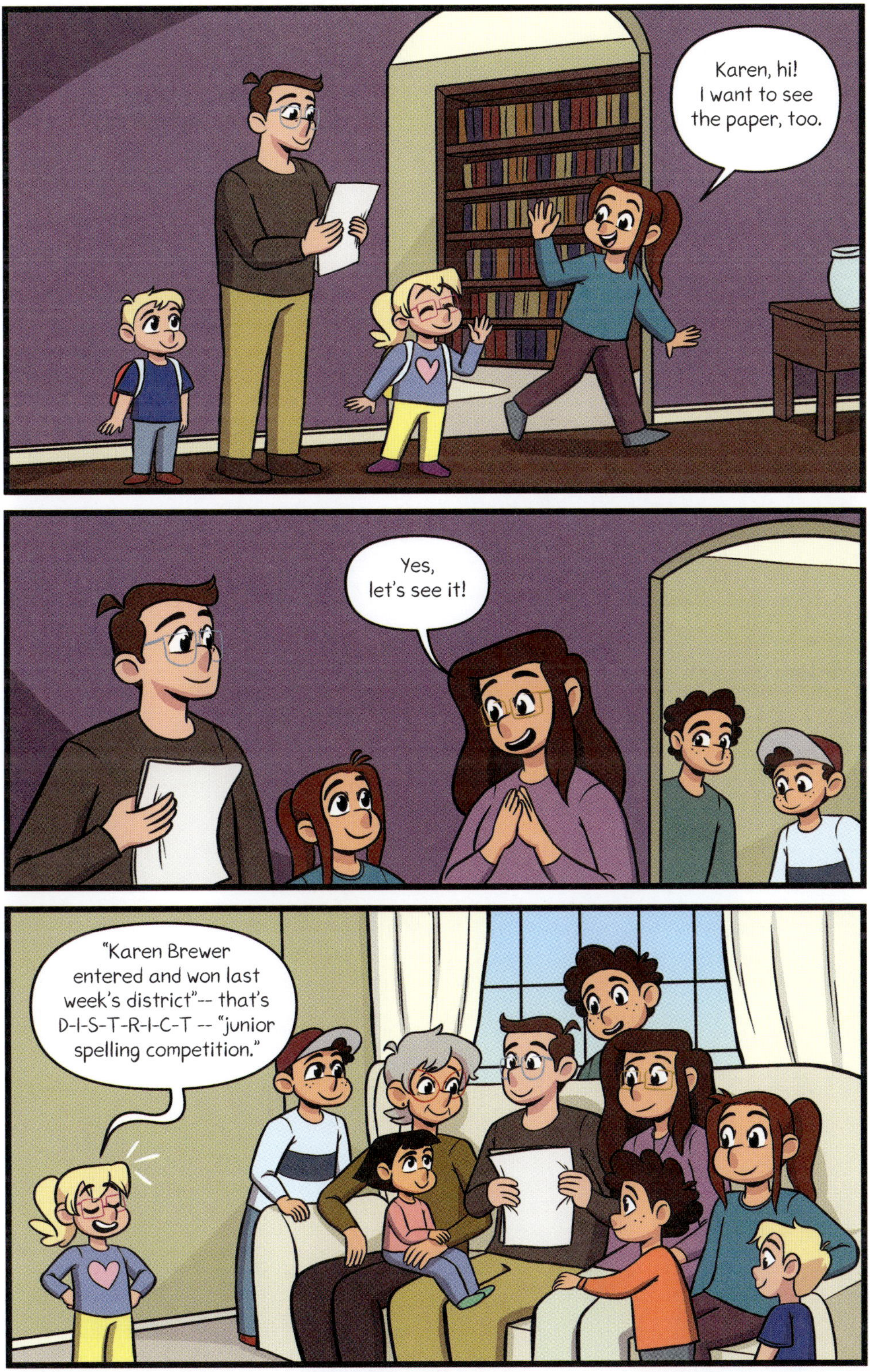
Karen, hi! I want to see the paper, too.
Yes, let's see it!
"Karen Brewer entered and won last week's district"-- that's D-I-S-T-R-I-C-T -- "junior spelling competition."

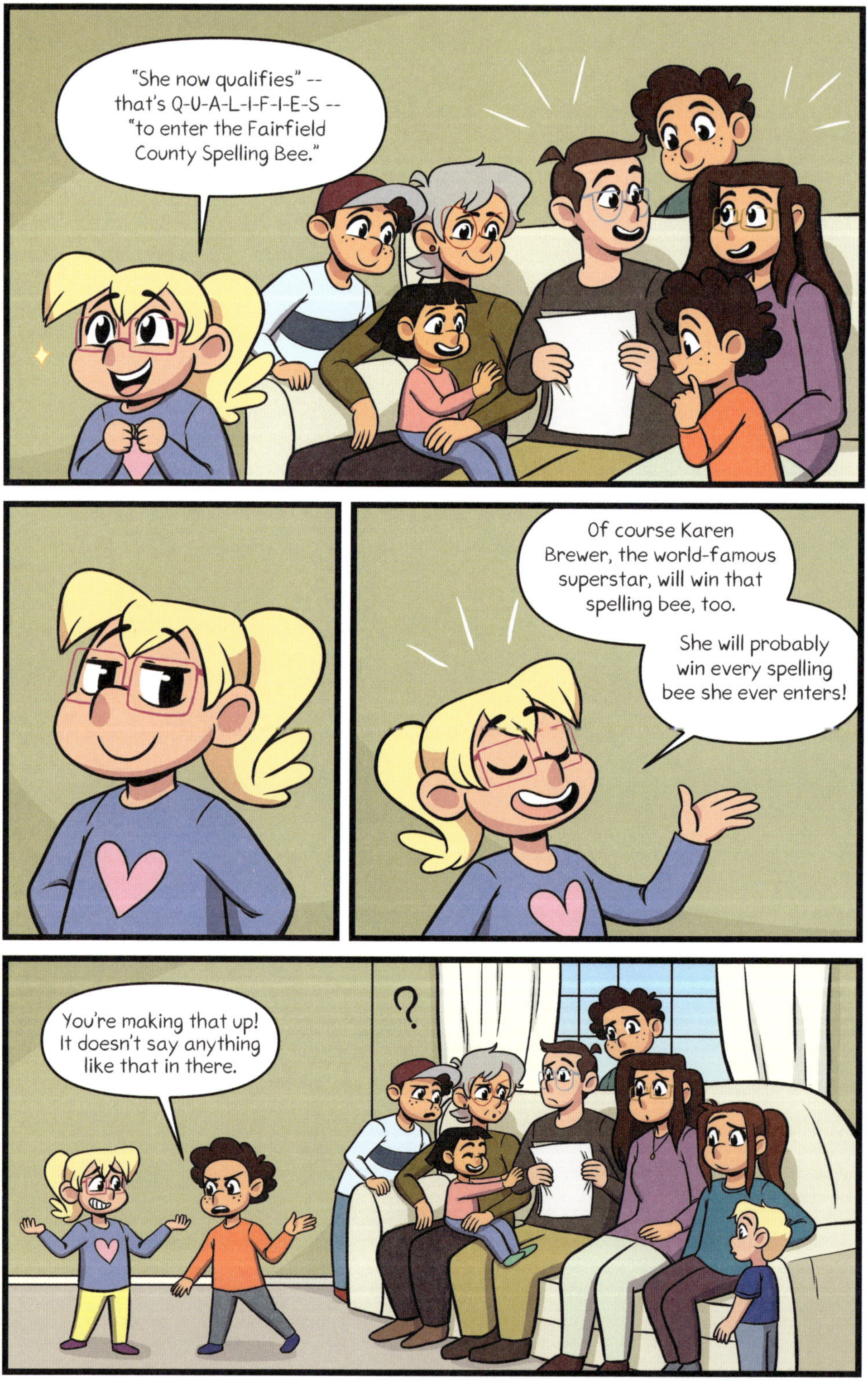
"She now qualifies" -- that's Q-U-A-L-I-F-I-E-S -- "to enter the Fairfield County Spelling Bee."
Of course Karen Brewer, the world-famous superstar, will win that spelling bee, too.
She will probably win every spelling bee she ever enters!
?
You're making that up! It doesn't say anything like that in there.

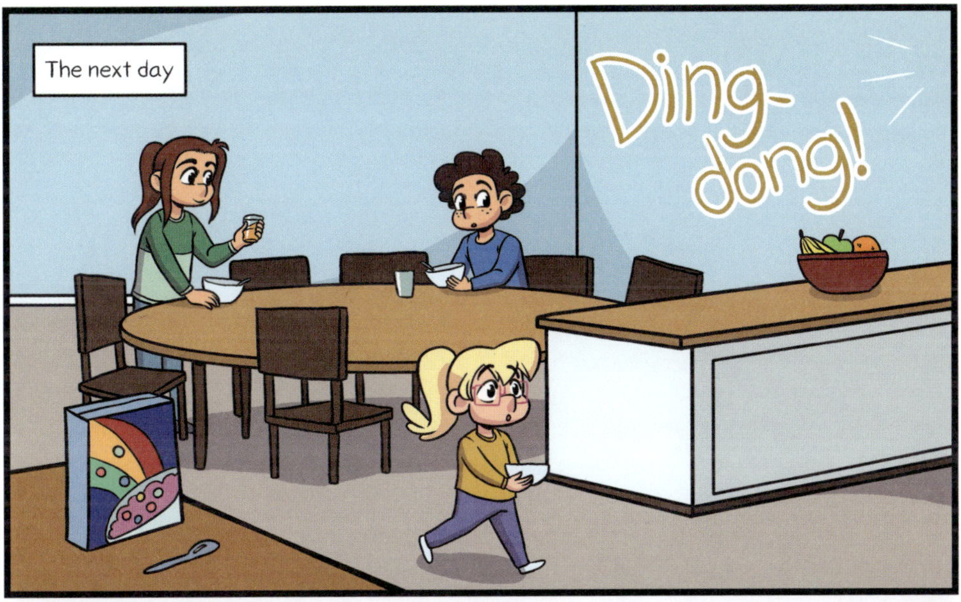
The next day
Ding-dong!

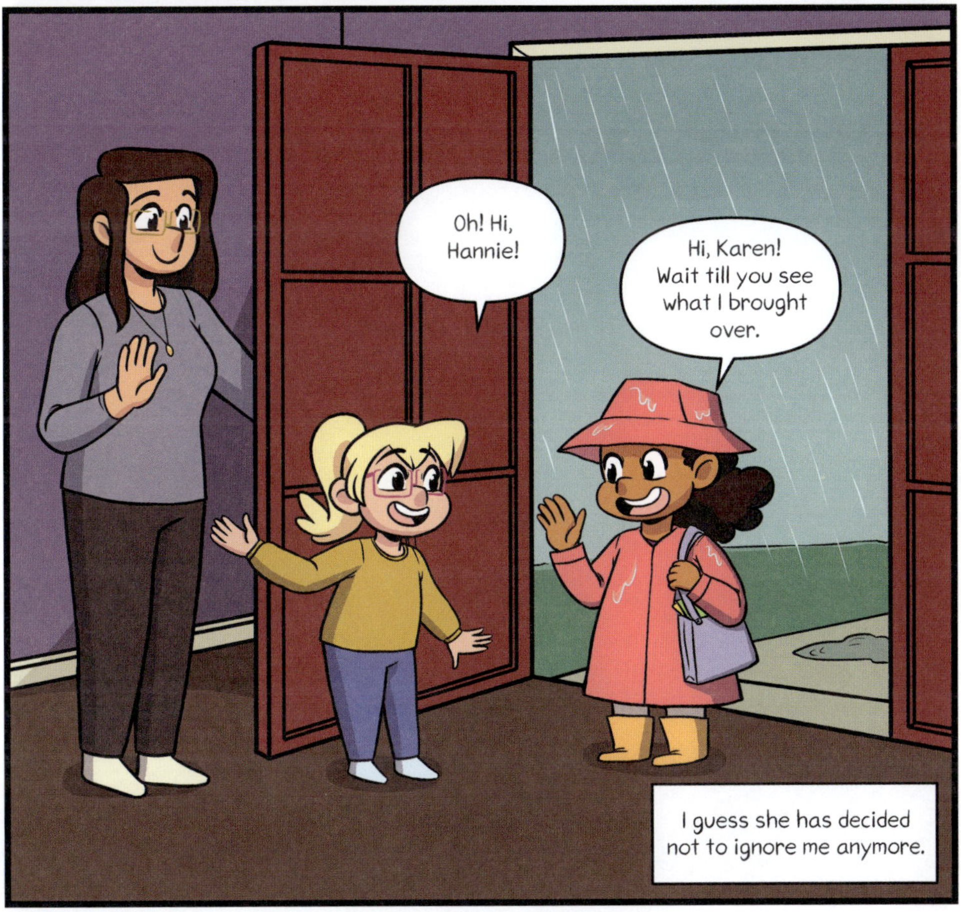
Oh! Hi, Hannie!
Hi, Karen! Wait till you see what I brought over.
I guess she has decided not to ignore me anymore.

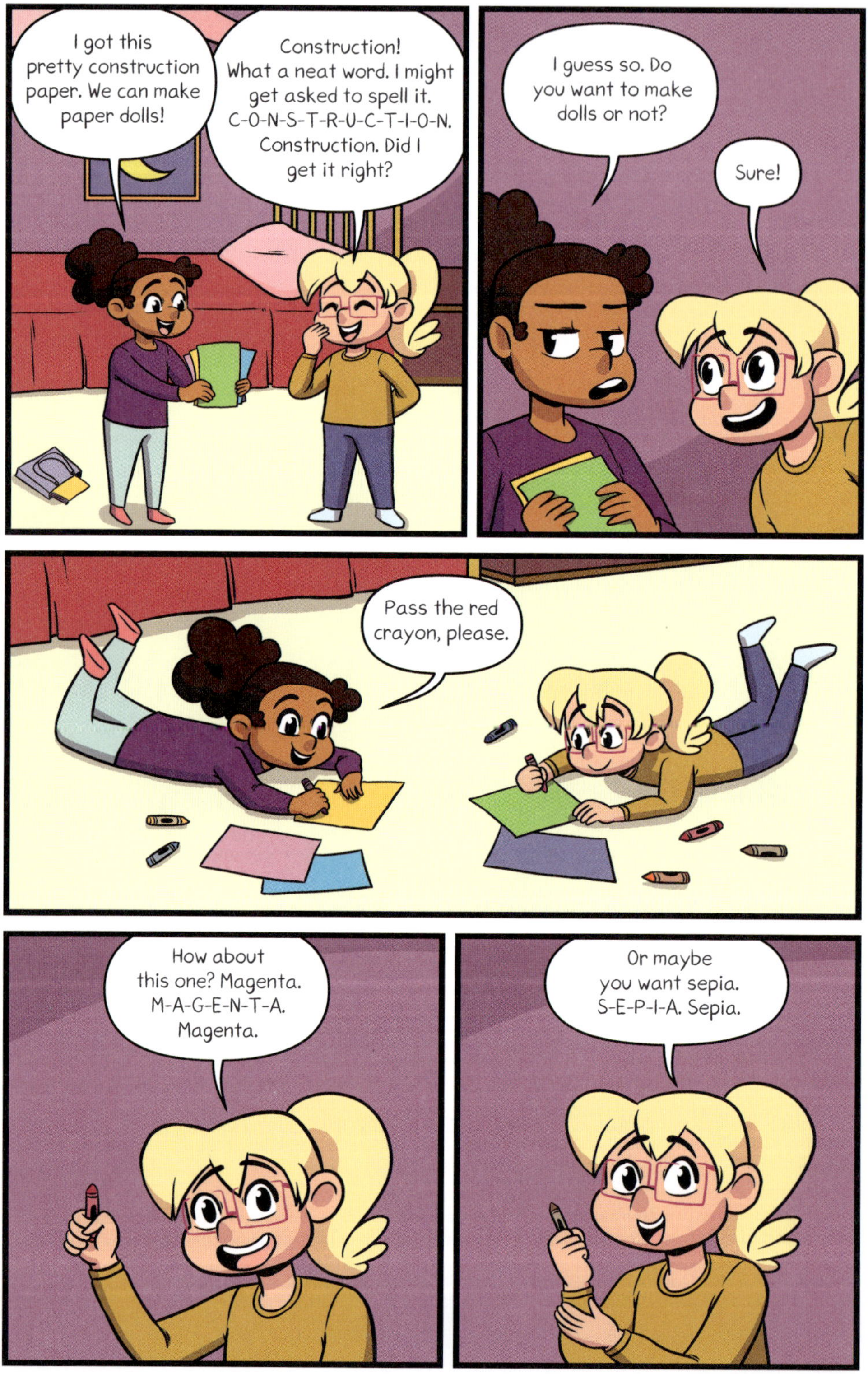
I got this pretty construction paper. We can make paper dolls!
Construction! What a neat word. I might get asked to spell it. C-O-N-S-T-R-U-C-T-I-O-N. Construction. Did I get it right?
I guess so. Do you want to make dolls or not?
Sure!
Pass the red crayon, please.
How about this one? Magenta. M-A-G-E-N-T-A. Magenta.
Or maybe you want sepia. S-E-P-I-A. Sepia.

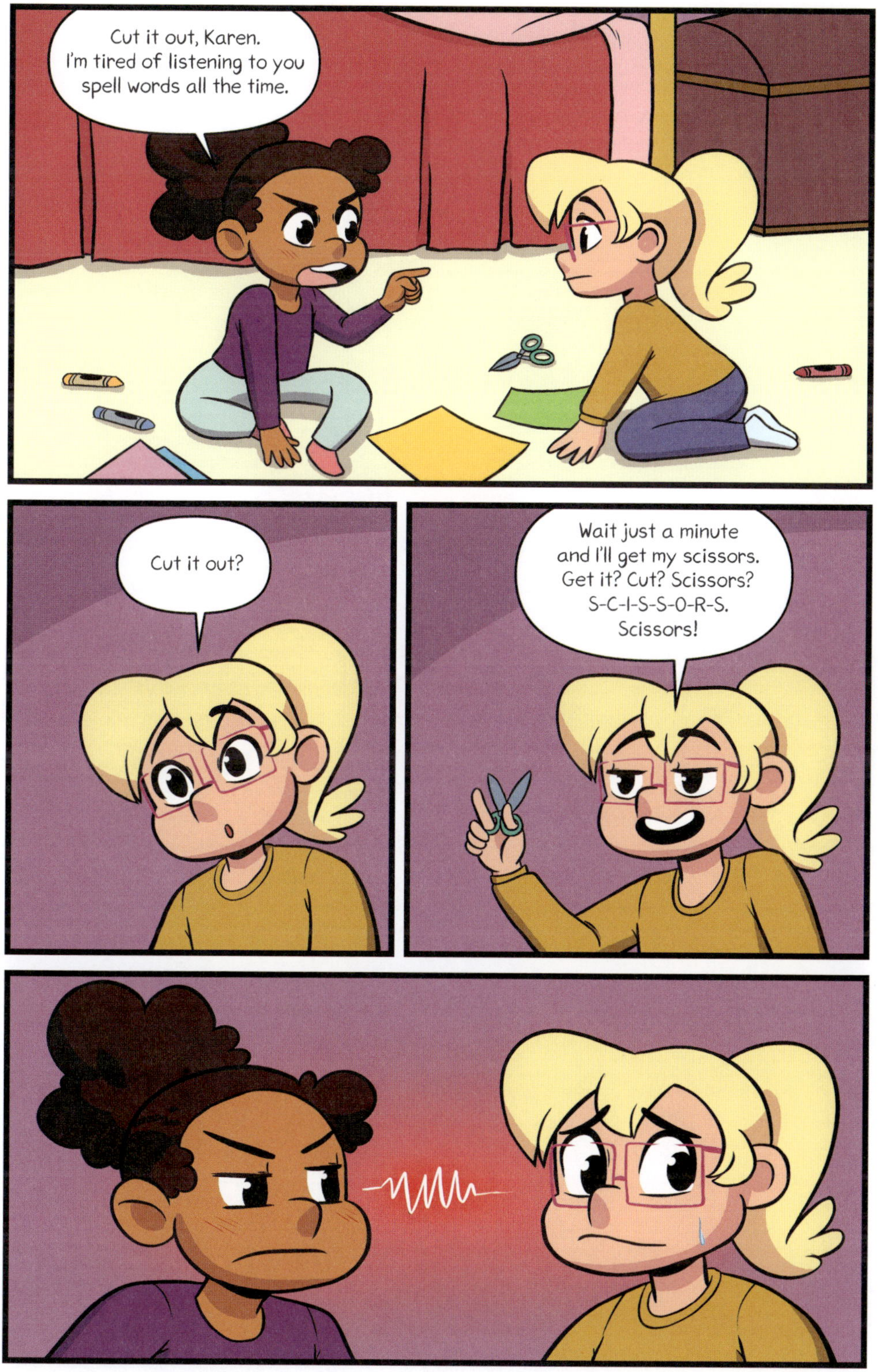
Cut it out, Karen. I'm tired of listening to you spell words all the time.
Cut it out?
Wait just a minute and I'll get my scissors. Get it? Cut? Scissors? S-C-I-S-S-O-R-S. Scissors!

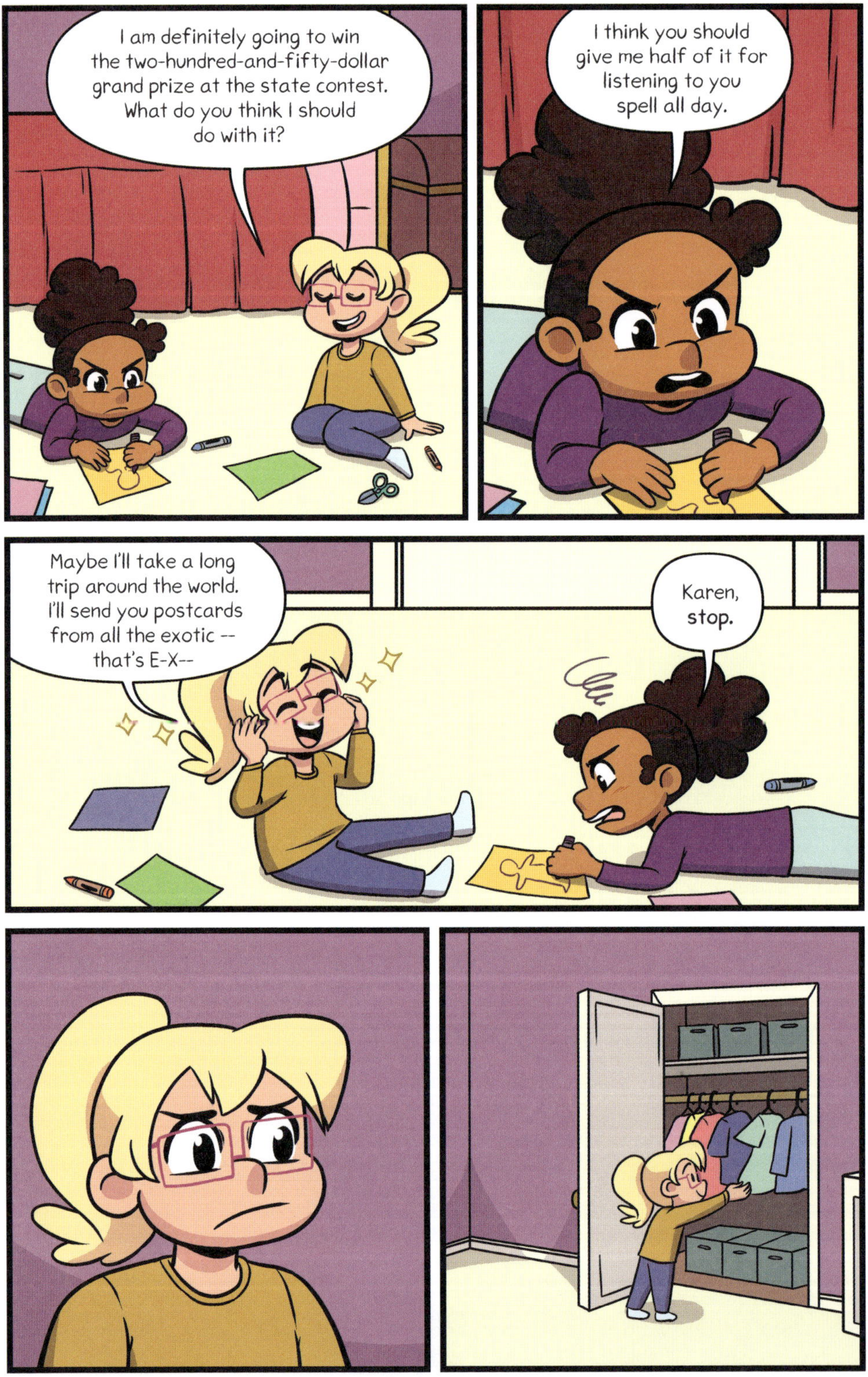
I am definitely going to win the two-hundred-and-fifty-dollar grand prize at the state contest. What do you think I should do with it?
I think you should give me half of it for listening to you spell all day.
Maybe I'll take a long trip around the world. I'll send you postcards from all the exotic -- that's E-X--
Karen, **stop.**

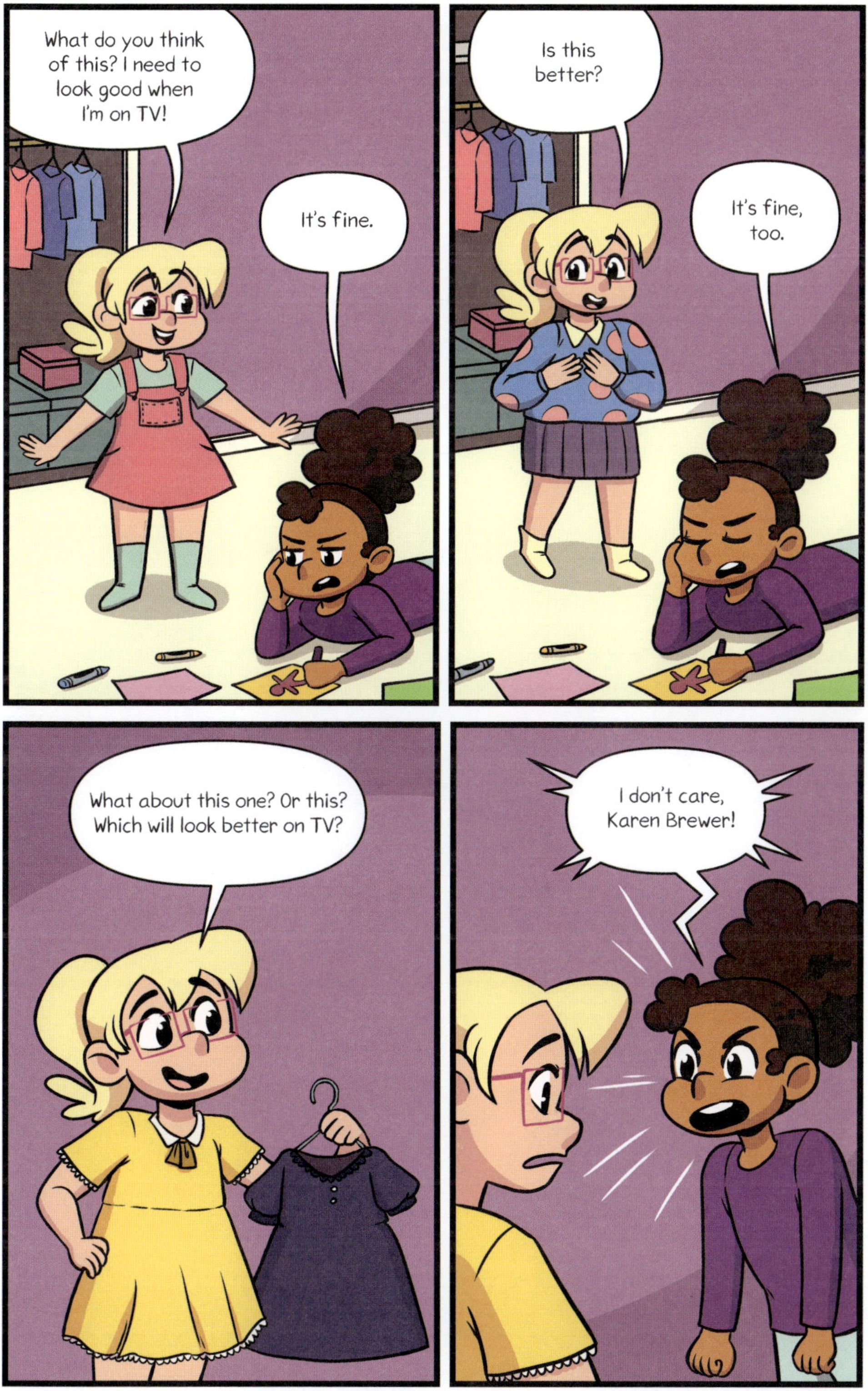
What do you think of this? I need to look good when I'm on TV!
It's fine.
Is this better?
It's fine, too.
What about this one? Or this? Which will look better on TV?
I don't care, Karen Brewer!

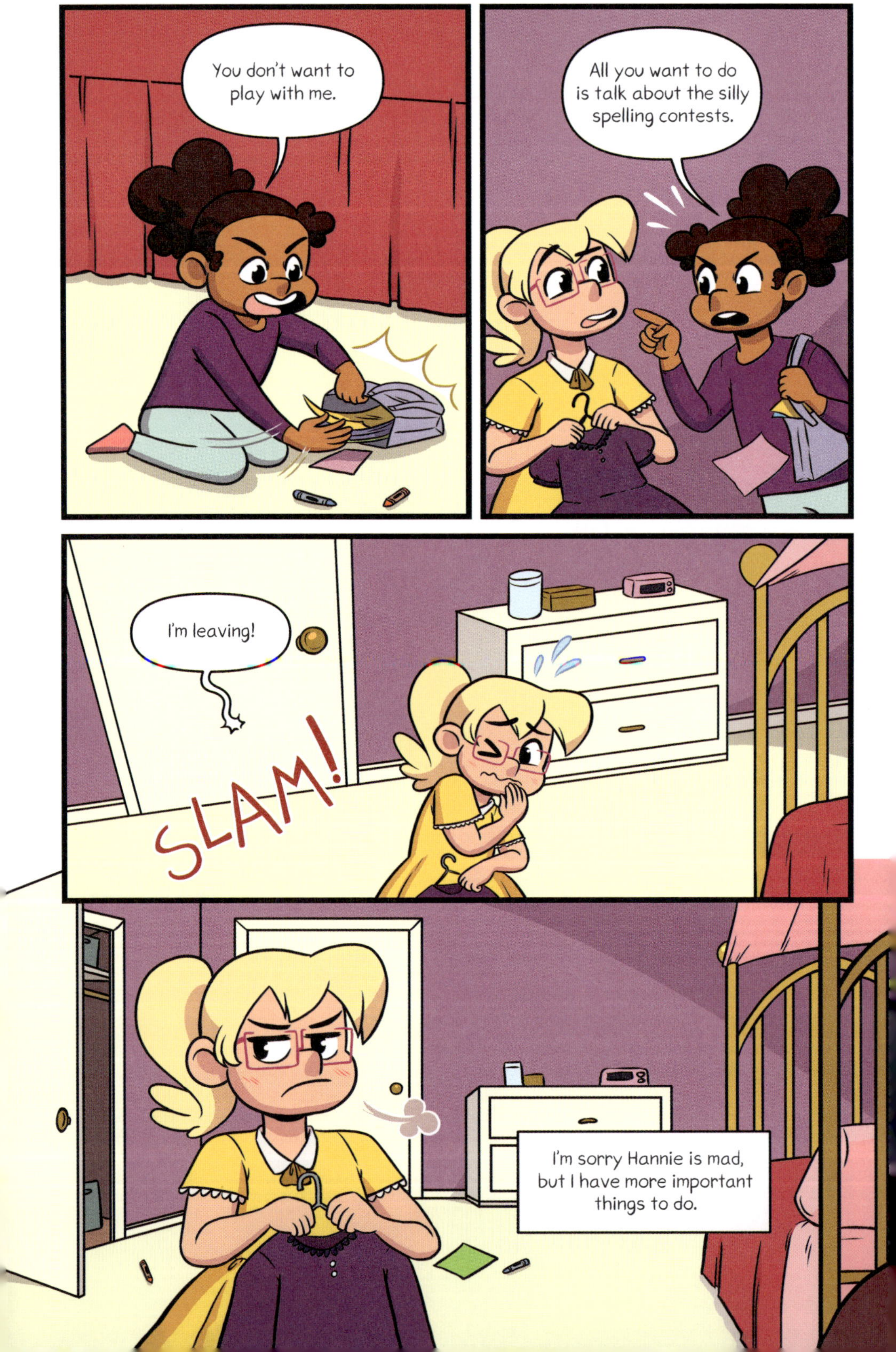
You don't want to play with me.
All you want to do is talk about the silly spelling contests.
I'm leaving!
SLAM!
I'm sorry Hannie is mad, but I have more important things to do.

# CHAPTER 7

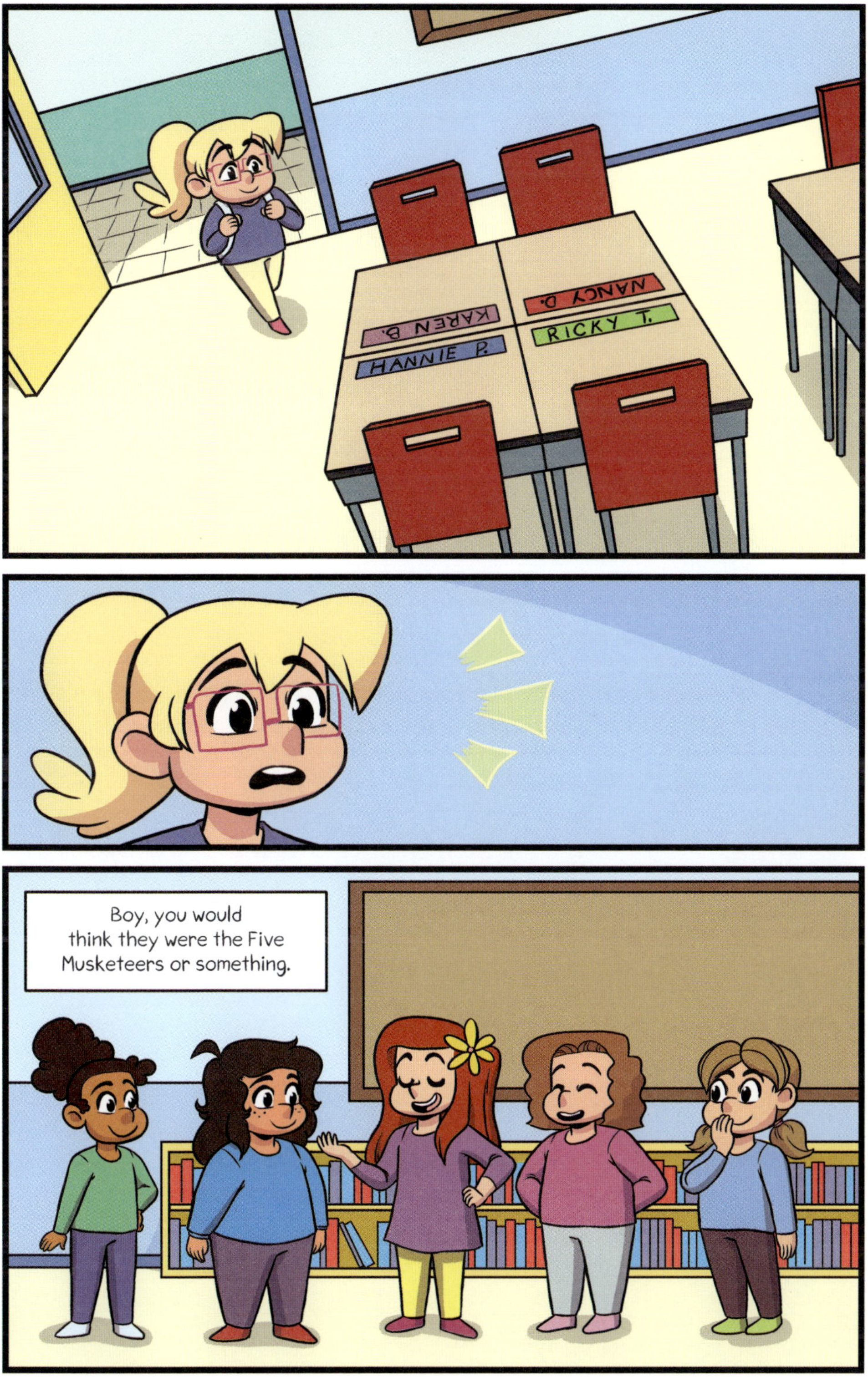
KAREN B.
NANCY D.
HANNIE P.
RICKY T.
Boy, you would think they were the Five Musketeers or something.

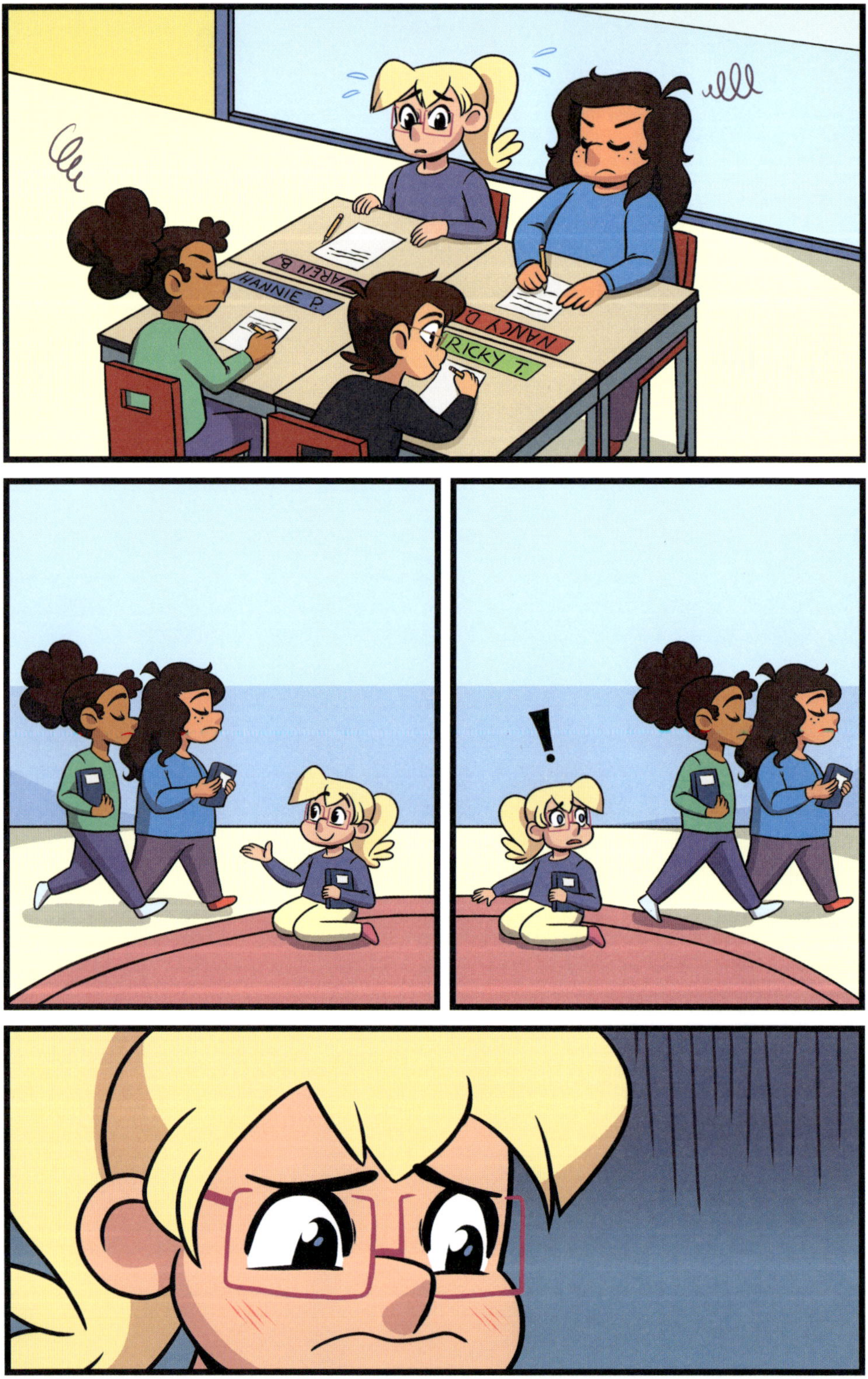
HANNIE P.
NANCY D.
RICKY T.
!

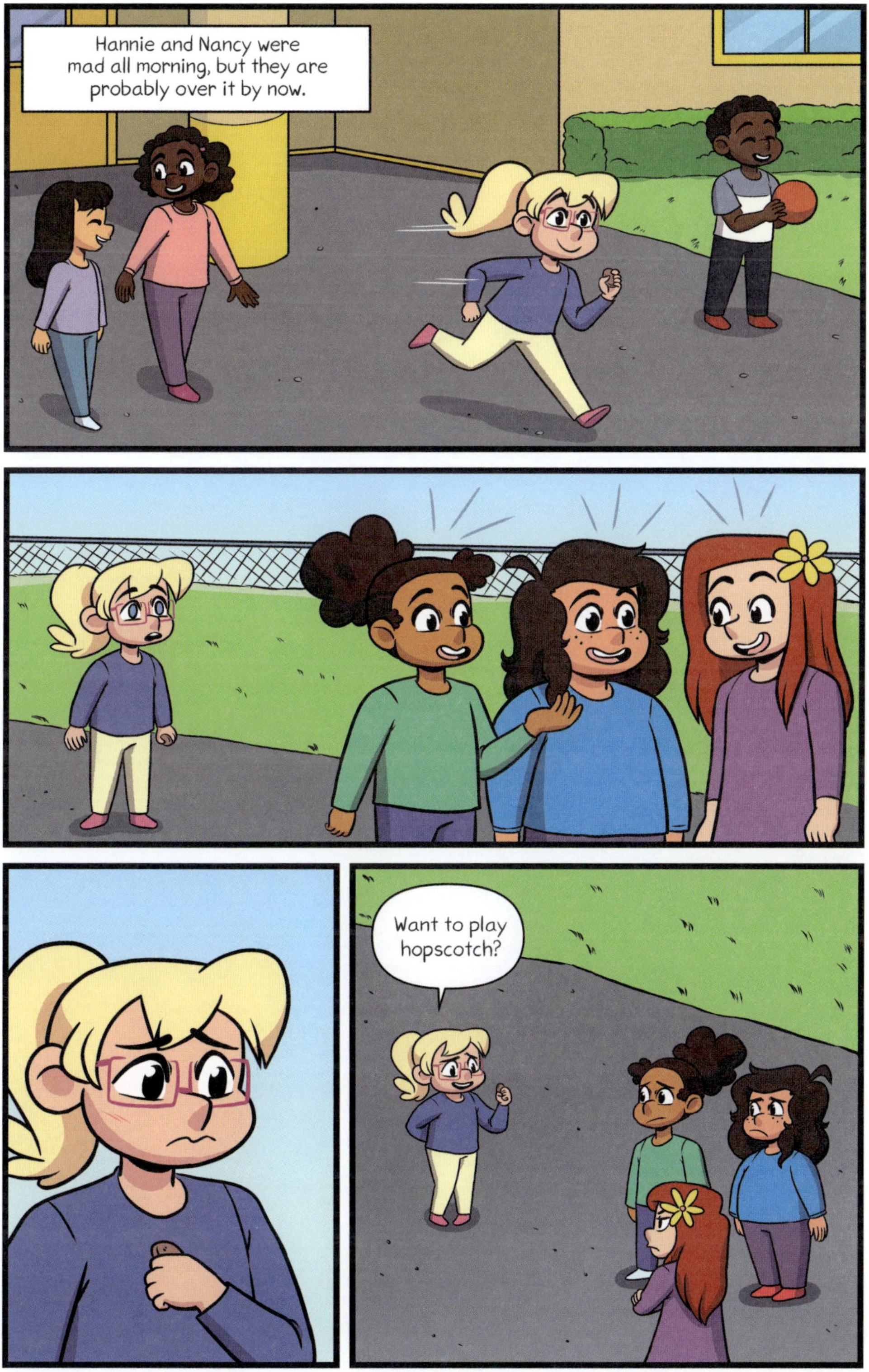
Hannie and Nancy were mad all morning, but they are probably over it by now.
Want to play hopscotch?

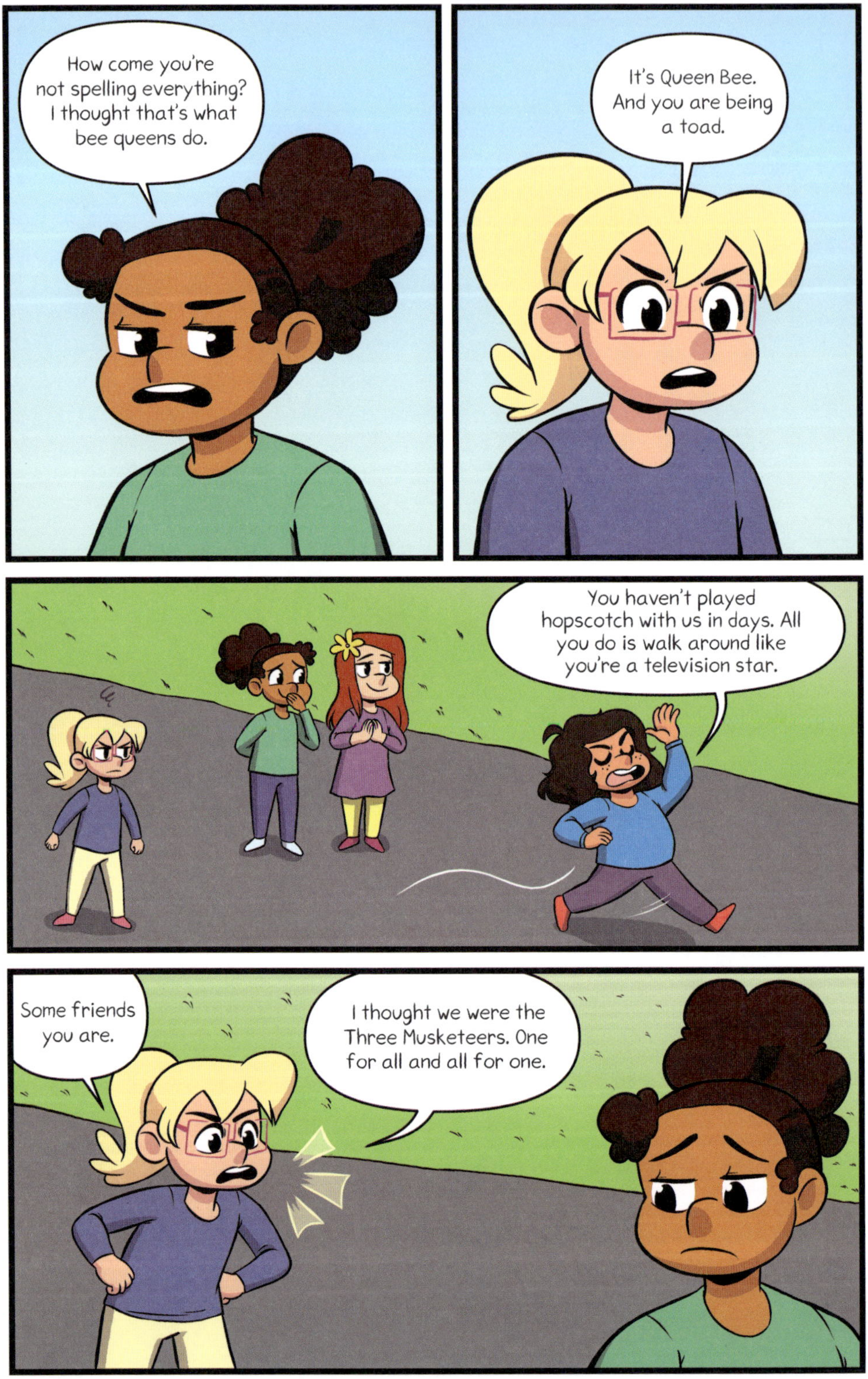

How come you're not spelling everything? I thought that's what bee queens do.
It's Queen Bee. And you are being a toad.
You haven't played hopscotch with us in days. All you do is walk around like you're a television star.
Some friends you are.
I thought we were the Three Musketeers. One for all and all for one.

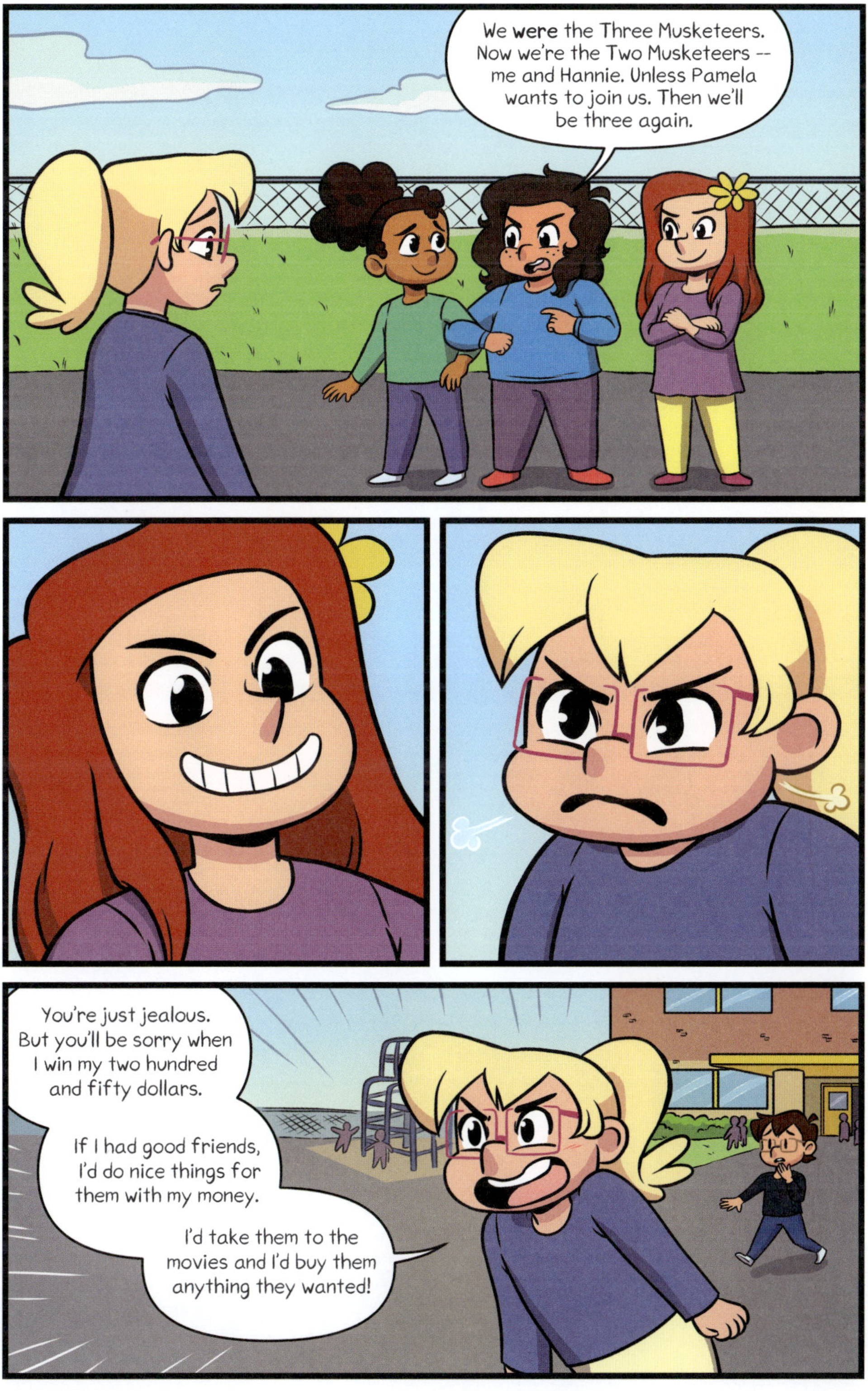
We were the Three Musketeers. Now we're the Two Musketeers -- me and Hannie. Unless Pamela wants to join us. Then we'll be three again.
You're just jealous. But you'll be sorry when I win my two hundred and fifty dollars.
If I had good friends, I'd do nice things for them with my money.
I'd take them to the movies and I'd buy them anything they wanted!

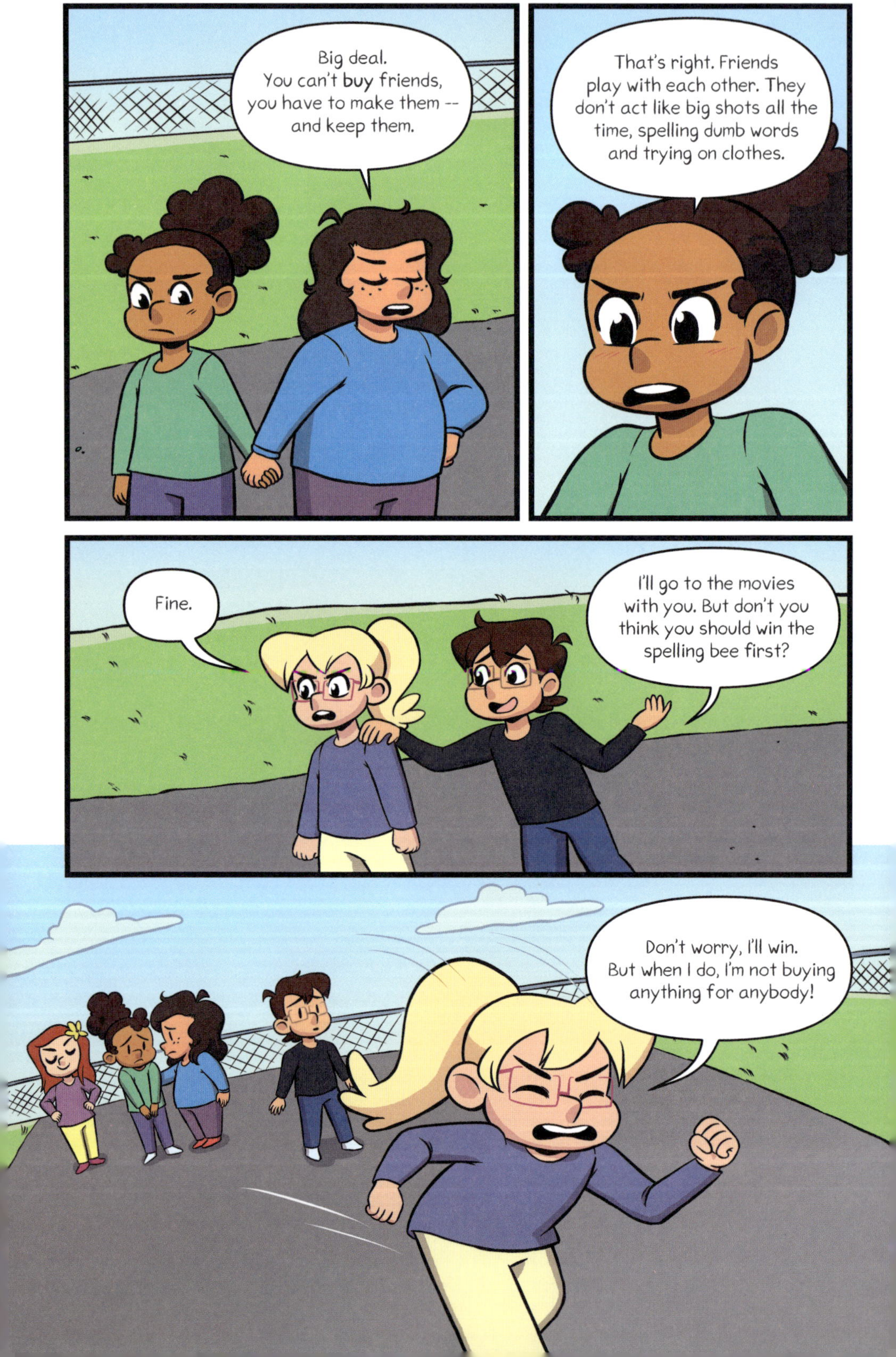
Big deal. You can't **buy** friends, you have to make them -- and keep them.
That's right. Friends play with each other. They don't act like big shots all the time, spelling dumb words and trying on clothes.
Fine.
I'll go to the movies with you. But don't you think you should win the spelling bee first?
Don't worry, I'll win. But when I do, I'm not buying anything for anybody!

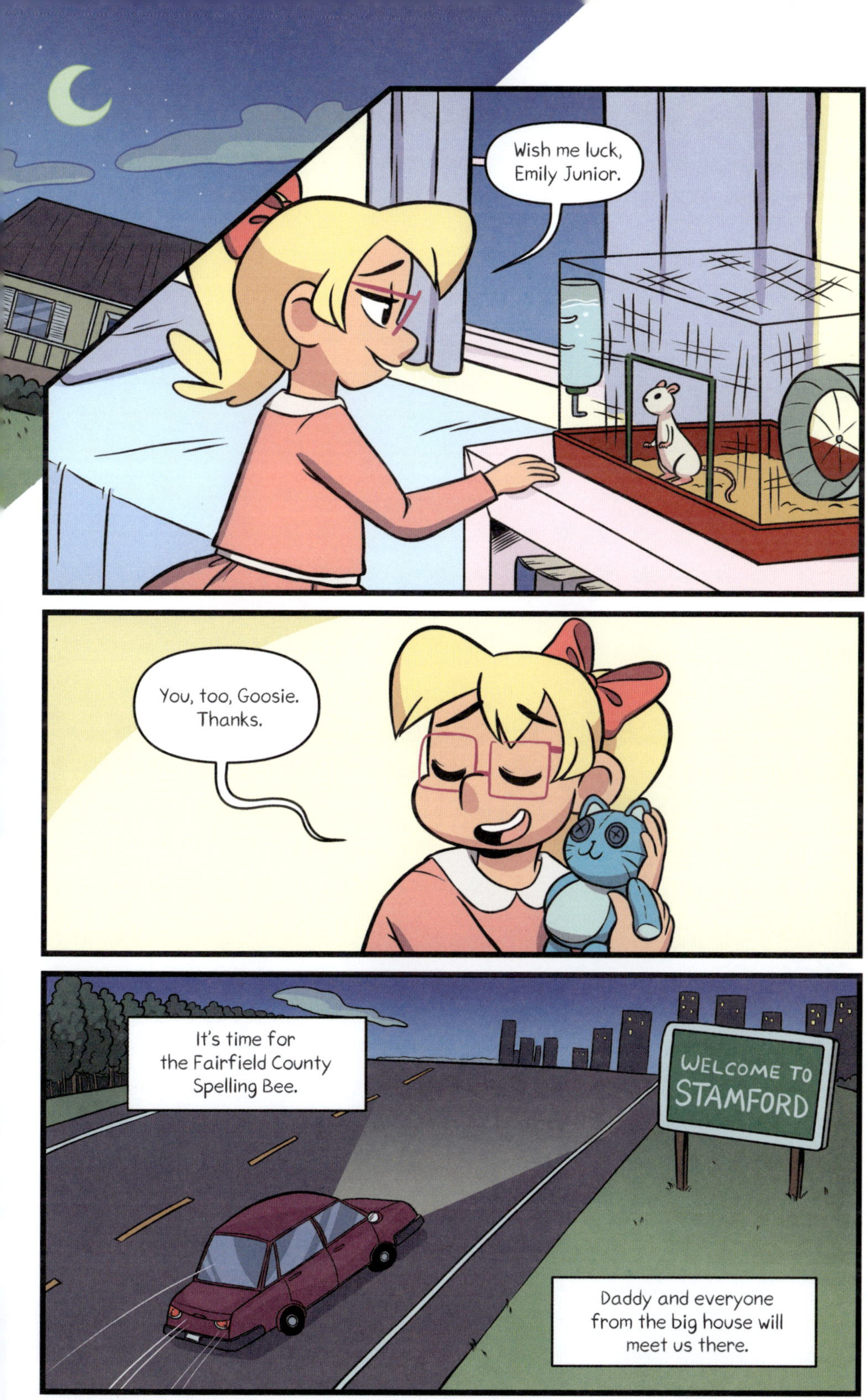
Wish me luck, Emily Junior.
You, too, Goosie. Thanks.
It's time for the Fairfield County Spelling Bee.
WELCOME TO STAMFORD
Daddy and everyone from the big house will meet us there.

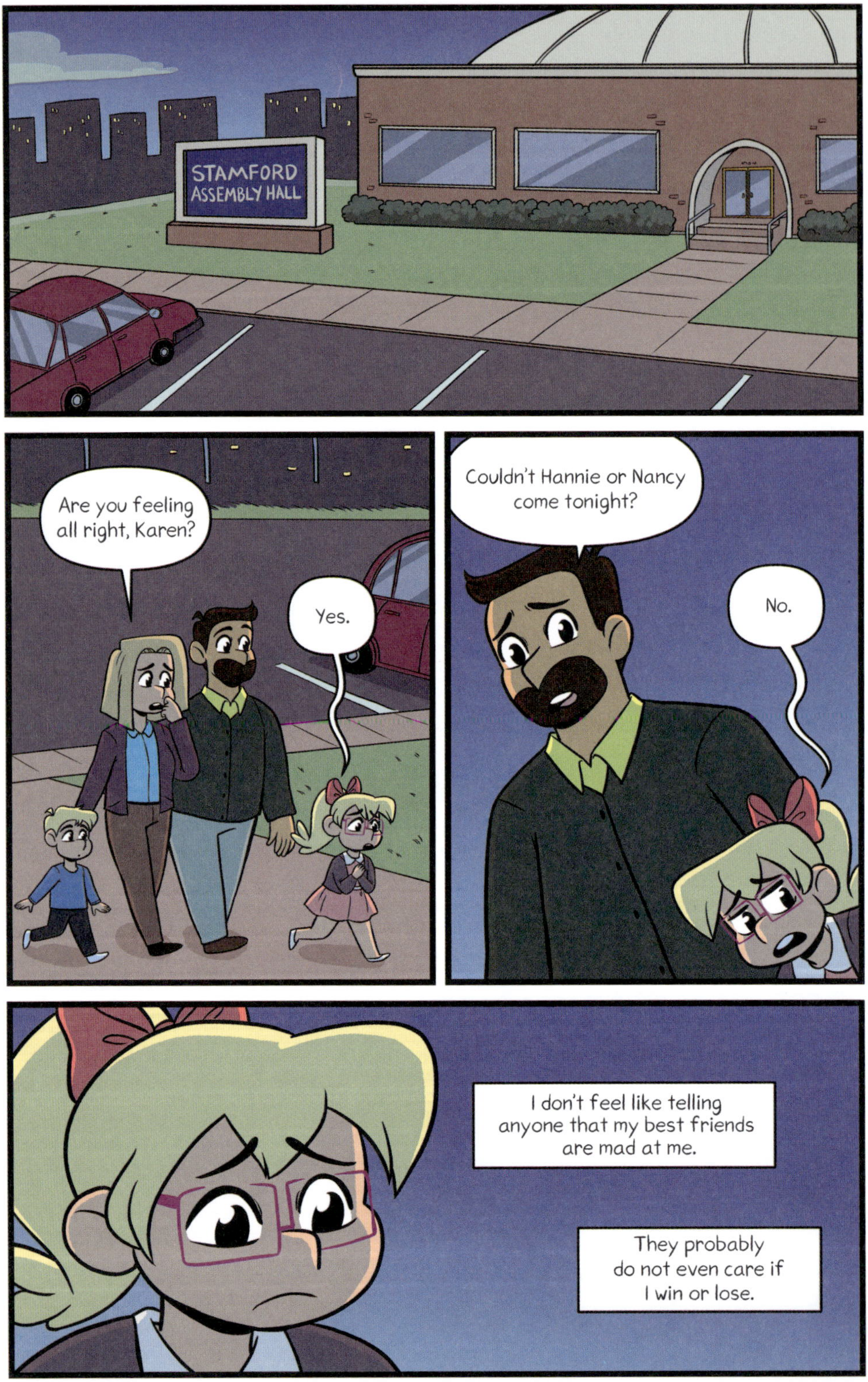
STAMFORD ASSEMBLY HALL
Are you feeling all right, Karen?
Yes.
Couldn't Hannie or Nancy come tonight?
No.
I don't feel like telling anyone that my best friends are mad at me.
They probably do not even care if I win or lose.

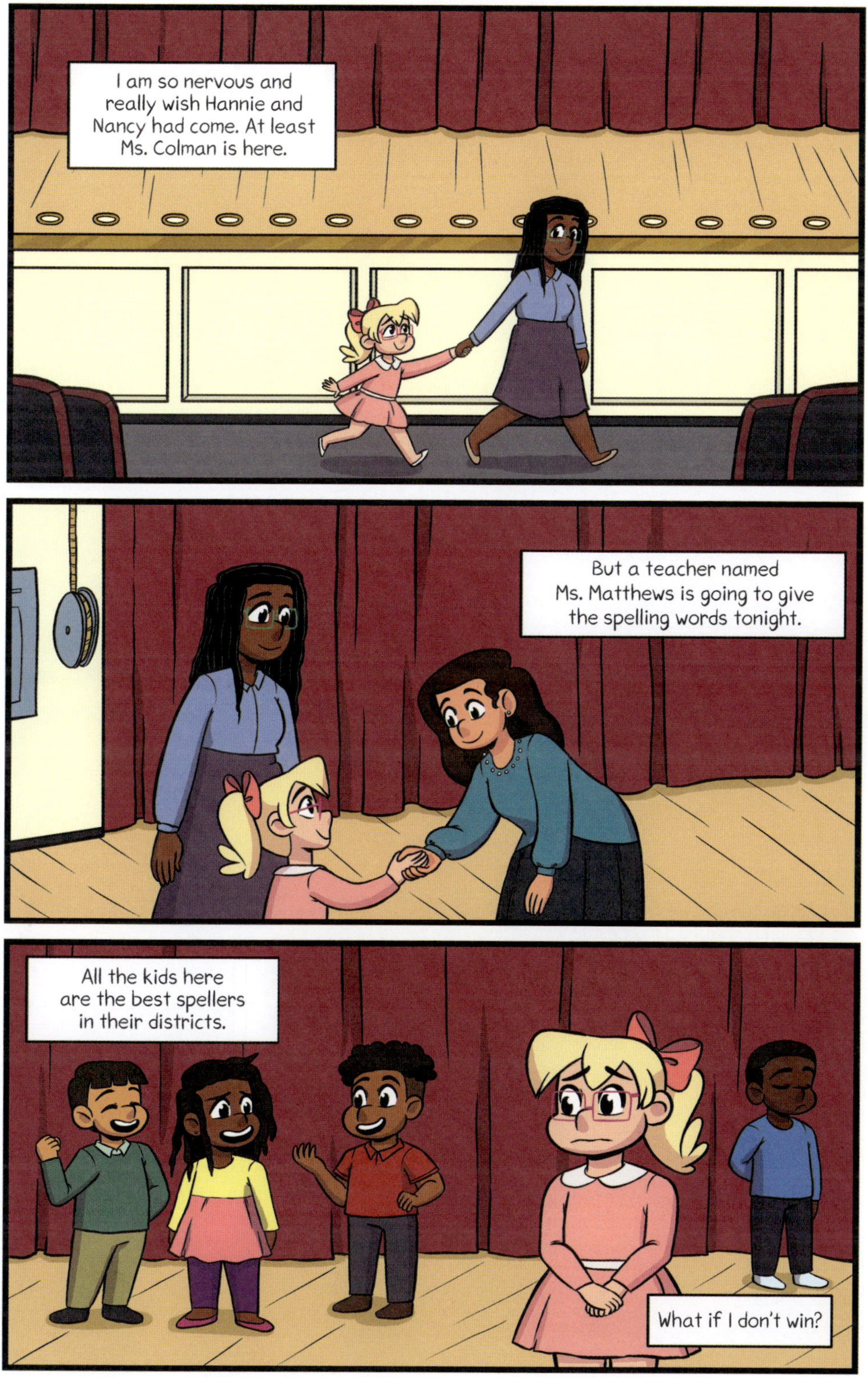
I am so nervous and really wish Hannie and Nancy had come. At least Ms. Colman is here.
But a teacher named Ms. Matthews is going to give the spelling words tonight.
All the kids here are the best spellers in their districts.
What if I don't win?

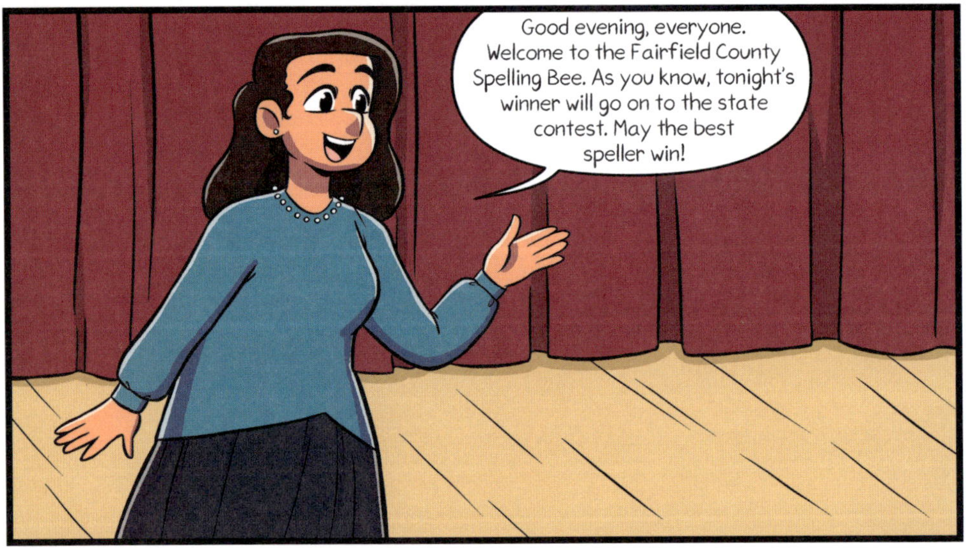
Good evening, everyone. Welcome to the Fairfield County Spelling Bee. As you know, tonight's winner will go on to the state contest. May the best speller win!

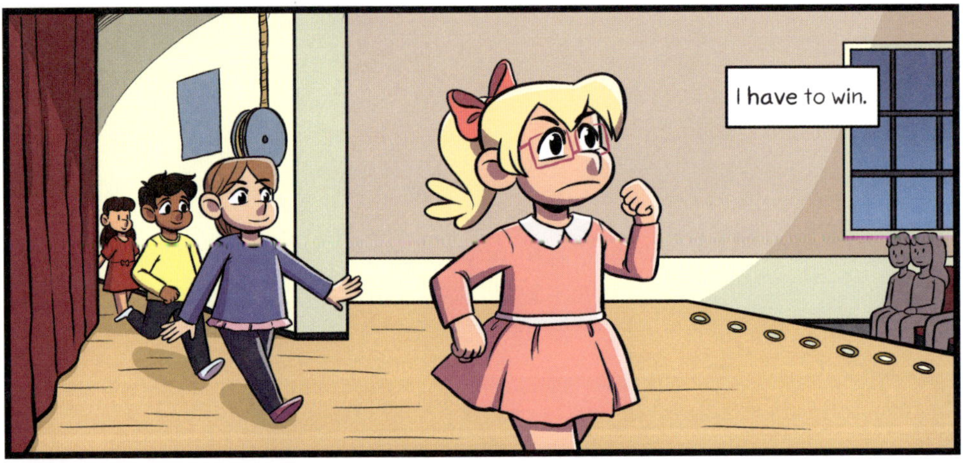
I have to win.

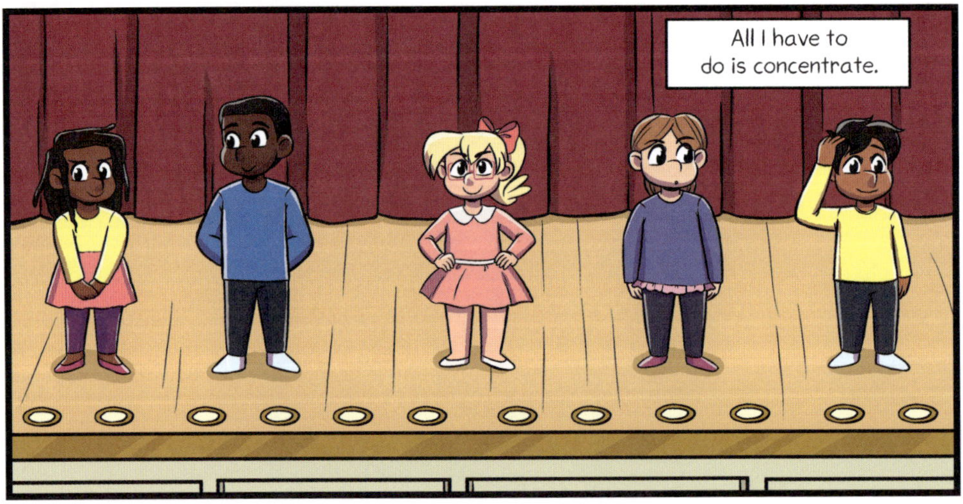
All I have to do is concentrate.

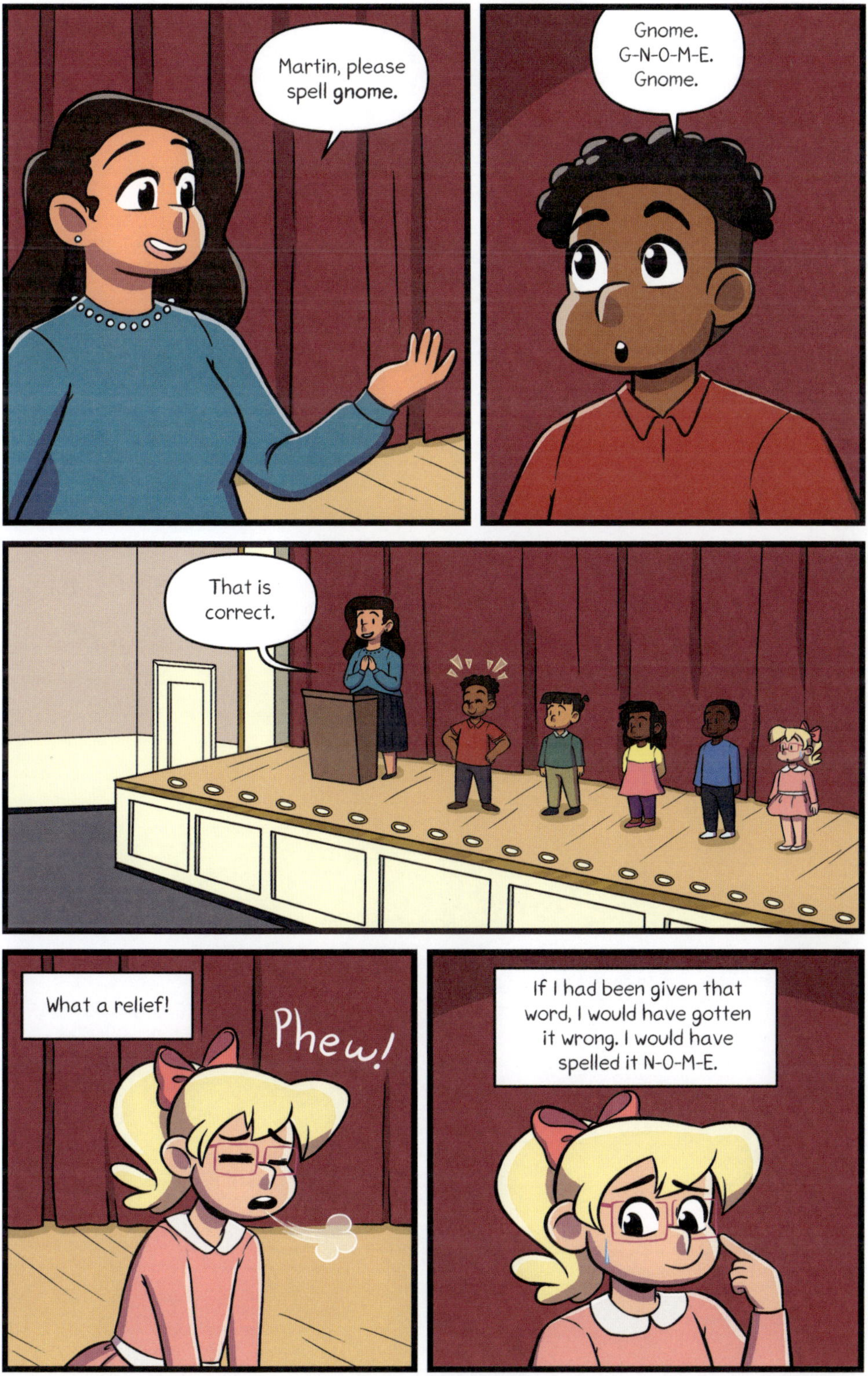
Martin, please spell **gnome.**
Gnome. G-N-O-M-E. Gnome.
That is correct.
What a relief!
Phew!
If I had been given that word, I would have gotten it wrong. I would have spelled it N-O-M-E.

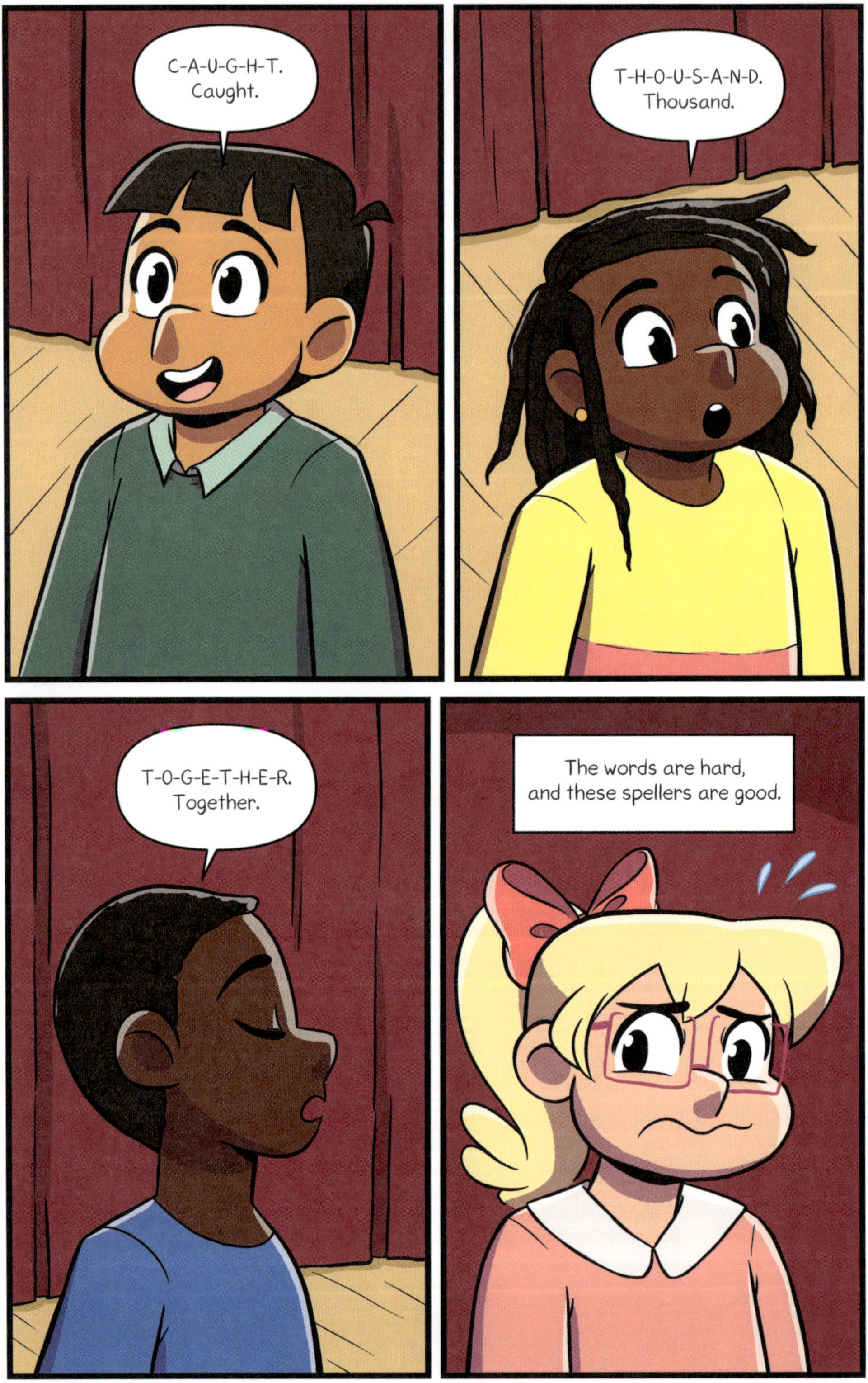
C-A-U-G-H-T.
Caught.
T-H-O-U-S-A-N-D.
Thousand.
T-O-G-E-T-H-E-R.
Together.
The words are hard,
and these spellers are good.

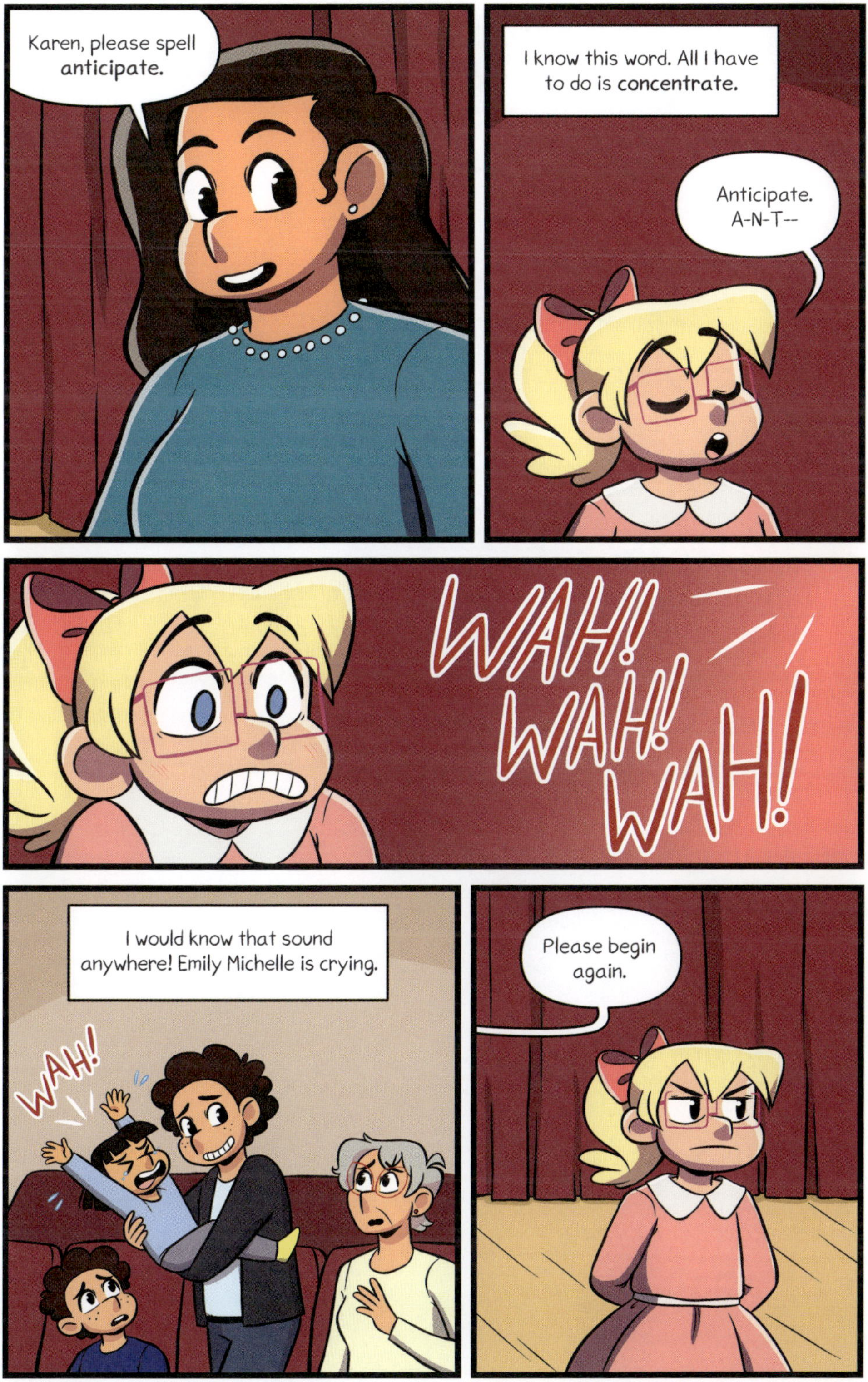
Karen, please spell **anticipate.**
I know this word. All I have to do is **concentrate.**
Anticipate. A-N-T--
WAH! WAH! WAH!
I would know that sound anywhere! Emily Michelle is crying.
WAH!
Please begin again.

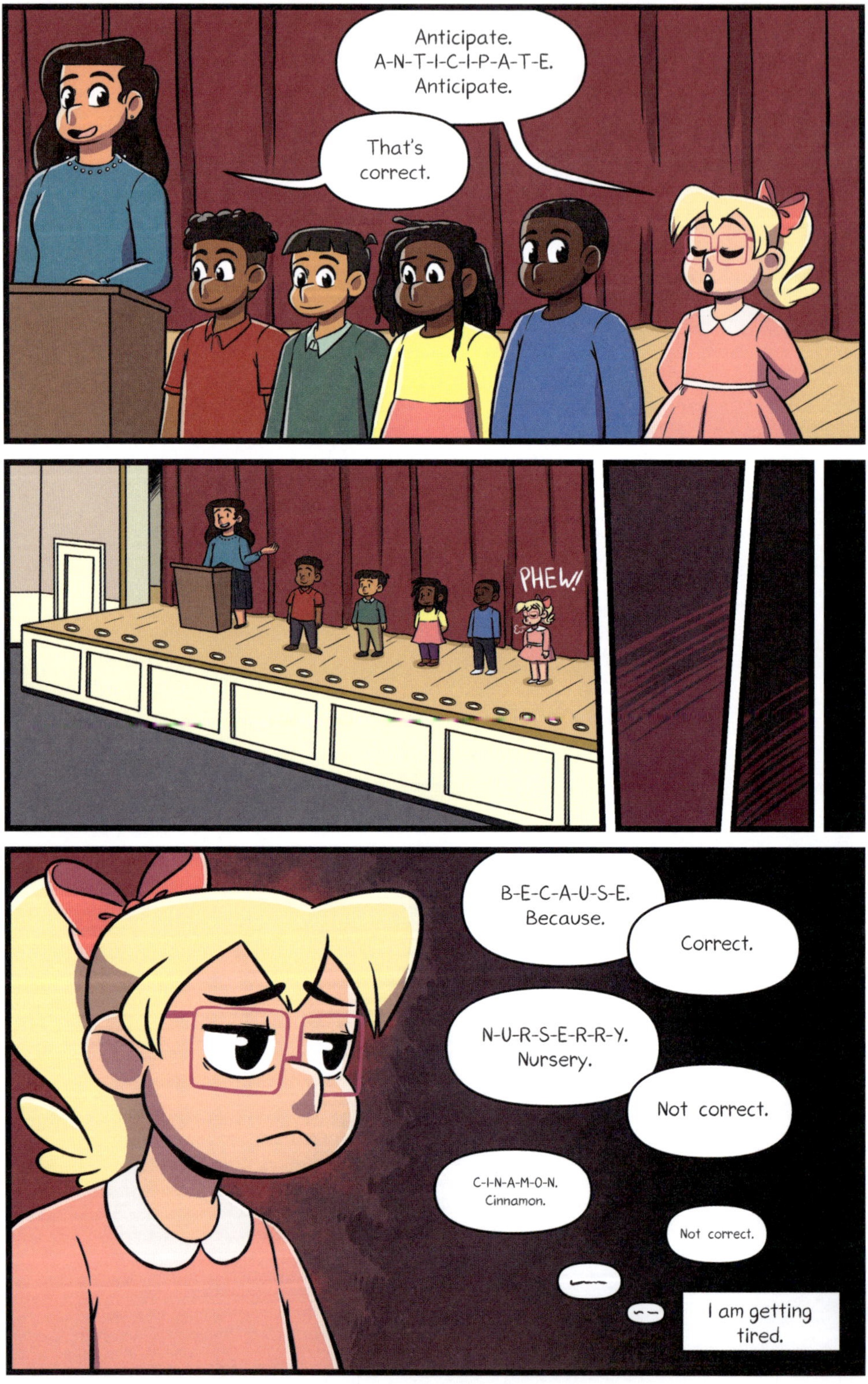
Anticipate.
A-N-T-I-C-I-P-A-T-E.
Anticipate.
That's correct.
PHEW!
B-E-C-A-U-S-E.
Because.
Correct.
N-U-R-S-E-R-R-Y.
Nursery.
Not correct.
C-I-N-A-M-O-N.
Cinnamon.
Not correct.
I am getting tired.

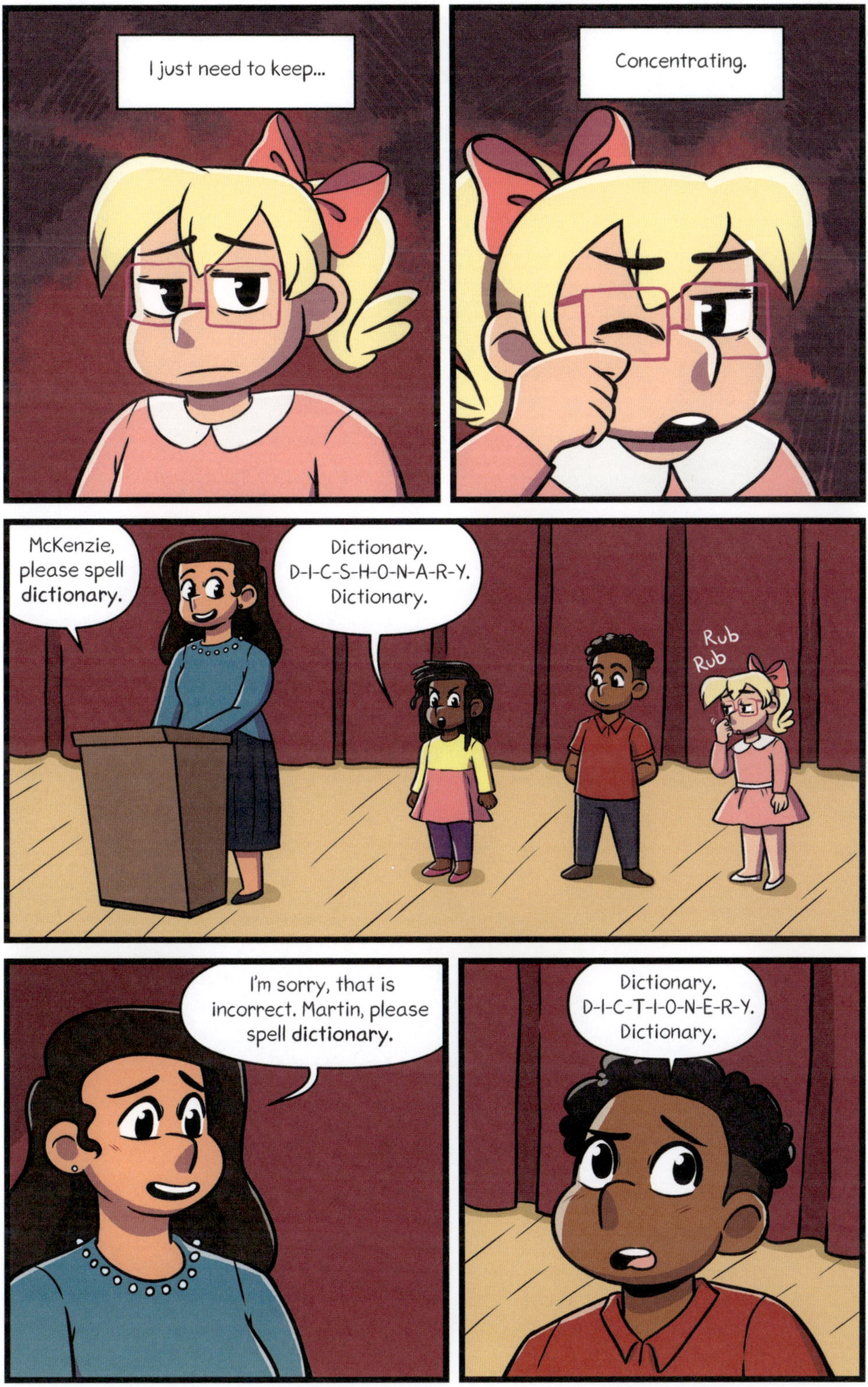
I just need to keep...
Concentrating.
McKenzie, please spell dictionary.
Dictionary. D-I-C-S-H-O-N-A-R-Y. Dictionary.
Rub Rub
I'm sorry, that is incorrect. Martin, please spell dictionary.
Dictionary. D-I-C-T-I-O-N-E-R-Y. Dictionary.

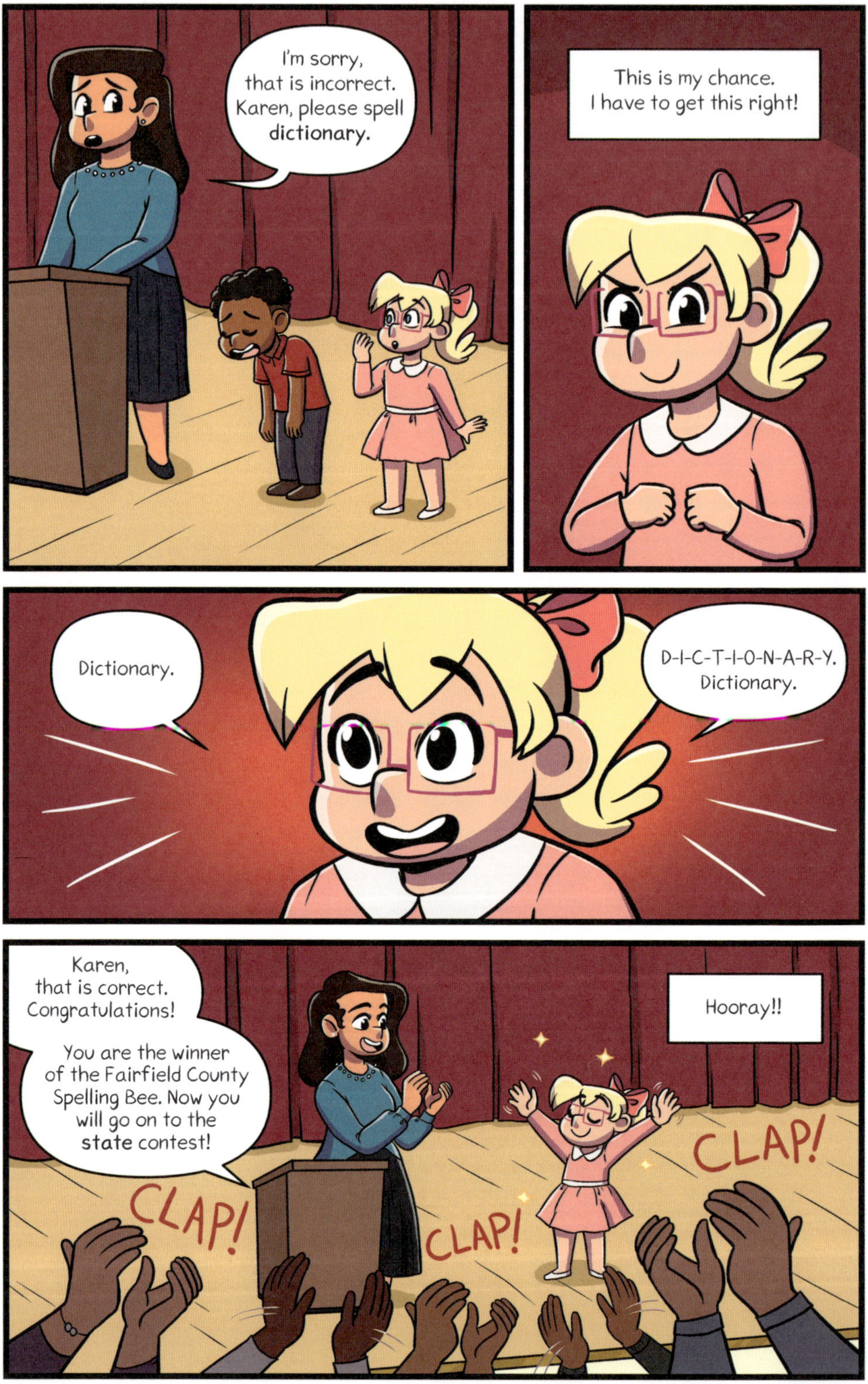
I'm sorry, that is incorrect. Karen, please spell **dictionary**.
This is my chance. I have to get this right!
Dictionary.
D-I-C-T-I-O-N-A-R-Y. Dictionary.
Karen, that is correct. Congratulations!
You are the winner of the Fairfield County Spelling Bee. Now you will go on to the **state** contest!
Hooray!!
CLAP!
CLAP!
CLAP!

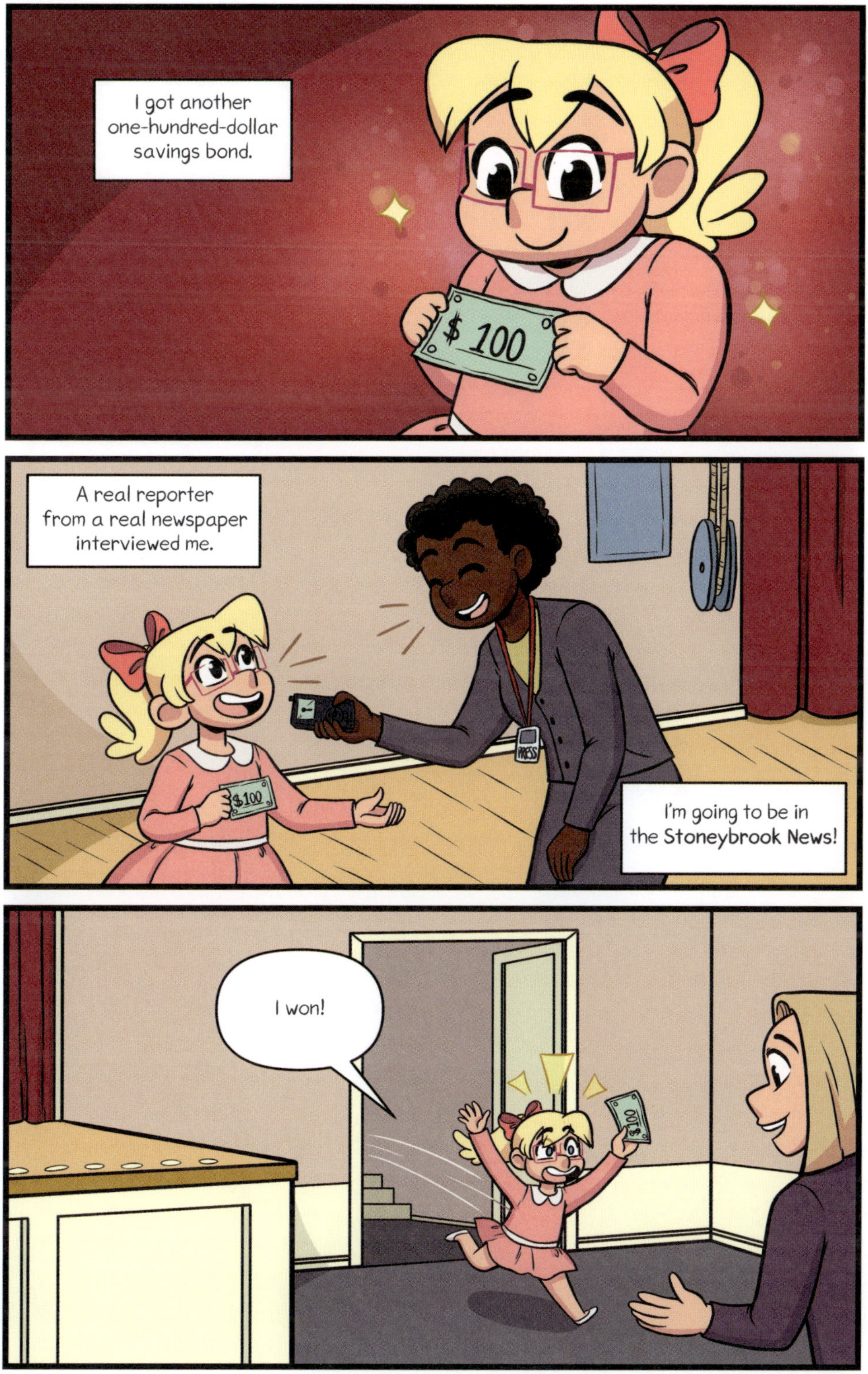
I got another one-hundred-dollar savings bond.
$ 100
A real reporter from a real newspaper interviewed me.
$100
PRESS
I'm going to be in the Stoneybrook News!
I won!
$100

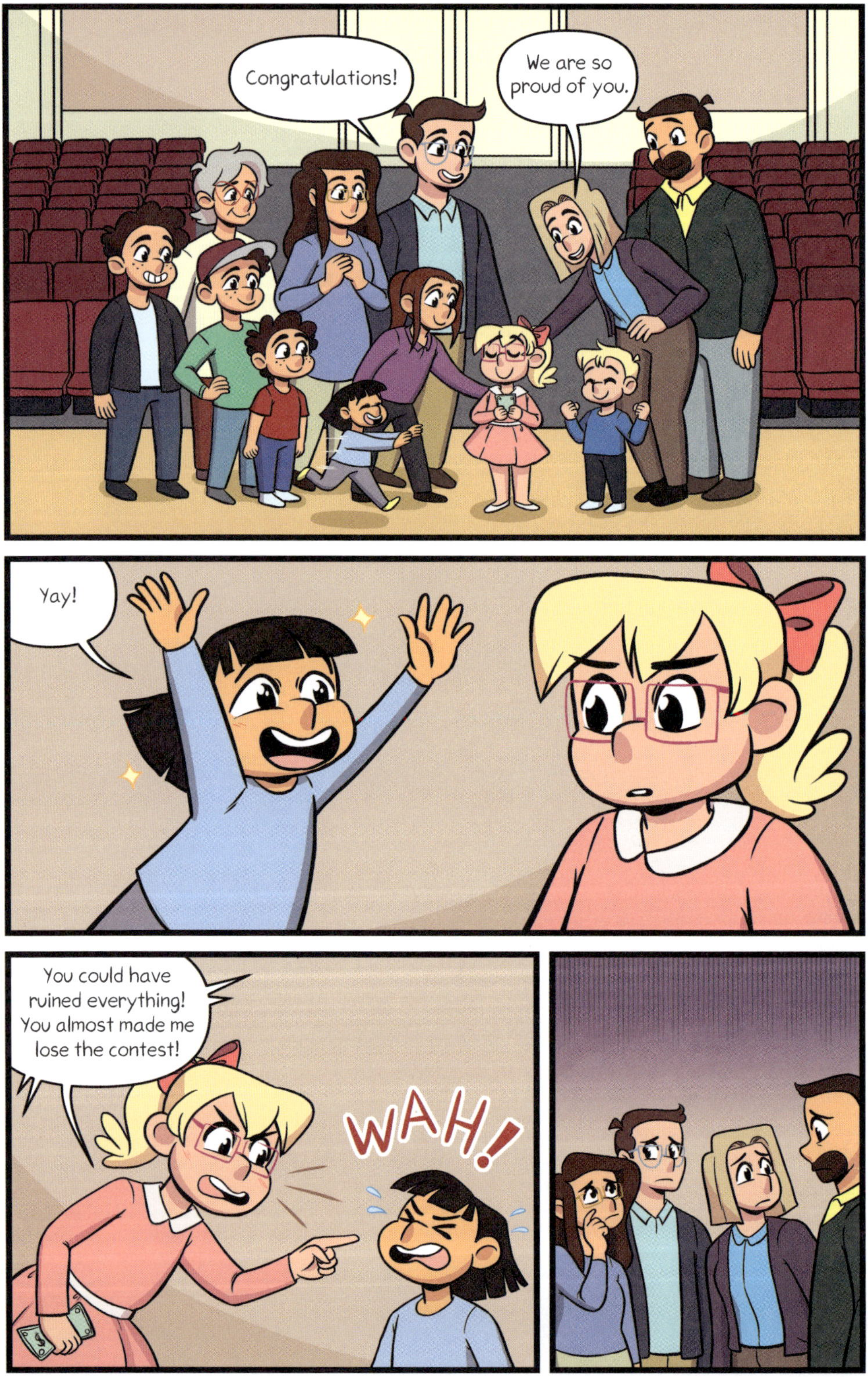
Congratulations!
We are so proud of you.
Yay!
You could have ruined everything! You almost made me lose the contest!
WAH!

# CHAPTER 8

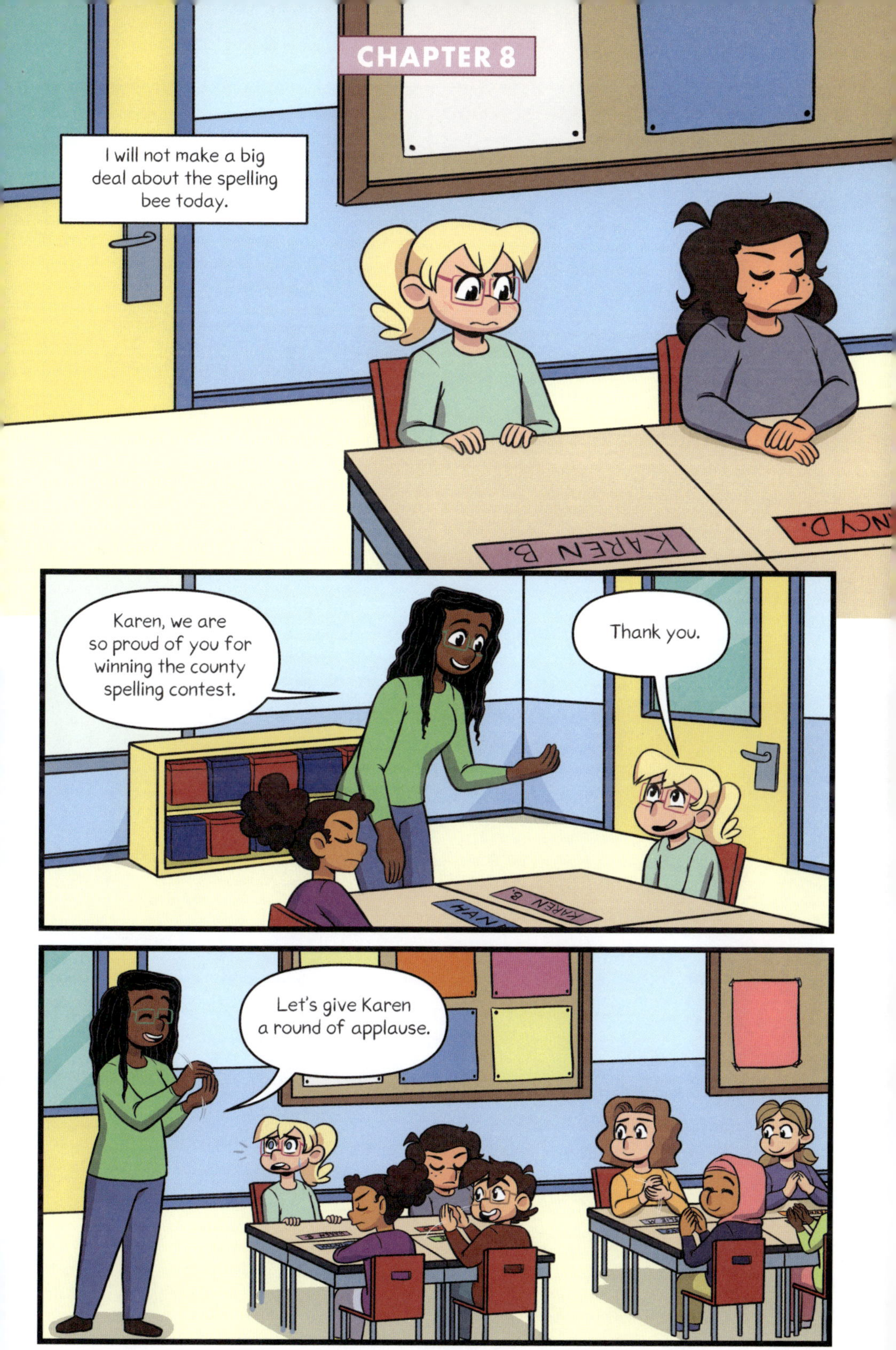

I will not make a big deal about the spelling bee today.
KAREN B.
Karen, we are so proud of you for winning the county spelling contest.
Thank you.
Let's give Karen a round of applause.

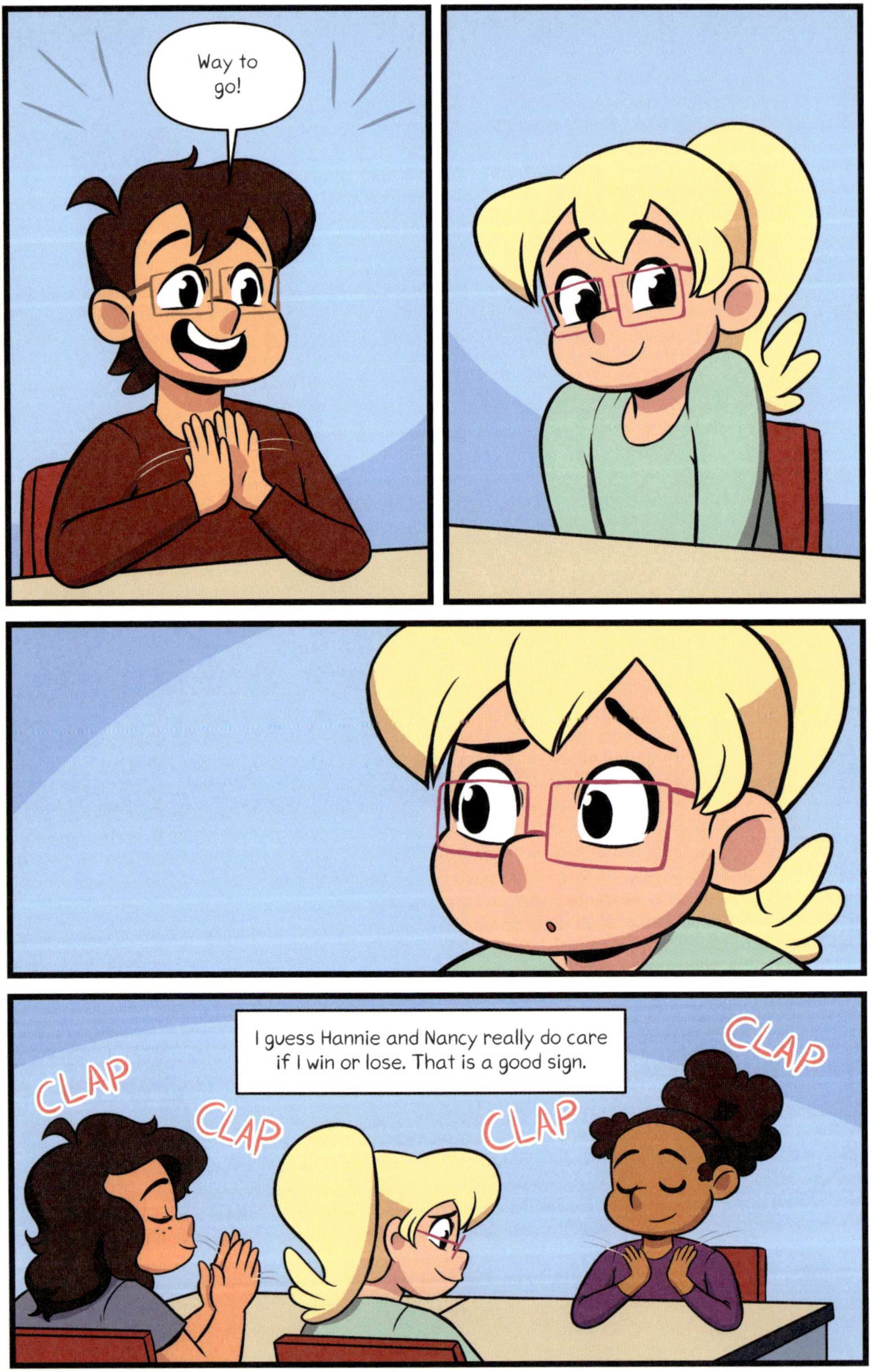
Way to go!
I guess Hannie and Nancy really do care if I win or lose. That is a good sign.
CLAP
CLAP
CLAP
CLAP

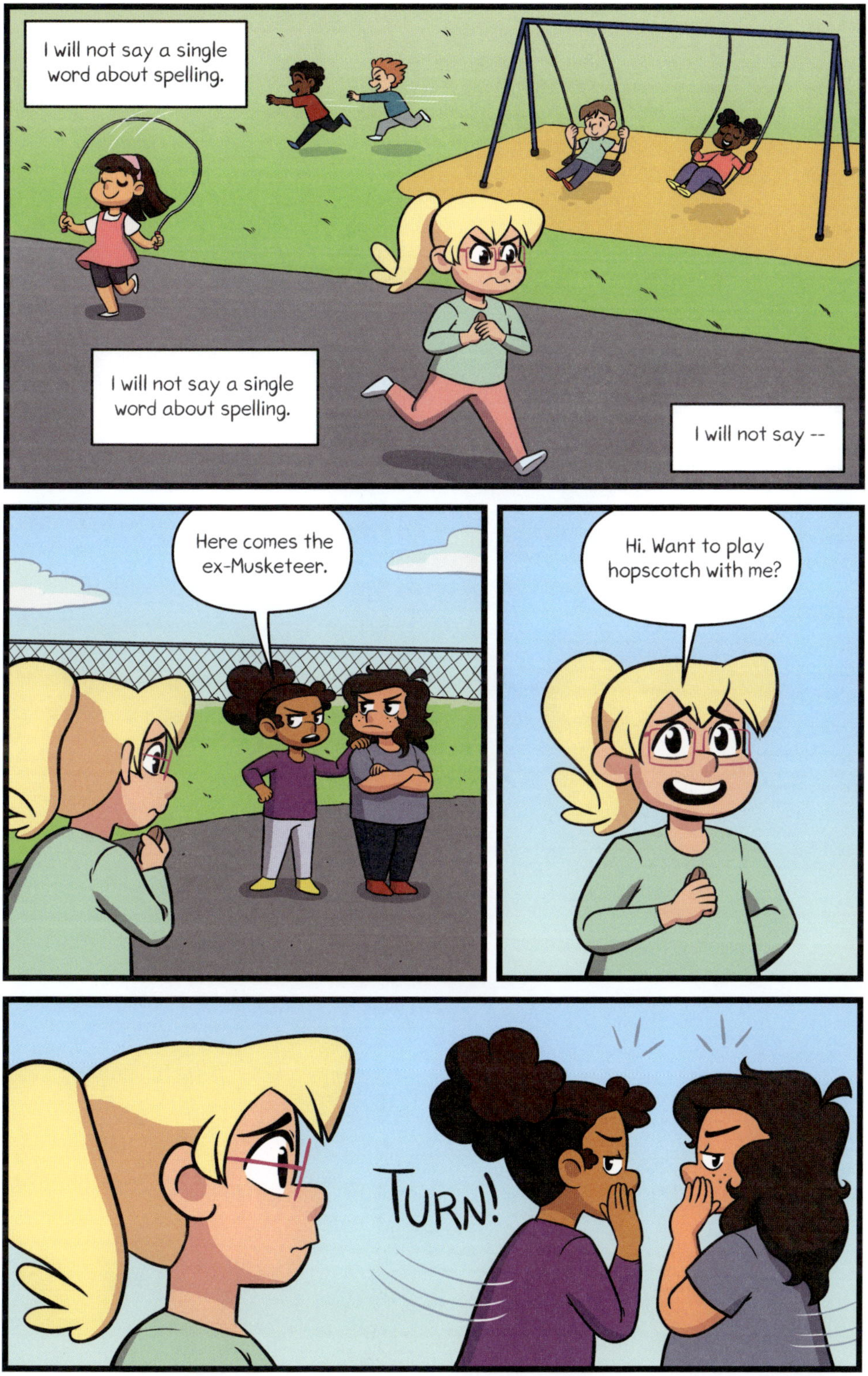

I will not say a single word about spelling.
I will not say a single word about spelling.
I will not say --
Here comes the ex-Musketeer.
Hi. Want to play hopscotch with me?
TURN!

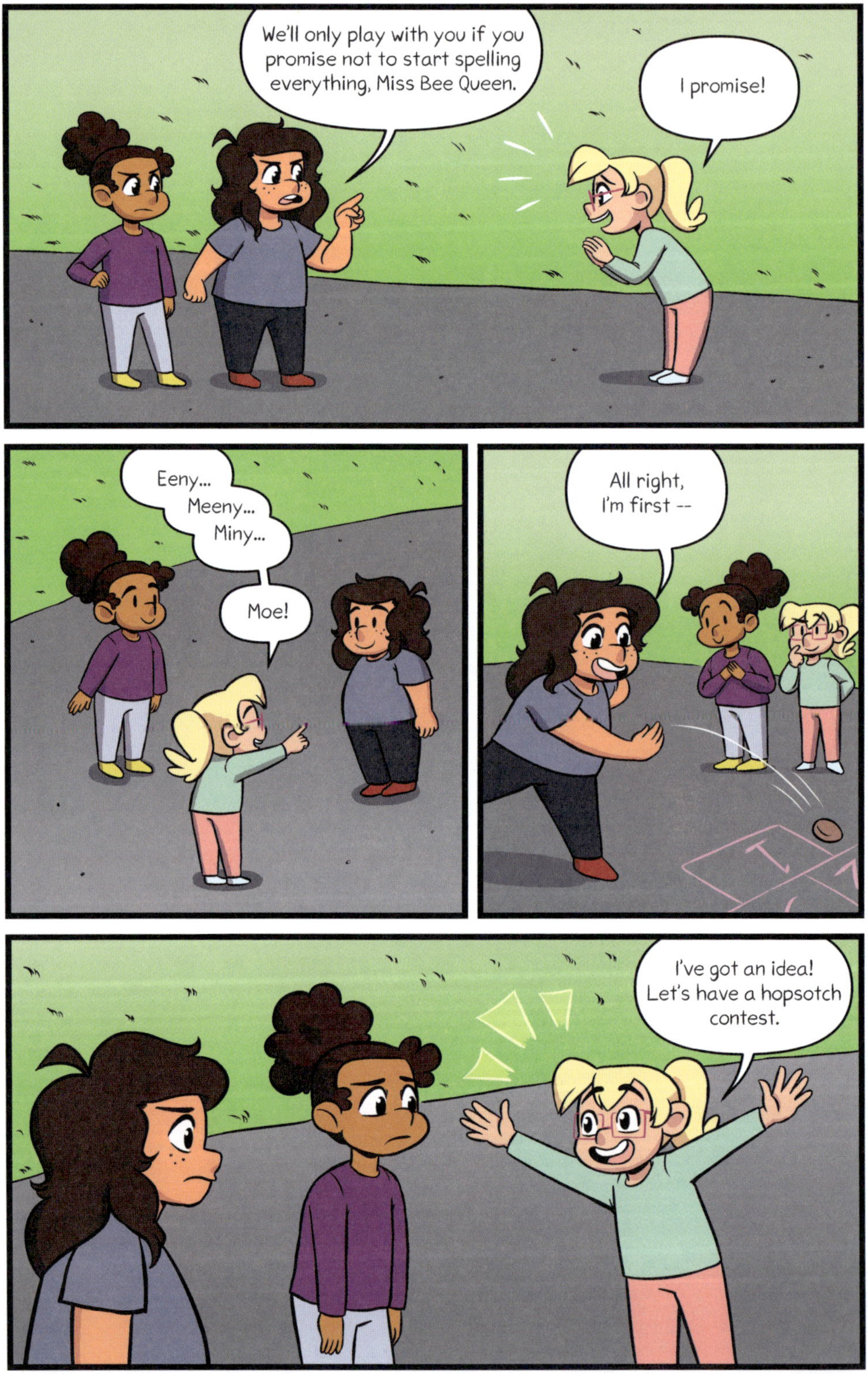
We'll only play with you if you promise not to start spelling everything, Miss Bee Queen.
I promise!
Eeny... Meeny... Miny...
Moe!
All right, I'm first --
I've got an idea! Let's have a hopsotch contest.

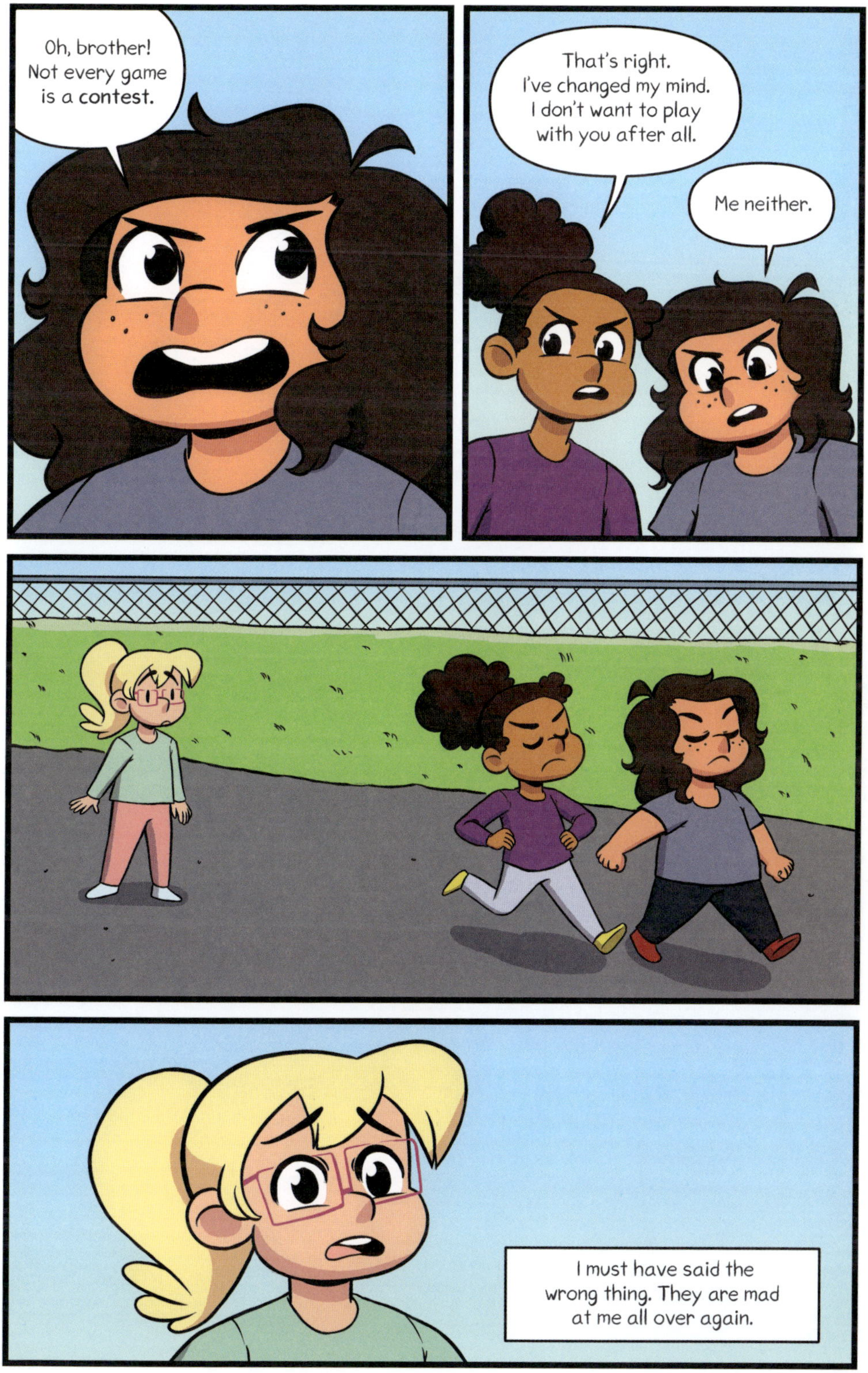
Oh, brother! Not every game is a **contest**.
That's right. I've changed my mind. I don't want to play with you after all.
Me neither.
I must have said the wrong thing. They are mad at me all over again.

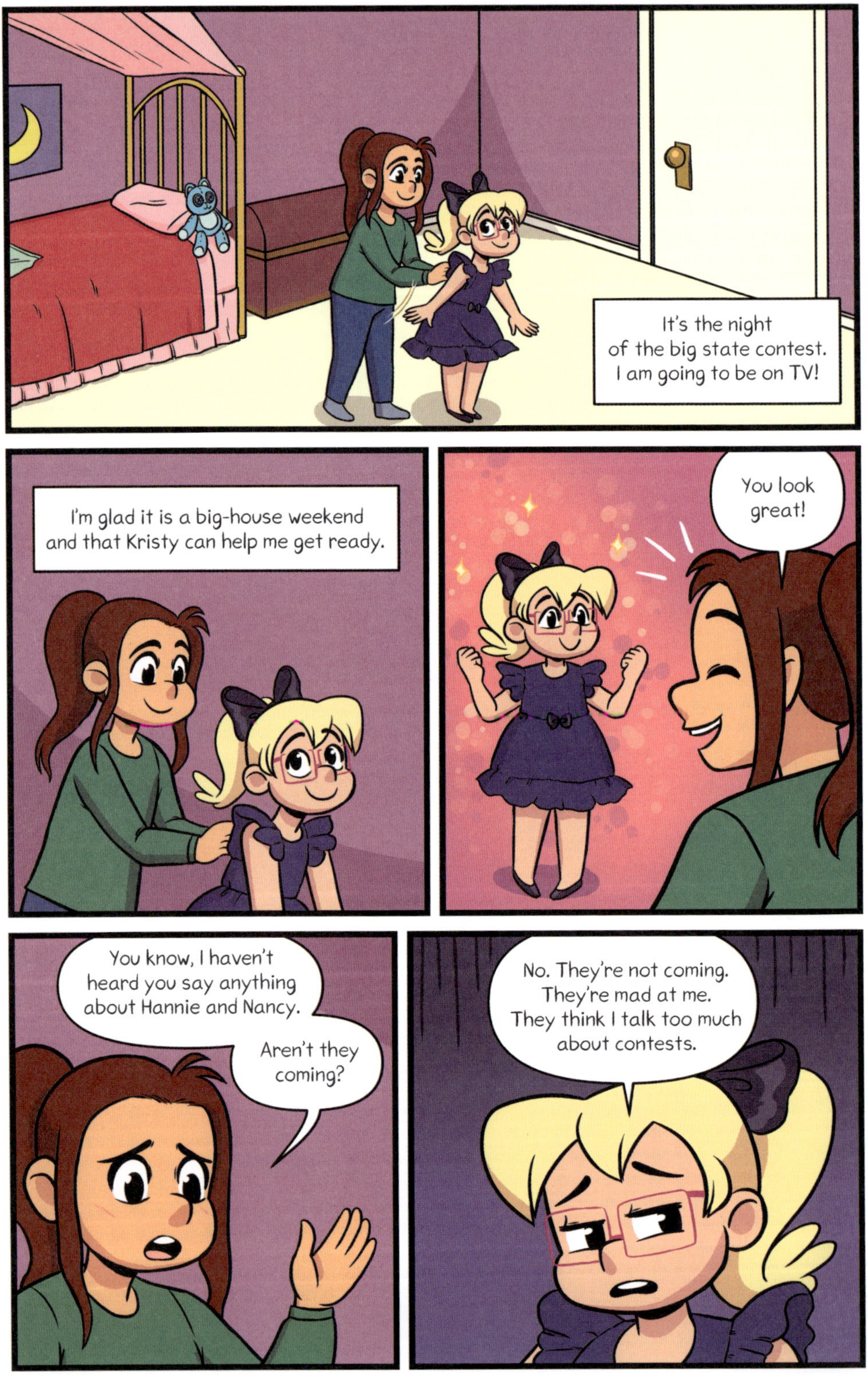

It's the night of the big state contest. I am going to be on TV!
I'm glad it is a big-house weekend and that Kristy can help me get ready.
You look great!
You know, I haven't heard you say anything about Hannie and Nancy.
Aren't they coming?
No. They're not coming. They're mad at me. They think I talk too much about contests.

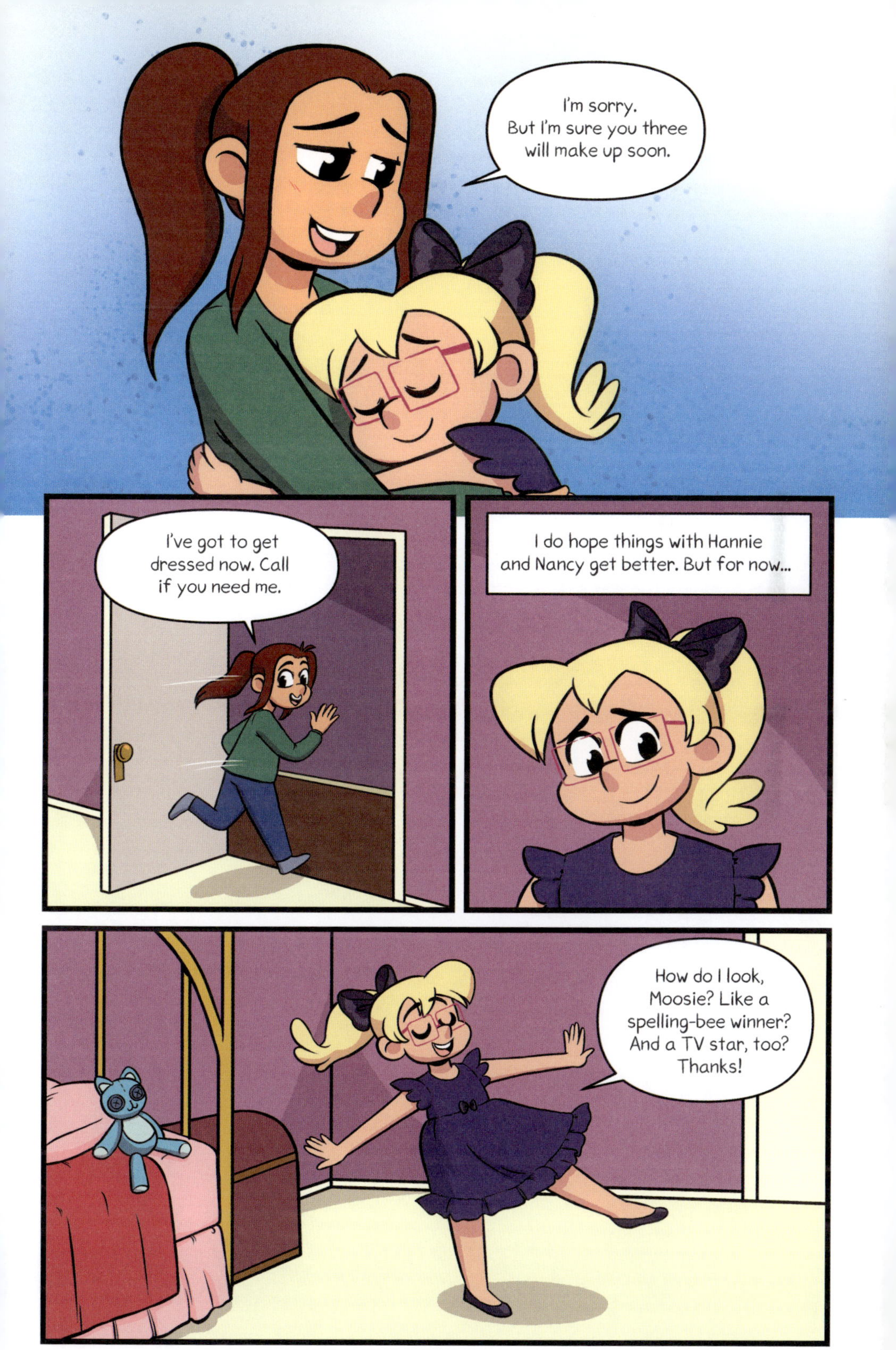
I'm sorry.
But I'm sure you three will make up soon.
I've got to get dressed now. Call if you need me.
I do hope things with Hannie and Nancy get better. But for now...
How do I look, Moosie? Like a spelling-bee winner? And a TV star, too? Thanks!

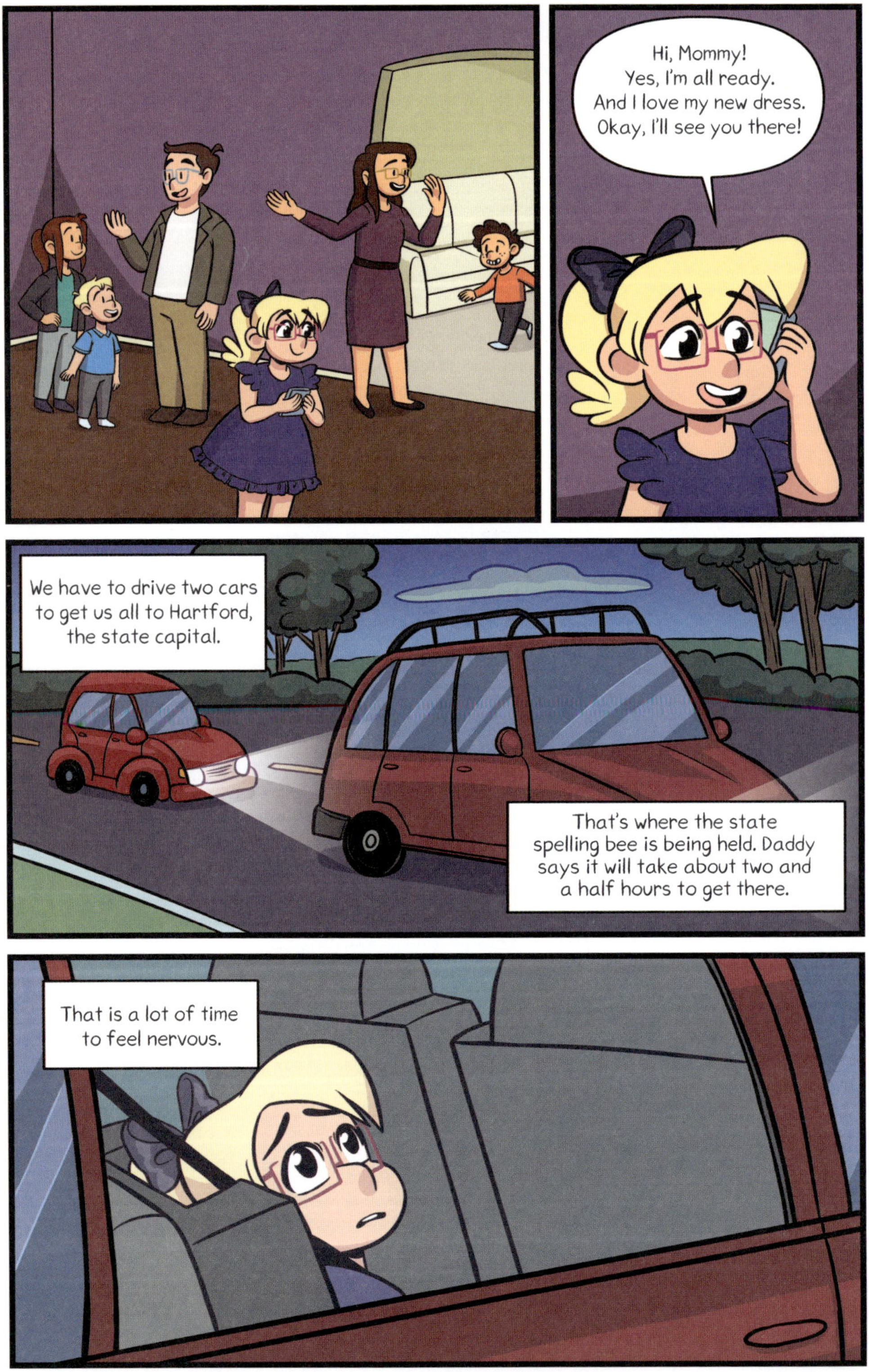
Hi, Mommy!
Yes, I'm all ready.
And I love my new dress.
Okay, I'll see you there!
We have to drive two cars to get us all to Hartford, the state capital.
That's where the state spelling bee is being held. Daddy says it will take about two and a half hours to get there.
That is a lot of time to feel nervous.

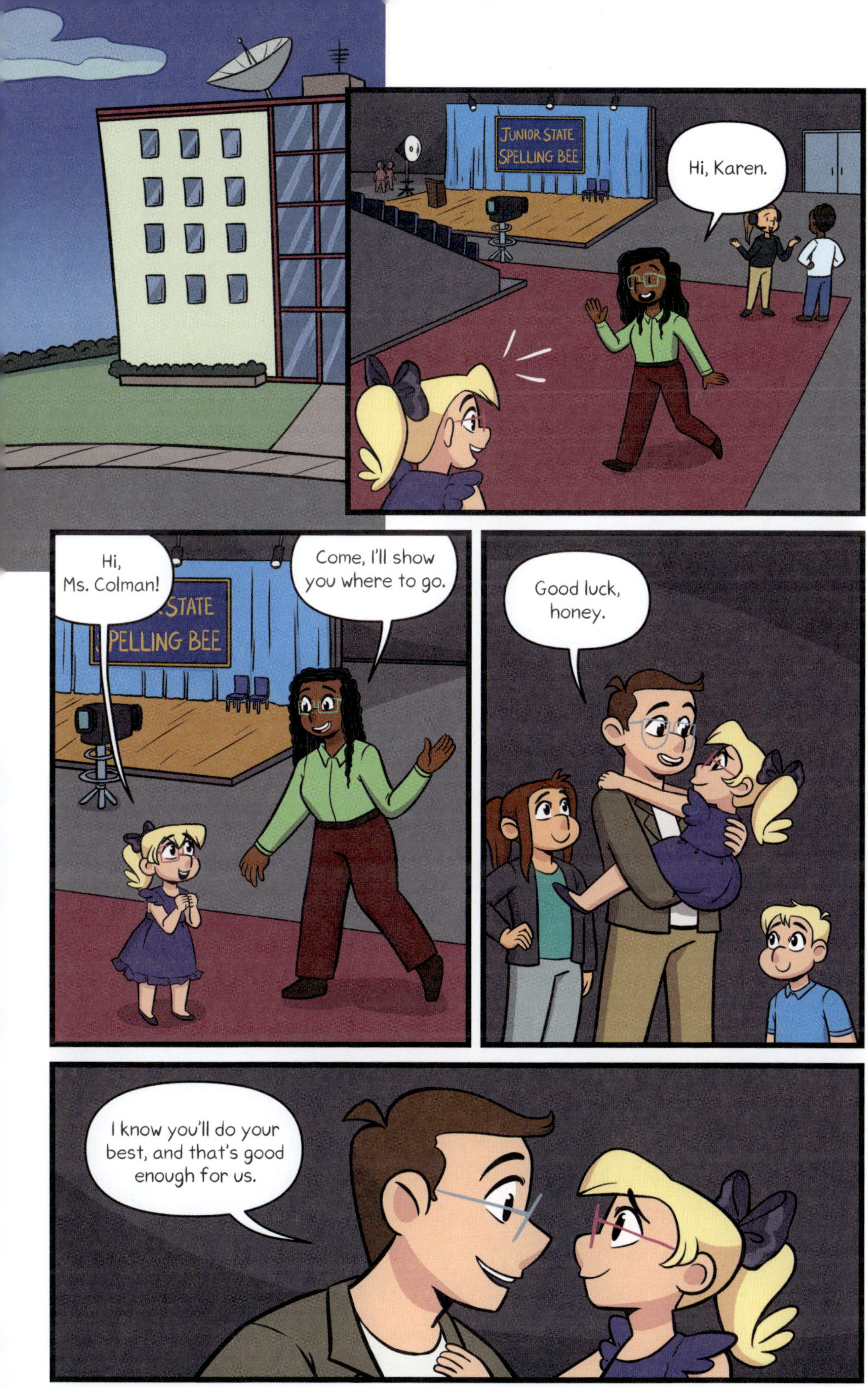
JUNIOR STATE SPELLING BEE
Hi, Karen.
Hi, Ms. Colman!
Come, I'll show you where to go.
Good luck, honey.
I know you'll do your best, and that's good enough for us.

# CHAPTER 9

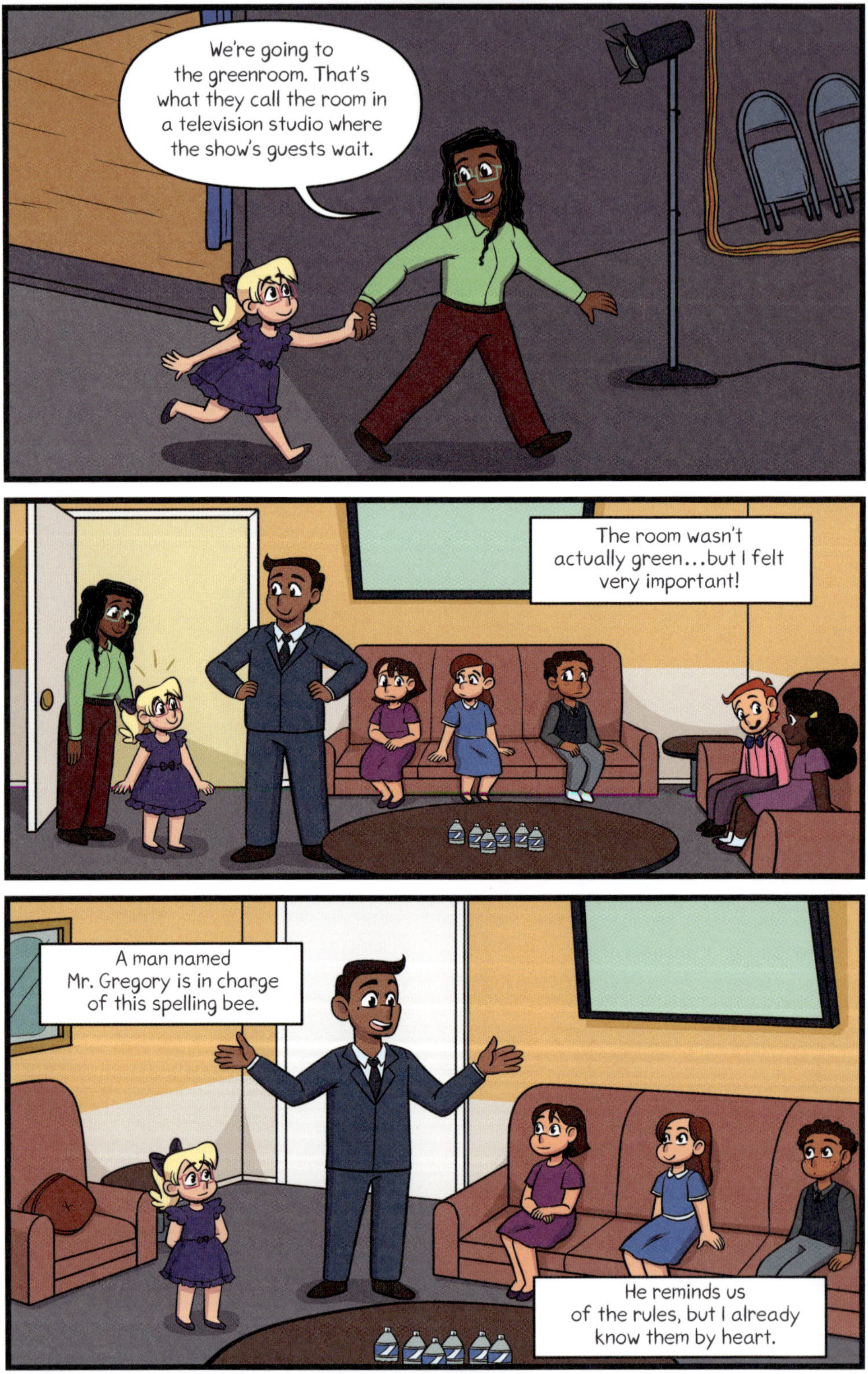
We're going to the greenroom. That's what they call the room in a television studio where the show's guests wait.
The room wasn't actually green...but I felt very important!
A man named Mr. Gregory is in charge of this spelling bee.
He reminds us of the rules, but I already know them by heart.

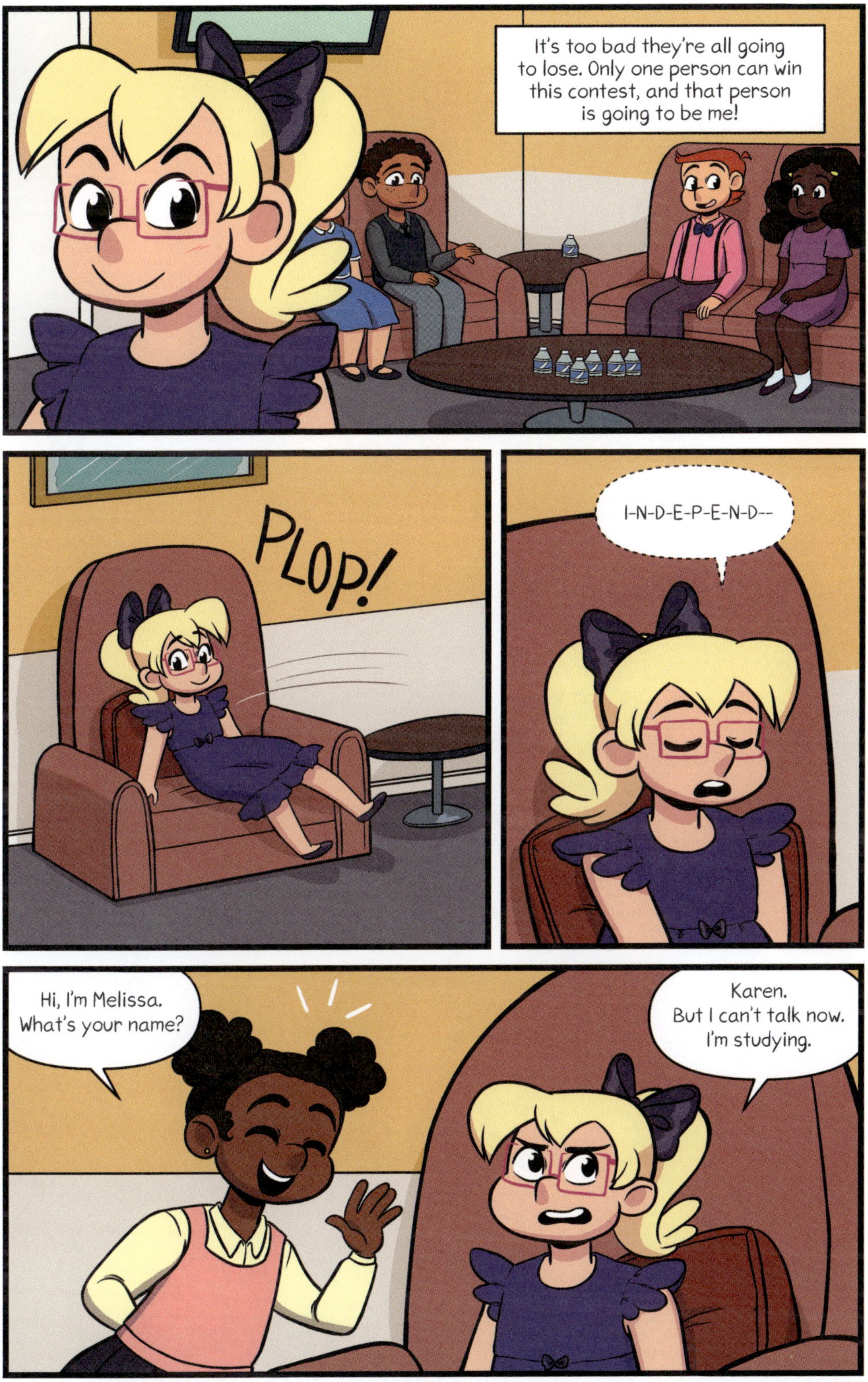
It's too bad they're all going to lose. Only one person can win this contest, and that person is going to be me!
PLOP!
I-N-D-E-P-E-N-D--
Hi, I'm Melissa. What's your name?
Karen. But I can't talk now. I'm studying.

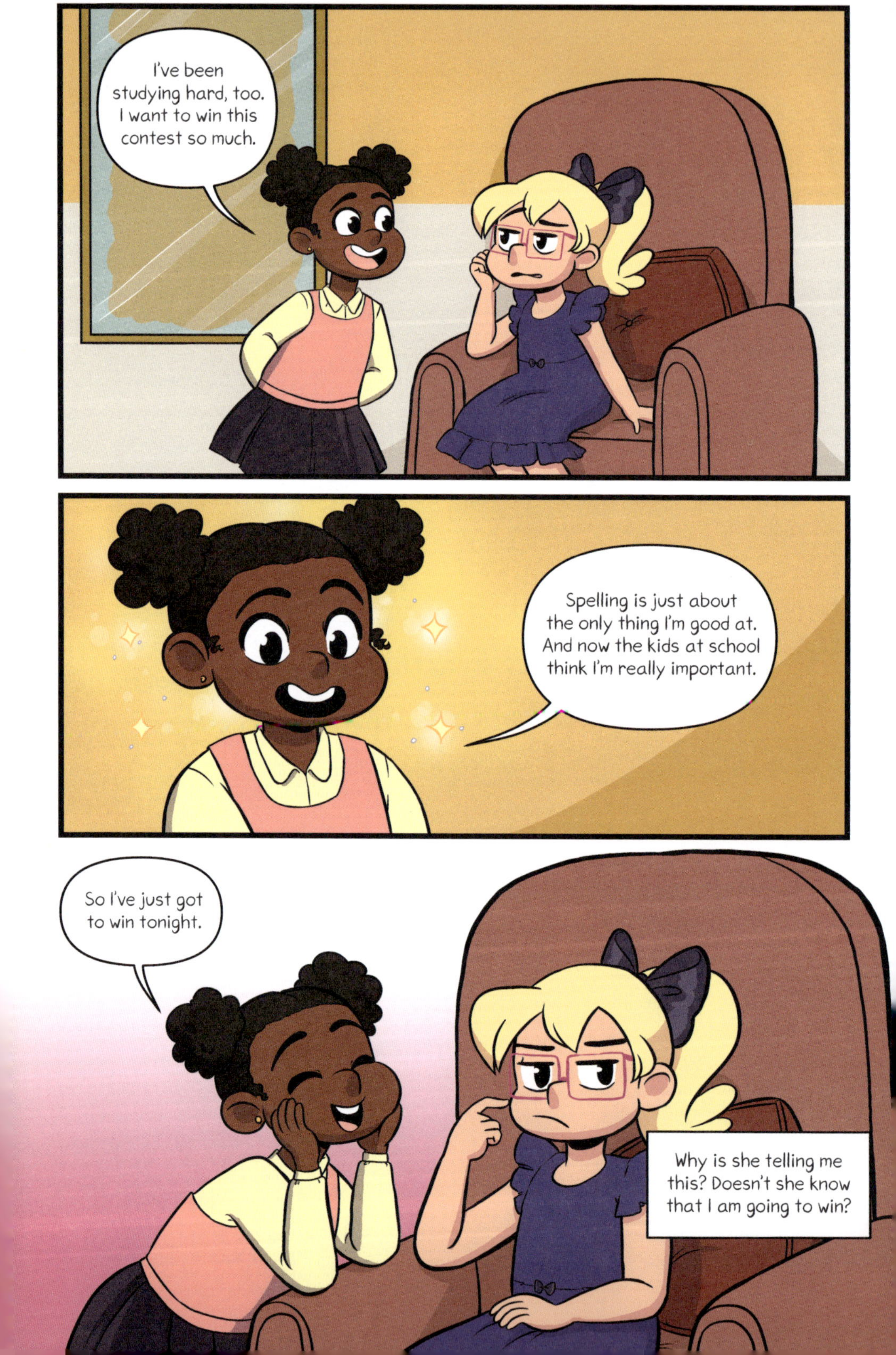
I've been studying hard, too. I want to win this contest so much.
Spelling is just about the only thing I'm good at. And now the kids at school think I'm really important.
So I've just got to win tonight.
Why is she telling me this? Doesn't she know that I am going to win?

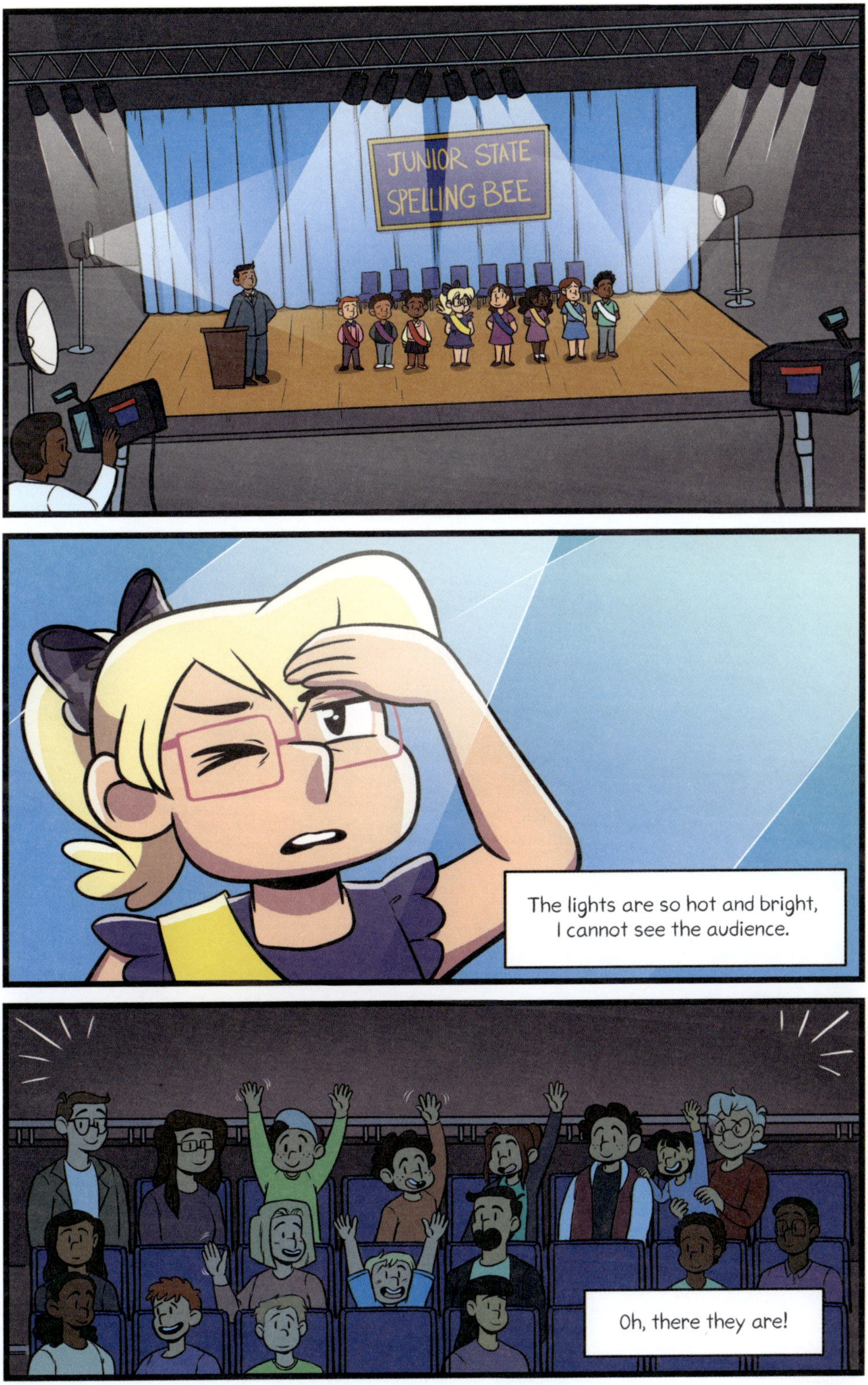
JUNIOR STATE
SPELLING BEE
The lights are so hot and bright,
I cannot see the audience.
Oh, there they are!

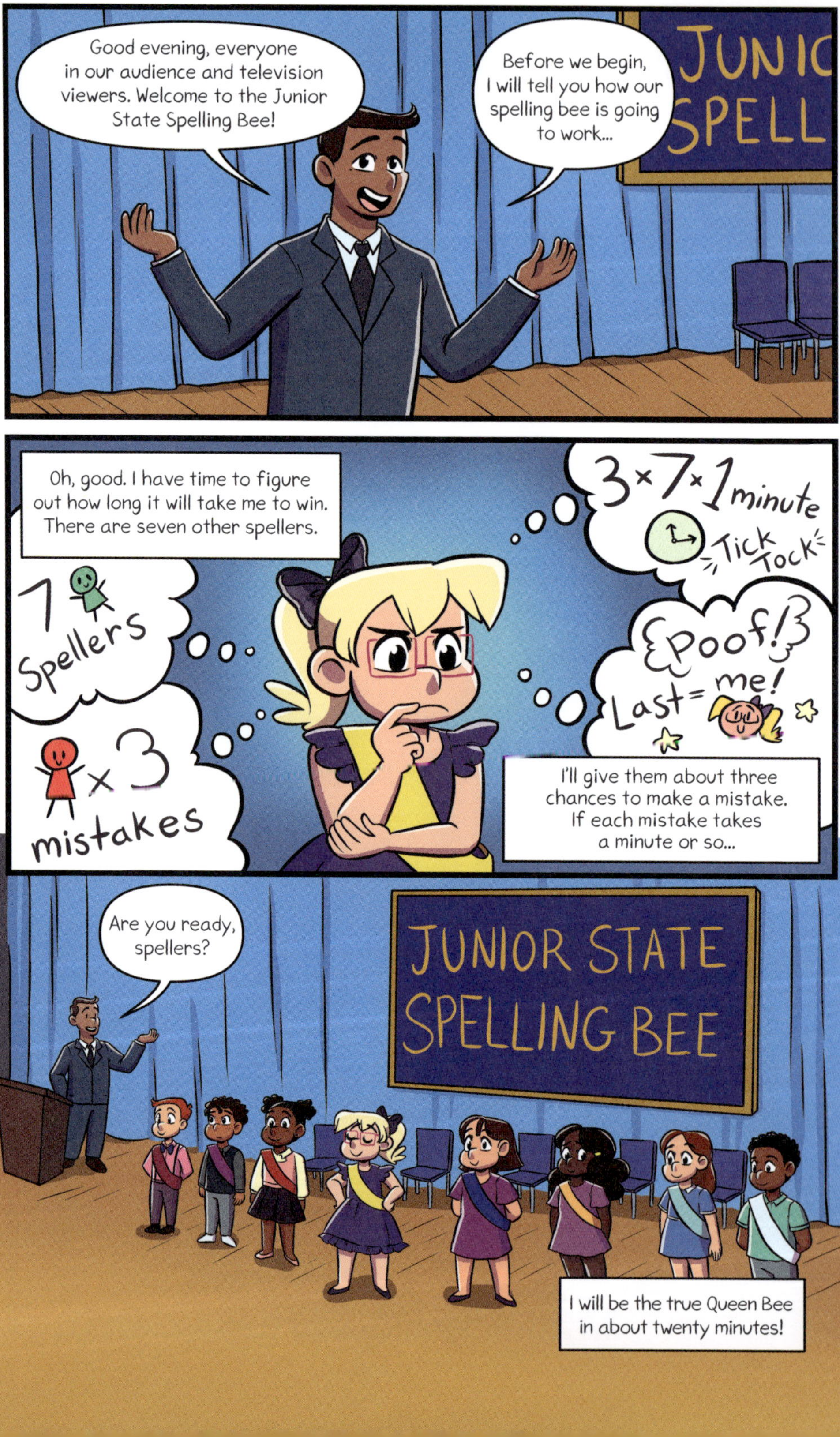
Good evening, everyone in our audience and television viewers. Welcome to the Junior State Spelling Bee!
Before we begin, I will tell you how our spelling bee is going to work...
JUNIO SPELL
Oh, good. I have time to figure out how long it will take me to win. There are seven other spellers.
7 Spellers
x 3 mistakes
3x7x1 minute
Tick Tock
Poof!
Last = me!
I'll give them about three chances to make a mistake. If each mistake takes a minute or so...
Are you ready, spellers?
JUNIOR STATE SPELLING BEE
I will be the true Queen Bee in about twenty minutes!

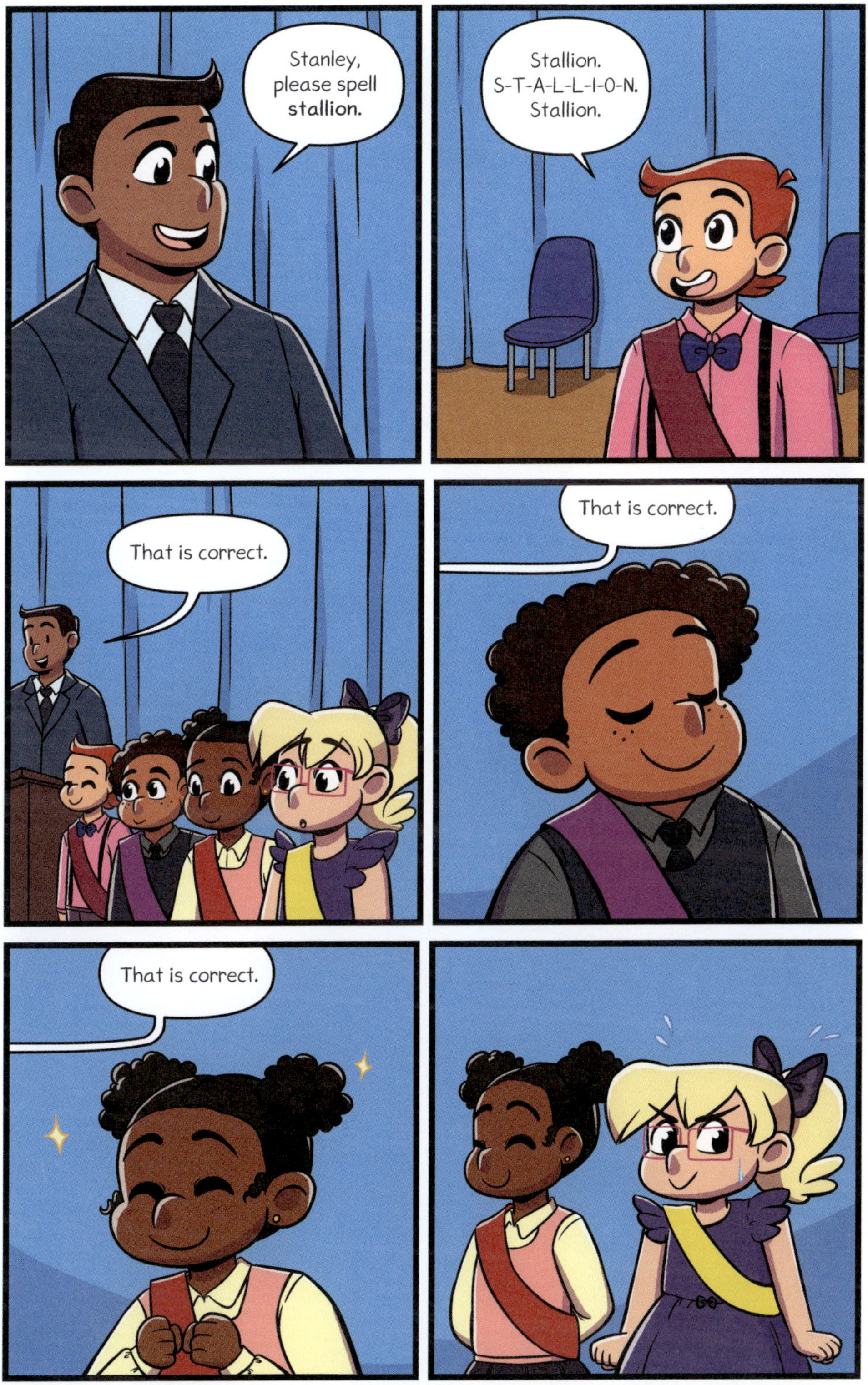
Stanley, please spell **stallion.**
Stallion. S-T-A-L-L-I-O-N. Stallion.
That is correct.
That is correct.
That is correct.

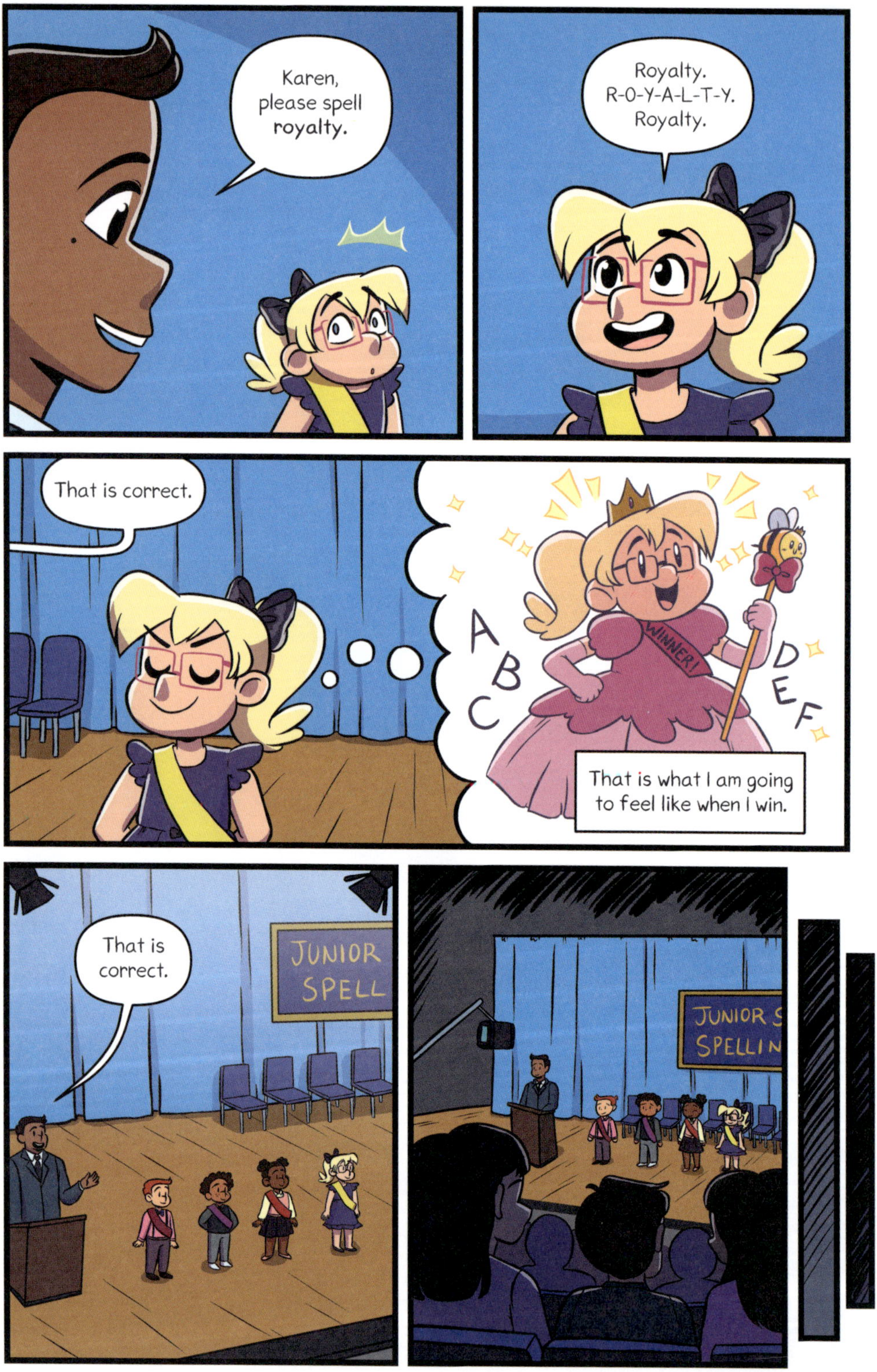
Karen,
please spell
royalty.
Royalty.
R-O-Y-A-L-T-Y.
Royalty.
That is correct.
WINNER!
A
B
C
D
E
F
That is what I am going to feel like when I win.
That is correct.
JUNIOR
SPELL
JUNIOR S
SPELLIN

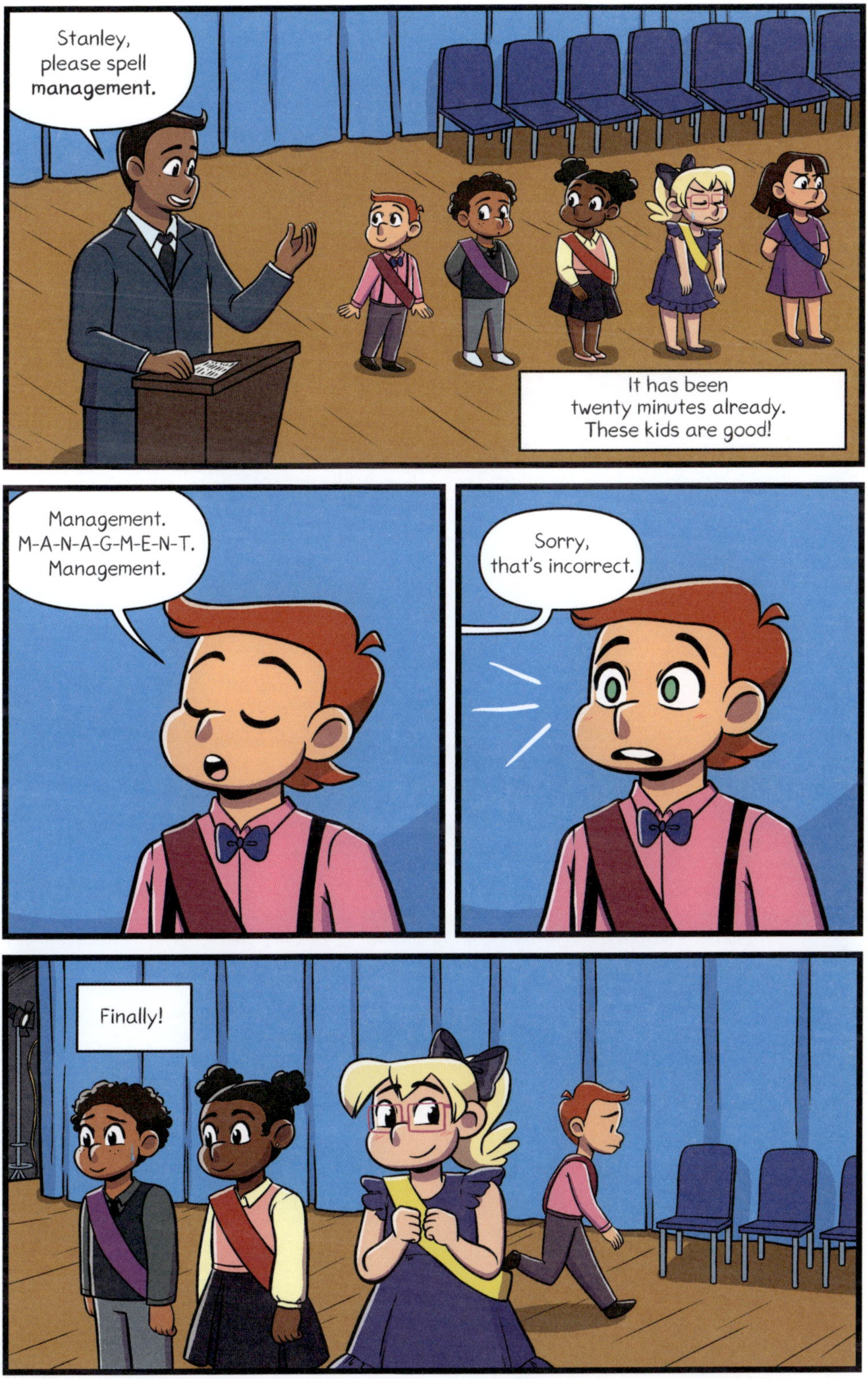
Stanley, please spell management.
It has been twenty minutes already. These kids are good!
Management. M-A-N-A-G-M-E-N-T. Management.
Sorry, that's incorrect.
Finally!

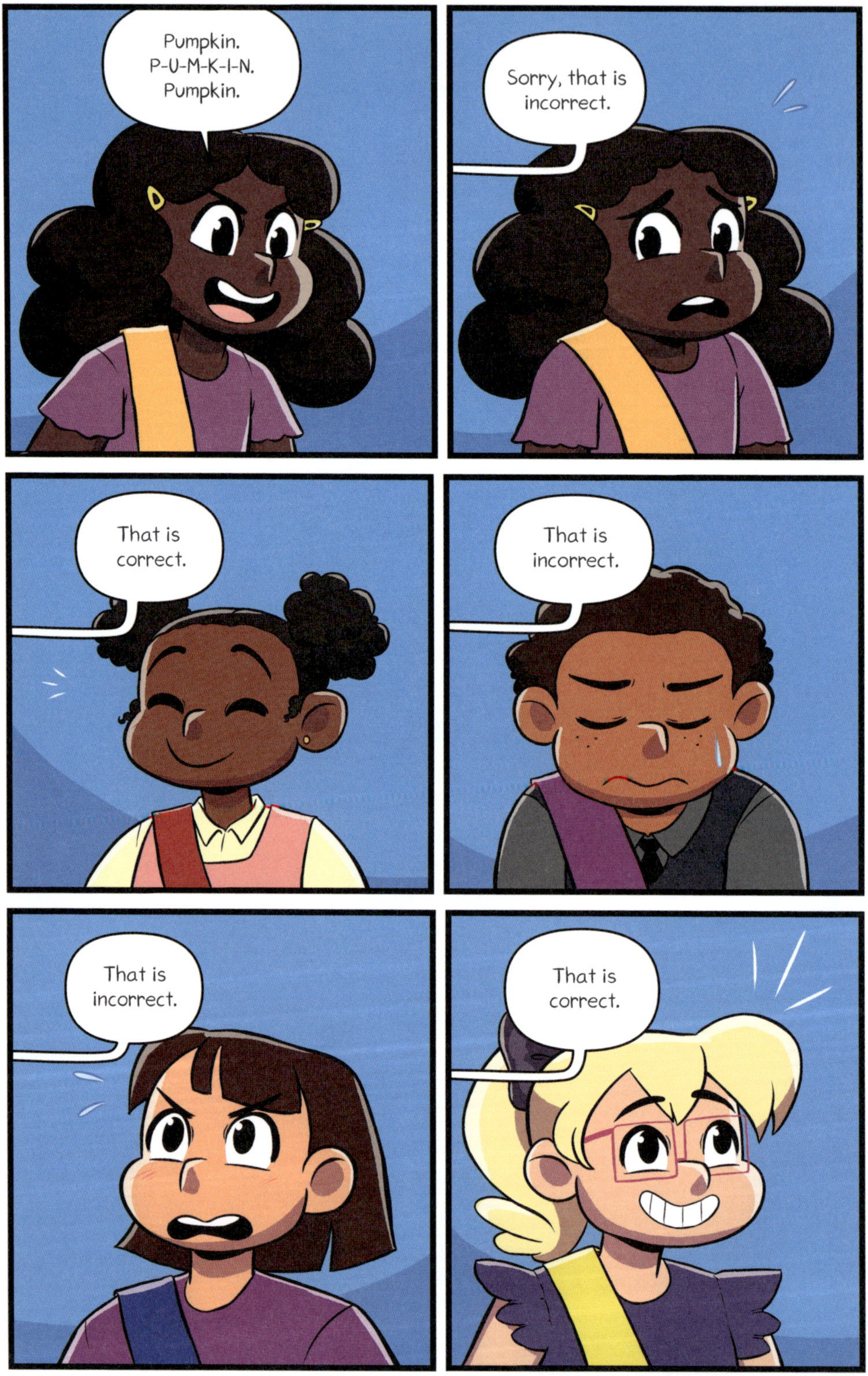
Pumpkin. P-U-M-K-I-N. Pumpkin.
Sorry, that is incorrect.
That is correct.
That is incorrect.
That is incorrect.
That is correct.

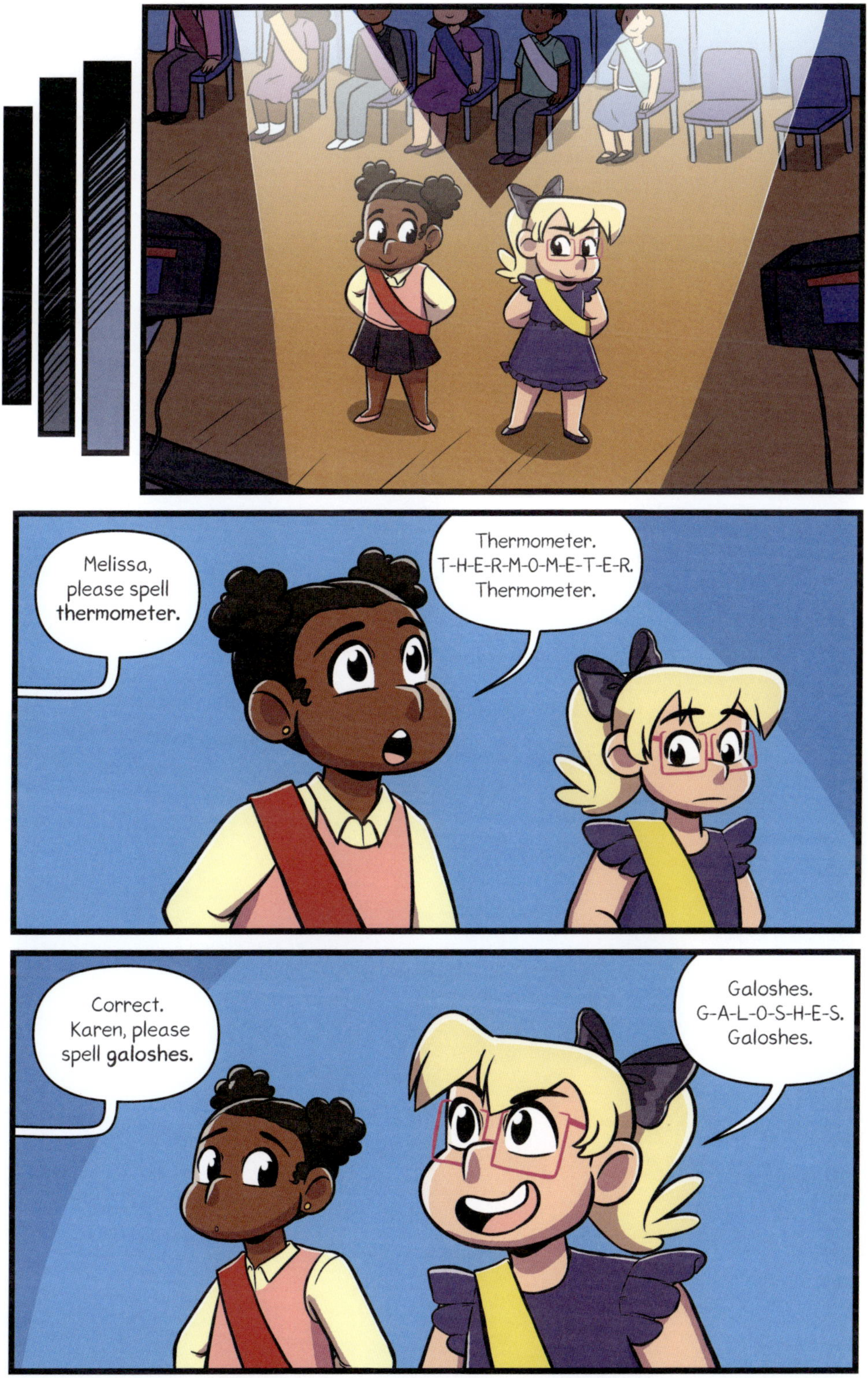
Melissa, please spell thermometer.
Thermometer. T-H-E-R-M-O-M-E-T-E-R. Thermometer.
Correct. Karen, please spell galoshes.
Galoshes. G-A-L-O-S-H-E-S. Galoshes.

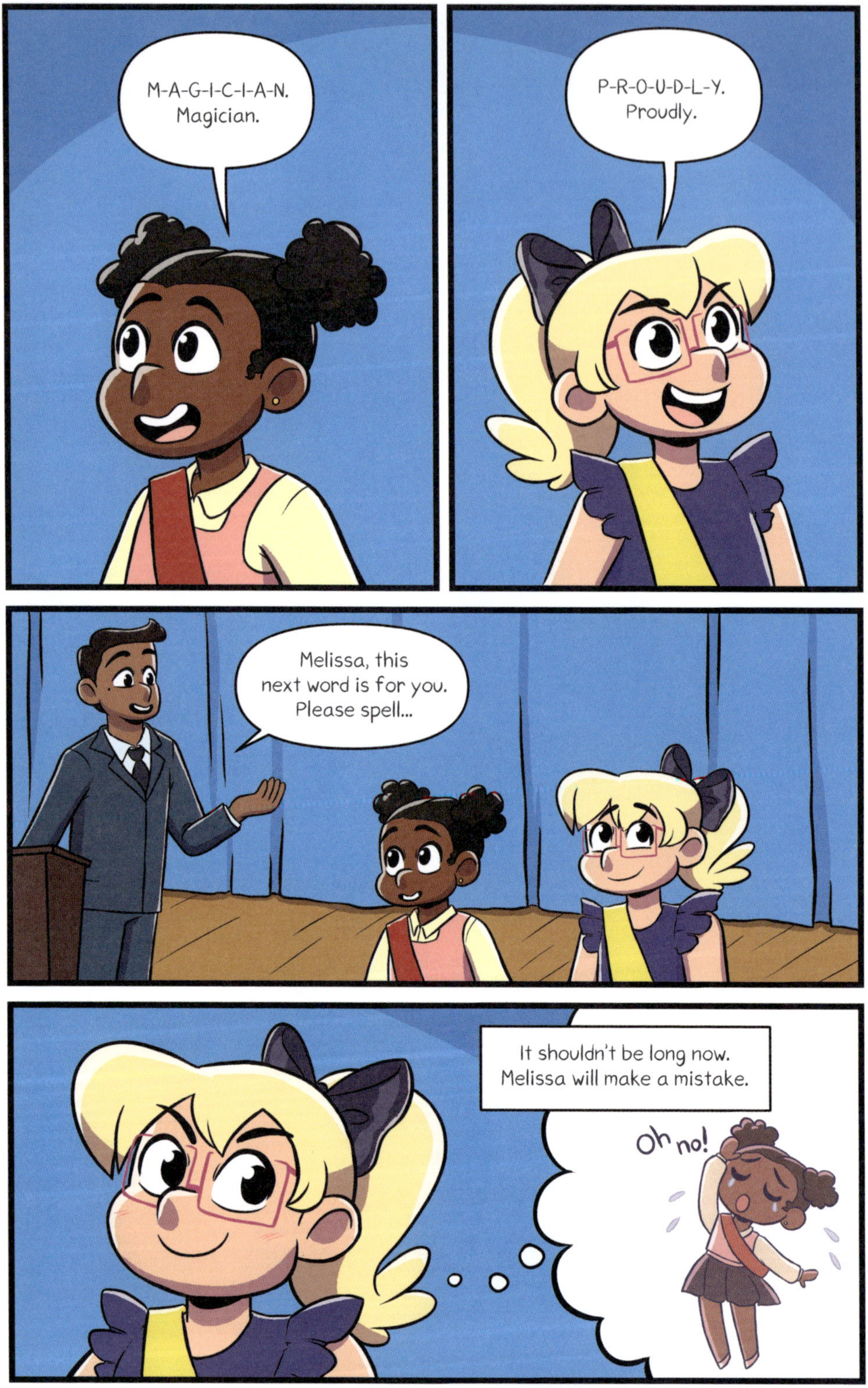
M-A-G-I-C-I-A-N.
Magician.
P-R-O-U-D-L-Y.
Proudly.
Melissa, this next word is for you. Please spell...
It shouldn't be long now. Melissa will make a mistake.
Oh no!

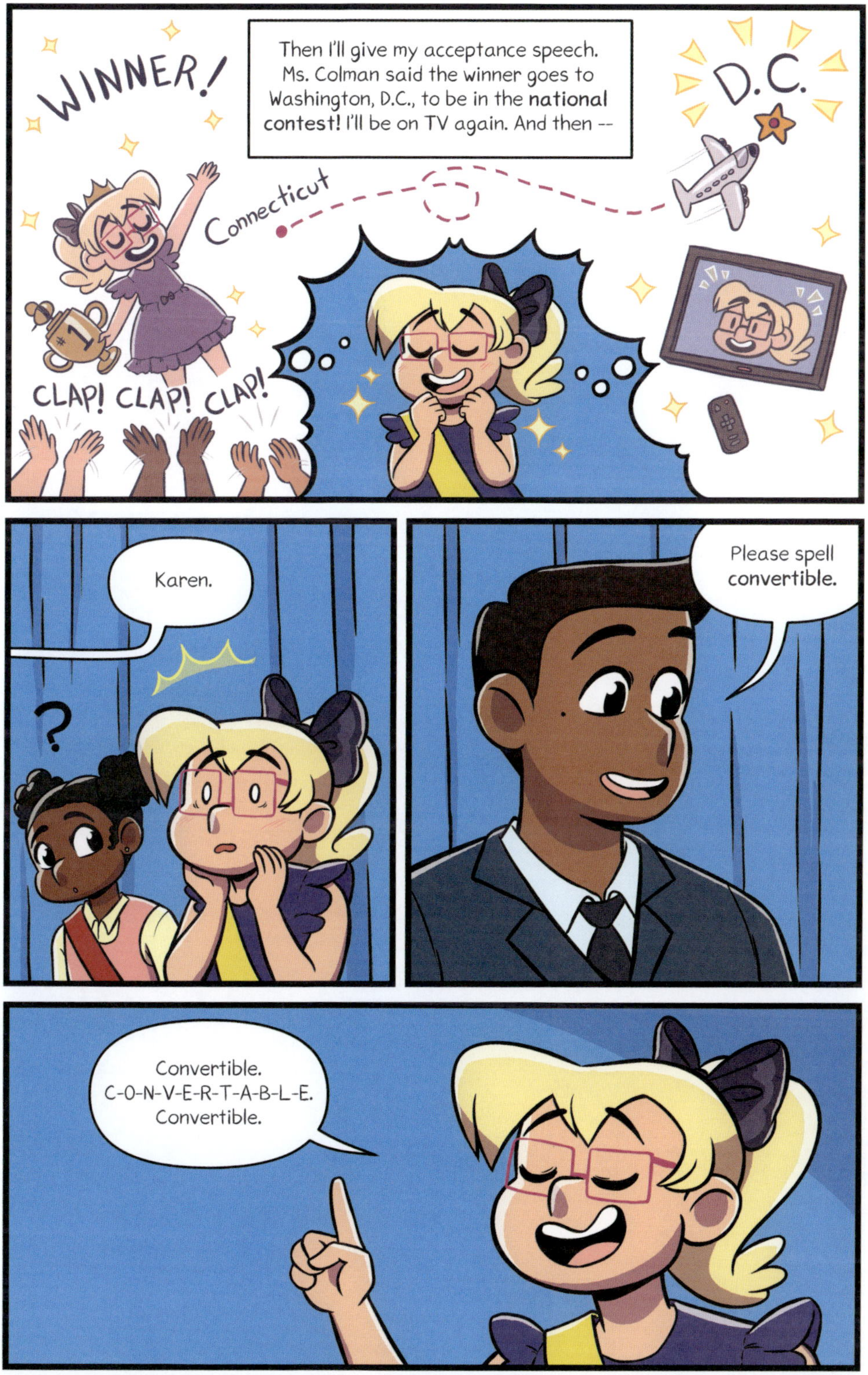

WINNER!
Then I'll give my acceptance speech. Ms. Colman said the winner goes to Washington, D.C., to be in the national contest! I'll be on TV again. And then --
D.C.
Connecticut
#1
CLAP! CLAP! CLAP!
Karen.
?
Please spell convertible.
Convertible. C-O-N-V-E-R-T-A-B-L-E. Convertible.

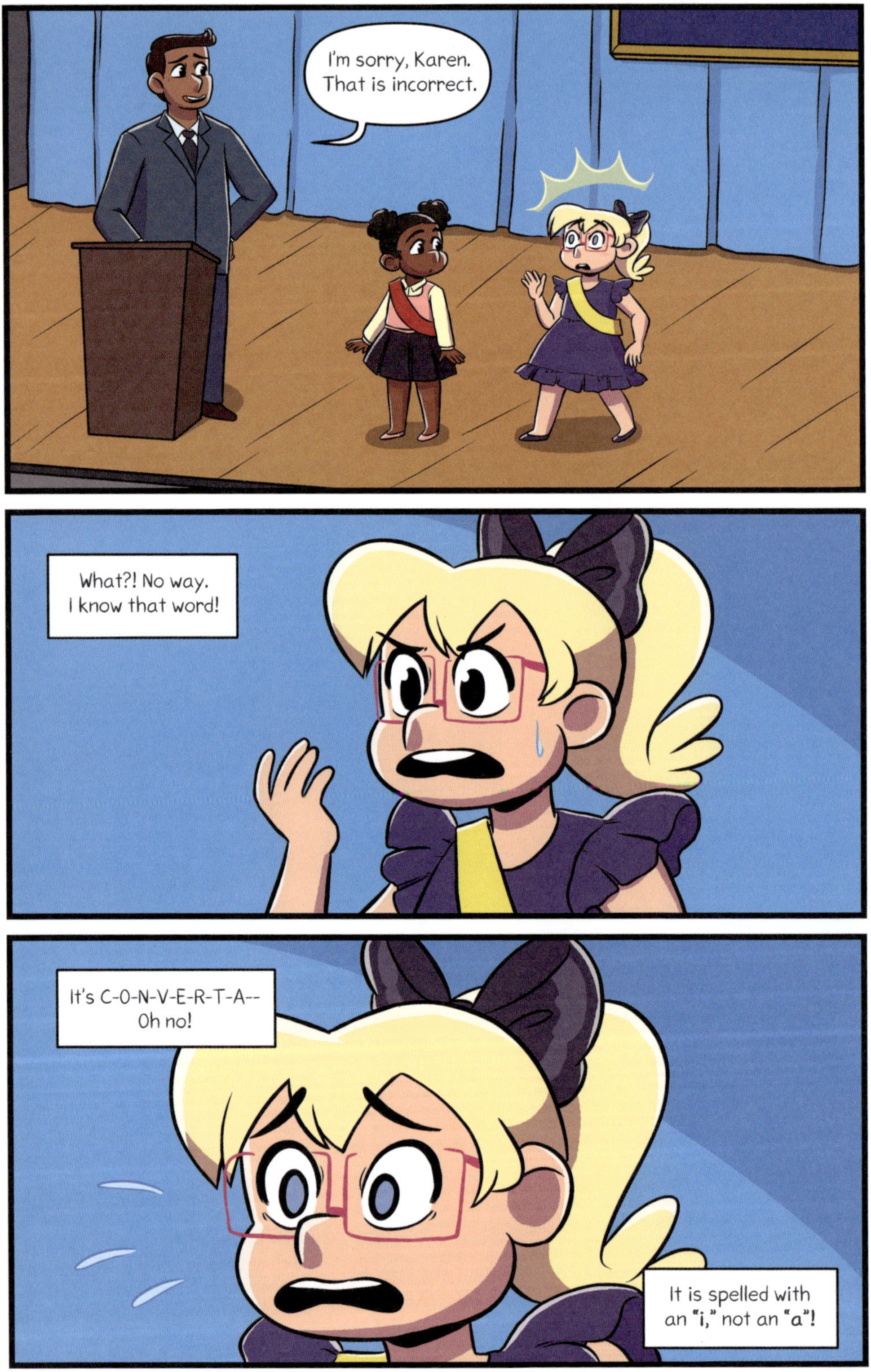
I'm sorry, Karen.
That is incorrect.
What?! No way.
I know that word!
It's C-O-N-V-E-R-T-A--
Oh no!
It is spelled with
an "i," not an "a"!

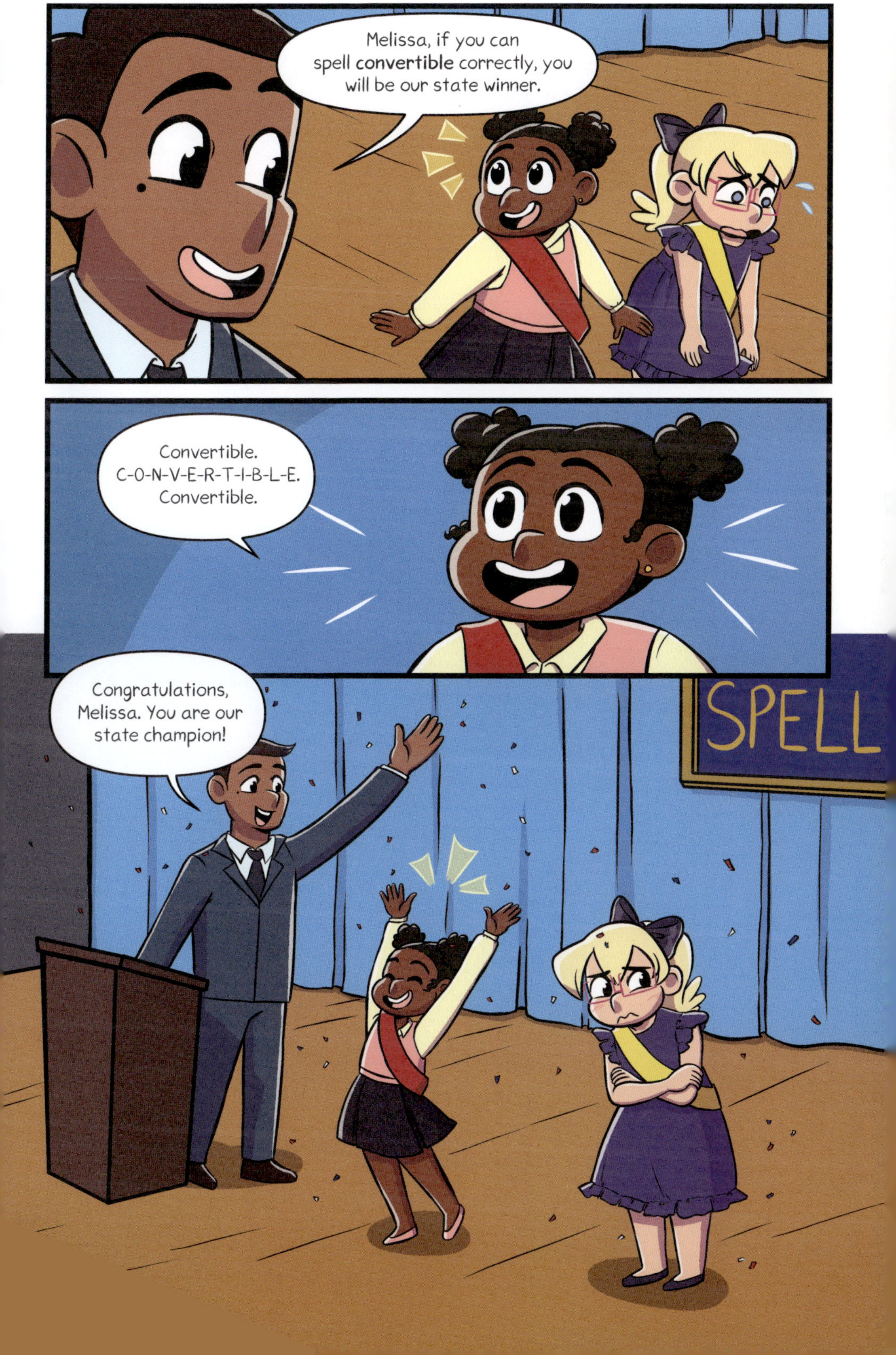
Melissa, if you can spell **convertible** correctly, you will be our state winner.
Convertible. C-O-N-V-E-R-T-I-B-L-E. Convertible.
Congratulations, Melissa. You are our state champion!
SPELL

# CHAPTER 10

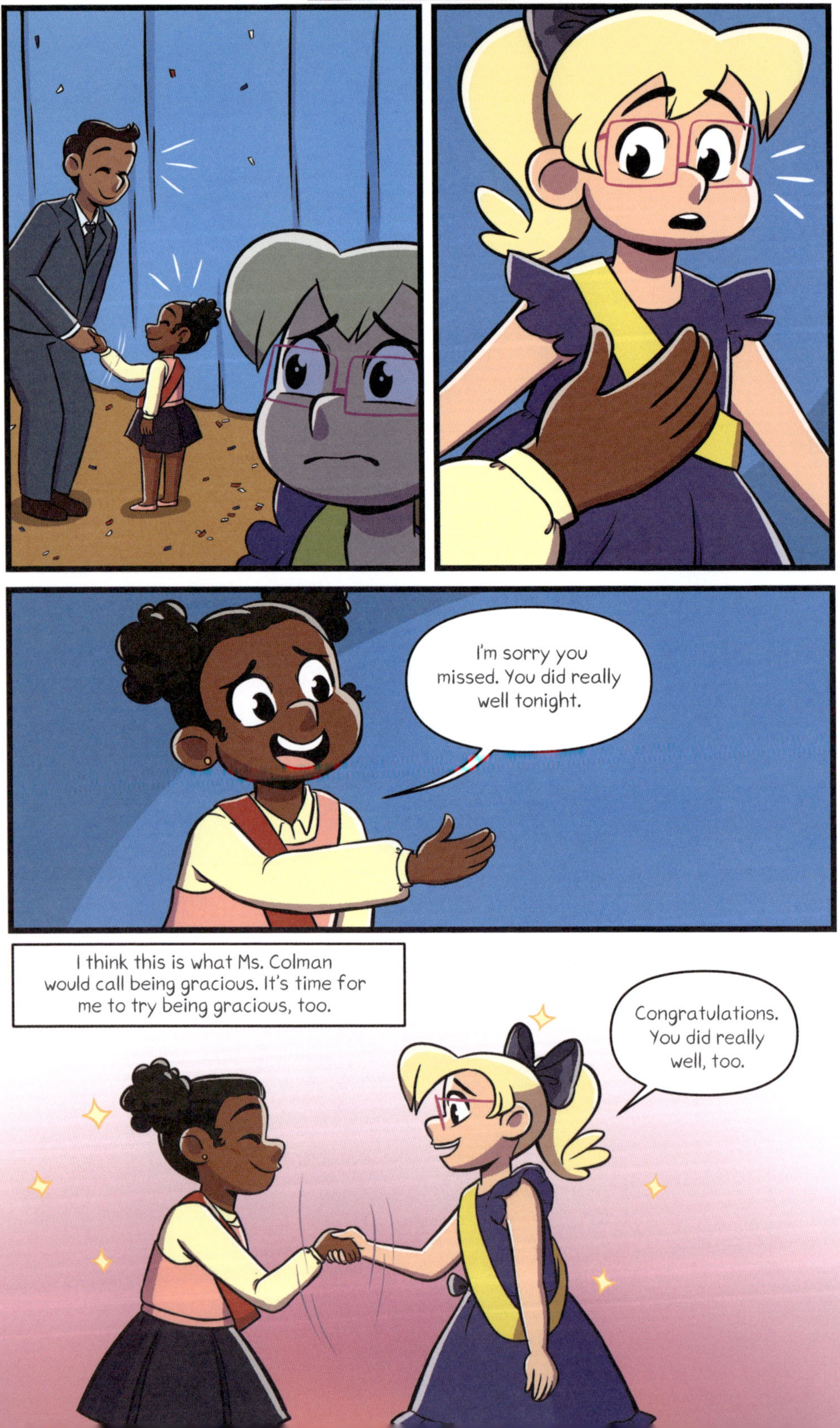
I'm sorry you missed. You did really well tonight.
I think this is what Ms. Colman would call being gracious. It's time for me to try being gracious, too.
Congratulations. You did really well, too.

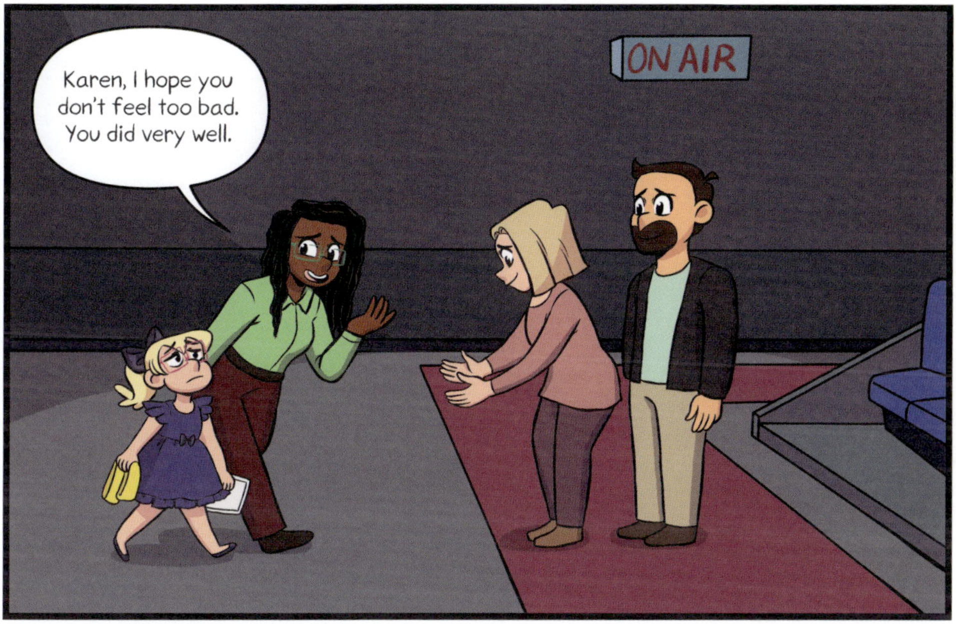
Karen, I hope you don't feel too bad. You did very well.
ON AIR

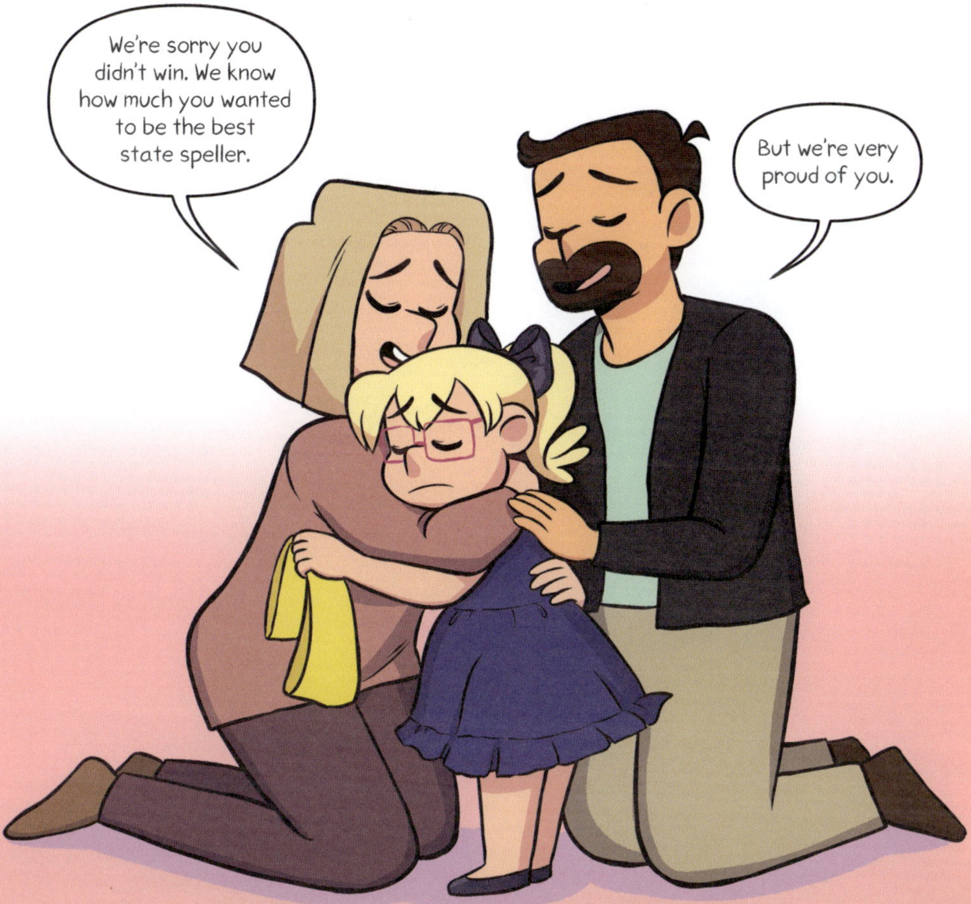
We're sorry you didn't win. We know how much you wanted to be the best state speller.
But we're very proud of you.

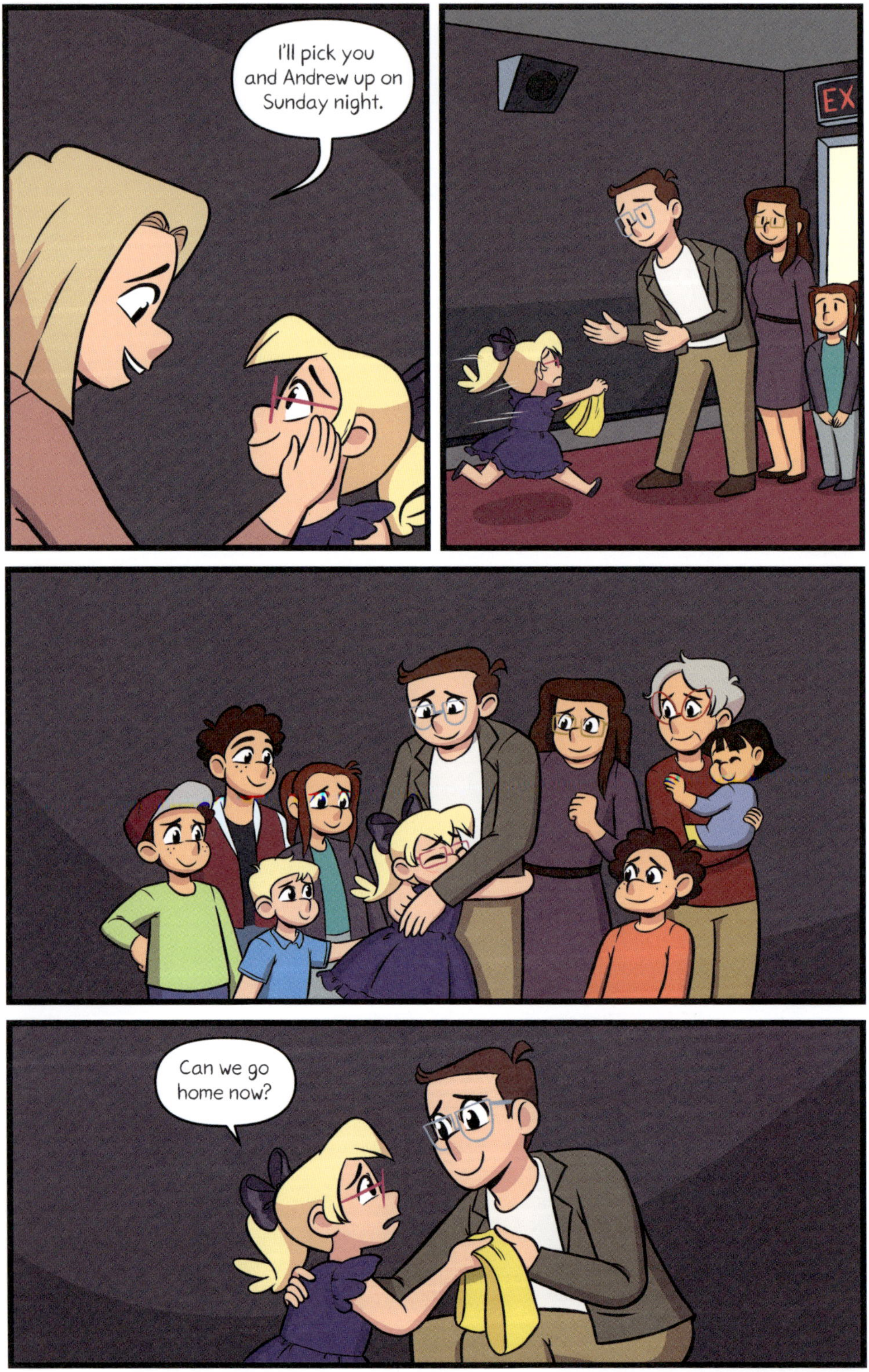
I'll pick you and Andrew up on Sunday night.
EX
Can we go home now?

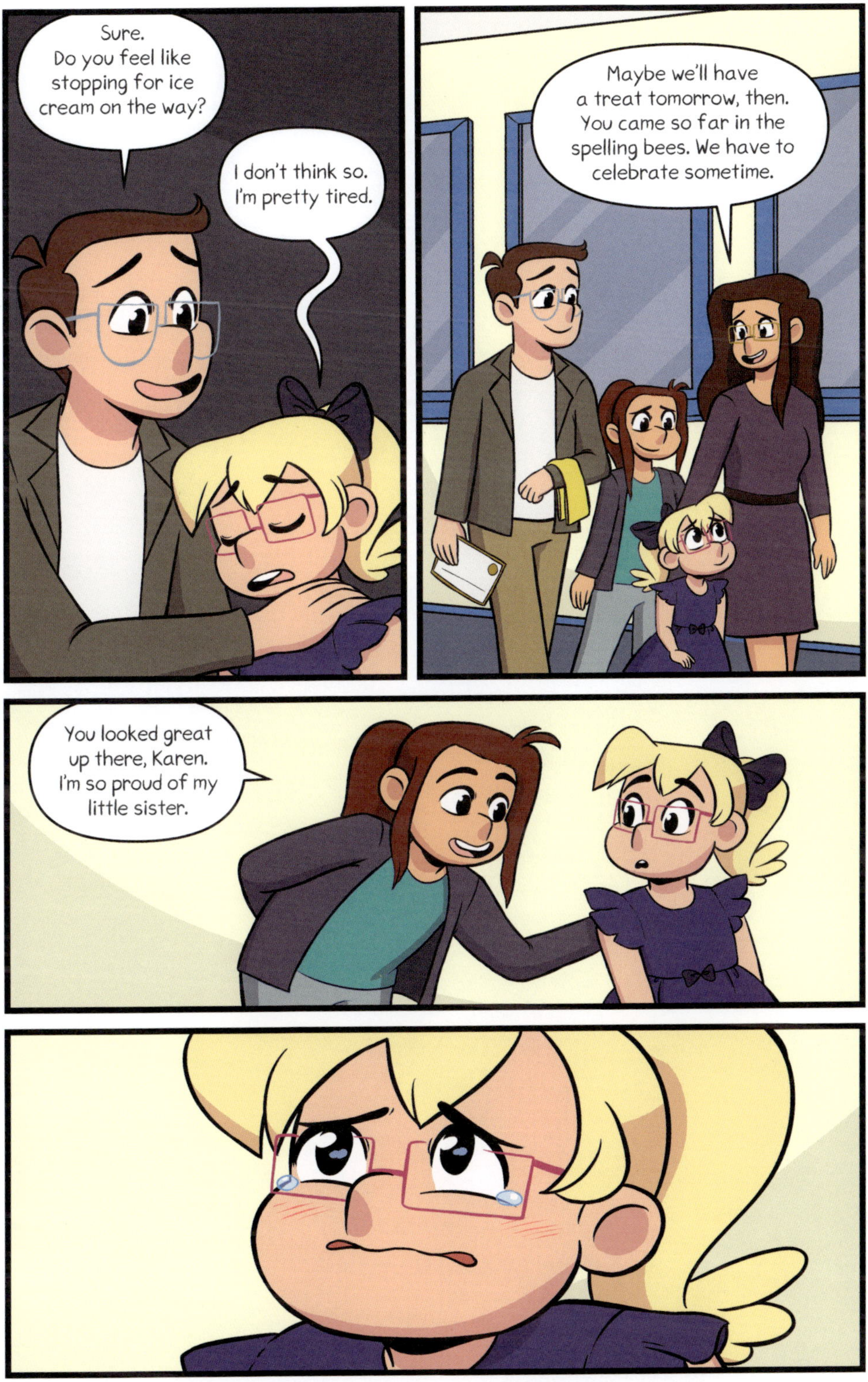
Sure. Do you feel like stopping for ice cream on the way?
I don't think so. I'm pretty tired.
Maybe we'll have a treat tomorrow, then. You came so far in the spelling bees. We have to celebrate sometime.
You looked great up there, Karen. I'm so proud of my little sister.

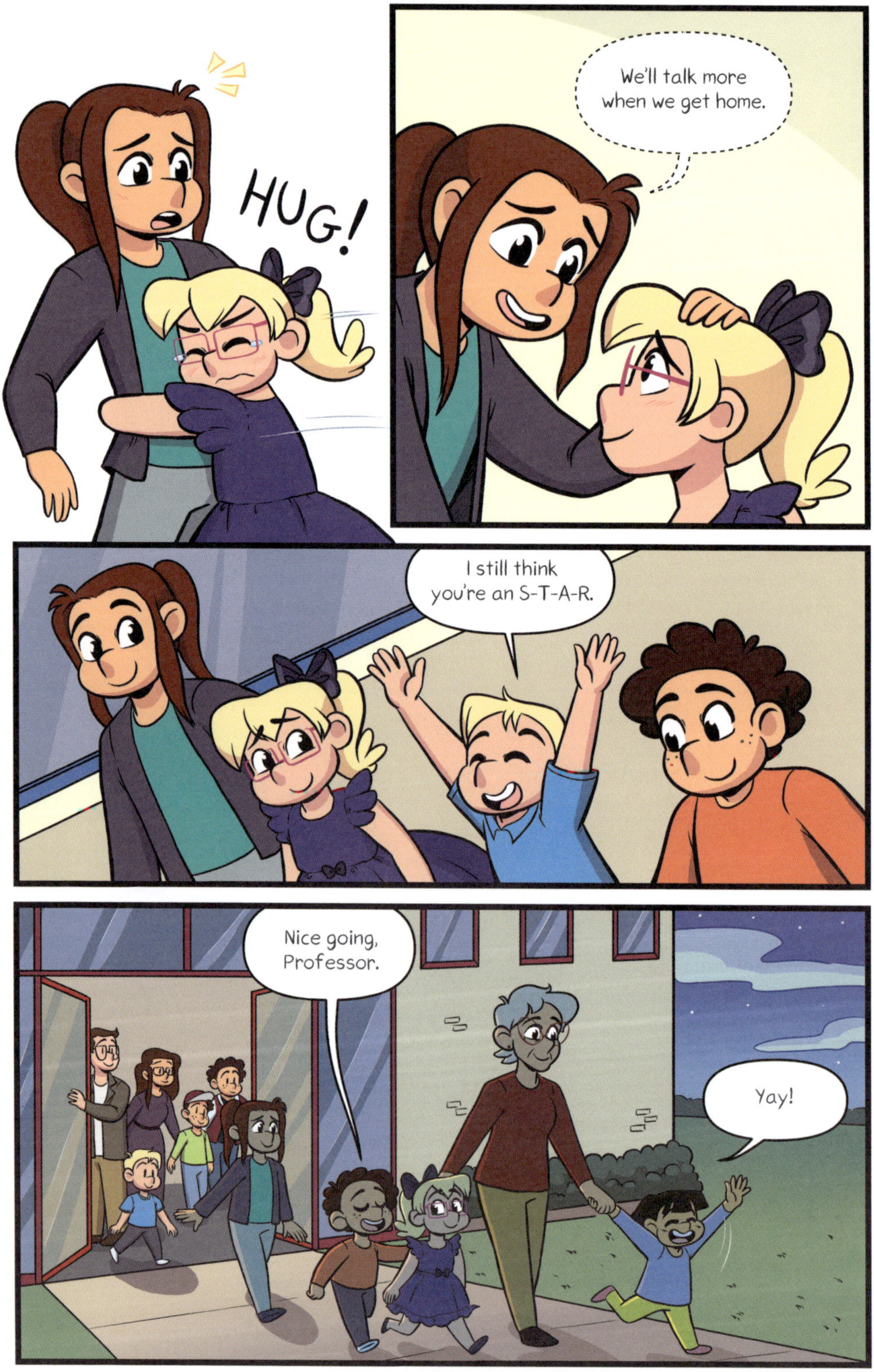
HUG!
We'll talk more when we get home.
I still think you're an S-T-A-R.
Nice going, Professor.
Yay!

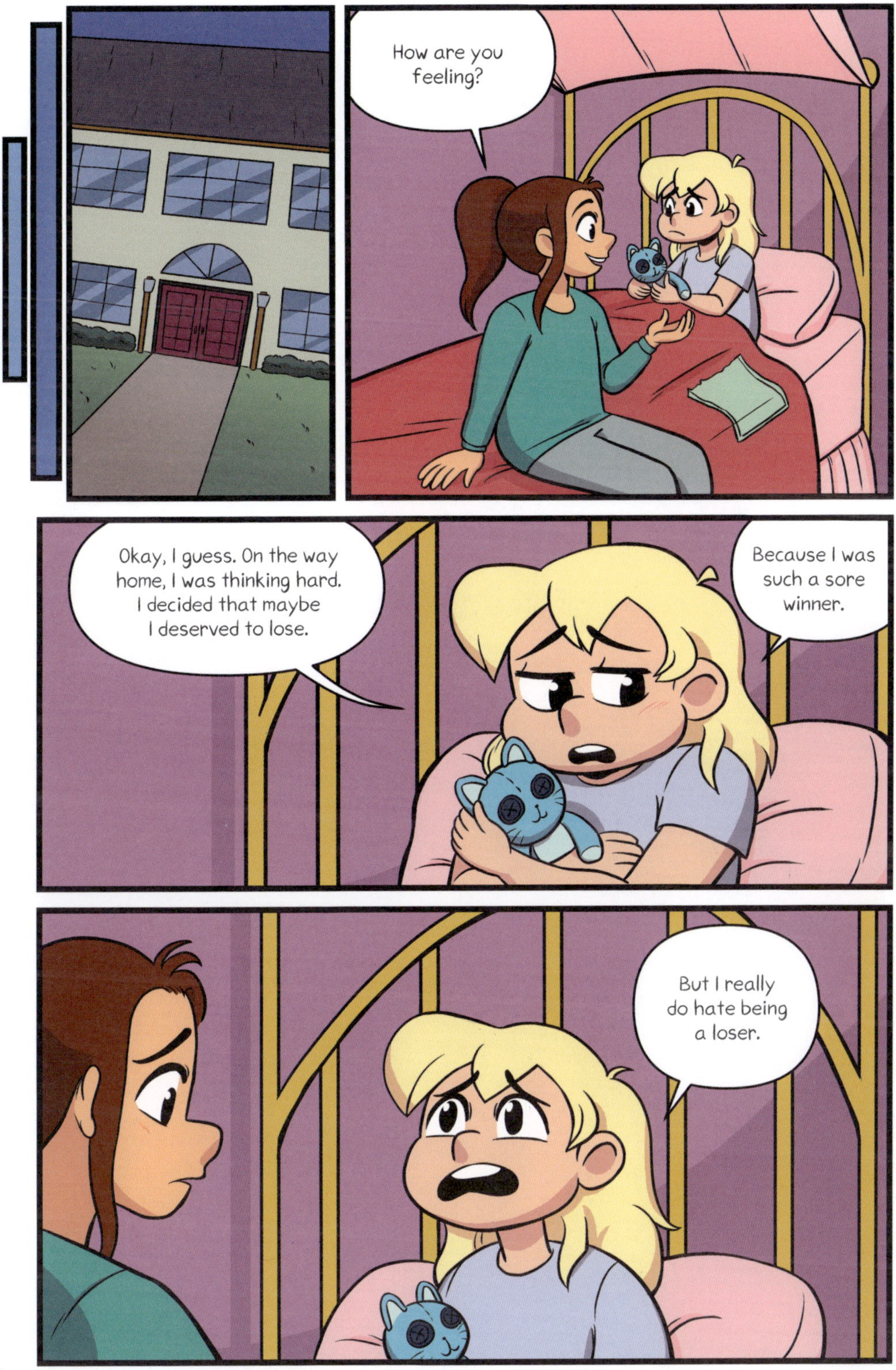
How are you feeling?
Okay, I guess. On the way home, I was thinking hard. I decided that maybe I deserved to lose.
Because I was such a sore winner.
But I really do hate being a loser.

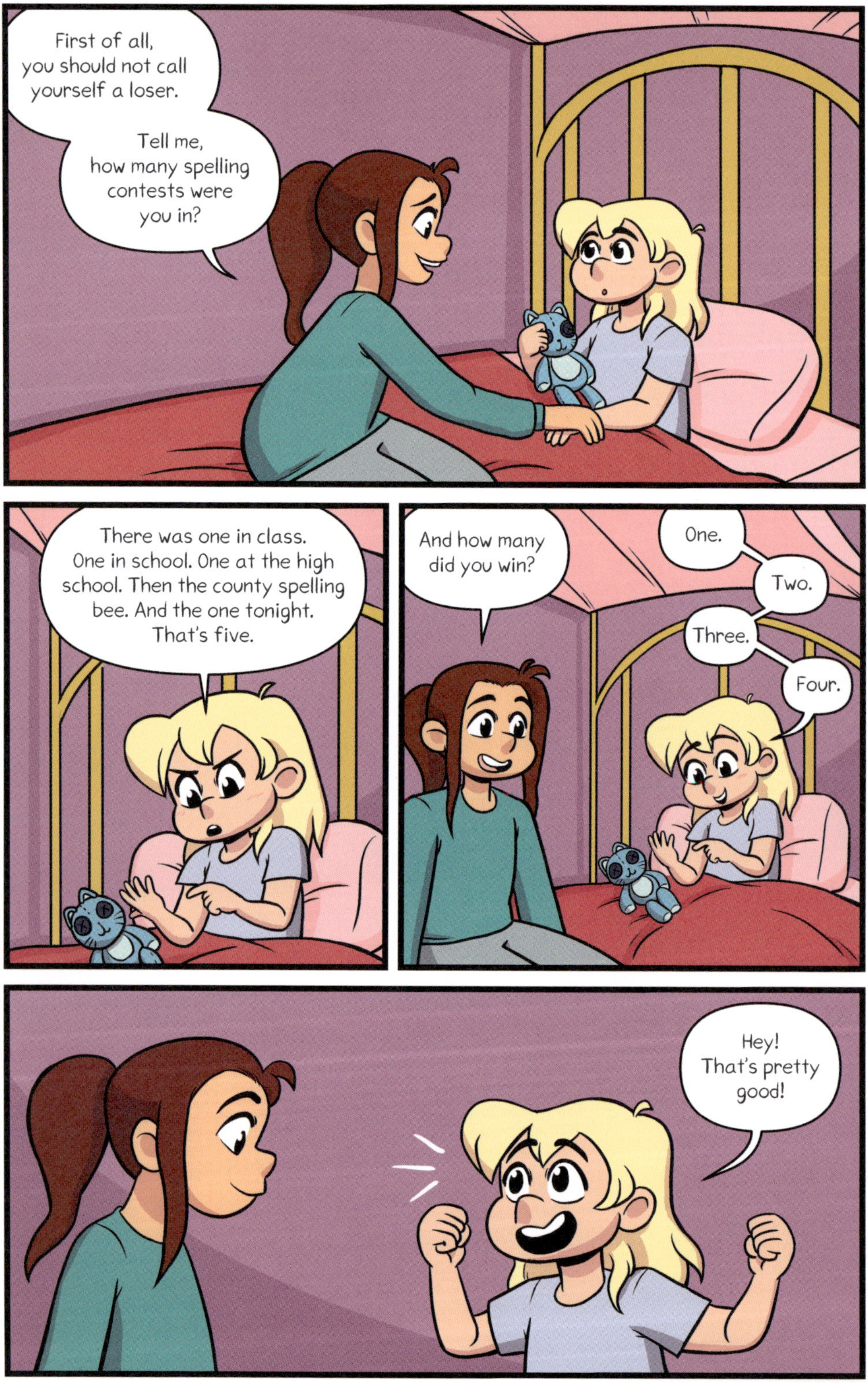
First of all, you should not call yourself a loser.
Tell me, how many spelling contests were you in?
There was one in class. One in school. One at the high school. Then the county spelling bee. And the one tonight. That's five.
And how many did you win?
One.
Two.
Three.
Four.
Hey! That's pretty good!

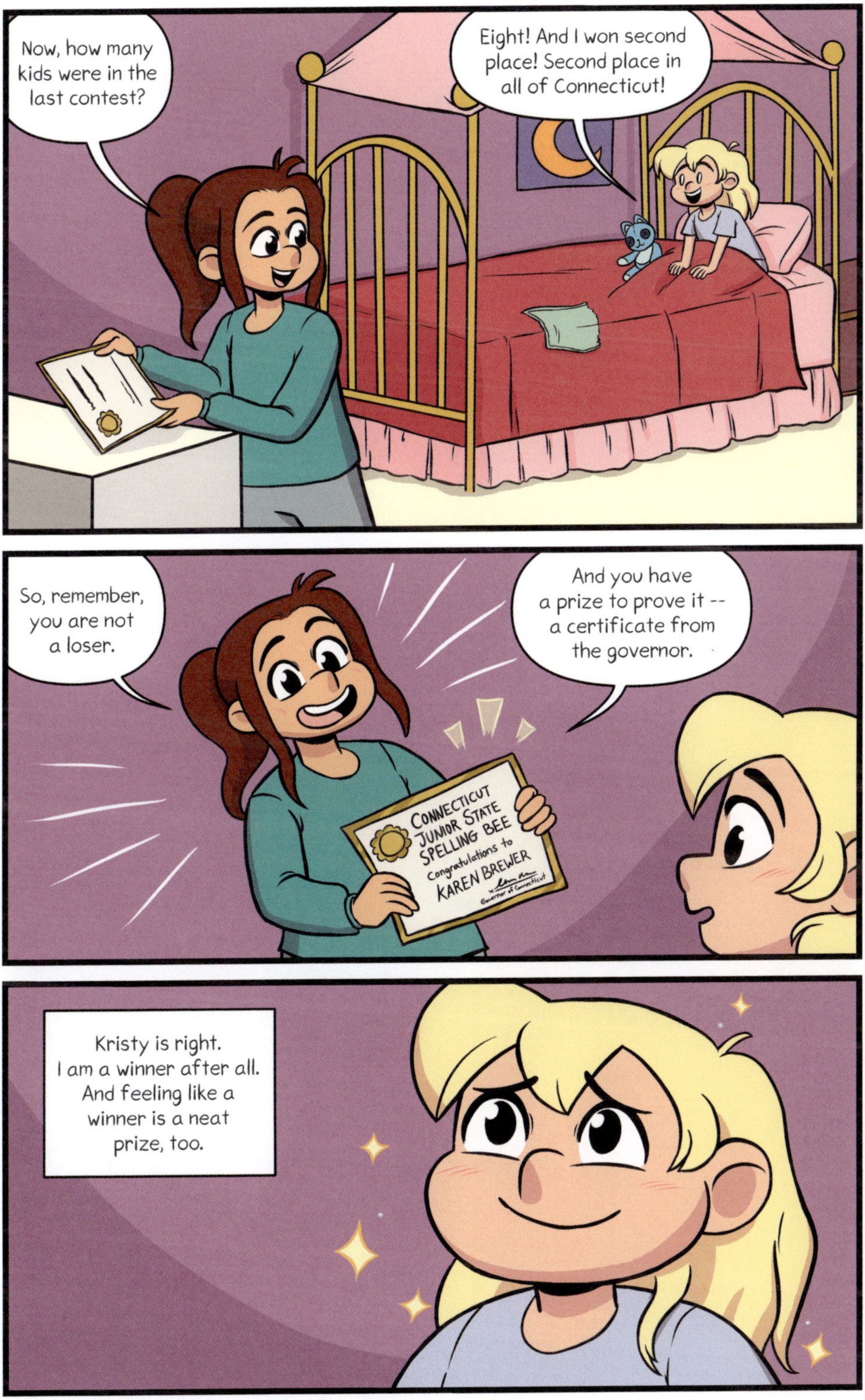
Now, how many kids were in the last contest?
Eight! And I won second place! Second place in all of Connecticut!
So, remember, you are not a loser.
And you have a prize to prove it -- a certificate from the governor.
CONNECTICUT JUNIOR STATE SPELLING BEE
Congratulations to KAREN BREWER
Governor of Connecticut
Kristy is right. I am a winner after all. And feeling like a winner is a neat prize, too.

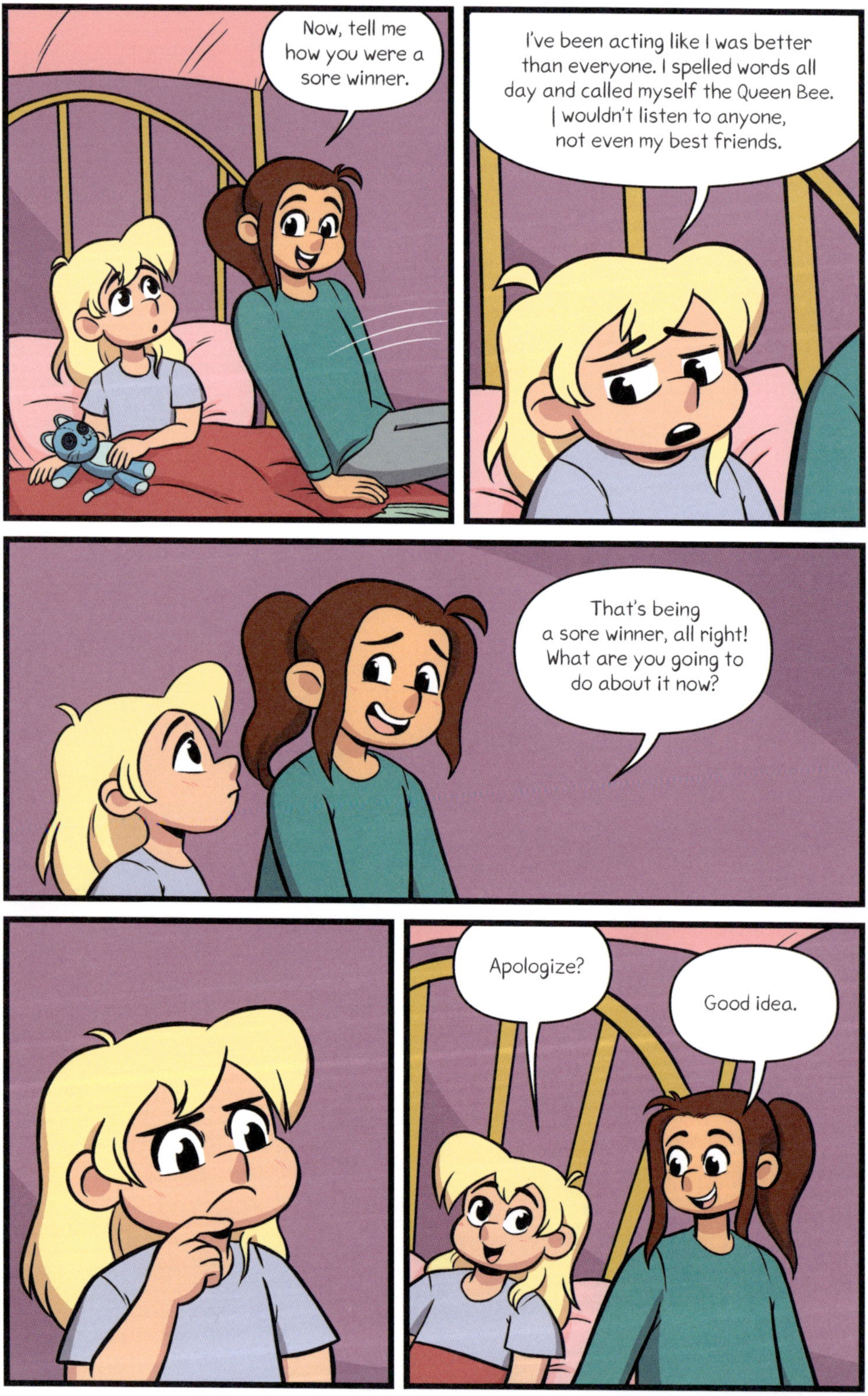
Now, tell me how you were a sore winner.
I've been acting like I was better than everyone. I spelled words all day and called myself the Queen Bee. I wouldn't listen to anyone, not even my best friends.
That's being a sore winner, all right! What are you going to do about it now?
Apologize?
Good idea.

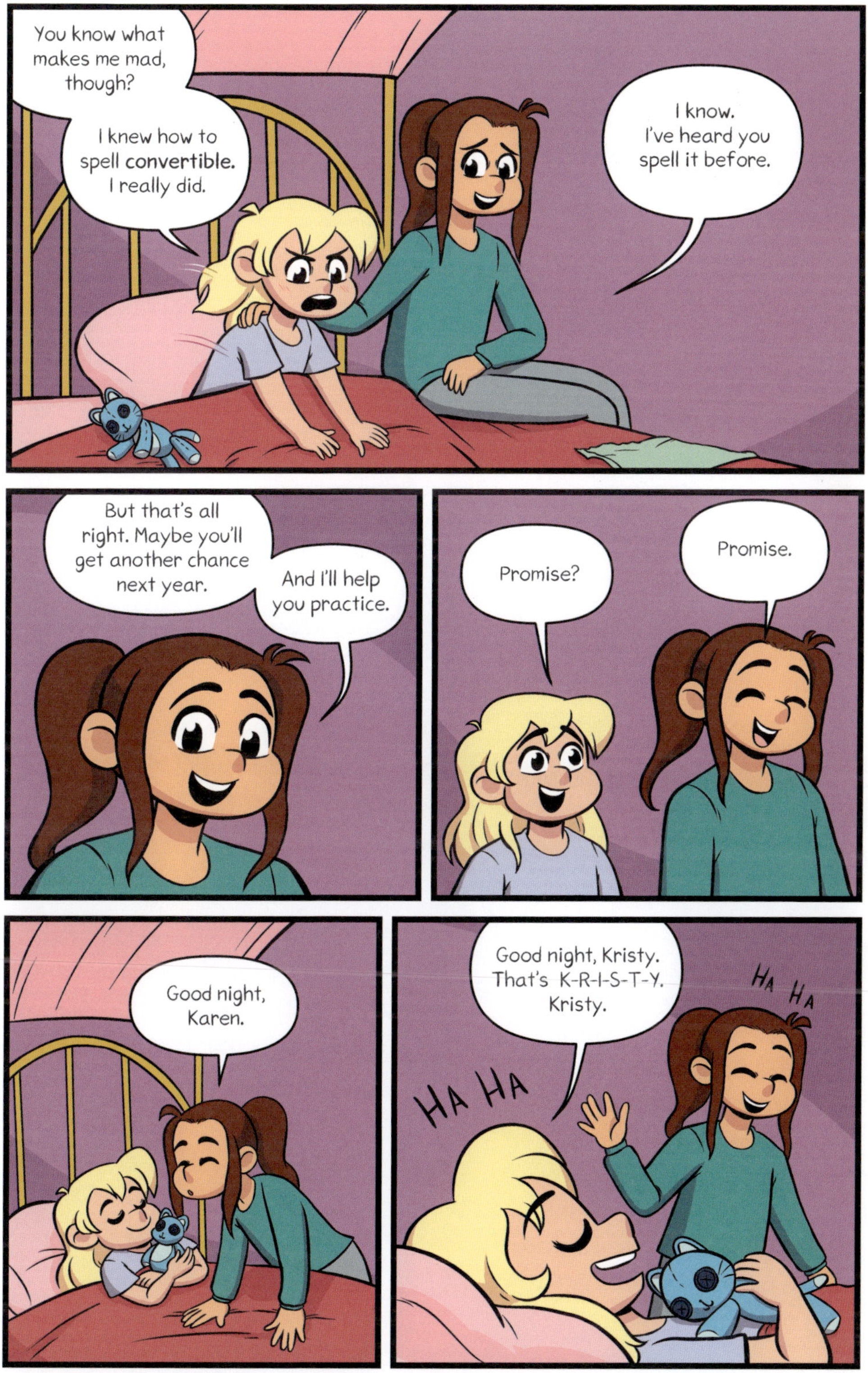
You know what makes me mad, though?
I knew how to spell **convertible.** I really did.
I know. I've heard you spell it before.
But that's all right. Maybe you'll get another chance next year.
And I'll help you practice.
Promise?
Promise.
Good night, Karen.
Good night, Kristy. That's K-R-I-S-T-Y. Kristy.
HA HA
HA HA

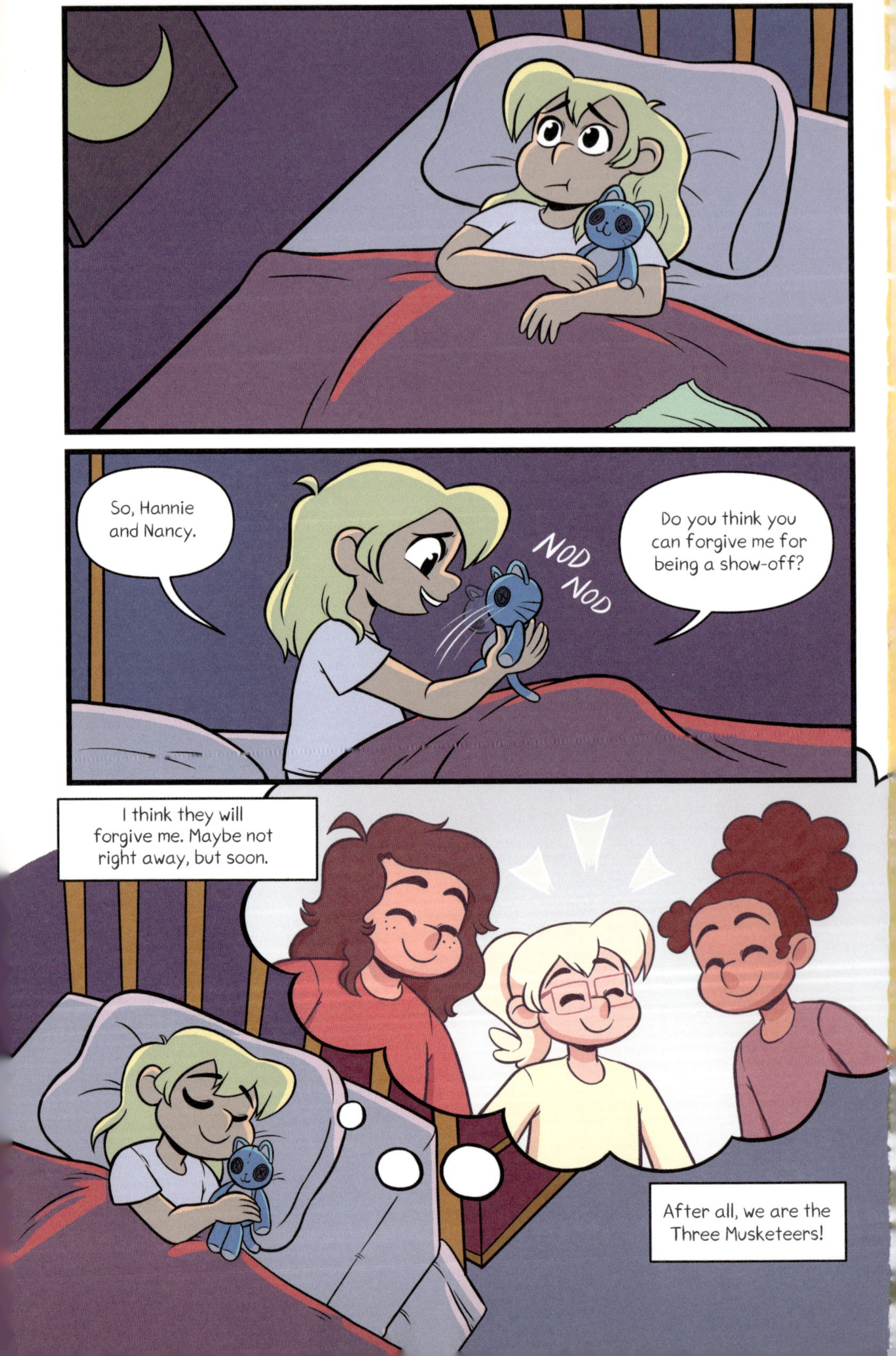
So, Hannie and Nancy.
NOD NOD
Do you think you can forgive me for being a show-off?
I think they will forgive me. Maybe not right away, but soon.
After all, we are the Three Musketeers!